BE QUIET

BE QUIET

Margaret Hollingsworth

BLUE LAKE BOOKS

Blue Lake Books acknowledges the ongoing support of the Canada
Council for the Arts and the B.C. Arts Council.

EDITOR
Luanne Armstrong

COVER DESIGN AND INTERIOR LAYOUT
Jane Lightle, Bibelot Communications.
Set in Context and Hoefler Text.

Published in Canada by Blue Lake Books
3476 Tupper Street
Vancouver, B.C. V5Z 3B7
604.874.1167

NATIONAL LIBRARY OF CANADA CATALOGUING IN PUBLICATION DATA
Hollingsworth, Margaret
    Be Quiet

ISBN 0-9730831-6-6

I. Hollingsworth, Margaret. II. Title.
PS8573.08633P62 2003   jC813.54   C2003-911250-0

Printed and bound in Canada.

For my family of friends and other mavericks.

ﻋﻠﻰ

"Life doesn't last, art doesn't last, it doesn't matter."
—*Eva Hesse*

Thanks to Valerie Snowdon, to Jean Rysstad for listening, to Luanne for believing in the book and to the New River Writers in London.

CHAPTER ONE

They faced off grimly across the expanse of tooled green leather, each waiting for the other to make a move. The doctor rested her elbows comfortably on the arms of the chair that had been specially made for her. She had cleared the desk, except for her blotter, a single sheet of paper and the large silver inkstand—a present from a grateful patient. She saw from Miss Carr's pinched mouth that all her skills would be tested, and it was far too hot a day.

Alice Carr was preoccupied with why she had been summoned back from the village. Her bags were packed, ready to be loaded on the cab that would convey her to the London train. She'd said her last goodbyes to Emily and she didn't want to make matters worse by putting in another appearance at her bedside and prolonging the departure. She didn't think she had anything to add to what she had already discussed with the medical staff, and she wasn't inclined to part with information freely. Her loyalty to Emily was absolute, but, though they had spent much of their lives under the same roof, (some in the same bed), she was not privy to the workings of her sister's mind, any more than Emily was privy to hers.

"You see, the more we understand, the more expeditiously we can effect a cure." Dr. Waller narrowed her cat's eyes.

Alice wondered why the English must always embellish when they wished to make a point. Expeditiously indeed!

"I feel we have not made much progress, Miss Carr, and, to be honest, I am disappointed." The doctor's beads chattered. Wisps of auburn hair escaped from her tortoiseshell combs.

"If you have made no progress, then why did you insist that she be taken out of my care and put into yours?" Alice asked.

"To be blunt, a woman with this condition sucks the pith out of the people around her. The first step is to remove these unfortunates from their home surroundings. By blocking up windows and keyholes when she complains of draughts, reading to her when she declares that the light hurts her eyes, feeding her with your own hand when she refuses to eat, you are prolonging her symptoms. It is misplaced kindness, Miss Carr."

"Then you are proposing to treat her cruelly?"

"Not at all. Our regime is strict, but it is by no means cruel."

Alice Carr was a mild woman, but she was stubborn. She hooked her heels over the rail of her chair and pressed down hard to keep her back erect. She glanced out of the window at the hummocky Suffolk fields and thought of the Fox and Hounds and the ride down the hill behind those skittish horses. Now she would be forced to put up for another night. It was a vulgar name for an inn and she had been forced to overlook the drinking that took place below her room, as it was the only lodging to be had in the village. "I think I've told you everything, Doctor Waller." She adjusted her pince-nez.

"Then let us go over it once more if you don't mind. The cause of your sister's illness is a mystery. I do not believe in simply treating symptoms, Miss Carr. We must prod and tease until we reveal origins. It is not always easy to distinguish between what is organic, and what is imaginary. We have ruled out physiological causes such as diabetes, infectious diseases or gout, so now we must look deeper." She dabbed at one nostril with a handkerchief edged with embroidered forget-me-nots; to Alice's experienced eye, they looked like the work of a novice. "Now, as far as you know, your sister has never suffered any trauma?"

"As I have said, none at all." Alice was in no doubt that the best medicine in the world was available in England, but perhaps their sister Clara was right after all when she wrote that they should brave the sea voyage and come home to clean Canadian air and freshly cured ham. Alice had argued that they couldn't take the risk. If Emily were to deteriorate and become completely paralysed there would be no one to help on the high seas, or, come to that, in Victoria. She deduced from the expectant silence that the doctor required more details of her sister's medical history. "We rarely suffer trauma in Canada, and my sister is no exception, apart from the amputation of her great toe, which was done some years ago, and appears to have been botched."

"That is disturbing." Dr. Waller observed that Miss Carr's hat covered her eyebrows, surely a sign that she had something to conceal. "It is distressing, but hardly likely to precipitate her present predicament, since she has nine toes remaining. No. What I'm talking about is some kind of abrupt trauma, a sudden death, a wounding, any disruption of the senses that might put a strain on her reserves."

"The foot took several months to heal." Alice pursed her lips.

"Perhaps a jilting, a folly, an unrequited love?"

"She was engaged to be married some years ago, but she never made a big fuss when it fizzled. I think she was relieved. I know that we were. He was adequate but he was a Presbyterian, and almost impecunious."

"And she has made a big fuss over other things?"

"It is not unknown."

"What kind of things?" Dr. Waller felt she was blowing on dead coals.

"Her blessed sheep dog ate the Thanksgiving turkey. No, that was my sister Edith made the fuss—Edith was the cook that year..." Alice gripped the gilt clasp on her bag, glad to have something solid under her fingertips. "Well, I'm not giving anything away if I say she's a bawler. Her lungs are stronger than all my other three sisters put together. Always were. She can bawl."

"Yes. We have noted that. So this 'bawling' has been long established?" Dr. Waller's eyes were drawn to the small woman's fingers, which were made for thimbles. She was grasping her ugly bag as if it were a weapon. Her English was strange, not quite standard, yet not unrefined. Miss Emily Carr claimed that her sister spoke excellent French, but this seemed unlikely. "Would you please take me back to the time when your sister was a young child, Miss Carr."

3

Alice shook her head. "All four of us took care of Milly, she was the baby after Richard passed on; Mother went into a decline, he was the only boy, you see." She paused. "I suppose she has what you'd call hysteria. That's what brings her down so low. It's not such a mystery, is it?"

"What she 'has,' as you put it, appears to be a classic case of neurasthenia. I believe it can be treated but it is, up to now, very little understood. Your friends were wise to recommend that she be placed in my care—I am the only doctor in England who can help you, though please understand that I must give priority to my consumptives." Dr. Waller looked down at the empty sheet of paper and dipped her nib in the inkpot. "Now, this is going to be a little embarrassing, Miss Carr. I suppose you have not heard of Doctor Freud? Doctor Sigmund Freud of Vienna? He has very modern opinions on cases such as your sister's, which he is not shy to impart. As far as I am concerned, his ideas are interesting but inconclusive. It is his contention that the condition is a product of a repressed—how shall I put it in terms you will comprehend? A repressed sexual appetite. What do you think of that?" The doctor put down the pen and made her fingers into a steeple.

Alice pressed down harder with her heels. She did not allow her expression to change, but she felt wings fluttering in her chest.

"This is delicate, Miss Carr, but can you tell me if there is any irregularity in your sister's monthly bleeds?"

Alice shook her head. "Perhaps you should enquire from Emily, herself."

"We have, indeed we have, but to be frank we cannot always be sure that she tells us the truth. Hailing from another continent, we feel she may have a slightly different perspective."

"Different?"

The doctor saw that this was obviously not the best line of inquiry, but having decided to embark on it she could not give up so easily. "At what age did she begin her courses, Miss Carr?"

Alice narrowed her eyes and took a dive back. They were both in the garden. Emily felt something, pulled down her bloomers behind the rabbit hutch and saw the blood. Chow the Chinese servant was no more than five paces away, his queue hanging down his back, not bound up as it usually was. Emily grabbed it like a bell pull and bawled as if someone had stuck her with a knife. Edith came running full tilt from the house.

"It's brown, does it mean I'm going rusty inside?"

What a to-do. The handing over of a pile of white napkins while Father's back was turned. And Emily rejoicing because from now on she could take part in the sisters' personal wash on Thursdays when Father had business in town. A double line over the lawn, all flapping like wet white sails. And on rainy days the barn, festooned with limp ghosts.

"I don't remember," said Alice.

"Well, let me ask you something else. We both know that your sister has lived an exemplary life and has never been guilty of excess, but are you aware that she may have—how should I phrase it? Has she ever stimulated herself?" The steeple of fingers collapsed.

"Pardon?"

"In the female regions." Oh, what a bother! "Onanism, Miss Carr. It is sometimes practiced with instruments other than the hands though the fingers suffice. Old wives have it that it will lead to blindness and it has been presumed to induce temporary, or sometimes permanent imbalance, or even insanity in some females." Dr. Waller watched Miss Carr's boater slip down, until it almost obscured her eyes. She laced her fingers, sat back and studied the offending hat through a cage of knuckles. "I would never allow it in my hospital without supervision."

"I suppose it is also a cure for T.B.?" Alice stood up.

"Not to my knowledge. My views are progressive, Miss Carr. You are fortunate that I am prepared to assume responsibility for your sister's case." She could not let the other woman see how much was riding on this.

Alice grasped her umbrella, her bag and the account for the first month of Emily's stay in the hospital. Surely everybody knew that the forbidden act brought on deafness, not blindness, what sort of a doctor was this? "Please refrain from any such treatments, Doctor, with or without supervision. If you have called me back to ask for my permission, you will not have it."

"Miss Carr, please do sit down. I'm sorry if I offended, but I must have your approval for the entire treatment or I will not accept your sister as a patient. If you do not agree, I must ask you to remove her from my hospital without more ado. Please understand that I am most hopeful. I have been conferring with a noted authority on neurasthenia, Doctor Hartenberg—he resides in Paris. He predicts that the invalid will be quite restored. We intend to follow his regimen. Miss Carr will receive every attention from our nurses—hers is the first case of its kind that we have admitted to this hospital. If we are successful, there will be others. Your sister is a pioneer." Surely, thought Dr. Waller, surely the small brain under the hat will comprehend this word.

"I'll not take responsibility," Alice whispered as she signed the paper and got herself out of the room. She could still hear the doctor's voice as she hurried down the corridor. The exit door was blessedly close.

Outside, on the drive, she examined the account and gasped. The family would be six guineas a week poorer, and this did not include personal laundry and pocket money for Milly's necessary treats such as cigarettes. She would have to confide the cost to her sisters, but she would not burden them with the diagnosis and would make no mention of the treatment. They would budget more stringently if that were possible. She would have to face the prospect of delaying the opening of her schoolhouse and postpone the day when she would at last be free to live alone, but she would dally no more in England.

CHAPTER TWO

§ 1999

The pink house with its thatched roof and leaded windowpanes reminded her of a teapot her mother used to have when she was a kid. There was no bell so she lifted the heavy iron claw and let it fall. Her ride had dumped her in the middle of the village and she'd noticed a pub called the Fox and Hounds that advertised rooms, so if the worst came to the worst she could use her Visa card and hope they didn't check her credit. She grasped the knocker again just as the door opened on a view of a monstrously protruding belly.

"Mr. Rintoul?"

The young woman behind the belly measured her up, looking down the bridge of her very straight nose. She was unnaturally pale, not much more than a teenager. "Do I look like Mr. Rintoul?"

'Snotty bitch,' Kit thought. A man materialized. He had a pink, scaly head the same colour as the outside walls.

The man ran his fingers through his beard. "I'm Roger Rintoul. Can I help?"

"Probably not. You haven't for thirty-five years."

"I beg your pardon?"

"I'm your daughter. I'm Kit."

Kit watched the smile freeze. His features seemed to implode very slowly; the last to go was his nose. It was a nose like you saw on drunks. His beard looked as if it was glued on. Her mother had no photos and she realized she had a blank in her mind where his face should be. This guy looked old. He took out a large handkerchief and honked. She wondered who used handkerchiefs these days, and who washed them? The young woman with the belly put both her hands over her mouth and doubled over. He grabbed her by the shoulders and pushed her aside a bit too roughly, wedging his body between Kit and the open door.

"Can I come in?" Kit toed her bulky holdall.

She saw him absorb the word Kit, which was stencilled on the bag.

Without a word, he bent and levered the bag onto his shoulder, turning his head away from it. She stepped past him into the hallway. He studied her back, her angular, butterfly shoulders, the halo of ginger hair, the dirty T-shirt. 'Not today,' he thought, 'please God not today of all days, not on the birthday.' The dining room table was still loaded with the contents of the Fortnum and Mason's hamper; there was a magnum of champagne, a jar of gentleman's relish, a chocolate cake. He'd lit the candles in the candelabra and Ilona had been about to unwrap her gift. He deflected the new arrival into the living room. How did this grungy, anorexic apparition have the nerve to claim to be his flesh? How old would she be? Mutton dressed up as lamb. He couldn't possibly have a daughter this age. How had she found him? Catherine wouldn't know his address. Catherine didn't even know he was still in England—back when they were an item he'd been threatening to move to Provence or Florence any day. He would have to play his cards carefully. She could be a fraud. She probably wanted money.

He glanced again at the letters on the greasy bag remembering that they'd nicknamed her Kit. She'd been registered as Kathryn, after Catherine, her mother, who was named after her mother, Catharine. How come he remembered all this now? They'd joked about the names, a clutch of Kates, a chimera of Kates...Catherine used to drive him mad with her word games.

A chimera, that's what this person was. A ginger-headed monster. With luck she'd disappear if he blinked three times. Ilona had dashed upstairs—he needed to go to her. He closed his eyes, but when he opened them the monster was still there, sitting on the settee, openly appraising one of his paintings. She licked her lips and he caught a glimpse of a tongue stud. Her skin wasn't smooth—she'd obviously suffered from acne just as he had. He fingered his beard again. It was a recent inspiration of Ilona's to cover old scars. He studied Kit's face more closely. The eyes. Yes, the eyes were Rintoul eyes, grey, completely clear, sparse lashes, pale eyebrows so wide apart they were ready to fly off her face. But she could still be an impostor. He could hardly ask to see her passport.

"What should I call you?" She nibbled her thumb nail.

"Call me? You don't have to call me anything. What are you doing here? How did you know where to come?"

"I traced you on the Net. I know where you work. You can track anyone down if you really want to."

This was suspicious. He hated the Internet.

"When's your birthday?" She told him, but he wasn't sure what date she'd been born. He knew it was summer. "Have you been in England long?"

"I was born here, wasn't I?"

"If you say so."

"You're amazing."

"What?"

"I mean, if I wasn't born here, how did I get a British passport? Don't you even remember that?"

"What's the name of your mother?"

"Catherine Van Duren, same as always, or at least it was last time I saw her. She has a boyfriend now." She waited for him to react to this news but he didn't respond. "She's retired."

That came as a shock—Catherine retired, Catherine as an old woman. "Then she's still alive?"

"You're down on my birth certificate as my father and you don't even know if my mom's alive. You're listed as an artist." She cast a scornful glance at the painting in the alcove.

Roger followed her glance. The painting had some significance when he did it, he couldn't remember what. It was a semi-abstract of decaying vegetation, after the style of somebody. Fortunately she didn't linger on it.

"Who was that pregnant woman?"

Ilona! "Forgive me, help yourself to whatever..." He jumped to his feet, gesturing vaguely, hoping there were some nuts or grapes in the bowl-things that Ilona scattered around, trusting she wouldn't attack the remains of the feast. Apart from a drop-in from Ilona's parents and his brother Sam, they hadn't actually had any visitors since they'd got married. He bounded upstairs as Kit picked up the package he'd wrapped up for Ilona that afternoon. Inside the pink and silver paper was a framed photo of a speedboat.

The mound of Ilona's belly shifted then jumped. It was entrancing. "Kick boxers," he whispered. "Are those two scrapping?" He knew his whisper was too loud. He almost toppled on top of her. Ilona pulled her smock down. She was sprawled on her back, naked except for the swath of polka dot material that was working its way up to her armpits. Her face was streaked with tears; when she felt Roger's weight, she launched into a new spate of sobs. He rolled off the bed and crouched down, stroking her hair and wondering what to do for the best. The hair was spread out on the pillow as though it had been ironed. It was so dark, a deep, peaty brown without a single grey thread. This colour always came out dead when you tried to paint it, unless you were Titian of course—that marvellous portrait of a man in the National Gallery, possibly a self-portrait—the hair impenetrably brown, yet full of life. If you couldn't get the light right, you'd have to cheat and add coppery undertones. He'd always had to cheat. Light was a problem for him; for Catherine it had been a gift. She'd never have let him buy a dark house like Golding.

He lay down on the bed and began working his nose along the pillow until it was within an inch of Ilona's earlobe. His nostrils stood by for the familiar scent of her shampoo, but he could only catch the damp smell of snot and tears. She was so young, too young for burdens. It was his duty to shield her, particularly now. He couldn't begin to come to grips with what was sitting downstairs; it was completely alien, bizarrely out of place. It had a tongue stud! He would have to face it. It didn't seem to be making any move to leave. But not tonight—he'd been looking forward to tonight.

"So, what's she supposed to call me? Mummy?" Ilona sniffed, and her belly dimpled.

"Of course not."

"Why didn't you tell me you had a daughter?"

"I don't know—I suppose I forgot."

"Forgot? How can you forget your own child? How many more have you forgotten? Are you going to forget the twins?"

"No, of course not. I haven't seen her since she was in nappies."

"She's horrible. How old is she?"

"I don't know—she must be over thirty."

"She doesn't look it. How did she get that hair? Tell her to go away."

"How can I? She's come all this way."

"All what way?"

"I don't know, from America or somewhere. She's my first wife's daughter."

"And yours?"

"I suppose so. She has the family eyes."

This brought on a fresh tempest. Ilona beat her fists on the duvet, defeated by the unresisting feathers. "Why did she come today?"

"I don't think she knew today was special. We're going to have to be civilized, I'm afraid. We'll have to ask her to stay. Do you think you could make up the spare bed? She can leave with me tomorrow morning. I'll book her a hotel in London."

"She's not leaving with you. You won't come back."

"Oh, don't be a silly Dumbo." Sometimes he couldn't believe how insecure she was. It was quite endearing, though it could be wearing, not to mention contradictory in a person with looks, family and youth on her side.

"She can make up her own damned bed."

Roger sighed, relieved. She'd accepted that Kit would stay. The birthday celebration was going to be a bit strained but they'd get through it. And now there would be someone to share the champagne. Pregnant women weren't allowed to drink, even on their birthdays.

"Why didn't you tell me you'd been married before?"

"It wasn't important," he said, helping her up.

🜊

Stranded in the dining room, Kit listened to the querulous falsetto and the deeper thrum of Roger's responses overhead. She moved round the table, weighing the heavy silver cutlery in her palm, examining the candelabra, the paper-thin china. There was money here, money her mother would drool for. She scraped some of the icing off the chocolate cake with her fingernail and thought about the meals they'd eaten when she was growing up—home baked pizza, chicken livers, day old bread—the birthday ice-cream cake from Dairy Queen that took them so far over their budget they had to eat soup for a week. She didn't like chocolate but this tasted deep and rich. She dipped a finger in some disgusting black squishy caviar then picked up a knife to cut a taster from the paté, longing for a hamburger. She heard footsteps on the stairs and dodged away from the table. Through the open door, she saw Roger go into a room across the hall without glancing in her direction. She went to the doorway. He was sitting in the bay window, staring out on the street. Suddenly she needed to pee.

She tiptoed upstairs. There were several doors along the landing, all closed, except one, no evidence of a bathroom. She looked through the open door and saw Ilona, propped up on one elbow, the drum of her belly exposed. The tightly stretched skin was mildly shocking.

🐜

Ilona couldn't control the shakes. She laid her hands on top of the sheet. They were empty gloves, dancing out of synch with her chattering teeth. She groped under the bed for her china rabbit—he was her good luck mascot, he'd been with her since she was six and he'd slept in this dark warren ever since she moved to Golding. Roger didn't mind—she didn't think he'd even noticed—he never looked under the bed. He didn't go where he wasn't wanted, that was just one nice thing about him. She turned the rabbit's painted eyes towards the photograph on the bedside table. It was a snapshot taken on their honeymoon in St. Agathe. She wore her going-away suit, silver grey with a high collar and Roger had an open-necked shirt and a stiff straw hat she'd bought him at a souvenir shop. They were standing by the gate that led into the old walled town, smiling like silly goats. Roger had given a boy some cash to take the picture. The boy smiled too—no wonder, it translated into the equivalent of £10.00, but it was worth it—it was the best photo she'd ever seen, (the wedding pictures hadn't turned out, her brother had been using his friend's camera). She got goose pimples when she thought of the honeymoon in St. Agathe. Was it possible that she'd actually walked on the rocking cobbles, gazed through the lace-curtained windows, visited the railway station? When she looked at the picture she felt much calmer. She knew there were no souvenir shops in 1911, no cars, or motorbikes, no tankers in the bay. People would have been wearing clogs and Breton costumes but this didn't make today's St. Agathe less than perfect. Before she met Roger, it had been a dream. "I'll make the arrangements for the honeymoon," she'd told him. She knew the ropes; she'd worked for a travel agency. She always managed to be bold with Roger, though it never worked with anyone else. Brazen, he'd once called her, my brazen hussy! She'd looked around to see if he meant someone else. He said he was thinking of a honeymoon in Tahiti or somewhere exotic but she saw he hadn't given it more than a moment's thought and she teased him. She knew he was more worried about when they'd get back than where they went. She was never afraid of overstepping the mark with Roger.

When they got to St. Agathe, he reassured her again and again that he liked the quaint fishing town, the good restaurants, the walks beside the water under the sweet-chestnut trees. Finally she believed him. He told her he was sorry he hadn't learned French at school, only Latin and Greek. The water was as clear as his eyes. Sometimes when she looked into his eyes she imagined fish swimming. Roger didn't know it yet, but they were going to buy a house and spend every summer here. The twins would have French lessons. She chose the house from Winifred Church's detailed description. It hadn't been easy to find—Bretons built so many homes in the same style. While Roger napped with the shutters latched, Ilona scoured the town and finally narrowed down three possibilities. None of the houses jumped out at her, so she tried eenie-meenie-minie-mo and rock, paper, scissors. She drew lots. The same one came up every time. It was built on a hill, surrounded by garden on all sides, facing the sea. She visited it every afternoon to make sure. (Roger was always exhausted after they'd had their fun—he blamed it on the heat.) There was a high hedge round the garden, just the way her great-great aunt described it, an apple tree, a grape vine, window boxes blazing with red, white and blue flowers, the colours of the French flag. One afternoon the woman inside saw her peeping through the hedge. Ilona waved at her gaily, trying to make out that it was the most natural thing in the world to be scrutinizing someone else's house. The woman waved back.

Ilona made sure Roger didn't read Winifred Church's diary. For the present it lived in a brown cardboard box in the walk-in cupboard in their bedroom, concealed under her shoe boxes along with a sheaf of letters and bills that Mrs. Martin said were of no interest. She kept the door of the cupboard open a crack so she could check that the box hadn't walked. The diary hadn't been discussed since she'd first found it when she was ten years old. Her mother had warned her not to read it. It contained things that were not suitable for a child's eyes. Not suitable for anyone's eyes. Family secrets, best forgotten. Mrs. Martin maintained that what was done was done, but it didn't need to be broadcast. Diaries were purely personal, if they were intended for public reading, the diarist would always be looking over his own shoulder.

Mrs. Martin assumed her injunction would be obeyed, but seeing that her daughter was still curious, she took the precaution of locking the spare room where the useless old sewing machine blocked access to the window seat. Ilona knew where she kept the key, waited for her mother to go out, then stole into the room, climbed over the machine and curled up on the window seat with the forbidden pages.

It didn't take long to have them by heart. This way, she wouldn't have to risk being found in the forbidden room. Winnie's secrets were safe with her, as were those of her friends, who, by this time, had become Ilona's friends too. They travelled with her, when she was sent away, though that was when she almost lost them. She kept landing on the picture she had in her head of her great-great aunt encountering a red-faced woman, dressed for winter in the middle of summer, at the railway station in St. Agathe. It never failed to make her giggle. She recoiled when she saw the railway station in real life. She couldn't be wrong about Miss Carr, too.

The first time she brought Roger home to meet her parents her father dominated the conversation and the two men shut themselves away in his study after dinner. They were both in banking, (Ilona met Roger at an office cocktail party, when she was standing in for her mother). While the men talked, the women loaded the dishwasher; Mrs. Martin was well into a hand of patience by the time they emerged from the study. Ilona grabbed Roger's arm and led him down to the cellar before they could stop her.

They lugged the heavy, framed pictures up the rickety stairs into what was left of the light.

"Oh, I'm so sorry, it's filthy down there." Her mother didn't bother to disguise her feelings. "They're just daubs, the poor old thing couldn't even draw. Look at those creatures with no necks. Are they meant to be women? I've been meaning to throw the things out for years. What were you thinking of, Ilona?"

"They're fascinating." Roger went down on one knee to tear off the plastic wrap and examine one of the vibrant canvases more closely. At that moment Ilona realized that she really liked him. "Who's the artist?" he asked.

"My great uncle. Geoffrey Church." Her mother's voice wavered, suddenly uncertain about her relative's prowess.

"You should find wall space for them," Roger said.

"Are they worth something?" Ilona's father was suddenly alert.

"Don't be silly, darling." Mrs. Martin ushered them into the drawing room for a nightcap, leaving Ilona to put the paintings away. Nobody mentioned that Roger had once been an artist, Ilona guessed it wouldn't endear him to her mother.

They sneaked back to the house one weekend shortly after they were married and scooped the paintings up, gabbling all the way back to Golding, like children with scrumped apples. They stowed them under the stairs, planning to hang them after the house had been redecorated. Ilona was sure they wouldn't be missed. Just before she was married, she'd found the door to the spare-room open, sneaked in and rescued the diary. Now she no longer had to search her memory, trying to retrieve fragments. She hoped her mother had forgotten it; the Martins prided themselves on being unsentimental; since she left home, she had begun to see her parents in a new light and it wasn't always flattering.

Roger knew nothing of the diary's significance to his wife. He'd moved his clothes to his dressing room and hadn't looked in the bedroom cupboard since he'd turned it over to Ilona. He knew nothing much about Emily Carr either, even though she dangled her birdcage on the wall opposite their bed. He hadn't wanted to hang the cartoon in their bedroom, but he bowed to Ilona's fondness for it.

"Oh, goodness!" The picture had jumped out at her the first time he brought her to Golding. It was lost against the precise red pattern of the William Morris wallpaper in the hall, but she made a beeline for it and ran her fingers over the faint signature.

"You know the artist?"

"Oh, yes. Emily Carr."

"Well done! I thought she went rather well with the wallpaper. There's a date on the back, 1908."

Ilona nodded, unsure what to say. No one had asked her opinion about art before. She was overwhelmed. Something had drawn her to the picture, something amazing.

"I think she may be one of the artists someone I once knew used to talk about. She doesn't add up to much, does she?"

"You mustn't lose her!"

"Oh, she's a keeper."

They were both tentative, walking warily, consumed with the newness of being together. He had yet to kiss her properly, but Ilona knew with a wave of certainty that she was going to move into Golding. "Where did you get that picture?"

"I picked it up when they were selling off the fittings from the asylum up the hill. I was after a filing cabinet but the ones they had were monsters, so I picked up a job lot of junk in an old beer crate to keep them happy—tools and old ledgers, nothing interesting. I gave them a couple of quid and beetled off as fast as I could. Place made me feel queasy."

This was the first inkling Ilona had that the hospital he mentioned might have been the T.B. sanatorium on the hill a few miles outside the village, the place where Emily Carr had spent a year and a half, long before she ever met Winifred Church. It confirmed that Miss Carr had lured her here. She would have liked to let Roger in on this theory, but to do so would be to betray Winifred Church by revealing the contents of her diary.

She'd found the crate when she was poking about in a corner of the loft, shortly after she learned that she was pregnant. She could hardly believe her luck. There were no other pictures in it, merely case histories of T.B. patients and treatments, medical notes that were hard to decipher, some spanners and a long length of perished rubber tubing that came apart in her fingers. She combed through the papers looking for references to Miss Carr, feeling closer and closer to the world of the sanatorium—if Roger was right, it had been turned into a mental hospital before it blossomed into luxury flats. She sniffed the papers and smelled chrysanthemums. Why did visitors always leave behind the pungent smell of chrysanthemums?

The day she found the papers, she walked the circuit up to the gates of the old hospital, and after that she went up there twice a week; the round trip took most of the morning. She usually sneaked down the driveway, imagining the building free of satellite dishes. She had no fear of ghosts; on the whole they were easier to deal with than the people she met in real life.

Emily had brought her to Roger and her parents were right, her husband didn't need to know about her past. She'd never felt better than in the last few weeks, so close to the birth.

CHAPTER THREE

᠅

E mily Carr burrows down under a knitted rug on a sweltering day.

The room where she lies is open to summer. Bugs, pollen, the swish of a scythe, the sound of a rounders game in progress have all invited themselves in through the gaping windows. Someone is caught out. There is a thin chorus of cheers. A nurse has pleated a paper fan and it sits on top of the mountain of Emily's left hip, disregarded. She will sweat it out. She is in Suffolk. In England. Everyone in the Dominion knows that England is not hot.

Word has it that she paints pictures, but no one asks. A nurse comes in with a chart.

"We just need to check your date of birth, Miss Carr."

"Check away," says Emily, "count the rings," and she uncovers her thigh. 'More than forty,' she thinks, 'more than half a life lived and what have I to show for it?'

The nurse frowns at the dimpled flesh, turns on her heel when she has no response and swishes out of the room. Emily tries to live up to expectations but her answers pop out from the wrong places. All but the bravest nurses steer clear of her. She knows she is not lovable, but today (and yesterday, and last week) she's exhausted and there's no breath left to expend on niceness. On good days, when she goes outside, she can crack them up.

"You're a bit of a sketch, you are." She remembers a young Cockney woman talking to her on one of her good days, "why don't you come out and play rounders?"

"I'm round enough."

The young woman laughed. Emily knew she'd seen her cracking jokes with the children who were here for the cure.

"Too bad you won't come down off your high horse and treat us 'ups' to a song, or maybe a hand of rummy in the Common Room of an evening. We won't bite, you know!"

Under the blankets, Emily is making an enormous pudding. She hurls the ingredients in, underarm, thwuk they go, thwuk, thwak, thwuk, like the solid rounders ball on the solid rounders bat. She can hear them shouting encouragement to the players as she makes her pudding. In go all the things a lady is not supposed to be. In her head she is arguing with Alice and, as usual, Alice wins. Of course there's no case for art. Alice insists that a lady's art is to care for others, (unless you're a lady with a capital L). Alice says a lady can paint but she can't be an artist. Alice says a lady can have talent but she can't have genius. Well, why not? Because ladies show in country fairs, or drawing rooms. Ladies dabble, so dabble goes into the pudding. Men experiment, men discuss and express, ladies gossip. In goes gossip. Ladies don't boom the way she does, they tinkle, and tinkle goes into the mix. It's getting massive, this pudding. That's too bad, because ladies don't take up much space. There's no more room, no room for desire.

When the time comes, who will cart the pudding away? She runs through the connections she has in England. Miss Brown, the Misses Walgrove, Mr. and Mrs. Carruthers, all friends from home, fugitives from the Colonies, trying hard to out-English the English. She likes them well enough, but desire is a word they dare not breathe. Cover your hopes like piano legs. The ladies from home have mastered the art of living up to other people's expectations so why cannot she?

Emily ices the pudding and encases it in a ring of ladies' fingers. She ticks off her virtues. She has always tried to be good and kind and generous, she believes in the Saviour with all her heart and soul, but she is forever tripping, and it has nothing to do with her bad foot. She is too intrusive. Her needs keep bobbing up though she does her best to bury them. Why does she have such a way of butting in where she's not invited? They turned a blind eye when she was growing up.

"Is Doctor Jameson a boy or a girl?"

"That's enough, Milly!"

"If he's a boy why does he wear rouge? And why doesn't he close his eyes when we say prayers?"

"Close yours and mind your own business."

She is close to forty and she still hasn't learned to ask the right questions or shrink into the shadows when it's appropriate, though the shadows try hard to claim her. The young woman was right. She is a sketch. She's a caricature. In a land of sparrows, she's a parrot. Into the pudding go all her colours. She screws up her face. She will shrink herself down to size and try once again to blend in with all the quiet people. Locked in this room, she knows she is fighting for life.

'Live!' she yells silently as the game goes on under her window.

This is her last chance. She's lucky. They are willing to tone her down one last time. Someone suggests that she write her story. Why doesn't she keep a journal of the treatment, they ask. It would give her stability when she feels herself slipping. But she doesn't want their stability. The truth of the monster she really is must never come out, not here and certainly not back home. Surely she can be forgiven for wishing to be important, when underneath she knows she is of no more consequence than the paper fan that has fluttered to the floor from the bed. She is a thing of rags and patches. It's all too confusing, and it cannot be told. She buries her face in the pillow and, as they dose her up to keep her down, she tries not to taste her own bile.

She dreams she is opening the top drawer in her mother's dressing table. She can smell the familiar almond oil, count the neatly folded lace collars. Now she is in the black and white tiled bathroom and she wipes her hands on the cross-stitched guest towel, but she's not a guest. So what is she? Her eyes are level with the second rung of the towel rack so she can't be full-grown. She claws at the heavy metal band round her forehead. Her hands are restrained. There are straps round her wrists so she can't reach the wires that have just delivered such a jolt, loosening her teeth and scattering them like piano keys on the floor.

Oldest sister glowers at the polished surface of the family dining table. Edith. Madam Vinegar Puss. She's wearing the frock she gave to the poor the year the Queen died. She has her belt in her hand ready to whack.

"Stay in your seat, Milly. Don't keep fidgeting."

And the other sisters are seated in their usual spots, Lizzie, Clara (without her husband and children), mild little Alice, her crochet hook flying; they are all assembled to thank God for the century just passed and to celebrate the new century which is barely half a day old; or is it a birthday they are celebrating? Is it her birthday? Then where is Mother? What's happened to time? The heavy curtains are drawn against the blinding Victoria sun and Edith is leading the prayers. She's placed the chenille cloth over the back of the rocking chair. And there's Father, twelve years dead, or is it twenty? He's looking down approvingly from the wall over the fireplace. No, he's not, he's striding from side to side on the hearthrug, his hands behind his back. He's displeased. Someone has hung a beaded pelmet over his picture. His beard brushes his waistcoat and she counts his buttons over and over. Each sister knows her place but she, who is the youngest, laughs louder, runs faster, gets more love than the rest.

She feels her thigh, cautiously. It's blown up. All of her has blown up, there's enough of her for three and nothing fits any more, not

23

even Lizzie's crewelwork nightgown, wrenched up around her hips. Yes, she is still here, she's been consigned to eighteen months of bed rest in faraway Suffolk, with three mountainous meals a day and she must be patient. Her chins are too numerous to count; her breasts hang like udders on her distended stomach. Nothing must be sent back to the kitchen, the minder sits by her pillow, watching every last crumb disappear. Six blankets don't keep out the cold winds that sweep across the Fens heading unerringly for her uncurtained, unglassed-in windows. All thoughts of art are long ago eclipsed. She's a captive of food, electricity, and the elements in this emporium where she is the only patient who is not suffering from T.B. It is winter. Snow accumulates round her bed, ice crumbs bounce off the bedspread and she half expects the minder to retrieve them and pile them on her plate.

No, it's spring. There are two new lambs in the sheep pasture below her window but she can't raise her eyes. Today, as always on electricity days, her body is water, there's something puffy, something rubbery, in her mouth; it's holding her teeth apart, she can't find a place for her tongue and there's no room to let anything through her throat though it's itching with words. The doctor is wheeling away the machine, the session must be over for another day, so what's that noise coming from her chest, straining to get out? The hot pig at her feet should be inscribed with her name. R.I.P. Emily Carr. It's a headstone, it's the stone they rolled up to Jesus' tomb—no, that's blasphemy. There are ten black currants on Father's waistcoat—he called it his weskit—ten currants down the front of the gingerbread men the big sisters bake every holiday. The men turn gold and they leave the oven. Gold. Ten more gold sovereigns—and more, they are heaped, cascading out of the sifter, into the flour. The cost. The cost of all this so-called cure. The cost of this sanitary airium. No! More! Food!

She stands on a cliff. She is home in British Columbia looking down at the waves as they chew up the rocks. The meadow behind her is impossibly blue. What is the name of those blue flowers? Cam...Cam...Cam—words are disappearing, drowned, engulfed by the rising sound, the roar, a huge wall of water—has to breach, has to breach her mouth, her eyes, between her legs. Electricity. Aaaaaaah!

Camas.

🜊

Ilona touched her lips to the rabbit's forehead and put him back under the bed. She jumped as the front door slammed. That couldn't be Roger going out—he always kissed her before he left the house. Swaying downstairs, clinging to the rail (stairs were hard when the treads were hidden), she saw the orange-haired Medusa standing in the dining room. She was just standing, not doing anything. Her greasy bag was still in the hall stamped with the word Kit. Kit Bag. There was no sign of Roger.

Ilona tiptoed into the living room, annoyed with herself for feeling ill at ease in her own house.

"I'm bushed." Kit screwed up her eyes.

"Does that mean you need to go to bed?"

"You bet."

"What about food?"

Kit shook her head. Ilona smiled with relief and left Kit alone while she mined the linen cupboard for the second best sheets and pillowcases.

When she returned, Kit pushed them aside, "I have my own stuff in my bag, thanks."

"I shall give you a tour on the way up." Ilona plunged upstairs again.

Kit followed, glancing around without bothering to feign interest.

The pink house was deceptive; it looked so smug and sunny from the outside but inside it was dark and a bit claustrophobic. Ilona explained the layout in detail. One room had been set aside for a nursery, the decorators were expected any time. She pointed out the closed door of the master bedroom, talking fast to cover the silence.

"We overlook the back lawn and a Beech copse," she explained. "There's a pair of nightingales out there somewhere—we keep thinking we hear them, but we don't really know what they sound like. Nightingales are dying out, you know."

Kit nodded. She didn't know. She wondered if Ilona was on something, her speech was jerky and she tossed her head in an odd way.

They toiled up to the box room on the third floor. This was where Ilona had decided that Kit should stay. It had once been the maid's quarters. Kit pushed past her, threw open the casement window and let out a low moan of pleasure. Ilona hadn't expected this. "You can have a bigger room if you like, this one gets hot," she said.

"It doesn't, it won't! It's perfect!"

Ilona stood in the doorway waiting for a sign that it was all right to leave, flinching as Kit dumped the bag on the bed.

"You should see where I've been hanging out. Last night I slept— no, dossed under Waterloo Station in a dump called Cardboard City. You have to watch out down there even if you have a dog."

"Have you got a dog?"

"Of course not."

"Why didn't you go to a hotel?"

"I wanted a genuine English welcome. Like this one."

Ilona watched for the smile that would show this was a joke, but Kit frowned.

"I've never been in a room with real roses on the wallpaper. I've never been in a room with wallpaper, come to that."

Why did she make every sentence sound like a question?

"What do they have instead of wallpaper in America?" Ilona ventured.

"I dunno. Walls, I guess?" Kit unlaced the bag and brought out a scrap of towel and a greasy sleeping bag that had once been light blue. She wanted out from this cut-glass person who seemed intent on standing here all night asking naïve questions. Hadn't she heard of jet-lag? "And by the way—it's Canada, not America."

"Canada?" Ilona was dumbfounded. "Emily Carr came from Canada."

"Of course. So does my mother. Actually my mom's not Canadian, but she's an amazing artist. Way better than Emily Carr."

Ilona couldn't believe her ears. "Look, let me get that bedding. Please. I mean, if you've come so far..."

"No. Honest. I'd rather stick with the bag, it's kind of my shape."

"Wasn't it uncomfortable, sleeping on the ground?"

Kit yawned. "Noisy. Trains rumbling through your head all night—the whole floor was jumping."

"Fleas?"

"Probably." Kit threw herself on the bed, hoping Ilona would take the hint, but she stood, looking down with her dense, unreflective eyes. She was thin as an eyelash behind the bump, arms so slender they'd break if you squeezed too hard. Kit saw that she was hiding her fear. She looked as though she was scared of her shadow.

"Are you scared?" The question popped out. Kit watched the pupils dilate. She saw herself through those eyes. A Hayseed. A Canadian Hick. She should have turned up in heels and a business suit, dressed like an air stewardess, or whatever they called them now.

Ilona fled.

She leaned back against the closed door gasping for breath. There wasn't enough air on this floor.

Safe in her sleeping bag, Kit heard the gasping and imagined Ilona's tongue, long and thin like her arms. She wondered if she should remove her tongue stud. It was a new acquisition—the hair didn't work, it made her look like the Lion King. How was a long lost daughter supposed to look, apart from young? She caved in to sleep.

Ilona made her way downstairs and loaded a tray with Lobster Thermador, Waldorf salad, a wedge of Black Forest cake, a beer mug full of champagne. She wouldn't be seen as a bad hostess, too bad if the person didn't want to eat.

Balancing the tray, she laboured back up the two flights of stairs. When there was no response to her knock she pushed the door open and found Kit curled up in her bag like a shaggy orange dog, apparently fast asleep. She'd switched the light on even though it was light outside. Ilona wondered if anyone would notice if she sprayed a little room freshener around and decided to compromise and leave the aerosol can on the window ledge. Five minutes later she was back. She removed the aerosol can and covered Kit with an Amish Log-Cabin quilt, a wedding gift from Roger's brother. She thought the quilt was ugly but she knew Roger prized it. She'd try to welcome this person for his sake, it wasn't asking too much, and she'd be gone by tomorrow.

CHAPTER FOUR

ع

The last echoes of 'For she's a jolly good fellow' died away—she saw that the room they'd chosen was too big for the occasion. Someone dinged their spoon against a glass and chanted "Catherine Van Duren. Catherine Van Duren." The chant echoed from table to table. Her stomach took a dive. Suddenly they were waiting, smiling encouragement. She knew they were expecting her to say something plucky, unassuming, redemptive. Lord, how she hated redemption, so sentimental, so impossible—so Canadian! They wanted her to be up-beat and positive, to allay their guilt by announcing that she was starting out on a new adventure.

She glanced around and made a mental note of who wasn't there. Seth Miles, the Head of Department, as bogus a practitioner as ever you'd fall over at a trendy opening, or vernissage (his word); he'd sent apologies as usual, the demands of his senile mother. Catherine had once remarked that if the old hag ever shucked off this mortal coil, he'd be punished by having to attend a duplicate of every gruesome event he'd missed because of her, till he followed her into purgatory. Catherine was known as a loose cannon.

Jennifer Yamagouchi, the department secretary, was there. That was surprising, she was a single mother with two kids. She'd expected to see Gilly Tannenbaum—Gilly, an Art Historian, was her only reliable ally in frequent departmental skirmishes, although she'd been out of touch since she rose to the rank of Associate Dean. Catherine finally spotted her at a table by the window, intense, arms flailing, talking something through with Big Bill Henshaw who was touted as the next 'name' in West Coast art.

It was a good turnout considering they had to pay for their own wine and considering she wasn't a tenured faculty member. It was their fault she'd been a thorn in everyone's side, they'd all chosen to live by the laws of Political Correctness. Before the singing, she'd heard people remark that she didn't seem to have any sense of danger and this was amazing since she was not tenured. She was the sole means of support for her family and had everything to lose by stepping out of line. Suddenly they were admiring. A young male faculty member remarked that there was something to be said for statistics since she'd only been kept on to meet the male/female quotas. She wandered around, smiling and nodding, thinking that if she wasn't meant to be listening, they must think she was deaf as well as past her shelf date. She was fairly sure no one in the room doubted her ability as an artist, though she hadn't had a show for years.

Everyone was aware she'd applied for all the tenure track positions that had come up since her appointment. This was the last night such knowledge needed to shame her. The faculty members who'd schemed for her to be laid off so near to her mandatory retirement date were scattered around the room. She picked out their faces; some were her own age, they were relaxed and smiling, unassailable.

Lay. Off. Catherine repeated the words to herself. Two such benign syllables. The gentle completion to be followed shortly after by the laying out. And then there was laying on—the laying on of libations so everyone would go away from her party feeling good. Here they sat, finishing supper after wolfing down canapés, laying aside everything they'd said in the past. Laying down. That's what they'd hoped she'd do. That way she'd have advanced. Lay down your litany of complaints, Catherine, lie down and let us walk over you. Play dead. Dead like a donkey!

"Speech," Jennifer Yamagouchi yelled, "let's have the Last Farewell."

"Positively her last farewell," someone murmured and the small flame ignited and jumped from table to table. "Let's hear it, Van Duren! Speech! The last farewell!"

Catherine scanned the expectant faces, willing her stomach back into its proper place. She'd written out a rough script and she fumbled under her chair for her canvas satchel. It wasn't there. She'd left it at home. She had no speech. Then she realized she'd transferred her stuff into her shoulder bag. For once in her life, she'd been worried about looking shabby. The purse was slung over the back of her chair.

She stood up, cleared her throat, and focused on Gilly Tannenbaum's smiling mouth with its small, childlike teeth set in a cushion of shiny pink gums. She noted that the first remarks went down well. There was a ripple of applause as she scattered a few remembrances of times past along with praise for former students who'd gone on to make more of a noise in the art world than most of the faculty. So far, so good. She began to work up to speed, thanking the Dean and Gilly for their support and now she was on level ground. All that was expected was a few quips about the joys of retirement and she could sit down and maybe half enjoy the rest of the evening. She had one last opportunity to live up to expectations.

"So what is power?" she asked, staring at Gilly Tannenbaum's mouth, watching the gums disappear. The loose page of her speech floated to the floor and she paused. Her hands stopped shaking. "I have no power." She waited. She thought she could detect a slight rustling in the audience. Let them stew. Here she stood, a life devoted to art and nothing of consequence to say about it, nothing to show, and not even enough to buy a few square feet of floor space in this, one of the highest priced property markets in North America. She scanned all the crinkled foreheads. People were wondering if she'd died.

"Is it possible that one day some one of you will give me my due?" She paused again. Did she dare go on? Someone lit a cigarette. Someone told him to put it out. "What is a due?" she asked. "What is actually due to us after forty-five years of making art, other than a dutiful party when we're laid off from our job with no pension, two years before closing time? We fill up our time making pictures. Good Art, Bad Art, Indifferent Art—who cares? Who cares? Drop one letter from paint and you have pain! What I'm asking is...what I'm asking is, what do you value in this place? No one talks about emotion or humanity or students. We're all posts. Post posts. Post post modernists. Post Colonialists. Trapped between ists and isms, trying to put the ball between the posts on the International scene. We've listened to the critics and abstracted ourselves from our own centres. There should be confessionals set up for critics—sort of A.A.'s where they can go for a cure."

She saw that she was getting through to them. "And where are the women in all of this? Toeing the line, of course. And where's the line? Not through the heart! We should have stormed the fortress; we've opened up a little gap in the stockade, but in the final tally we still don't count. Look at this pathetic department. Walk the galleries—see how many of us are headlined. Who's to blame? White men? Give me a break! All you white men are busy protecting and re-inventing your own, and all the time kvetching about being undermined—and why shouldn't you kvetch? Show me a dog who shares his dinner when he's hungry. And now it's not just women—there's all the other under-classes snuffling at your trough!" She drew a deep breath. The hush was so intense it creaked. Just a few short strides and she'd cross the finish line.

"I've come into this place three times a week and I have nothing to show for it. I haven't made it because I don't know how. I've stopped trying to find It. I don't even believe in It. I don't know how to please you—I don't know how to say please. I paint (well, I used to paint); I paint because it satisfies me. It's the only thing that does. And I hope I'll paint again now I'm out of here. I've been thinking that maybe my work's ahead of its time but I'm not sure what it means to think in terms of time. It's the excuse we all use, isn't it, when we can't get to sleep for worrying about being ignored? When we don't fit? Maybe I'm actually behind time. One thing I do know, I'm not running to catch up. No Sir, no one's going to see me run."

She sat down abruptly, her heart thudding. All she'd shown them was a shrivelled little pea, full of envy and disrespect. The art scene was much more complex and she was a bigger person. No wonder they were laughing at her now. She fingered the nitroglycerin spray in her pocket. Someone pushed a glass of champagne into her hand, and she downed it without tasting it. She heard clapping. Clapping, not laughing. And they were on their feet. Gilly Tannenbaum strode over and shook her hand, and others followed. "Brave, Catherine, bravo, you finally put us straight!"

She made it to the washroom, threw up, swilled her mouth out and spat into the pale pink sink. Then she rushed up to the cloak-room, grabbed her coat and umbrella and hightailed it out into the ever-reliable Vancouver rain. She looked down at the keys in her hand. There were keys to the office she shared with two other sessionals, the key to the storage rooms, keys to the art complex. She took them off the ring, jingled them in her palm and hurled them into the shrubbery. She wouldn't be back. Sliding into the driver's seat of her Valiant she found a paper streamer trapped under her collar.

Headlights and street lights shimmered and rebounded off the wet surface of the road. She was dazzled and reminded that her night vision wasn't good. Luckily she found a parking space outside the house.

She stepped from the car into a deep puddle and stood for a moment, shocked by the chill, looking down at her only pair of dress shoes, waterlogged, probably ruined. She grinned. She didn't need them. She'd never have to make the journey up to the university again. She glanced up and saw the upstairs curtain twitch. As usual, Ernie Last had recognised the sound of her engine and was checking that she was safely home; as usual, she felt mildly irritated by his concern.

She'd rented the basement and first floor of this old house on the east side of town since she first came to Vancouver when Kit was a baby. She'd stayed on because the place fit, and Ernie had only increased the rent twice since they moved in. He was a bootmaker. Catherine thought of him as an oddball, but over the years they'd evolved into a sort of family. He'd helped out with babysitting and driven Kit to after-school classes and he'd always been free to come and go in their apartment uninvited, though he'd never overstepped the mark. They'd seen each other through countless crises, like the time he fell off the roof, or the time Kit was arrested for shoplifting. Now they were both retired. Catherine had no idea if Ernie found it as hard to grasp as she did.

After Kit left home, they'd blocked off their shared entrance to give themselves more privacy. She'd turned Kit's basement playroom into a studio. She only had energy for painting in school breaks, and even then it was sporadic; teaching and being a mom took precedence. Ernie made her mad when he said she had a cushy job. He couldn't grasp what it took to do it well, and how much time she needed to recuperate after the term was done. She always felt guilty for not spending more time with him; she knew he wanted to learn from her but she only invited him down to the studio when the work wasn't going well and she needed distraction. He sat silently, unless invited to talk, whittling a piece of wood as if the feeble creative sparks he gave off would feed some fire in her. The sound of the blade annoyed her but she needed it. Because he never minded being asked to leave she was all the more determined to let him stay and the repressed anger fuelled her work. Lately Catherine felt the weight of his solitude upstairs. She ignored it.

"I'm back from the long farewell," she called up, as she stepped over the threshold onto the worn linoleum and breathed in the quiet. "It went okay, I'll tell you about it some other time. They gave me a book token." She'd shared her anxiety about the retirement party, so now she owed him a report, but not tonight. It was a relief that there was nobody in the apartment to greet her, no one to tell her not to light a cigarette or say she couldn't play Céline Dion as loud as she liked, no animal to rub round her legs claiming attention. All she could see ahead was a wonderful absence of expectations. It was like a giant sigh.

The only person she wanted to talk to was Kit, but she had no idea where to find her. She'd given up reminding her where home was. Kit had been independent from kindergarten, insisting on selecting her own clothes, packing her lunchbox and walking to school alone when she was still in Grade Two. It was amazing how she breezed through life; she was sassy and outgoing, and, to everyone's amazement, she'd never shown any interest in visual art. Catherine had tried to follow her acting career but it wasn't easy. She was always on the road, even after she started her own company, always broke, always on the verge of breaking into the big-time. After Kit reached thirty she'd stopped trying to stay in regular touch and tonight she admitted to herself they had nothing in common but mutual love, and Kit found her painting boring. In art classes at school she produced boxy houses with coiled springs of smoke coming out of the roofs. She'd brought them home and taped them to the living room walls. Taunting. Catherine touched her index finger to the drawing of a stick man that was tacked up to the wall over the record player with its bold signature—K I T. It was dated 1971. She reached up and tore it down. The face had no features except for a large nose and two round eyes with a sunrise of hair. He was holding something in one hand, a cushion, or perhaps a drum. In the other he brandished a stick, or was it a knife? The lines were crisp and precise, not fuzzy as you'd expect from a young child. The background, lightly sketched in, was more interesting than the foreground. It was a desert, or a beach. There were some nicely realized shells scattered around, a single lost cactus or a leafless tree on the skyline; a psychologist would have a field day with it. She wondered if seven-year-old Kit had felt as lost as she felt now, at the age of sixty-three. Kit never gave the impression of being lost, and she probably wasn't as hopeless at drawing as she'd always made out. Catherine longed to confide in her, spend a few hours in her company working out a future.

Roger sat in the bay window, looking out on their almost Japanese front garden, thinking fondly of how Ilona dreamed up the project based on a picture in a travel brochure of Kyoto. They'd drawn up the plans together. He'd feared the worst, but he hadn't expected what met his gaze. He'd been at work when she ordered the concrete fences designed to look like wood; the nymph was definitely not Japanese and the bamboo was half dead when it arrived. He hadn't had the heart to correct her—he'd even agreed to keep the climbing rose though it hardly spoke of the Orient.

Beyond the fence a neighbour walked a waist-high poodle, which sported a diamond-studded collar. He didn't know many people in the village though he'd lived here for so long. He knew he should make more of an effort now he was about to be a father, his children would soon be playing with their children, there'd be sports days and parents' days and other kinds of days he had yet to imagine. Ilona would take care of most of it, but he didn't want to be left out the way he was last time; that was a mistake and mistakes always caught up with you.

The party had been a mistake. Every detail was calculated and timed to go off without a hitch. It was his first surprise party, and he'd organized it without once having to call on the good graces of his secretary. How could he have anticipated what arrived on his doorstep just before the gift giving? He practised risk management at the office, there was no alternative in these days of uncertainty, but he'd fallen down badly on the home front, left too much to chance, trusting there were no outside dynamics to factor in. He hoped Ilona guessed how filled with love his preparations were. Perhaps she was considering this while she was working herself into a state upstairs in their newly decorated bedroom, ignoring the need to keep calm for the sake of their babies.

One knee locked suddenly as he stood up. He shuffled out into the hall and stepped onto the front porch, screwing up his eyes against the blast of light. The house had always been too dark and clammy. He slammed the door behind him and turned towards the village.

The name of the landlord of the Fox and Hounds was painted on a removable board over the door with the date 1803 carved into a stone lintel above it. The place blended with the mellow stone of the village, though it was easy to see it was of a later vintage than many of the surrounding buildings. The red-coated horseman on the sign had been retouched recently. Inside, the saloon bar was welcoming but unremarkable, with bits of polished brass and a display of badly foxed hunting prints. Two men sat at the bar watching a cricket match on a huge monitor; apart from a courting couple in the corner and an old man hawking into a Kleenex, they were the only customers.

He ordered a gin and tonic and was about to make for a table when one of the two men patted an empty bar stool. "You're the chap from the pink house, aren't you?"

"Yes."

"Nice property," the red-faced one looked well fed, a proud advertisement for middle England with his small moustache and cable stitched cardigan and sandals; his friend would have slotted comfortably into the fifties. He wore a cravat, a blazer and a blue and white checked shirt.

"Bit of a hermit, aren't you?" There were rags of froth clinging to his interrogator's moustache.

"Not really." Roger thrust his hand out. "Rintoul. Roger. Never had much time to join in local activities."

"I gather your daughter's expecting. That'll be a happy event."

"My daughter?" He realized they were needling him. "My wife, actually. My second wife." He should have thought of a quick comeback. He noticed the landlord had his ear cocked and he tried to remember the name on the board outside. He needed to make a quick exit before he made a fool of himself.

"Have another?"

"No thanks. Just looked in on the run." He glanced up as the tarpaulins were being pulled over the cricket pitch on the T.V. monitor.

"Rain stopped play," the landlord announced.

He stepped into the parched street and turned in the direction of the road to Colchester. Why had he told those clowns he'd been married twice? The divorce was in the dark ages, Catherine had disappeared into the northern wastes. There'd been a couple of cards from her, then silence, apart from the exchanges with lawyers. And now there was Kit.

The woman with the poodle was sitting on a bench at the bus stop. She had a walleye and he wasn't sure if she was looking at him. He knew her from somewhere but her name evaded him, like the landlord's. He realized he'd left his hat in the pub, his straw hat—the one Ilona gave him.

The hat was still hanging on an antler beside the bar. The two men introduced themselves. He felt trapped into ordering a second gin. They ordered another round before he'd drunk half of it. He ignored the moderating bell that sounded in his head. He was in charge and the future was in place. The men were looking at him expectantly.

"My wife doesn't know I'm out."

"She's a good-looking girl," one of them remarked. This was a bit close to the mark, but he was right, Ilona was a head-turner, he always felt proud to have her on his arm. "She bought me this." He reached over and worked his finger under the band of his straw hat. "In France."

"You should bring her down here after she's had the baby."

"Babies."

The man with the moustache, who was called Tom, whistled. "You've been working hard!"

They laughed. Roger fished the ice out of his third drink. The landlord offered a spoon but it was too late, the ice was already forming a grey slurry in the ashtray. He stirred it with his finger. He saw that these three men were genuinely interested in him. They would see the truth, whatever it was, where a woman might miss it, and better still, they were strangers. It wouldn't hurt to open up a little, it was the least he could do to repay their impartiality. He wasn't such a terrible person, whatever Kit thought.

"I have a daughter. I was at art school with my first wife—and with the Pop Art crowd." He waited to see if they understood the significance of this. "David Hockney—he was there. Freud was ahead of us. They've made it, of course. Part of the Establishment now."

"Have another?" Tom placed a comforting hand on his arm. "Freud as in Sigmund?"

"Lucien. His grandson."

"I always thought he was a bachelor." He pouted, as though he'd been left out of a secret.

"I was talking about Pop Art, wasn't I?"

"Pop Tart?"

Roger joined in their laughter, though he didn't know why. He felt a bit dizzy. "They never had any doubts, those establishment types. I've always been a doubter." It was true. This was the first year he'd ever felt safe enough to express himself. Ilona never judged him. She'd approve of him making friends. He emptied his glass and ordered another. "It was a crapshoot back then. Any one of us could've made it. I used to drink with Francis Bacon. My wife wasn't welcome in his circles. She was brilliant. More than you can say for me, I can admit that with hindsight." He had to make sure they kept up with him. "I suppose you're married?"

Tom grinned. "This young man's still waiting for Miss Right." Maurice Thomas shifted under the weight of his friend's arm; Roger noticed he looked unhealthy, his liver-coloured skin stretched taught and shiny across his cheekbones.

The landlord changed the channel to a soccer game.

They ordered another round. Roger eyed the upside down bottle. They gave you such small measures in pubs. "Make that a double," he heard his voice, sounding more confident than he felt. The three men cheered for a missed goal. Roger spoke up. "They said I was an imitator. That hit home. Critics have to put everyone in boxes don't they? It was my one crack at the big time." He felt the hurt as keenly as if it had been yesterday.

"We all end up in boxes." Tom didn't take his eyes off the screen. "Ssssh!" The referee was blowing his whistle and waving his arms.

"My wife left with the baby, just before the show."

"What happened to them?" the landlord asked, without looking at him.

Roger clapped his hat on. It was a mistake to think he could talk about his family. He'd left Kit alone with Ilona—so many mistakes. With luck she'd be off after breakfast. "Catherine baked croissants for breakfast long before the English got a taste for them. I don't suppose anyone here knows how to make a pancake?" His throat felt stiff and full of unpronounceable words. There'd be no croissants, but he'd send Kit off with a North American breakfast, it was the least he could do. He took a paper napkin from the glass on the counter. "Do you fellows work in London? Face me, will you?"

"Retired early." Tom swivelled round from the screen.

"Moi aussi," said Thomas. "Yourself?"

"Still commuting. I used to stay in town and come back to Golding at weekends—the Garden at Golding. It's a painting. By Constable."

"He was a Suffolk man!" Maurice Thomas thumped the bar. He had their attention again.

"Did you get married here in the village?" Tom asked.

"In Surrey."

"I'll bet half the women had Kew Gardens on their heads!" His laugh sounded like a ticking clock.

"It was a nice wedding." That was the truth. It had been nice. It was still nice to wake up in the old bed with a new wife. He wanted to make them confess that they envied him. "She's one of a kind. She makes me think of a Watteau painting, you know, that creamy skin, tiny feet, dark hair, well, you've seen her. We all deserve a second chance." Of course they didn't understand, two old duffers screwing themselves into the floor on their barstools. "I recommend it. It's a fairy tale with no wicked witch and no poisoned dart. You can call me a fool, but you can't call me dead!" He got up and grabbed the bar to steady himself. The toby jug beer mugs leered from their privileged position over the till, the ranks of dimpled glasses were suddenly dancing on their hooks. "My daughter's at the house." He shook his hand out of Tom's paw.

Outside, the light seemed even brighter than before, though the sun was gone. He pointed himself towards home and set out in a straight line, counting the paces, fetching up in front of the bus shelter where the walleyed woman was still sitting with the twinkle-collared pink poodle sprawled at her feet. He stopped and took off his hat. "Good evening, I think we may have met."

"Enid Benton Brown," she said. "I was your housekeeper for two years."

He remembered her dog. She used to leave kibble in the pantry and he'd dipped into it once, by mistake, when he was searching for a snack.

"Sorry, so sorry," he backed away. It was true. Mistakes always came back to haunt you.

Four hundred and six, four hundred and ten—he passed his studio. The windows looked both blank and accusing. That wasn't plausible.

He sat in the hollow on the worn stone step leading up to the patio, waiting for dark. The stone was worn. His eyelids drooped. He remembered how he'd come by this place, how much he'd always enjoyed his Saturday morning sleep-ins, and then, one Saturday not so long ago, Ilona had perched on a chair beside the bed waiting for him to wake up. He'd finally opened one eye and she'd hopped up behind him and blindfolded him with her hands before he could reach for his glasses. She'd pressed a key into his palm—he could still feel the shape of it—and when he was dressed she'd led him out of the house and up the road, admonishing him to keep his eyes closed. To his astonishment, the key fitted the door that was right behind him, the door to a worker's cottage at the end of a row of how many—four? Five? One, two, three...he counted them slowly. Their lights were going on. He was tempted to duck inside and lie down. It was not much of a space but the owners had updated it, they'd laid new floors and installed skylights before they put it up for rent. The light was perfect for a studio. Perfect, as long as no one expected him to paint.

What did she expect? What did anyone expect? Was he supposed to remember names, recognise people he'd hardly laid eyes on? He'd talked to her about starting to paint again because he thought it was something she'd want to hear, and suddenly he had a studio. And now he had one more thing on his plate. Kit.

He slipped and almost fell as he got to his feet. One, two, three paces, he was at the front door of the cottage. It opened with the magic key. The first time he'd set foot in the place, he'd taken Ilona in his arms and made love to her, coming instantly on a camp bed that had somehow found its way into the corner of the downstairs room, the room she'd picked out for his studio. Thinking about it gave him a hard-on. He sank down onto the bed. It had seemed like a milestone. They were both certain it was the moment when Matthew and Alexander were conceived.

Roger tiptoed upstairs without bothering to put the light on. He was clutching a glass and the bottle of champagne, which had been losing its bubbles on the dining room table while he'd been out. She wasn't asleep. There was a light under the bedroom door and a light on the third floor too. He pushed inside. Ilona lay on her back with her eyes wide open and

43

the sheet pulled up around her chin. She didn't turn to greet him. He sat down carefully and massaged her toes.

"Did Kit get to bed?"

"Yes."

She still didn't look at him. "I was thinking I'd take the day off tomorrow, whoops, no, today—it's after midnight isn't it—maybe show her around."

"I thought you said she wouldn't stay."

So far so good, at least he sounded coherent. "I'll get one of the secretaries to book her in somewhere tomorrow night. We'll have a nice lie-in, and I'll make you breakfast in bed." Surely this was an offer she wouldn't turn down. "We'll show her the village, take her up to the pottery, maybe have a sandwich in the restaurant."

"It closed last year."

"She could eat with us here."

"And the pottery's not happening."

"Oh—too bad."

"You smell."

"Do I?" He poured half a glass of champagne very carefully and held it up to the bedside light. There was nothing like it, clear and hopeful as an early summer morning, full of energy and promise. Things would turn out. It couldn't be all bad having a daughter, even if she was years older than his wife. She might even be made to look presentable if Ilona could persuade her to have a bath and visit the hairdresser. If it turned out all right, he'd introduce her to his brother Sam. There was nothing like gaining a child to stand you on your head, and here he'd been thinking this new phase was about being a husband and the father of twins. Inside a year, he'd be moving from being a bachelor to 'father of three.' It was about as likely as backing three winners on Derby day; there'd be three people with claims on him, four, with Ilona. If she was still here in the morning, he'd take time out to show her London, Madame Tussauds,

44

treat her to one of those mega-musicals that tourists raved about. She looked as though she could do with a good feed. He let his eyes wander up along the sheet, following the ridge of Ilona's shin. When he reached her face, he saw that he was still out of favour. "Aren't you cold, darling?" No response. "Shall I get us some lobster? You're eating for three you know."

"Oh, for heaven's sake!" She jumped up. She was still fully dressed. "I want her out of here tomorrow. I don't want her touching any of my things. I mean it, Roger, mean, mean, mean, mean. I mean it, I do. I do." Her voice had a strange edge that he'd never heard before. He dismissed it. His two girls would learn to hit if off. And if they didn't? If they didn't, he'd write a cheque and ship Kit back home to her mother. Express. He went downstairs to tackle the lobster.

Ilona crawled into the cupboard, shifted the shoe boxes and reached into the brown cardboard box, noticing the smell of soap powder. The beam of light from her torch illuminated the pages of the diary as she mouthed the familiar words.

§ ST. AGATHE, May 20th, 1911

My husband insists that I decorate the house with wild flowers. This is easy in May, there's an abundance of bloom in this part of the country, many of which, I am ashamed to admit, I can't even name in English let alone French. They grow profusely along the railway line and I always start out there. On this particular afternoon I happened to glance along the line to the station. The Paris train had left five minutes ago—all but one of the passengers had dispersed. The lone woman was marooned full square, surrounded by bags and boxes and a vast trunk. There were two large bird cages at her feet; I was too far away to discern the contents of the cages but not too far to catch one bird's frustration which erupted in a shriek as I adjusted the tie on my hat. "*Merde, merde, merde,*" it shrilled.

I could hardly believe my ears; I have always considered animals incapable of blasphemy. The woman did not look in the least disturbed or apologetic; something about her spoke to the fact that she was not French and therefore not responsible.

Since we first came here several years ago, I have taken it upon myself to help out the foreigners who land up in our community. Obviously this woman was expecting to be met, yet there wasn't a soul in sight on the ribbon of road that unwinds down to the sea and the stationmaster had retired into his office to continue his interrupted nap.

I made my way towards the station along the path used by railway workers. I was wearing my tatty old gardening clothes and the veil on my hat was snagged so I didn't feel ready to introduce myself to a stranger. "Hello, I'm Winifred Church, your everyday common or garden frump, wife of Geoffrey Church, the revered artist."

I crept a little closer and observed that the woman was vastly overdressed for the time of year. She was pear shaped, and her reddish face bloomed above a fur ruff. Her purple floor-length coat appeared to be made of a good thick worsted. In addition, she wore several scarves and a large unfashionable hat. I concluded that she did not have room enough to store her wardrobe and had decided to transport it on her back, or that she was intending to stay for more than one season. She was leaning heavily on a walking stick, and she appeared to be about fifty years old—certainly not a comfortable age to be left standing in the hot Brittany sun.

I was about to step up onto the platform when I glimpsed the red trap meandering up the hill. I recognised it without difficulty. It belonged to the Hotel Bon Amie—and Frances Hodgkins was perched up at the front beside Raoul, their driver. I realized with a start, that the person on the platform must be Miss Carr. Either my eyes deceived me, or the woman had aged more than twenty years since she was at our house in St. Eflamme, a few summers ago. It was my husband who recommended that she come to St. Agathe this year. When she wrote proposing to study with him again, he suggested a fresh approach, a course in watercolour. (He does not teach watercolour.) I think he was a little frightened of her, as he is of all his exceptionally gifted pupils.

It so happened that one of the best teachers of aquarelles in all France is summering in the town, and Geoffrey wrote that Miss Carr should not be put off by the fact that Miss Frances Hodgkins is a woman. She is renowned in her field, being the first woman ever to teach at the Academie Colarossi in Paris, and she is very open to the new art. (I should note that I know exactly what he writes, since he dictates his letters to me. He treated me to a course in Sir Isaac Pitman's shorthand writing which is normally reserved for men; since then I have been more than equal to assisting him.)

Fanny must have seen Miss Carr, but she did nothing to urge the driver to increase the pace of the two horses. She appeared to be in lively conversation, she has a tendency to be easily distracted. I concealed myself, and kept an eye on the situation. The meeting, when it came, looked frosty. I didn't want to pry so I turned my back and applied myself to a clump of pale blue Scabious that were growing obligingly beside a pile of abandoned railway ties.

CHAPTER FIVE

ٱللَّه

Suffolk". Kit said it aloud. "Sounds like suffer. It's 1999 and it feels like 1920." Her watch told her it was eight o'clock in the morning, no one was up, and she was perched on the edge of the birdbath in her father's back yard. She'd left her stash under the bridge at Waterloo. She shivered and blinked at the blunt edged fields, the geometry of pine plantations, a distant sliver of water. It didn't feel cosy and forever like the pictures in the English Countryside calendar she bought every year. It was over-exposed. She needed green. Vancouver green. She hadn't actually lived there for years but it was always at the edge of her eye when she was in unfamiliar territory. This green was crisper, more insistent. She was used to light, she'd grown up on it; her mother was obsessed with it. Nothing could get done till the light was right. This morning's light bounced her around unmercifully.

She was still wearing the T-shirt she'd slept in, it smelt boggy; there was an expensive-looking dressing gown hanging on the back of the bathroom door, but she'd ignored it. What time did they get up? Roger. It was such a rabbity name. She wondered if he'd expect her to call him Dad? Would she ever get into the habit of taking him for granted like other people took their fathers for granted? He was different than she'd imagined. It was obviously okay to look old here, there were so many grey haired people on the streets. Back home, if you were over forty you dyed your hair and drove everywhere. And time was more drawn out, things happened later here. The night she arrived, she'd seen people going into restaurants at around midnight. Back home, eating that late gave you indigestion.

She wondered how long it would take to get used to the changes. If it was only about adapting, that was easy, she'd been adapting all her life. There was never enough work to keep her in one place, she was always scraping by, but she loved it; even when her belly was empty her head was full. She was always challenged. How would she manage without challenge?

She used to make up stories about her dad—he was a handsome devil of an Englishman, a sort of highwayman in a black cape, a cross between Batman and Robin Hood. He was going to turn up on the doorstep, probably in the middle of the night and he was the exact opposite of Uncle Ernie, who crept around upstairs like a mouse in thongs. When she was small, she'd wait for her mother to go to sleep then tip-toe to the front door and unlatch it so her father wouldn't be locked out. She'd slept with the light on in case he showed up. She used to dash into the arms of every man who fitted her picture and she called complete strangers daddy, though she knew they didn't belong to her. If she was lucky, they gave her quarters or candy. She had two imaginary friends called William and Ralph who spoke a secret language made up of words like 'tosh' and 'flipping' that no one else knew, and she read English books and recited English poems. She enunciated like a real English Lady. "Fayer daff—o—dils, we weeeep to seee theee haaaste awaaaay so soooon."

When she turned eleven, she'd transformed her father into a Zombie. No one but a low-life scumbag would stay away forever and never send a Christmas present or a birthday card or even a note. Sometimes he was Dracula, or her most feared school-teacher. He stood in doorways with a stick in his hand, and later the stick was a gun. But she'd kept up the English fantasy talk into her adolescence, replacing it eventually with a hip drawl. Later, she wiped him out completely, but she still had to sleep with the light on.

She took off her T-shirt, rinsed it in the birdbath and wiped under her arms. Being half English had its uses. It helped her C.V., she'd often been cast as a Brit. She'd played a Scot once in San Francisco in an under-rehearsed version of Trainspotting—fortunately the show wasn't reviewed by anyone important and she got away with murdering the accent till the last night, when an angry drunk from Aberdeen crashed the communal dressing room and called them all a load of wankers, singling her out as never having got nearer to Scotland than the Golden Gate Bridge, and he was right.

She was proud to have started her own theatre company and run it successfully for ten years. No one could take that away. The shows were well-practised improvisations, audiences loved them and their reputation was still growing when she'd called it quits. What a stupid decision! She swiped the water with the wet shirt. All that book-keeping, hunting for venues—the eternal squabbling! For weeks on end they were dark, and they had to search for other gigs, but when they were on, it had really worked. She'd found the formula, but not without the help of a fix to kick start every day. Was that so terrible? Not nearly so terrible as the day after she called the gang together and told them the final curtain was dropping. They'd hated her. Goodbye. Dream over. So easy. So much pain. Keep moving on.

She picked up a stone and skimmed it. Was it possible to make it skip on smooth English turf? She turned and asked the question of a clump of purple flowers. They were unlikely listeners. She needed an audience—that was her real fix!

Before she left Canada, she was rehearsing a threadbare musical. She'd woken in her motel room on the morning of her thirty-fifth birthday to the sight of a fiddle leaning against the chest of drawers, so she knew the guy she was bumping up against when she rolled over must be in the orchestra. She didn't recognize him. She always partied on the night before her birthday. Two of the musicians had scored a last minute gig in Toronto and opted out of a summer with Anne of Green Gables. He was one of the replacements they flew in from Halifax. There was a half-finished bottle of wine on the floor by the bed and she picked it up and took a swig. It tasted of tobacco. She didn't drink when she was in rehearsal but birthdays were an exception. The guy was thin, he didn't have a roadie's beer belly, but he did have a two- or three-day growth of stubble. Red stubble. He had a sweet face. She grabbed his earlobe. "Hello you," she woke him. "It's my birthday and as a present I'd like you to get the hell out of my bed."

"Hi Annie, hi doll."

She punched him. "I'm not playing fucking Anne, and I'm not called Annie."

"Right, Kitty Kat." He smiled and threw his arm over her, acting like they'd known each other thirty years.

"Excuse me, did you hear what I said? What's your name?"

"Cary Grant." His front teeth were missing—a hockey player, who'd have guessed?

"Everyone wants to be Cary Grant. Even Cary Grant wanted to be Cary Grant," she said.

"Oh, you know my secret?"

He was nice. Too bad. She got up, showered and dressed and hiked over to the coffee shop where they were out of everything except bacon and beans.

Breakfast had always been special—it was one of the best lessons Catherine ever taught. Lunch and supper could be dropped but for as long as she remembered, breakfasts were special. At weekends they'd had hot croissants. She was the only girl in her class who got to call her mother by her first name.

She eyed the mound of baked beans on her plate and she wanted Catherine. She wanted someone to sing Happy Birthday. Thirty-five was so old! She dragged herself back to her room. Cary Grant had decamped. She dialled home. The phone rang a couple of times then cut off. She tried again. Same story. She called directory assistance and they said the number was disconnected. She panicked. Something was terribly wrong.

Back in the restaurant she squeezed into the booth again. Her baked beans had a skin on them. She bit her knuckles. The tears came. Real, dreary tears—not improvised. She hadn't grizzled like this since she was an angel in the school nativity play and her wings dropped off before she got to deliver the Good News.

Roger caught a glimpse of his daughter sitting in the bird-bath, topless. Was she going to turn out to be a nutter? If she was, she could leave right away. There was no room for someone who was falling apart, not at this crucial time. He was relieved to see that Ilona wasn't up. It wasn't likely she'd looked out on the back garden. He threw the kitchen window open and motioned to Kit to cover herself up. She responded by waving a white rag then pulling it over her head.

He'd spent an uncomfortable night in the studio, the first night he and Ilona had been apart since their wedding' and he was filled with remorse and regret as he set about clearing away the remains of the party and preparing breakfast. He suddenly remembered Ilona's birthday present, still sitting on the dining room table.

He tiptoed up to the bedroom. The bedclothes were ruffled but there was no sign of his wife. He looked down at the bed. The folded duvet was hollowed in the shape of his body exactly where he'd sat the night before. He could smell her light perfume. Perfume made him sneeze but hers was an exception. He noticed that the Emily

Carr sketch was missing from its hook and he hung his gift on the wall in its place. It was a framed photo of 'Lady,' a motor cruiser moored at the marina in Ipswich—sleek, high powered, waiting for her to get behind the wheel; Lady was possibly dangerous, but she was something he knew Ilona would love. She was full of surprises, he'd learned that the first time she'd picked him up at work and driven him up from London at speeds of over 100 m.p.h.

✤

Ilona was toiling up the hill to the old sanatorium, buckling under the weight of the twins. There were beads of dew on the seed-heads of long grasses along the hedgerows and beads of sweat trickled down from her hairline into her eyes. The hawthorn berries were green and shiny, the flower stamens powdery gold. The world seemed fresh and open. As the incline increased, she had to concentrate on each step, trying not to falter, afraid of back-flipping down the hill. She had no time to think about what she was doing; she had just enough energy to do it. Her shoes were rubbing, making blisters on her heels, she hadn't given herself time to put socks on. She'd slept in the cupboard and her lungs felt scratchy. She closed her eyes between paces to shut out the pain.

When she reached the iron railings, she stopped and glanced up the wide paved drive. It was relatively flat, the going would be easy from here, but suddenly she had no spring left, so she sank down on the bank on top of a starry white patch of Stitchwort. One of the babies was kicking, he'd been at it for ages—she thought it was probably Matthew, he was the boss. She pulled the cartoon from her shoulder bag and set it down on the grass beside her. Miss Carr was well. Miss Carr always took care of things.

No cars had passed on the long climb up the hill and she listened closely to the birdsong; she'd promised herself that she'd learn the different calls. It shouldn't be hard to distinguish a nightingale, all you needed was a musical ear, but a musical ear wasn't something you could buy in Sainsburys. Miss Carr had listened to the birds, she'd reared them—her fledglings were possibly relatives of today's birds, their song hadn't changed. She and Miss Carr were both listening on the same green bank.

She shut her eyes. Gradually things were beginning to fall into place. She was meeting the carpenters today—they had roughed out plans for the conservatory, and the painter was coming with colour samples for the nursery, definitely not pink or blue—maybe lavender—it should have been finished two weeks ago. There was so much to do, but everything was organized, there was no need to panic, she just had to move forward one step at a time, the way they'd taught her. Matthew kicked again, hard, jabbing up into her diaphragm. He was aiming at her heart. Could the twins hear the birds? Soon she'd bring them up here, and they'd make an audience of four—five if Roger joined them. There was no room for a sixth. Behind the glass, Miss Carr held up her birdcage. 'Steady on,' she seemed to be saying, 'You can do it, my girl.'

⚘

Symptoms. Deadening of sensation. Feeling of disconnection and remoteness, as if there is a barrier between the object and the perceiver, a screen, layers of muslin. (The patient has noted her symptoms as they occur on a notepad she carries on her person.)

'My body is tremulous, feels empty, unfinished. Dead. Don't know myself, I am someone else looking on from far away.'

Miss Carr experiences severe pain with the application of heat and cold. She complains of tingling in her extremities, intermittent paralysis of the legs, shooting pains in the hips and up the back, headache, constipation and tinnitus in the left ear.

She exhibits severe melancholia, which is sometimes augmented by periods of euphoria. In general she has no interest in the world, is fearful and somewhat bad tempered. According to our consultations with Dr. Hartenberg the above can all be considered classic symptoms of neurasthenia. In other words, the diagnosis is correct, and it only remains to effect the cure. Dr. J.C. Waller, January 21st, 1907.

Emily watches clouds of flour puff up from between the floorboards, cover the bed, waft out of the gaping windows and turn the lawn white. Jerry the donkey is plodding up and down the white lawn, pulling the mower. Can he be wearing a diaper and two pairs of some old tramp's boots on his feet? Yes, he can. This is matron's idea of decorum. Jerry turns white in the time it takes to sneeze.

She can hear Hilda the gardener. (Matron believes the female presence to be cleansing and calming, no worker of the opposite sex sets foot over the threshold, even the delivery boys are girls. Jerry the donkey was a mistake.) "Me, I got eyes like a hawk," says Hilda to someone, "I can see a sparrow break wind." But she hasn't seen the flour. She turns the corner and Emily watches as it sifts. She's covered from head to toe, so are the men patients, the 'Ups' who are filing back from their walk to the village with their noses pointed at the ground; their black coats and their mufflers and their black homburgs are all caked in flour. Someone should tell them they shouldn't weep, for the flour turns water into paste and the tears stick to your cheeks like flies on sticky buds.

She sees the meadow of blue flowers behind the Ups. Camas. But Camas only grow in Canada. The flowers are deeply blue, the dust can't dilute it, they shake their blue heads and say no, no, we are Canadian, we will resist your English flour.

Oh the longing she feels. The plain old longing.

Treatment:

Open air.

Temporary relief from all physical activity. (The patient complains that she cannot reach up to comb her own hair.)

Complete bed rest, to be reduced to 12 hours per day, with minimum one hour rest (no sleeping) after meals and very slow walking when the condition begins to improve.

Hydrotherapy, very gentle, tepid overhead douche, (no cold douche, no jets under pressure), to be followed by dry rubbing with fibre glove and Eau de Cologne.

Daily massage.

Electrotherapy with brush or pad, but avoid all strong muscular contractions.

Psychological treatment. The patient should be encouraged to entertain joyful thoughts, introduction of the idea of hope and patience. Reassurance that symptoms will disappear. The doctor will be the confessor.

Hypnosis, but only as a last resort, (this will await the visit from Paris of one of Dr. Hartenberg's assistants).

Dr. J.C. Waller, 3rd day of June.

Emily slides down onto the floor and rolls in the flour. It turns to paste, thick paste for wallpapering, and she's stuck to the boards. She can't move, her legs are glued together and her arms are pinned to her sides. Her lips are sealed. She's shrinking down to her eight-year-old size. She knows she must get up; she must get back on the bed before someone comes in, be a brave little soldier. No one must hear the cries for help, for someone to take her home.

The sanatorium is built in a giant C. Its rooms look out over a good portion of Suffolk. Emily stands at the open window where far away in the valley, people live everyday lives in the village where Alice put up for two nights when she brought her here. She can see the church spire but she can't pick out the inn. She has the room on the tip of the C; she is the last to be served. Behind her head, in room after room, a long line of 'Downs' bounce their bedsprings with bone-breaking, shuddering, unending coughs. Crowns pound against bedsteads, the ring of iron on plaster peals through every wall and the coughs echo and re-echo along the C as far as matron's office where they come to a full stop. There is only improvement where matron lives. She takes the patient's wrist and feels the patient's pulse. "Ah yes. Much improved." And on she marches, on to the next Down in a snap of starch. Do as she says or she'll tell you off. Be as she says, or she'll see you off. Emily heaves herself back onto the bed.

Medicines:

Arsenic to be administered as drops of Fowler's solution, or injections of cacodylate of soda.

Iron.

Iodine, 5 drops administered with chloroform, with meals.

Phosphorous (phosphate of soda).

Injections of artificial serum.

Phosphate of codeine to counteract symptoms of extreme apprehension. Bromide of potassium is also useful to counteract irritability.

Tonics: Mineral water for liver and kidneys (not effervescent).

Strychnine in large doses, i.e. one thirtieth to one eighteenth of a gramme per day. (Be bold with this.) Hypodermic injections of strychnine are preferable, be aware that they can induce a state of intoxication, vertigo, stiffness of jaws and legs for about half an hour after administration, but these symptoms then pass and a state of well-being ensues.

Dr. P. Hartenberg. Paris.

Bottles. It seems to Emily that life in the San is all bottles. She likes the colour of the blue milk-of-magnesia bottle on her bedside table. Then there's the smelling salts, green glass—the expectorant—blue glass with a silver cap, one each to revive the Ups.

Mustn't spit on the ground don't want the grass to get germs. The hot water bottle in her bed is called a pig and it is made of stone. She's looked through the door into matron's office and seen that all the jars are brown glass, a container for every eventuality. Try a little infusion of...a tincture of...some liniment, a poultice. Constipation? Cascara. Headache? Senna pods. Insomnia? A drop of laudanum, milk of magnesia, camomile pills, horses' rubbing oil, goose grease...the smell of soap, the smell of ammonia.

Diet:

A dry diet is to be strictly adhered to, no drinking with meals. Between meals the patient should be given sugar water, 8 to 12 oz of sugar dissolved in one quart of water, (sugar possesses all the tonic qualities of alcohol, but does not cause excitation or drunkenness).

Judicious superalimentation is recommended. Large helpings of meat, (underdone), and 6 to 8 eggs with every meal. The patient should be encouraged to eat slowly. Fish of all kinds is not recommended since it is too difficult to digest and is rarely fresh enough. Salads and raw fruit are indigestible as are farinaceous foods such as pastry. Vegetables must be well cooked and fruit should be administered as jams or compôtes.

The cure of Guelpa is recommended, this consists of three days of fasting with saline purgation, and in the evening, purification of blood with 500 grammes of physiological serum.

In the morning the patient should lie on a hard bed and raise her body without the help of her arms 20 times, to aid digestion. If nothing is passed, a suppository should be given, electrics will aid severe constipation.

Dr. P. Hartenberg. Paris.

The flour settles finally as Emily knows it must, and she can see more clearly. Sister Alice has been gone a long time, taking the two parrots with her. She will be a Down for the duration and there is nothing more her sisters can do, other than provide the inducements for little extras in the way of care. Finally everything will right itself. She will see them all again and parrots often outlive humans.

There are regular letters from home but she scans them and pushes them aside:

'The Autumn Crocus have spread this year, they never appeared under the willow before, the snowdrops are out; the buds on the camellia are like pop eyes, ready to burst; the pink Dogwood is a picture; that Broom they brought from Scotland is now at home on all the cliffs, so we have banks of gold to make up for gold in the bank; the fool from Ontario who introduced the European starlings into the grounds of our Legislature must be well pleased, they are bossing all our native birds about; the goats send their love and Miss Sugar has just had five darling kittens, all black, so we know who did it; the wives of two of the members of the Empire Club have enquired about painting lessons, and Edith has told them Miss Carr will be happy to oblige as soon as she gets home from her engagements in the Mother Country...' There is no mention in any of the letters of Camas.

The sisters send Emily new sable brushes and she uses them to drop milk down the throats of the nestlings that have been brought to her window. The birds multiply, huddling together to keep warm. It's a cold, overcrowded country. The landscape wears stays and the trees have good manners. Only the hedgerows are wild. She tries to see the day when she'll be well enough to make her own search for nestlings. Meantime the Ups disturb the nests and filch the eggs. Words pin all this down too coldly, so she gives up on writing and draws cartoons. Everyone in the hospital is dying for want of laughter and when it comes, it's brought to the surface like a long-suppressed sigh.

She is not improving. She is beginning to believe she will never go nesting. She never gets up now. She is told there is a new treatment that will restore her. While she waits for the onslaught, she lashes out with her tongue. "Leave me in peace can't you?" she tells the children who have always been welcome at her bedside. "Leave me in peace to get better."

So peace is what she gets, and then she wants war.

CHAPTER SIX

అది

Catherine's shoes were stiff with water, she eased out of them and plunked down in her favourite black leather armchair—the leather was filigreed with age and she ran the tips of her fingers over it, feeling the tiny cracks. This action always soothed her. She yawned, trying to expand her lungs. The only thing she'd ever asked for was time, and now, by God she had it. After almost thirty years, she was no longer tied to the clock. If she wanted, she could sit here, stroking the arm of her chair until next week.

She looked around, idly assessing the room. It didn't give much away about the occupant, just a table, a couple of chairs, a few shelves of books, a T.V. and the old fashioned stereo. Nothing added since Kit was in school. The only pictures on the walls apart from Kit's drawings, were a few prints by Käthe Kollwitz, the German artist whose grim, extraordinary renditions of workers, particularly working women, had provided her with a second wind in the months after she left Roger. Life had been grim when she first came to Vancouver, with no job and a small baby to feed. These relentlessly realistic black and white pictures of intense suffering with the odd splash of joy had helped corroborate her loneliness. The pictures were no more than wallpaper now. "I have never worked coldly," Kollwitz said, "but rather, in a certain sense, I have worked with my own blood." The power and spirit in the exhausted women's faces hit the mark tonight. The absence of colour was so right. "I have never worked coldly." Catherine thought of how the Nazis removed Kollwitz's pictures from museums and galleries and now one of her sculptures was the centrepiece for the freedom monument in Berlin. Anything was possible. Did she believe that? I have never worked coldly.

She felt the gap where the buttons on her blouse were straining. It had been a while since she'd looked at herself closely, was she putting on weight? She slid her hand under her bra strap feeling the weal and the damp place where she'd scratched herself. She sat on her hand to stop it from returning to the raw skin and tried to empty her mind, but the worries didn't want to be dismissed. Did she have enough to live on? Would she find the energy to start painting again—the kind of painting that was all-consuming—the only kind that mattered. Right now she was just a number, another unsold lot in a grab bag of auction consignments. She knew she had work inside her that was just as strong as Kollwitz's, but did she have the energy to pull it out? Something had to connect her with the old joy of putting paint on canvas, the joy she'd felt before she started to teach, when she'd trusted the outcome and never questioned her ability or worried about what people thought. All that stuff she'd spouted tonight about women and their problems—did she believe it, or was it a smoke-screen? She scratched. There was blood under her fingernails.

She dimmed the light, peeled off her tights, then stripped off the rest of her party clothes, flung them round the room and followed them with her bra and panties. She flopped back into the chair, feeling the rough leather on her buttocks, not bothering to draw the blinds. She tried to look down the length of her body but the folds of her belly blocked her sightlines. The flab under her arm felt like an old boiler hen. Her armpit was dry. The question was, how to portray the feel (not the look) of dryness in a wet medium? How to reveal all the sap in what seemed so drained?

She got up and went into the kitchen without flicking the light switch. By the light of the open fridge, she uncorked a bottle of white

Australian and filled an ugly blue and yellow striped mug, watching the level go down in the bottle. The mug wasn't hers. Back in her chair, she raised it and drank to unanswered questions. This house was ugly too. Ugly and safe. The illuminated dial on her watch showed 11.20, the neighbourhood was asleep, there was no sound other than the quiet hiss and occasional gurgle of rain.

By three a.m., she'd gone through a pack of cigarettes, started on a new bottle of wine and decided to move back to the States.

When she left Roger, she'd applied for jobs all over North America. She'd wanted to get herself and Kit as far away as possible from the voraciousness, the petty jealousies and insecurities of his world. She'd come to Vancouver because someone wrote her a kind rejection letter. She'd loved the city right away—it made her precarious situation more bearable because it was undemanding and peaceful. She'd never felt comfortable in Beatles London and hadn't set foot in Carnaby Street. Vancouver's natural beauty, its beaches and mountains were overawing and she welcomed the snail-like pace of life. Later she loved it for providing a haven for the young American draft-dodgers. It was the ideal place to bring up a child and before long she'd found a teaching job. In those days they actually welcomed Americans. Now, Vancouver had lost its allure. Everyone at school complained about it. Andy Warhol was rumoured to have said you can't sell art in Vancouver, and they all agreed, no matter how much they sold. She always took the opposite tack when her colleagues competed in the demolition derby, but right at this moment, as she popped her stuck skin from the hot leather, she was ready to bomb the place. The mould that was attacking the city's rain-soaked high-rises was attacking her, too. She'd stayed on in Vancouver out of inertia. If she wasn't careful she'd descend into a sort of Emily Carr existence, that fat white woman whom nobody loved, a wanna-be painter with a few successes under her belt, locked in a cycle of poverty, never enough strokes, wandering the look-alike streets pushing a baby carriage full of animals with a monkey perched on her shoulder.

She put the mug down beside her chair. It was so easy to lie back and drift, let your anger eddy in little pools like art departments rather than run for a canvas. It was as if she'd spent every night in a hotel room with permanent room service, oh so comfy and bland. That's what she'd been trying to tell them at the Last Farewell. None of this was their fault. She was to blame. As an immigrant, she'd allowed herself to remain a visitor, always on the edge. She could have capitalized on this, seen it as an advantage instead of learning to rub along with a perpetual sense of displacement, like living with a mild case of shingles. British Columbia was a good place to not quite make it, a good place to be disconnected, and that was probably why she'd stayed. Cowardice. She chugged the dregs and poured some more wine.

She remembered a worldwide study of colour preferences. Blue—blue like the stripe on the mug—blue was the hands-down winner and next was green. But in Canada, the third favourite colour was beige. It was the only country in the world where anyone had put beige on the list. She was living with people who were in love with beige—people like Ernie Last, asleep upstairs under his beige quilt, dreaming beige dreams.

The drink was giving her a sort of woozy clarity. You grew out of places the way you grew out of favourite painters or favourite writers. Canada had met her needs, England never would. The end of the search brings us back to the place where we started out and finally we recognise it. Where had she read that?

So she was going to end up in the U.S.A.! Where? Since she would be a rookie again, she'd have to choose her place carefully. Definitely not the Midwest, where she grew up. L.A.? Too glitzy. Boston? Too rarefied. New York? Possible, but impossibly pricey. There was always the South—she'd never spent time there. She tried to imagine herself in New Mexico, tramping the desert in the footsteps of Georgia O'Keeffe. When she was young, she'd got a buzz out of O'Keeffe's renderings of the sexuality of nature, and above all her colour. There was a picture in the Albright Knox gallery in Buffalo that was her own personal doorway. She'd walked towards it in her imagination over and over, wanting to vanish through it, to be consumed by the colour. It was a colour that didn't belong in any palate, an entry into pure turquoise light. It was lodged behind her eyes, unattainable. O'Keeffe was a master. How would it feel to startle people into joy over a cheap print of the open throat of a tulip—people who cared nothing for pictures?

Catherine padded back to the kitchen and opened a bottle of burgundy. The red wine tasted sour after the white. She was out of cigarettes. Slowly she fitted her legs back into her panties. She doubted if there were any stores open at this hour. Movers probably stayed up late, what was to stop her from hiring one and decamping right away?

She heard a noise at the window. It sounded like throat clearing. She zipped her pants and checked outside the window, but all she could see was darkness, so she pulled down the blinds.

Ernie tried to swallow the frog in his throat, but it escaped. She looked up immediately. He stepped back from the window as she zipped up, his legs almost buckling under him; he'd been standing in one position in the rain for hours, waiting, hardly daring to breathe. He wondered how long a naked person could continue to scratch between her breasts without moving her hand to some place more interesting. She'd left her blinds up—she'd never done that before, so he knew it was deliberate.

He'd thought something was about to happen when she switched off the light. He tracked her from window to window as far as the kitchen. Her naked body was outlined in the light from the fridge, unfamiliar, the breasts flattened like leather wine flasks, the protruding stomach, the veined legs, and behind this a glimpse of wire shelves, bottles and parcels of food. She was familiar, yet completely new. He watched as she walked back to her chair, then crossed her ankles on the stool as if she were fully dressed. The square horn rimmed glasses stayed on her nose, nothing disturbed the spiky grey brush cut, her toes barely twitched. Everything was in place, yet everything had shifted. She swigged wine from one of his mugs and moved her lips silently. She was talking to him, playing him like a yoyo.

He kept his hands deep in his pockets. His rain slicker leaked, his shoulders were damp and he feared her image would dissolve in the rain-streaked glass. He thought of a woman he'd seen through the window of a moving train years ago, dancing alone, naked in an empty upstairs room. It had filled him with rage. One summer, when they'd been sitting together in the backyard, he'd described it to Catherine, though he couldn't convey the powerlessness it evoked. She hadn't seen it as shocking—she'd pointed out how he'd edited everything else out to come up with the one perfect visual image, the train, the passengers, where he was going were of no importance—the image must have been central for him to have hung onto it so long.

He started to make connections as he stood at the window. The videotape, left out on top of the T.V. was linked to the unseen thoughts spooling through her head. The blank screen of the T.V. was dead but her square spectacles were alive. According to her, you didn't have to explain, you just had to see. There was no code to crack, no right or wrong. The challenge was to get past mere looking, to see what is not immediately visible. His talks with Catherine changed his approach to his trade. His boots were no longer standardized. Each pair was slightly different; each contained an indecipherable signature. Later, he treated each boot as an individual. Rather than straining to make matching pairs, he began to make them different in ways that only eyes such as Catherine's would detect. If there was a flaw in the leather, he incorporated it into the work instead of disguising it. Under the insoles he inscribed designs of such detail and complexity that the orders were often weeks late. The waiting period increased his orders. People knew they were getting something special. He even filled an order to make boots for Prince Charles from a paper pattern whose accuracy he doubted. Was it possible that the prince had one foot two sizes larger than the other? He changed the sign outside his shop to read Royal Bootmaker. Before he retired he satisfied himself that there'd never be any boots to match his. He'd always made sure that none of his assistants followed the entire process through from heel to toe, and, when he locked the door of his shop for the last time, he destroyed his templates. This was the sum of Catherine's teaching.

She didn't often talk to him about art, but when she did he listened. She said painting isn't like a story; you don't have the luxury of letting time unfold. Everything you want to express has to be there at once. When you're looking at art, you know when the work's good because the artist's given you everything you need for a sense of completion. Even the fragment of a line can be complete. She had given him completion as he stood in his yard; there was nothing he could add to what he had seen. He followed her instructions and didn't look for meaning. There was no beginning and no end to the image. From the train there had been rage, but this time there was longing. She said that when you're working on a painting, you hear a pop in your head and you know it's done. He'd heard the pop.

He'd observed all her moods as he stood in front of pictures with her. She was transformed when she liked what she saw. She quivered. In front of her own work she was stony, hardly present. She rarely let him sit in while she painted, and when he did, he tried to seem disinterested, taking care to bring something to whittle, so he could occupy his hands. When she was nearing the end of a painting he hardly dared breathe, for fear that she'd miss the pop.

Now he owned something of hers, something she could never take back. He could return to it as often as he wished. He could place her in any shaft of light, leaning over slightly, spectacles on top of her head, with a wine bottle in her hands. She reached up for the cord of the blind and he saw a muscle strain under her breast, her nipple was no more than three feet from his face.

He adjusted the hood on his rain slicker, stepped back into the darkness and crept upstairs, to the warmth of his kitchen.

Catherine got up late, went out to pick up the weekend paper, and met Ernie at the gate. He walked up the path with her, sheltering her from the rain under his black umbrella. She gripped his wrist. "Ernie, I've decided to get the hell out of this place. Go home. Can you believe it? I almost did it last night. With luck I'll be out of here by the end of the month, but I'll pay next month's rent in lieu of notice. It's going to be a new millennium in more ways than one!" It was said. She was committed. All of a sudden she was calling the country she'd always loved to hate, home.

Ernie shook her hand off his arm and stood erect, beady-eyed in his black rain slicker. Tears spurted and ran unchecked down the deep vertical gullies in his cheeks. She watched with horror as they dripped off his chin, and onto his shirt collar. Ever since she'd known him, he'd worn a clean white shirt every day, with a navy tie, like a commissionaire. She always thought of him as a small man, but she realized he must be almost six feet tall. She moved her eyes to the thick white thatch of hair—he was an eagle. She put out both hands, wanting to comfort him. He pushed her aside.

"So much water today."

She had to acknowledge the tears. He was a bald eagle, standing in her path, silent and watchful in his black slicker. He didn't move, so she had no permission to go into her house. "I thought I should let you know right away. I made the decision after the Long Farewell. I have to work out the logistics later, but I thought it would be fair to tell you, you've always been so good."

"So that was what you said?" He looked away.

"What I said?"

"I saw your lips move last night."

"I didn't see you last night, Ernie. Last night was my retirement dinner, remember? Definitely my last performance! I have to tell you about it soon. I made a complete fool of myself. You're the only person who'd understand."

He turned and walked towards the side entrance. She watched his back, not knowing why the hairs went up on her neck. He was her good buddy, wasn't he?

The next day she drove down to Seattle. She hadn't crossed the border for years though it was only an hour away from Vancouver. She parked in an expensive multi-storey parking lot and wandered downtown. Seattle felt odd, a little foreign. The mix of people on the street was different, more black, less Asian, but this didn't account for the underlying throb, the electricity. She took short, sharp breaths, sniffing things out. The atmosphere was distinct. Those who despaired looked more despairing, those who prospered looked more prosperous, they advertised themselves, lived outside their skins; the air was headier. She felt a rush of recognition. From this side of the border, Canada looked like a country of modifiers, law-abiding, and untroubled and for this she had loved and cherished it. If she'd stayed in the States she'd have been bigger—she'd have had to puff herself up to make them notice her. In British Columbia, she only had to open her mouth to rub people the wrong way. She studied the lunchtime crowd. The real difference was the unseen presence of guns and pepper spray, a sense that the quiet scene was fermenting.

On impulse, she took a ferry to the San Juan Islands. Even the ferry was different, clean, but less manicured than the boats that plied between the islands in British Columbia. The announcements were more casual. "Stay clear of the rail folks, we don't want you to end up in the water." You could even buy beer. Idly, she picked up a sheaf of the latest listings from a display of real estate flyers, thinking she might glance over them when she got back to Canada and get some idea of prices.

She got off at one of the stops without paying particular attention to where she was and drove away from the dock through a small community, then past fields studded with sheep, alternating with thickly wooded bluffs. She flicked on the radio, searching for some kind of news or local programming and hit on the CBC. She turned it off. After about twenty minutes, she noticed a For Sale sign on a cottage perched on a cliff overlooking the sound. The name on the sign matched the name on one of the flyers she'd picked up on the ferry. The listing described the cottage as a small, two bedroom, one bath dwelling; she did a quick calculation of the currency conversion and realized that, even with the bottomed-out Canadian dollar, the price was just about within reach. She lifted the gate, which sagged on a broken hinge. The sign read 'Viewing by Appointment Only,' but the house looked empty. The garden was overgrown, though it had once been landscaped. A white jasmine growing up against the wall of the house scented the whole yard. The trees and shrubs bore all the signs of providing breakfast for the local deer. A large, rusty oil drum on legs fed a stove inside the house. It reminded her of a stick insect.

Squeezing through the gate, she followed a path round to the back where she found the structure that was referred to as a workshop. It was a square rickety box built from sea-silvered wood; the ancient asphalt shingles were covered with moss and it had a dangerously angled tin chimney, but the north wall was entirely made of glass. With a bit of work, it would make a perfect studio. She gulped at the view from the cliff-top, then she peered into the kitchen. It was empty, the lino was scuffed, the windows dirty, the appliances ancient.

She got into her car and drove on, but she couldn't take in her surroundings. She made a detour, driving aimlessly, then turned back and pulled up in front of the real estate office.

The realtor was a local, friendly, but in no hurry. She did her best to sound disinterested; he asked about her background and said he had keys to the property. He picked up the phone and made a series of calls to people who sounded like children or very slow adults. Finally he announced that he could fit her in.

By five o'clock she'd viewed the house, walked the perimeter of the small lot, half listening to explanations about liens and property lines, heard news about the local school, which was all set to build a new gymnasium, the Dramatic Society, the Rotary, the Cancer Survivors Club and the reading circle, and returned with him to his office to complete a conditional offer, terrified in case she'd knocked too much off the asking price.

She pulled the car over just north of Blaine, Washington and rested her forehead on the wheel. It was almost dark. In darkness, every place looked the same. If things were to continue at this breakneck pace, she would be a property owner tomorrow. She'd own land for the first time in her life, on a sliver of an island in a country she'd abandoned forty years ago. What did she think she'd live on? How would she pay medical bills outside the shelter of Canada's social insurance system? She'd probably have to grow her own food and she'd never planted as much as an avocado pit. She'd have to take good care of herself, exercise—she hated exercise—cut down on the smokes, limit the wine. She doubted if any of this was possible, but as long as there was enough left over for paint at the end of the day she'd make out. It would mean she'd have something to leave to Kit—not that Kit would be remotely interested in a shack on a nowhere island.

A State Patrol car drew up behind her. Two cops got out and one approached her, shielding himself; he had his hand on his gun. Welcome to America.

CHAPTER SEVEN

ﻋ

K it stooped and tried to pick the purple flowers that were her only audience. The plant came up by the roots. She wandered through a rustic gate between two trees and into the field that bordered the garden. She would keep her distance from the dark house for a while longer. Holding the flowers like a bride, she made her way along the humpy path dividing whatever was ripening in the field from a boundary hedge.

She had to concentrate to keep her footing and finally she crouched down in the shadow of the hedge, shook soil from the roots, and laid the flowers round her in a circle. The insects seemed to have quieted down in the shelter, but something was snuffling and a bird sent out a warning call. It sounded unreal, like a recording, she felt she was being put on hold while calling some ecological do-good organization. She grabbed the flowers and plunged into the corn.

The place was chock full of unseen animal eyes, birds' nests, all the wildlife had a home and she imagined them watching as she made crop circles with her ass. It felt very far from Vancouver. After the phone-call home, she'd taken the first flight west, bent on discovering what was amiss. The house was still standing, but the lawn wasn't cut, the gate was wide open, and there were no blinds on the windows of their downstairs apartment. The drapes in Uncle Ernie's upstairs windows were drawn. She'd always been ambivalent about Uncle Ernie. He'd named himself Ernie Last—he'd once told her his real name was Ernesto Zapata. He was kind, but she never quite believed him. He had a strange smell, a sharp smell that used to prickle her nose. But now she wanted nothing more than to have him hug her and welcome her home. She'd lost her key somewhere in the thousands of miles she'd travelled since she was last out west, so she had to ring on the doorbell. The chime clamoured. She knew that sound so well. She peered through the letterbox. The hall was empty, the mirror was gone, no table, no coat rack. She edged along a crumbling wall to get a look in the living room window. The room was bare, the carpet had the indentations of all their furniture, but there was nothing on it, not even a packing case. She clung onto the windowsill. The only thing that was left in the room was the drawing she'd made when she was in Grade One.

Back on the doorstep she attacked the bell again. A woman appeared on the path next door.

"You look Mrs...?" she said.

"Yes, where is she?"

"She gone. She and mister upstair. They both gone. Yestairday."

"Yesterday? Did she leave a forwarding address? I'm her daughter."

"Oh, dotter!" The woman cleared her throat and looked her up and down. Obviously no one in the Chinese community would make the mistake of taking off and leaving their daughter behind. "She gone United States."

"How long have you lived here?"

"Live here? Two year."

Kit shook her head and turned tail—Catherine and Ernie Last? After all these years?

The neighbourhood had changed. She didn't know any of the people who lived in the old wooden houses on the clean streets. Who had painted them such bright colours? When had the trees grown so high? A man at the bottom of the hill was attacking the sidewalk with a hose as if he were sluicing down an abattoir. She needed to track down her mother's oldest friend, Aunt Mary, who used to live on the next block. Like Uncle Ernie, Mary had played a relative's role when Kit was growing up. She'd moved to a house near a cemetery in the rain belt under the mountains in North Vancouver. Kit hailed a cab.

Mary was packing for a vacation when she arrived. There wasn't a big welcome, but she offered the couch for the night and she supplied the information that Kit was dreading. Catherine had run off to an American island with Ernie Last.

How could it be true? Catherine was anti everything American, so why would she go there and why would she go with Ernie Last?

"We were all stunned." Mary folded a shirt in tissue paper. Kit had never seen anyone pack with tissue paper. Her shoes were lined up neatly, stuffed with crumpled newspaper. She'd been clipping coupons.

"Where is she? What's her phone number?"

"I've no idea. She hasn't been in touch with anyone."

"But, Ernie Last? You're sure?"

"Yeah, he called and said they were leaving. I thought it was weird, he never calls me and I never heard him sound so excited. He said they'd be in touch. I guess she needs company now she's finished with teaching. Best not to go looking for them for a while. Give them time to settle, eh?"

"Don't worry, I won't disturb them. You're sure it was him?"

"He didn't sound like himself, if that's what you mean."

"I can't stand him!" A fist of dislike punched her in the stomach.

"Oh, don't be silly." Mary was too preoccupied to provide any kind of buffer.

The following day Kit cashed in her Canada Savings Bonds and bought a one-way ticket to London.

She used the rest of her money to stock up on supplies for the journey, stowing them in a small backpack. Then, on impulse, she gave the bag to a couple of burned out cases, squatting in front of the liquor store. They tried to give it back when they saw it was only food, but she moved on. She didn't want things. She didn't need food. She wanted... What did she want? She wanted her theatre company back. What had possessed her to wind it down?

She eased herself up and saw a woman walking a huge poodle along a lane at the bottom of the field. She was crooning something to the dog; Kit couldn't make out the words. The woman threw her head back and laughed. The dog must have a sense of humour. When they were out of sight Kit got up and ploughed a trail to the path abandoning the last of the purple flowers.

Back in the garden, she rippled the water with her fingers and looked at her reflection. A fractured orange wraith. This hair was such a no-no—acceptable in Cardboard City, but no good for life in a teapot. She undid one of the hair extensions. It was going to take hours to fix.

She'd known that quitting Anne of Green Gables was her death knell. She'd done it after the rehearsal, on her birthday, after the musician, after the disgusting baked beans, after the abortive phone call home, before she went to Vancouver. She licked her lips. They tasted bitter. Disillusion was probably good for you, like quinine.

The theatre scene was so small that if word got round you were difficult, or that you'd reneged on an agreement for any reason other than life-threatening illness or a lucrative film deal, you were out of the loop forever. She'd stepped out of the loop without a thought, and now she'd kissed goodbye to the stage. She thought of her friend Barb who'd been hanging round Hollywood for years, waiting. Waiting tables. At least there'd be no more grim auditions; when Hollywood came to cash in by filming in Canada, everyone turned into donkeys, braying for bit parts and she always brayed loudest. There'd be no more weeks spent burnishing two lines in a nonsense script, hoping it would lead to the Big Break. There was no starting again—not there, and certainly not here in Britain. It was over.

A new bird appeared, a precise, little blue and yellow bird. He pecked at a lump of fat hanging from a branch. He made her feel hopeless, he was so neat and watchful, peck, peck, peck. Did anyone let anything hang out in this tidy, hideously green country? Where was the passion? She'd broken up the company because she was afraid of becoming a junkie, and now she needed a fix more than ever.

CHAPTER EIGHT

࣮ؖ

Ilona swerved from side to side of the road, trying to concentrate on her feet. The walk down the hill from the San was usually easy, but today the road was a switchback and it seemed to have doubled in length. She thought of a straight white line down the middle and this helped. She rounded the bend past the farmhouse with its walled, secret garden, and found it was easier to keep her heels down and slide her feet forward, so she skied through the housing estate, out onto the flat where the six-lane expressway scythed through the county. There was a notice warning that eight pedestrians had died here in the last five years. She waited until there were no cars in sight, glancing towards Colchester in the direction of the spiritualist church she attended on Wednesday nights when Roger worked late. Lost souls sometimes chose living bodies for company and some of their messages were spine-chilling; they tapped and groaned and made the lights flicker. She found this intriguing. As she waited for the traffic to clear she imagined herself, sitting at the back where she always sat, (she never talked to anyone, it was important not to be recognised), rehearsing what she'd say, should someone like Miss Carr or Winifred Church make her presence felt.

She skied past the village church, pulled up and went inside. Approaching the altar, she felt a blast of cold air coming from the chancel (the last time she'd been in an Anglican church was on her wedding day). She dropped down on one of the blue tapestry kneelers, and rested her joined hands on her stomach. It was a very old building, Saxon or perhaps Norman she decided, filled with centuries of prayers and promises. She closed her eyes, but it was wrong to pray that a guest should be made to leave, so she said the Lord's Prayer twice, then she tried the twenty-third psalm, stalling at green pastures. The people who'd knelt here before believed there were black souls, living and dead. She would light some candles when she got back home to clear them out.

Within sight of the house, she turned tail and doubled back to the studio. She was feeling better now. She hung the cartoon on a handy nail on the upstairs landing—Emily had earned a new view of the world; she promised to visit her every day. Roger had made it clear that he wouldn't be using the studio till after the babies were born, but he'd slept here last night, she saw that he'd wrapped himself in the travel rug from his car; it was hunched on the end of the camp bed like an old dog. It had been nice to have their bed to herself, last night, nice not to have him constantly tapping her belly. If she could manage it alone, she'd move her uncle's paintings from the house and store them here. Emily would appreciate being closer to Geoffrey Church.

Roger greeted her with a yelp of pleasure before she reached the door. He had breakfast ready—a strange spongy concoction that he called a pancake. It had been sitting under the grill, so its edges were brown and curly and he'd stuffed it with last night's smoked salmon. She sat down obediently and nibbled on a half slice of cold toast, watching as he poured the herb tea that had been stewing in the pot. She hated herb tea, why did everything that was good for the babies taste so awful? He didn't ask where she'd been, and she didn't ask where he'd slept. He knew nothing of Miss Carr, even though they'd walked in her footsteps in St. Agathe and he lived so close to her, here. He insisted they should concentrate on the present and the future. He was right, except that the present was the person who had been sitting on their birdbath, half naked when she came in. The future was their house in France, and the twins. She yawned.

Roger pulled her chair back and helped her to her feet. "You're tired, sweetheart."

"I went to church," she said. He nodded. She saw that she'd pleased him.

꙳

Up on the hill in her room, Emily hears the rattle and squeak of trolley wheels on the stone flags outside her door. She knows that half the hospital will have heard as well. They'll guess that it's time for her electrics. A nurse she doesn't recognize clunks the large battery into the room and starts to prepare the pads.

A pad is soaked in a solution of sodium salicylate and another in dilute zinc sulphate. The pads are placed in contact with two metal plates, the zinc to the positive pole, the salicylic to the negative pole. With ionization we go deeper than diffusion.

The circuit is closed by depressing the switch. A 16 m/a current is applied at first and muscles contract. The patient feels a painful sting. As the current rises it causes a disagreeable tingling. It can produce thermal changes. Fat will be heated to a much higher temperature than muscle. Blood is heated least of all.

The nurse places one of the pads on Emily's left ankle, she works with precision but she is no more involved in what she is doing than if she were counting pillowcases.

"You're new, aren't you?" Emily sits up, dislodging the first plate.

"Don't worry, I know what I'm at. I galvanize for Doctor Waller in Harley Street." The nurse's fingers are red and her nails are purplish. She has no wedding ring.

"Where's Frith?"

"Day off, I suppose."

"No it's not, she took her day off on Tuesday."

The nurse pinches Emily's hip. "You've got a lot of packing on you, that should make it easier. Come on now, relax, it doesn't hurt more than an ant bite."

"Ant bites hurt."

The new nurse pokes Emily's thigh and looks at the places on the inside where the skin puckers over the fat. There's a blue vein throbbing under the surface of the skin and the nurse places the second plate over it. "We generally see thin ladies in London, poor things, shutting their systems down. They've stopped eating, they've just about stopped breathing. The electricity works wonders for them. You don't have a problem with your eating, so that's a help."

"They feed me up like a prize porker."

6a.m. 10 oz. raw meat soup. 7a.m. cup black coffee, 8 ladles oatmeal porridge, gill of cream, boiled egg, 3 slices bread and butter, cocoa. 11a.m. 10 oz. milk. 2.00 p.m. half a pound rump steak, potatoes, cauliflower, savoury omelette, 10 oz. milk. 4.00 p.m. 10 oz. milk, 3 slices bread and butter, 6 cups of gravy soup. 8.00 p.m. Fried sole, roast mutton (3 large slices) French beans, potatoes, stewed fruit and cream, 10 oz. milk. 11.00 p.m. 10 oz. raw meat soup.

The nurse touches Emily's knee and she screams, "Don't! Don't touch me, I don't want to be touched. It hurts."

"No massage then?"

"No. No massage."

"It's good for you, 'specially if you're not getting about. See here..." The nurse puts her hands on Emily's distended belly, smoothes the skin, gathers it up and begins to pummel and vibrate it, as if it were laundry.

Emily holds onto the bed, momentarily stunned into submission. The nurse continues to knead, and Emily opens her lungs to their fullest. The nurse jumps back and bangs her elbow on the corner of a cabinet.

"All right, let's get it over with." She stoops over the machine, grimacing.

Galvanisation. The treatment works best for disorders not too far below the skin. It relieves pain and spasm, lowers blood pressure, resolves inflammation.

The room is darkened. There's an animal inside Emily's chest and it's called Fear. She screws up her eyes and tries to picture herself at home in the room above the barn she once used for her studio. She is leaning out of the window with her nose over the Geraniums. They spill out of the window box. In the distance, a sparkling sheet of water reaches out to the Olympic mountains. They flute the horizon like white peaks of meringue. The sky is flecked with scraps of tissue paper. British. Columbia. The flowers fade, the scene darkens until only the shimmer is left, and then the shimmer cuts out. Everything goes black as the room closes in. She can smell electricity, acid, acrid. The three cells of the battery glow, the glass receptacle is filled with glowing violet gas. She reaches out and a shower of sparks explodes between the glass and her skin. The nurse tugs at her knee, the cable dislodges and sparks, the spark seems to come from the nurse's hand, from her purple nails, it is divided into numberless fine little lines, a jumping, darting violet flame. Emily's scalp contracts. "Nooooooo—oh!"

Dr. Waller rushes in. "What's going on, nurse? Oh Lord, you've got a brush!" She pushes the nurse aside. The contact is re-established and the flame is quelled. "Why didn't you call me?"

"But Doctor, I was only following instructions, she keeps on wriggling and calling out."

"She's a bawler." The doctor takes Emily's hands. "You'll have the whole hospital on its head with your bellowing, Miss Carr. This would be quite enjoyable if you would only lie back and let it do its work." She slips a rubber gag in Emily's mouth. "I think we'll vary it a little." She turns to the nurse. "How long since her last meal?"

The nurse unclips the chart from the head of Emily's bed. "She was given milk at eleven. Breakfast was at eight." Emily rolls her eyes and tries to spit out the gag.

Dr. Waller has made a decision. She lifts Emily's nightdress, "Take these things off, nurse, she mustn't be constricted." The nurse struggles to inch Emily's bloomers down. She doesn't resist, but she offers no assistance. The doctor pulls a sheet over her.

'I am a whale,' thinks Emily. 'I am lying at the bottom of the sea, and above me is an entire city the size of San Francisco and it is pressing me down, causing a giant wave.'

Dr. Waller changes the pads. She checks her notes, and swallows her nervousness. There is a first time for everything and it is as well to begin on a patient who is an old hand at illness, who doesn't respond to being gentled by galvanization. A few years ago, Leduc produced a general anaesthesia with electrical current. Other men have been able to produce catatonic states, stupor or convulsions by changing the intensity or placing the electrodes on different parts of the body. Progress is the most important word in medicine and if this doesn't work she has one more ace up her sleeve. If ever there were a patient so stuck, so in need of a forward-looking therapy, it is this one.

The nurse brushes back Emily's hair, and Dr. Waller motions her to daub some jelly on the end of her extended finger. This she applies to Emily's temples. The nurse hands her two gauze pads soaked in witch hazel, which she places over Emily's eyes. The nurse tapes the pads in place.

Now Emily is in a deep trench and the sides are so close they are touching her hips. She can feel air on her cheeks, she can breathe, but all she can smell is the witch hazel and over it some kind of chemical, a rough, caustic smell. She tries to rub her nose but the nurse is binding her hands to the bed and shoving a pillow under her head. She is raised up. Something damp trickles over her right cheek and down her chin. She wants to wipe it away, she tries to ask for help but her tongue is wedged back in her mouth and the taste of the rubber gag is terrible. She gasps for breath, and then something else happens—they're putting something over each temple, something cold and hard, and a tight band to hold whatever it is in place. It feels like a thick rubber strap. This is not the same as galvanization.

"Try to unclench, Miss Carr, it will soon be over and you're going to feel like a new person. You have nothing to fear, nobody wants to hurt you." The doctor's voice booms. Then she feels a roar starting, she tries to shake her head to let the sound out, but she's pinned down. She must get to the surface before... And then it comes, a huge burst of something that is neither outside nor inside. It engulfs her, her body is stiff as a rod, her back will break in two. It's not light, not pain, not pressure, it's...something else. Then it goes black.

The convulsive threshold cannot be predicted. Low resistance patients sometimes need higher currents than those with high resistance readings. To start, the time can be set at one tenth of a second and the voltage at 60.

Dr. Waller notes with satisfaction that the patient appears to have suffered a grand mal seizure of the type induced by a major epileptic episode. She tells the nurse to wipe the saliva from her neck and chin and check the sheets for faeces. The patient must not be aware of any indignity.

Later, when they remove the gauze pads, the room is so bright that Emily shuts her eyes immediately. She feels loose and slithery—completely free to move forward and backwards and sideways, in and out of time. She smells dog mess. Turning her head, she can see beyond the garden to the tussocky fields dotted with sheep and the familiar clusters of trees folded into the dips, copses they call them here, beech and ash and elder all in full leaf, copses alive, not corpses dead, this green and pleasant land where she will get better, this England, so well described by her poets. The whole room, the whole building the whole landscape is rocking gently, as if in a light breeze. She floats on the soft, summer air.

On the far side of the lawn a pregnant cat was stalking a butterfly, its tail straining with concentration. Kit thought of Ilona, popping out of her skirt, brimming with babies. She'd never paid much attention to children. When her friends got to be mothers, they always changed. They couldn't concentrate on ordinary conversations and they kept beating the drum, telling her she should follow their lead. She'd laughed at them. Maybe that was wrong. Her best friend Betsy Jensen had been cast in Twelfth Night at Stratford when she got pregnant. Rehearsals started in March and the season ran through to November. Kit had urged her to have an abortion and stay with the show, but she hadn't listened. And she'd never worked since. Betsy said that being a new mother was like taking part in an endless rehearsal for an incomprehensible but supposedly brilliant play. You didn't sleep. You were drugged and one-tracked and completely focused so there was only the world onstage, and the world outside was like a washed-out movie. Kit couldn't square it with passion, but it was surely better than a summer spent with Anne of Green Gables and an audience of reverent Japanese tourists. She gazed up. The blue and yellow bird had made steady progress, the remains of the lump of fat dangled precariously like an endangered bungee jumper. The trees on top of the hill in the distance were rimmed with yellow light, the air shimmered, a dragonfly, or maybe a wasp, zoomed by and disappeared. The landscape was zigzagged with energy lines.

There was the small question of a father, of course, but there were lots of sperm out there lying in wait. She was hungry. She wanted breakfast, a good English breakfast with fried bread and sausages. She felt excited, slightly heady, and the amazing thing was she'd achieved it without any chemicals.

⚶

Roger helped Ilona light her candles and saw her into bed. Downstairs, he found Kit perched on a bar stool, tucking into his pancake. It took an effort to smile and bid her a good morning. She was wearing threadbare jeans and a clean T-shirt that said *we are what we eat, I'm fast, cheap and easy.*

"Hi. I was out in the yard. I went into the field."

"Yes." Roger couldn't think what to add. "Do you like croissants?"

"Absolutely. Do you have some?"

"No."

"Mom makes them. Hers are C.P., whoops, that's her word—off limits!"

"Copacetic." He didn't need any more reminders of Catherine. "Look, I don't know if Ilona explained the arrangement last night— she's my wife, you see."

"Yes. She's a bit young, isn't she?"

"I'm sorry you think so." He swallowed.

"No, what I mean is, she's young to be pregnant."

"Yesterday was her birthday."

"It was mine last week. It was a big day for me."

"Really?"

"Yes. Really."

He wasn't ready to pursue this, so he focused on Ilona. "She's expecting—well, I'm sure you noticed. That is...we're expecting. In about month—they say first babies often arrive late. Or early."

"I thought it was next week by the size of her. That would have made us both Cancer. Both your kids."

"Cancer, oh no! Perish the thought. Are you ill?"

"Not that I know of."

"It's twins."

"Oh, you mean Gemini?"

Roger frowned. What was she talking about?

"Just teasing. She's really expecting twins?"

She looked ill, but most young women were underweight so it was hard to know. Ilona was thin, too, her hips weren't wide enough to support a birth without cracking like a wishbone; the midwife had reassured him, but he wasn't convinced.

He applied himself to making coffee, thinking he must have satisfied his obligation to be helpful.

"I was thinking I might have a baby myself."

The coffee beans spilled onto the draining board. "You're pregnant? Is that what you're trying to tell me?"

"Not yet, would it be a problem?"

Roger turned on the coffee grinder and drowned her out. It was a classic case of North American self-absorption. Me, me, me. They always wanted the limelight, they couldn't even bear anyone else to give birth without trying to go one better.

"You have a neat place here. I like the pink walls." Kit waited for the noise to subside. She knew she was getting off on the wrong foot; he wasn't giving her any clues as to how to talk to him. The walls were hideous, but he lived with them so he must like them. He seemed to expect her to butter him up. She should say something about his pictures, once she'd established they were really his. His silk dressing gown hung open to reveal his nipples and a spurt of silvery chest hair. He was hairy. She'd never liked beards, men grew them to disguise their weak chins. "They say it's the woman that passes on the baldness gene," she remarked.

Roger covered his head. He placed the cafetiere carefully on the table and adjusted the tie on his dressing gown.

"I was just thinking I'd probably inherited your baldness gene, or would I inherit it from Mom?"

He scraped some marmalade into a cut glass dish. It wasn't too late to put a rose on the table to welcome her and send her on her way. He wondered if he could snip one out of the bunch he'd given Ilona without her noticing. He went through to the living room, glad to escape for a moment, and pulled a red rose from the bouquet. Why had Ilona insisted on re-lighting the candles? Someone should do something about the remains of last night's meal.

He brought the flower back to the kitchen and offered it.

"You look like Olivier when he played Othello, except he was all painted up. He'd never get away with that today. White men in black face? Someone asked him if he really felt like a Negro and he said 'what's wrong with acting, dear boy?'" She took the rose and tucked it under her plate.

"Why did you come here?" This sounded petulant, but if she didn't want acting he needn't bother to put on a false welcome.

"I needed to see you. I've always thought I'd find you one day. I'm having a terrible time, and Mom's gone off to the States with a boot-maker."

He wondered if he could trust this information. Had she meant to say bookmaker? "Look, about today. We thought we'd show you around a bit, you know, the village, the pottery, oh no, there isn't a pottery. Grab a bite in the pub and then maybe you and I can go up to London. I'll drop you off at a hotel..."

"Oh no, I can't afford a hotel."

"Don't worry, I'll take care of it. We don't want you sleeping rough again. You've no idea what goes on in London after dark."

"Do you?"

"I did once."

"I thought I'd stay here for a while."

"No, I think you'd be terribly bored." It was impossible! She was impulsive. She got it from her mother. She was deliberately trying to make him feel uncomfortable and she knew unerringly how to press the right buttons. He'd have to make it so she'd want to leave; he wouldn't cook any more breakfasts. But how else did you scale down when she was so completely at home with the low life? She even liked the terrible pink walls. He'd been meaning to get them painted for years, but he'd never got round to it and people like those jokers in the pub kept telling him how they liked the colour. She was mopping up the last of the marmalade. "We could get to know each other better in London," he said, hopefully.

"But you won't be there, you'll be here."

"I work there. I'll show you my office if you like. We have a mixed dining room at the club so we can have lunch together. I'm afraid they won't put you up, the sleeping arrangements are strictly unisex."

"Oh, you mean it's a gay club?"

"No! Where did you get that idea?"

"Mom said you used to hang out with David Hockney."

Catherine had talked about him! What else had she said? He should be picking Kit up bodily and throwing her out, but he was actually feeling a vague sense of guilt, or was it regret? "I used to be an artist." It sounded so final. "Why don't we both get ready? I'll show you the village myself, if Ilona's not up to coming with us."

"That's fine, I'll just hang out here if you don't mind."

A scream rang out. He jumped up and took the stairs two at a time.

Ilona was sitting up in bed, her eyes shining. She'd discovered her present on the opposite wall. "What's that?"

"It's for you. It's for your birthday. Her name's..." What was the bloody boat's name? "We'll take her out, but only when there's no swell. We're too close to risk calamities."

She pulled him down on the bed. "I'm so, so lucky."

CHAPTER NINE

Catherine was surprised at how understanding Ernie was once he got over the initial shock of her move. He helped with the garage sale, made trips to the dump and the Salvation Army, sorted, sized, packed and provided coffee. The main decision she needed to make was what to do with Kit's stuff. Kit had fiercely resisted any changes to her bedroom. As always, Catherine respected her wishes—it remained exactly as it was when she was growing up, with the addition of the stuff she'd moved out of the playroom to make way for her studio. She unscrewed the little porcelain plaque that she'd fired and painted so lovingly, KEEP OUT. KIT'S ROOM. As she watched it shatter against the side of the garbage can, she was overcome with the first pang of sadness she'd felt since making the decision to leave Vancouver. Her efforts to track Kit down had failed. It wasn't unusual for them to stay out of touch for two or three months when Kit was on the road. She thought back to their last encounter. Kit had shown up on the doorstep with a tousled young man and a young couple in tow, wanting to spend the night.

"We're heading up to the Okanagan tomorrow to check out the fruit picking and see if I can firm up venues for a couple of shows. We thought maybe Julie could stay on here. She has hepatitis."

"Then Julie should be in a hospital."

"You don't go to hospital for jaundice, Mom!"

"Well, I'm not a nurse. It's not on, Kit, stay tonight but then you have to make some other arrangements for them. You're always welcome, but..."

"Too bad."

She'd turned tail and herded them all back into her beat up Volkswagen. Catherine didn't lose much sleep over it, and the next day Kit phoned to apologize, but not to explain. "Why don't you get a cellphone, Mom, that way we could keep in touch?"

"Why don't you?"

"I have one, but it always needs charging."

As she dismantled the shelves, and threw the books and toys into boxes, Catherine wondered how she'd managed to get off so lightly in the parenting stakes. She'd made so many wrong moves, but still it seemed to her, they had an easy, permissive relationship, though it was never completely free of tension. She bagged the broken guitar, the books, paintings, school reports and essays, the first box of grease paints—they were important markers for both of them but she was determined not to allow herself to be nostalgic. Kit was thirty-five, practically middle aged. It was too late to be weeping over childhood relics. She realized with a jolt that she'd never truly acknowledged that she'd lost her, though the parting had happened when Kit left high school. She balanced a patent leather tap shoe on her palm. She hardly thought of Kit as grown up and she'd never indulged in hopes of being a grandmother. Was this what they called denial? She hadn't saved any leftovers from her own childhood, so there was nothing to pass along.

Over Ernie's protestations, she hired movers to help pack her artwork; it was a delicate job, there were sculptures and installations that needed expert attention. She'd stored everything she hadn't sold and, though she wasn't prolific, the stuff had mounted up. The men were almost too careful and the job wasn't finished when it came time to decamp, so she left them to it, warning them that nothing was insured.

The final papers for the house purchase were signed and she was behind the wheel of a U-Haul cutting adrift from Vancouver. It had all taken exactly twelve days. She marked this on the calendar as Day One. Ernie was full of smiles though he'd been tetchy and difficult the day before. He tailed her in her car, piled to the roof with household effects.

She negotiated customs and the ferry crossing in an agony of apprehension in case there was a quota on returning refugees. The interview went without a hitch, the young man at customs had red hair, he reminded her of a boy she'd known in high school. He said, "Welcome back ma'am." She wondered if she was dreaming.

She was tired out when they arrived at the house. The place felt different. Something was missing. Ernie set about dusting and sweeping right away while Catherine sank down uselessly on the rickety steps of the shack, which would serve better as a dog house than a studio. A peeling fence and a fierce tangle of blackberry bushes hid the cliff edge. She'd be making jam alone this year; it would be too soon to invite Ernie to come back and join in the harvest in September.

Kit sat at the kitchen table unravelling her hair extensions, trying to shut out the racket upstairs. One bellow was all, but that was all it took. It was followed by eerie mewling—Ilona's contribution to the shindig. She'd never felt so lonely, never wanted her mother so badly. No matter how old you were, how much you'd lived, no one should make you listen to your father making love to a pregnant child. Through the open door, she saw that someone had lit the candelabra on the dining table. She pulled the petals from the rose Roger had given her. For better, for worse she was here now. "He loves me, he loves me not."

⚜

Catherine crossed her fingers, hoping Ernie would stay and help with the unloading. He'd already been so kind, she knew she shouldn't expect it and she'd seen him consulting the schedule so he knew there was one more return ferry before nightfall. When she got up the nerve to go out to the truck and ask about his plans she found he'd already started to offload the boxes.

Between them, they hefted the heaviest furniture into the empty rooms. He carried the lighter things in on his own and then began unpacking boxes, folding and saving them, stowing the newspapers in plastic garbage bags that he'd brought with him. It was almost midnight. Catherine was hungry and she was beyond tired so she could only watch as he continued relentlessly. He kept his face turned away from her, apologizing for not having had time to shave.

He stopped briefly when she insisted they should eat the sandwiches she'd packed and open the beer he'd put on ice. The enormity of the move was hitting home and she wanted desperately to take time, but Ernie slogged on. He'd hardly opened his mouth since they arrived on the island, but they'd spent so much of their time together in silence that she hardly noticed it. A group of people were having an early morning party on a boat in the bay. She heard the shatter of glass as bottles hit the rocks below the house. Their voices were magnified by the water, odd phrases floated up. "It refused to fuckin' function...real returns are...forgot about soy beans..."

Collapsed on the couch, Catherine listened, incurious and detached. It was like being in the sauna at the local community centre in Vancouver, disembodied forms shrouded in steam, a constant chatter in half a dozen languages, none of it connected, sometimes clashing, sometimes harmonizing, sometimes spontaneously hushed. She was falling asleep. This toiling had to end.

"Tell me about your husband." He had come to sit on the couch beside her. The request was so out of character that she was immediately awake.

"You mean Roger?"

"Was that his name?"

"It was." Ernie had never showed the slightest interest in her past. "He's probably dead."

"What was he like?"

"He was English."

"And?"

"That about sums him up, I guess." She saw that he wanted more. "He was a student when I married him. He liked my legs. I used to have legs, I mean, legs that people liked. Now I'm just glad they hold me up, or let me down, like now."

"What did you like about him?"

Catherine swallowed her irritation. "I can't remember. I guess it was his...absurdity. He was absurdly—you know, he was a sort of puffed up...what can I say? He was absurd. I liked that."

Ernie frowned. "What does that mean?"

"I guess it means he took himself seriously."

"Like me?"

"Not a bit like you, Ernie."

"Why did you break up?"

"He started to make a name for himself."

"That was the reason?"

"Oh, I don't know. He had this show—it was so long ago. I just remember it was the end of the road. I was a new mom and...and he had this show. It was all he could think of."

"Well, didn't you make a name for yourself, too?"

"Oh, I did okay, but I didn't think it was very important. He thought it was. He thought I was a coward. The jury's out on that."

"What does that mean?"

It was too early in the morning for this. Too late and too early. Did he want a confession about how insecure she felt? She wasn't going near that one, and certainly not for him; he'd never been a confidante, he was essentially a stranger, a wonderfully familiar stranger but he was nothing to her, and what was she to him other than a space-filler? She'd always been someone he took for granted, like the no-name tree in the front yard. She knew she was being ungenerous, especially after all his kindness, but she hadn't asked for kindness, hadn't asked for anything. She was too tired to think and he was waiting for her. It was safer to stick with the past, her first marriage was long enough ago that it wouldn't come back and haunt her.

"Roger was always looking for the 'scene' and I hid from it. He showed in a group exhibition in New York. He streaked at an Andy Warhol opening once, and got a mention in *Time*. There were magazine spreads about all his buddies—he grooved the scene. Remember the sixties jargon? I couldn't do it." Ernie looked mystified. She wondered if he'd ever been part of the sixties. It didn't matter. "How about we turn in for the night?"

"What did he look like, your husband?"

She sighed. "My ex-husband. Ugly. He was ugly." Ernie recoiled. "It's okay, ugly was in, even for the beautiful people. He slouched and he swore. He was a big farter, he liked to let them rip at cocktail parties. He was Upper Middle Class, so rudeness was sanctioned, but I think he had to work at it. And he never shaved, but he never could grow a beard, just a sort of coconut mat. I thought that was copacetic. That was our word for all the grotty things we approved of. It's a forties word actually. We thought we were really hip." She glanced over to see if Ernie was following. "I don't know why they make such a big fuss about the sixties today, they were torture. I never wanted to be a hippie and I didn't want to be a dolly bird either.

I didn't do drugs. I just wanted to paint, and I was better than most of the posers who were getting all the press. I guess that made me sort of smug. He knew I was better, but he only let on when he was drunk and feeling okay about himself."

"Do you think you're smug?"

"Why, no." The question startled her. Was that how he saw her?

"Why did you go to England?"

"To study and get away from the Midwest. Kennedy had been shot; America was getting sucked into Vietnam. England was happening. I never thought I'd stay. Well, I didn't stay did I? I decamped to Canada. And now I'm back. Full circle. That's it in a nutshell—isn't it ironic?"

"I want you to come home." Ernie reached across and touched her knee. "I love you."

She focused on his hand, reached down for the beer bottle and topped up his glass.

He got up. "I think you're right. We should call it a day."

She stored away the curve of his back and his deft movements as he leaned down to unroll the scrap of mattress he'd found in the shed. She wanted to tell him to use the bedroom, but if he preferred this disgusting piece of foam, this bed of nails—why couldn't people be trusted to leave things unsaid?

Sleep didn't come easily. She lay stiff with outrage. Her bed felt lopsided and unfamiliar in this featureless room. Did the floor slope? How could Ernie have blown it so stupidly? It was no good pretending he didn't mean it—he never spoke unless he meant it. She wrapped the pillow round her head to muffle his asthmatic wheezes. Or was he sobbing again? She hoped he would be gone before she woke.

When she got up he was showered and packed, ready to leave. He'd rolled the mattress up neatly and tied it with one of his navy knots. They sat across from each other at the kitchen table. Catherine tried to be cheerful and he did his best to respond. The place looked even more unloved and derelict in the morning light. She squeezed orange juice but he didn't touch it. The plan was for him to drive the U-Haul back to Vancouver, but he said he'd changed his mind and he'd try to drop it off in Seattle and take the train home.

She watched, sleepy-eyed, as he pulled away from the house. She hadn't wanted it to end like this. She hadn't wanted it to end. What would she do without him? It was all too complex, there were too many invisible lines. It was just as well the thing had come out in the open and been implicitly denied. The chapter was over and there was no going back now. She was free to unpack slowly. Alone.

When Roger came downstairs, knotting his tie, he found Kit still sitting at the kitchen table in front of the dirty dishes, playing with her hair. She didn't look up.

"Care to go out?"

"Not right now."

He didn't challenge her. He'd already rung his secretary and told her to cancel his appointments. He needed to take a break and think what to do next.

He sat in his car, his mind blank, listening to a phone-in programme about disciplining children, then sat in the parking lot of the pub, watching children play in the garden. He didn't go inside for fear of running into Tom and Thomas. His head felt heavy, his mouth was still furred from yesterday's over-indulgence. He listened to the start of a radio programme called 'One Minute Please' in which the contestants were challenged to have their say about a given topic in a minute without pausing or repeating themselves. He gave himself the topic of Kit, but he hadn't enough information to fill a minute, even if he repeated himself over and over. "She acts like an ingenuous teenager and..." "She's from another planet. What am I supposed to do with her if...?" False starts. He eased himself out of the car and began to walk in the direction of the highest hill in this part of the county, crossing the highway and sauntering through the Council Estate. It was an affluent estate, there were expensive cars at the curb, the lawns were well kept and some attempt had been made to differentiate the copycat houses from one another. They'd obviously been sold off. He wondered what they'd fetched? His oxblood leather shoes weren't suited to hiking, and his briefcase was heavy (he picked it up automatically whenever he got out of the car on weekdays).

He pulled up short in front of a farmhouse gate. Daunted by the steep rise in the road beyond it, he turned and retraced his steps. An elderly man who was bent over a blazing bed of red flowers looked up suspiciously as he passed. Roger quickened his pace, thinking he must look like a salesman. Back at the car he tuned in to 'Round Britain Quiz,' a radio programme he remembered having to listen to when he was a boy. He still couldn't answer any of the questions but the fact that it was still running was comforting. He decided to risk it and pick up a sandwich, but as he pulled up in front of the pub he spotted Tom getting out of a BMW. He took out his fountain pen. His secretary had been urging him to plan how much leave he would be taking for the coming birth and how things should be organized while he was away. He opened his date book, booked himself off for two weeks, then crossed this out and drove to Ipswich, where he sat by the new marina gazing at the sleek lines of 'Lady,' daring himself to take the boat out on the water.

He got home in time for supper, and Ilona served the paté and left over Seville-orange-and-stout ham. He didn't think it had been refrigerated, but he ate it cheerfully for fear of upsetting her. Kit appeared as they were finishing. She said she didn't want to eat, which was probably wise.

Next morning, he walked with her to the village where they bought a stack of newspapers on his tab and she spent the rest of the day on the window seat, going through them article by article, snipping and stuffing the clippings into a Harrods' carrier bag she'd ferreted out. She seemed indifferent to his offers to show her the sights of London and showed no interest in going further afield. She made him tongue-tied. He felt both hopeful that her refusal of his offers of hospitality meant she did not intend to stay, and hopeless at his inability to please her. She didn't acknowledge his discomfort, or that he was staying away from the office on her account. He saw that she could contort her limbs and hold the most extraordinary poses for hours.

On the second evening, they all sat in the lounge, silenced by the television. She had no opinion on what they should watch—he presumed she thought everything was C.P., even the weather fore-cast. He tried his best to maintain the peace between his two ladies as they sat straight backed at either end of the settee, one like a fat Buddha, the other a Yogi princess. He'd always managed to keep things calm in the office by insisting that the women who worked for him dealt with emotional matters in their breaks, but for once he wished for a blizzard, a blow up—anything to fracture the frosty silence. It wasn't getting easier to believe he'd fathered this twitchy young—or was she middle aged?—this twitchy person, who took up so much room in his mind while occupying so little physical space. He dismissed his earlier qualms about her being ill.

※

Ilona always ate lunch on the run these days, there was so much work to finish off. It was easy to ignore the guest. She quickly discovered that she wasn't expected to make conversation, though for the first three days of Kit's visit Roger introduced stupid topics for them to discuss over dinner. It was like a school debating society and she was glad when he gave up. In the nursery, she painted the undercoat on the skirting board, carefully avoiding anything that required her to stretch. She stripped the wallpaper to waist level. She liked the little curls of paper that sprang off the wall, and saved them to build fanciful nests, which she set fire to in the garden, watching them curl in on themselves then burst into quick life as the flames licked the edges of the spirals and galloped towards their heart.

By the fourth day, she realized that this was going to be a long siege. She hadn't lit any more candles since she was in the village church, but now she placed the candelabra on the sideboard in front of the mirror so the five flames multiplied to ten. She kept them burning all day and into the night.

Roger watched Ilona as she sat on the edge of the bed, stroking her belly. It was a gesture he loved and he thought that if he ever painted again he'd capture it.

"What's she cutting out?" she asked. He pushed the question aside. He was thinking of a spread of some of Lucien Freud's latest portraits in one of the weekend Colour Supplements. The old faker was still putting his energy into beautifully executed, exaggerated renditions of hideous women—the seamy side—he'd fathered children by several, by all accounts. He'd obviously never been overcome by the queasy tenderness that Roger felt at times. Freud didn't try to translate female fragility into paint. His women were mostly buxom and substantial, not friable. Roger couldn't come up with an answer to the problem of avoiding sentimentality. He was living in the wrong age—five hundred years ago men got around it by painting Madonnas, but there was no call for virgins today. He spent a good part of every day sitting in his studio on one of the plastic chairs he'd bought from the hardware store, pondering his first brush stroke. Men who were still in the art game at his age generally moved away from realism; it was a question of refining the spirit when the flesh gave out. Wispy stuff, this old man's abstraction. Trying to pass off a few scant lines or a daub of colour for depth of experience. Old age was parcelled up in reflection, loss, but he was bent on renewal. If he painted another landscape it would be fleshy. He'd try to convey the mystery of flesh, never mind if it was another cliché. The very idea of it upended him, made him feel nervous—too nervous to embark on anything new. The baby kicked and he leaned over and feathered Ilona's skin. She pushed his hand away.

He couldn't remember how Catherine looked when she was pregnant. He remembered a scarlet kimono she used to wear, and she'd pinned her hair up with blue plastic clips. Funny how colour stayed in the mind after everything else faded. How was it possible to forget so much? He'd jotted down a couple of memories. Kit's first word was pooh, but he couldn't remember when or where she was born. Men weren't expected to be present for the pain and gore in those days. Remembering was the woman's job—birthdays, anniversaries, thank-you letters—they were all taken care of, and if you didn't have a woman you were forgiven for passing them up. He was going to reform. It wasn't too late.

Ilona's navel protruded like a badly fitted bung. The aureoles round her nipples had darkened from the delicate slightly greenish tone they used to have; he supposed it happened to all pregnant women. "I don't know what Kit's cutting out. Does it matter?"

Ilona seemed to have forgotten she'd asked the question. He didn't want her to speak any more, he wanted to keep looking at her.

"Well, it's too late to ask now," she said, crossly, "it would look rude. We should've asked when she started."

"Why don't you peek in that bag of hers?"

"Without asking?"

"Ask if she'd mind."

"No I couldn't. I want to know what the clippings are for. I don't want to look at them. And it's my bag anyway. And why does she have to sleep with the light on?"

"Maybe it's the same reason as you keep candles burning." Roger got into bed and sighed.

Ilona didn't dare ask Roger how long he intended to harbour the guest. She dreaded the equivocal answer, the hot look. Sometimes he reminded her of her father, he'd dig in and it was impossible to budge him. She had to find ways to get around him, making him think he'd made decisions that were really hers, like deciding to change the colour of the outside walls of the house. It was stupid to call a house Golding when it was painted pink. The scaffolders were due to arrive any hour, and after that she had to start interviewing nannies. She'd never conducted an interview before, so she spent a day drafting a list of questions. She wasn't sure whether she wanted someone who was already a mother or someone who'd never had children like one of those educated young women from the expensive nanny schools in Knightsbridge that she'd read about. Why would a mother want to be someone else's nanny? And why would a single woman want to look after someone else's children rather than have her own? Maybe it would be best to hire someone who couldn't have children—but how did you ask such an intimate question? Roger had left it to her and she didn't want him to have an excuse to criticize. He was always criticizing her these days. She shouldn't light the candles, she should get interested in newspaper clippings, she should be a better hostess. He'd even commented on the burning nests of wallpaper in the bird-bath. It was better when he wasn't hanging about the house, watching. They had this much in common—they were both watching—watching Kit. For his sake she'd forced herself to call her by that name. Kit. And now she'd got started she couldn't stop. She tried to think of Kit as a trial nanny, sent to show her what it would be like to have a stranger in the house. She knew Kit wasn't being purposely intrusive, but when she moved from room to room, Kit left a trail in her wake, a trail of used up space. She was always there. A nanny would take up space too, but it would be neutral space. She decided there was no need to be impolite or unwelcoming, she would treat Kit as if she were an unwanted domestic pet that had to be fed, but not loved. Roger's pet. She rocked on her heels when Roger pointed out that Kit was actually her step-daughter.

Kit was blocking Ilona's path to the front door as she was about leave. "Do you need anything from the shops?" she asked politely, motioning to the empty string bag on her arm.

"Not right now."

The alarming eyes saw right through her. They saw the water. Roger had the same eyes, but his didn't see.

Shopping had become an ordeal. Ilona found it increasingly hard to squeeze behind the steering wheel of the car and she'd had a couple of bad dreams lately about the air bag deploying and puncturing her uterus, catapulting the babies through the roof in a great whoosh so that she was left with two placentas in her lap. Or did twins share a placenta? She made a mental note to ask the mid-wife. There were still so many unanswered questions.

She loved driving. She'd loved it from the first moment she got behind a wheel. She liked to take risks in the narrow lanes around the village, driving like a champion, screeching to a halt with split-second timing. She always drove over the speed limit but she knew she had to be more careful now. She'd read about Isadora Duncan who was strangled when her scarf caught in a car wheel, then her children died. She thought about Isadora a lot. Ilona and Isadora. Ilona never wore a scarf when she was driving, and now she was too scared to drive, too scared and too bloated.

"Why don't you hire someone from the village to take you where you need to go?" Roger asked, after he watched her foot-slogging up from the bus with a cargo of plastic bags. He was so far off the mark that she didn't bother to respond.

"Well, if that doesn't suit, take a taxi. Or ask Kit. She'd probably be happy to drive you."

"In my car?" Ilona reddened.

"What's wrong with her using your car?"

"Because it's mine!" She tried to stop her lip trembling. "You could help—I'd make a list for you—you could pick things up. You wouldn't have to do it every day." She saw that Kit was listening and decided to have another go at driving. She'd had plenty of practice at overcoming fear. It wasn't hard if you put your mind to it. She guessed that Roger had never set foot in a grocery store.

"Okay, I'll do it," he barked.

Ilona watched Kit sipping a glass of water, her eyes wide and innocent, making out she was unaware that she was the cause of all these rows. They'd never had a row before Kit came into the house. She sat down and made a list of basic food items on the magic slate. Roger picked it up and went straight to the phone. He telephoned the village shop and arranged for a delivery.

Ilona unpacked the boxes when the boy delivered them on his bicycle. The bags were full of horrible plastic bread and withered fruit and veggies, battery eggs and tins of green beans. She saw Roger smiling as she piled the cans on the counter, but he made no move to put them away.

The next evening he ordered in pizzas. She didn't comment, nor did she comment on the take-away curries (they arrived cold because they'd travelled so far). She reflected that precooked food might be bad for the babies and cancel out all the efforts she'd made for the last eight months, but if they didn't develop properly it wouldn't be her fault.

She put her foot down when Roger suggested placing a standing order with Harrods. She supposed they could afford it, but it went too far. "Do you expect them to drive all the way up from London to deliver it?"

"No. I'll pick it up when I'm in town."

"You'll get on the train carrying a bag of groceries?"

"Why not?"

"Does that mean you're going back to work?"

Ilona didn't know how to tell him she didn't want him to touch her. She had asked the midwife if touching down there was bad for you when you were so far advanced. The midwife laughed and said it was fine to carry on as they were, whatever was comfortable as long as they were careful. She'd said something about rear entry that Ilona didn't understand. Before they were married, her mother had tried to talk to her about intimacy; she'd made it sound like injury. Ilona remembered how she'd confessed that she was a virgin on her second date with Roger. It was a measure of how easy she felt with him in those early days. She hadn't expected to actually like sex. At first, she thought it was only nice because they were in France where everything was new and enchanted, even his snoring. But when they got back to Golding, she never wanted to say no to him. Before she got so big, she was even beginning to pluck up courage to tell him what she wanted, and nudge him when he made it clear he'd rather go to sleep. He tasted of fresh oysters—her brother James once told her oysters were an aphrodisiac and she'd looked up the word in the dictionary. She looked up intimacy, but the meaning didn't convey any of what it felt like to actually melt into someone, to trust him completely. There was only one thing she hadn't confided to Roger. Soon after they were married she'd started to touch herself. She always waited till he was at work; it was strange, so strange and so lovely to feel open as a quartered orange. But since Kit had arrived, everything had closed down—even that. All her old friends were deserting her. She couldn't even imagine walking up the hill to the San any more. It would take too long. It would be too hot. It was just too far away.

When she was in Suffolk, Dr. Waller rarely strayed far from the grounds of her Sanatorium. She was a great believer in balance, she dwelt on it whenever the staff were gathered together, she exhorted the chaplain to be sure to mention it at Sunday prayers. She lectured to doctors and medical students when she was in London, and generally began by pointing out that Dis was the Roman god of the underworld. When his name was joined with ease, it created unbalance—disease. The physician's job was to put the body back into balance and this is what she attempted to do, regardless of whether the patients were suffering from T.B. or some less easily diagnosed sickness such as the one that had been variously described as neurasthenia, or, in the old terminology, hysteria.

Medicine was Elizabeth Waller's life, but she tried to maintain her personal balance by reading widely and paying particular attention to her appearance. The world saw a well-groomed, meticulous woman but her work was so absorbing and all encompassing that she often had to dose herself with laudanum in order to sleep. Increasingly, opiates were her balancers.

Her interests were not widely shared by the medical profession. They were suspicious of unmarried women, particularly those who were so single-minded and so ready to speak publicly on issues that were not in the female domain. Her lectures and informal talks were popular, in spite of the opposition, although no one admitted to wanting to attend. She made it a point to invite nurses, but they knew they were secondary, and not many were willing to break with the status quo and come to hear what she had to say. She grabbed her audience's attention when she followed up her definition of disease with a definition of masturbation—ma meaning manus or hand, and, sturbo—possibly meaning to defile. This definition had its root in the passage in the Old Testament when Onan, son-in-law of Judah was struck dead for spilling his seed rather than coupling with his sister-in-law as ordained by the law. Onan gave his name to the word onanism, a dark, and self-defiling act. There were unspoken reasons for Onan's death sentence. The second syllable of the word mastur-bate could be turbo, not sturbo—turbo, to agitate by hand. The soli-tary sin.

She always paused at this juncture and glanced up at her audience, noting which of them reddened and shifted their feet. They would not be recruited as her assistants.

"Until recently I believed, as do most of my colleagues, that onanism, the solitary sin, caused rather than cured conditions such as hysteria, as well as epilepsy, asthma, paralysis, melancholia and insanity. Now, following my reading of the Greek physician and philosopher, Galen, I am proposing that the opposite is true, that the so-called sin is necessary to keep us in balance." She always paused there, waiting for an intake of breath from the nursing fraternity and adding "I have no opinion on the sinfulness of the act—I am a doctor, not a cleric." Some of the doctors smiled at this.

"Over time we have investigated many cures for this sin—removal of the clitoris or burying it under the labia, blistering the thighs, or, more recently, mesmerism or hypnosis. The fact is that there is foreign matter lodged in the body and the patient needs to expectorate it, much as a tubercular patient must expectorate phlegm or a writer must expectorate words; while it remains in place there is no hope of balance. I'd like to suggest that healthy males, and also females, have maintained their sanguinity throughout the ages by means of masturbation." The intake of breath at this point was always audible.

"Masturbation is most suitable as a medical treatment for those patients who have shown a stubborn resistance to accepted cures." She cited case studies of patients at her London clinic who had benefited, naming each sufferer silently, for she had developed a fondness for most of them. She did not include the name of Emily Carr. No one had been more challenging. There was no patient with whom she had worked harder to banish Dis and restore ease and no one had been less receptive.

"By means of rigorous self-examination, I have confirmed Galen's findings that the female, when coaxed, emits a secretion, a form of milt which can, at times be abundant. I have disengaged from Galen's theory that this milt is impregnated with an evil essence but I am in no doubt that its retention can be harmful—it will putrefy if it is not flushed from the body." With a long and measured glance she challenged the nurses to leave. Nobody stirred.

"Galen asserted that in all things physicians must find the right beginning. In order to find the beginning, one must dig, dig and dig again. Some time ago a young bitch from the farm close to my Sanatorium in Suffolk started to hang around the grounds. She was a working dog and I wouldn't allow her to approach the patients, but she persisted in visiting my quarters and I gave in and fed her. Finally she ventured over the threshold and would lie by the fire, though she was not in the least domesticated. She was not displeased by my attempts to manipulate her manually, though I could never induce her to secrete. (Animals such as camels, and elephants have been observed to masturbate intentionally, this may account for their long lives.) After several weeks I gained her confidence, and, under light anaesthetic, I applied an electric current to her clitoral area as she lay before the fire. Now the secretions were manifest. After that, the dog became quite tame, she would follow me with her eyes and wag her tail whenever she heard my voice. Unfortunately there was no opportunity to follow up on the experiment because shortly after, she was shot for killing a sheep. Far from being *dis*-couraged, I extended my investigations. Now the time had come to work with human subjects—a word of warning, before I go into detail. While most patients tolerate the treatment and some appear to welcome it, some females are recalcitrant. A recalcitrant patient is not beyond help; patience is needed to persuade her to submit to manipulation, and she will often protest that she would prefer to undertake the task herself. This cannot, of course, be permitted since we need to measure the secretion. The best way to reassure her is to isolate her. There is still another reason for this. On occasion a patient will find the experience pleasurable and her cries could be disruptive to the daily functioning of the wards. In the absence of more suitable rooms at my Sanatorium, I repaired to the chapel until the chaplain intervened. Now I have found a quiet corner in the mortuary. Provided there are no cadavers in evidence, this serves well as it encourages the patient to dwell on her mortality and the urgent need to recuperate and diminishes the merely pleasurable aspects of the cure."

At this point Dr. Waller always took a sip of water and eyed the audience, knowing that there were ill-wishers in every crowd. "If I may backtrack to the source of my investigations. During the long evenings in the quiet of the Suffolk countryside, I delve into my library. My reading is not confined to medicine. I've long been fascinated by the hidden world of Japan and at some point in my reading, I came across a description of a method of self-manipulation called Ben Wa which is apparently ancient in origin and was widely practiced by ladies of all classes. It has been left to the English to find a practical use for Ben Wa." She pinned her audience down with a proud smile. "Evidently news of Onan's 'sin' did not spread to the Orient." She failed to reveal that she was unsure of her motives in commencing this hitherto untried treatment with Miss Emily Carr. There was a saying about killing with kindness and, in a moment of brutal honesty, she once admitted that this would not be an entirely unwelcome outcome. Miss Carr was not her first subject. "With the help of an assistant, I experimented on myself." She held up the two hollow balls, one of which was filled with mercury. "These are inserted into the vagina and gently manipulated. The movement creates vibrations, which are transmitted from the labia to the clitoris to the uterus. The experiment results in a copious stream of milt. It leaves the patient exhausted and exhilarated, and brings about huge relief."

Emily Carr lies on a narrow bed in the mortuary with a warm pad positioned over her stomach and a sheet around her waist to keep the lower portion of her body from view. Dr. Waller sits on a chair beside her, wearing a glove and preparing to position herself between her legs. Miss Carr remarks that she feels as if she were about to be milked, and she also expresses some discomfort at the proximity of a small empty coffin that has been readied that morning for a child who will be dead by evening. The coffin is removed. A vase of Sweet Peas is set down in its place, a phonograph is brought in from Dr. Waller's own private quarters and the introduction to 'Sheep May Safely Graze' by J.S. Bach fills the room. At the first touch of the doctor's hand, Emily bellows and she continues to yell until Dr. Waller and her nurse lock eyes, fearing that the entire hospital will conclude that a haunting is taking place.

It happens again when Miss Carr is persuaded into a rocking chair with warm bandages applied to her thighs. She agreed to the continuation of treatment, and admitted that she had no cause for complaint, but when it comes to the point, she refuses all intervention. She laughs at the effort, etched on the good doctor's forehead. She notices for the first time the scattering of freckles dancing across her nose. She laughs loud and long. Shortly after, she pronounces herself cured and discharges herself from the hospital.

Dr. Waller was glad to see the back of Emily Carr, though she missed the money-order that arrived punctually each month from Canada. The wretch was unable to submit to pleasure, and the doctor concluded that she may have been correct in thinking that she was cured. The course of this kind of illness was unpredictable, but it had to be admitted that something must have triggered her remarkable recovery. Could it have been the mirth? Who else would have had the gall to laugh at such a moment? Laugh or die, the old adage said. She sometimes had to content herself with the knowledge that the patient had returned to the world in balance due to circumstances that were entirely beyond any doctor's control. However a cure was achieved, it must be counted as a success.

Elizabeth Waller wrote up the case in detail, but she would not publish such equivocal results. After her encounter with Emily Carr she taught that some people's very nature militated against treatment, and it was always necessary to carefully assess their humour before commencing care. She suspected Galen would probably have diagnosed Miss Carr as having an excess of yellow bile—hot and dry. He had a man's certitude. He would have advised her to return to her outpost immediately; she was not equipped to tackle the unstinting demands of life in the Mother Country.

CHAPTER TEN

꜀ℓ꜀

K it did her best to make herself invisible in her first few days at Golding. It was a difficult adjustment after so many years in the driver's seat, but she saw that it was the only way to go, until she made other plans. She'd improvised ghosts, but they were always substantial ghosts and she'd usually managed to steal the scene. This situation was volatile. The leading man kept out of her way, disappearing for hours on end without giving her a chance to interact with him. The whole place felt like a set for an Agatha Christie play, the lives of the characters were tense, shrouded in secrecy and they had stilted lines—the only thing that was missing was a body. Roger was rich. She studied him and made a mental inventory of the house and its corpsy furnishings. She sniffed the clothes in his closet. Five or six business suits, a rack of shirts, socks, striped ties. The whole thing smelt of man. He didn't leave much around the place except for his old paintings and they weren't as bad as they'd looked at first. A couple of them leapt off the wall—one was a female figure with a tiny crucified man nailed to her armpits. Kit wanted it.

When insight came, she was sitting on the john. The relief was instant. It was so simple, so hokey! She didn't want—had never wanted—to birth a child. Her inner child was wailing to be let out! She was here to find out how it would be to ride on her father's shoulders, to have him run a soapy wash-cloth over her ribs, tuck her up in bed, sing her a nursery rhyme. She wanted him to butter her toast and cut it into soldiers and feed them to her one at a time. She wanted him to admit he'd been wrong to back out of the deal after he'd fucked her mother that one fateful time. And it wouldn't be a one-way street. She would show him what it was like to have a daughter who loved him. Her inner child was crazy to know the real him, not the man he presented to the world. Underneath his indifference, she was sure he was the solid, stable older man who would protect and advise her, provide treats and pocket money. He was the magician who'd line up the pins after she'd knocked them down. It shouldn't have taken so long to figure this out.

If he wanted it, she'd be beautiful. She'd be enigmatic and glamorous. She'd show him that she'd grown into a beautiful woman, inside and out. She was beautiful. She'd dump the hair extensions, the tongue stud—the craziness. Dump the drugs. She didn't need them. Of course he wasn't interested in the person who'd slept under the bridge in Cardboard City. He needn't know that some Texan had brought her there from the airport. Who cared that they'd dropped a couple of tabs, and she'd had to jerk off a complete stranger in exchange for a corner of his box, while his dog looked on and licked up the cum. It was disgusting and it had nothing to do with who she really was. The real child was the one who'd wandered over Waterloo Bridge as morning was breaking. The river had looked thick enough to walk on. She'd marched to the beat of the rising sun, crossing and re-crossing the river by different bridges, experiencing the Houses of Parliament when it was dressed in a single cloud, and finding out that the hands on Big Ben actually moved. She'd absorbed it slowly into the map of England that was etched inside her body. This was home. A big arrow on the map pointed to Suffolk.

She focused on the bathroom ceiling, attracted by the sound of mice. The house dated back to 1784; this made it the oldest house she'd ever stayed in and Roger and Ilona lived in it like it was a brand new suburban townhouse. At night the mice in the thatch kept her awake; she thought they'd probably been up in the attic for three hundred years, generation after generation of the same mouse family, skittering down the same pathways.

She wound a wad of toilet paper around her fist, fending off a sudden pang of homesickness for strip malls and grow-ops, grids, multiplexes, electric power stations behind wire mesh fences, driverless trains—the familiar down-home joylessness of Whalley. Ilona reminded her of one of Henry VIII's wives, all grave and frosty, head held high, knowing she was destined for the block. If that was what Roger liked, she'd be frosty, too. Meantime she'd keep her head down and keep clipping the newspapers. They had the best murders in the world here, juicy intrigues and abductions, and there were so many, they often didn't make the front pages. She was learning about the English way of doing things while she was coming down. Forcing her hands to stay steady.

She got up, flushed and unlocked the door. Ilona rushed in as if she were ready to tear out the bathroom fittings.

"She was in the loo for an hour." Ilona catapulted into the den without knocking. Roger had his nose in the *Financial Times*, snatching a moment with the FTSE Index. The only time they ever talked to each other in private these days was in bed.

"Well, so what, you could've used the en-suite." He was crabby. He was a morning person; six a.m. was his best time on weekdays and he'd spent half his life getting up early to avoid the traffic even when he was staying at his club, which was around the corner from the office. Kit's hours were starting to take their toll on him.

"What does a person do in the loo for an hour? I thought she'd slit her wrists." Ilona hopped from one foot to the other.

He thought he heard the twins' heads clashing, and put his arm out to steady her. "Why would she do that?"

"Because!"

"Well, why didn't you bang on the door if you suspected she might be committing suicide?"

"I couldn't." And that was as much as she could say without confessing that she'd been rather hoping for deep cuts and an ocean of blood.

⁂

Catherine felt the transition from Vancouver to the island was happening without her. She was so absorbed by the new house and her plans for turning the workshop into a studio that time had lost all meaning. Every day the lists of things to tackle grew longer. The wiring was ancient, the floorboards in the workshop were rotting, a couple of windows would have to be replaced and she needed to have a sink plumbed in and some kind of heating system and insulation installed. The wooden exteriors of both buildings cried out for caulking and a coat of paint. She thought the cedar shakes on the roof of the house might hold up a few years if she could detach the moss gently, but the chimney pointing was almost non-existent. She hadn't noticed any of this in her rush to buy. This was the first time she'd ever owned a house and she hadn't prepared herself for the excitement. She'd never had a moment's fear that Ernie might turn them out of their apartment in Vancouver, but she'd never felt the desire to put her stamp on the space. It was just a place to hang out, a set of rooms; there was no pride, no real sense of belonging—now she was finally wearing her own clothes instead of someone else's cast-offs.

She decided to tackle most of the work on the house herself. The move had cost more than she'd anticipated, and, while materials and labour were cheaper down here, the exchange rate wasn't in her favour and she'd be hard pressed to find money for art materials, let alone luxuries. The non-essential repairs and alterations would have to be put off. Her first priority was to get the studio together. She knew she wouldn't make much progress with any of the large jobs without outside help.

It only took a day or two to fathom the local work ethic. Tomorrow. Tomorrow meant 'possibly next month,' or 'don't expect me unless I show up.' After a couple of attempts to hire handymen, she set about trying to unravel the unwritten rules that signaled how to get what you wanted in paradise.

At the end of her first week, the Welcome Wagon lady showed up. She was a young woman, heavily made-up, dressed like a matron. Her badge read Ida Mae Dawkin. She was armed with a cornucopia of samples and coupons for everything from sanitary napkins to bug repellent. "Call me Ida" was in no hurry to get through her spiel, and Catherine waited in vain for a pause long enough to ask a question. She finally understood that the welcome was from the island merchants, not the tradesmen. There were offers of free hair-dressing, free aromatherapy and free brake inspections, but there was no free plumbing or glazing or roofing and no guides or maps that might point out how to pin these services down. By the time Ida Mae left, Catherine had put her name down for library duty and agreed to help paint scenery for the Community Players' production of Oklahoma. She'd been 'red flagged' for school art visits and volunteered to serve on the ladies committee of the fire department, but her questions remained unanswered. It seemed that everything on the island was volunteer.

It was the same story in the post office where the mail was sorted prior to being placed in the ranks of boxes at the roadside. If business was too brisk, sorting went by the board unless someone volunteered to help. Nobody worried about bills and catalogues arriving on time. The postmaster waved vaguely when she asked for advice about good carpenters. He told her the man he used had taken off for Tacoma last month.

At the general store where she asked to have the *Vancouver Sun* delivered, the frizzy woman who served her wore a badge that read 'Have a Dandy Day.' She guffawed at the idea of bringing in a Canadian newspaper. No one had ever asked for such a thing. Catherine gave up and bought a copy of the *Post Intelligencer*. The paper felt thin and foreign. She craved the bulging Vancouver papers. She purchased two large chocolate bars—how long since she'd eaten chocolate? On the way out of the shop, a customer stopped her. "Did you get the pun?"

"What pun?"

"Why, Dandy Day of course. Her real name's Danuta Day, but Dandy's kinda handy! You're new here, right?"

Catherine turned in time to catch Dandy Day's wink.

She realized she had to move carefully. She didn't want to be seduced into community life, but it wouldn't do to be labeled an uppity foreigner, or worse, a tourist. She'd need to rely on islanders for everyday necessities. As she drove home, she was aware of the proliferation of American flags on flagpoles and mailboxes. She needed to update her ideas, take a crash course on the country she'd landed in. It didn't feel the least like coming home. She decided to make Canadian radio off limits, along with the newspapers. She'd plug her cultural leaks by tuning into the local radio stations and try out some American T.V., sitcoms and talk shows. There'd be no more trashing American icons.

She drove past the real estate office and pulled up. The realtor who sold her the house wasn't there, but a young man was chatting on a mobile phone, his feet neatly crossed on the desk. He grinned when she walked in and beckoned her to sit down while he regaled the person on the line with news of a recent boat fire. He seemed to expect her to listen in. When he switched off, she explained who she was and asked his advice about hiring a carpenter. He pulled out a Chamber of Commerce directory, the same one Ida Mae had in her cornucopia.

"What I need is advice on who's reliable. Who can I trust? Who can I trust to even show up?"

"Aw, man, that's not something I can tell you." The man grinned. "That's the fastest way to lose friends around here."

"So what am I supposed to do?"

"There's the local rag—comes out every week. Some of them advertise in that, but most people are backed up with work, so if they have to advertise you might want to stay clear of them."

She thanked him and turned tail, wishing she'd stood her ground and told him the agency owed her, considering the commission she'd brought them. But she was still too polite, too Canadian. She drove carefully, avoiding the potholes. Evidently there was no money to fix the roads in this corner of the state.

It was clear that the island was a secret society populated by two classes, old timers and outsiders. It all felt too familiar to Catherine; the university was exactly like an island and as a sessional she was forever in the wrong camp. How much energy would it take to figure out the secret handshake, the open sesame, without taking out an expensive membership?

The car engine missed a stroke as she rounded a bend and she was so badly thrown by what this might portend that she almost ran over the man who stood with his hand up in the middle of the road. She stopped—there was no choice.

"I'm not going far," she said, winding down the window.

"Me either." He hopped into the passenger seat. "Mel Mantova."

He held out his hand. "Can't get the darn truck started so I left her at the Bakewell's. I was over tidying their lawn, thought I'd get home for a bite to eat and finish off later. Your wheels have seen better days." She drew a breath, ready to defend her ailing car, but he didn't give her time. "So, if you don't mind dropping me off."

"I'm afraid I'm not familiar with the island." The words came out stiff and formal.

"That's okay, I been here fifteen years and before that we farmed outside Yakima, know it?"

"No. I'm from Canada."

"Canada? Well, now." This seemed to be a conversation stopper.

She followed his directions and deposited him by a mailbox labeled 'Meg n' Mel'. "Why don't you come in and meet the wife? She keeps her eye out for newcomers." Catherine shook her head. She'd spotted a sign, nailed to a tree—MANTOVA HAULING— GARDENING, ODD JOBS, CARPENTRY, NOTHING TOO SMALL.

"What kind of odd jobs?" she asked. He had one leg out of the car.

"Oh—you know, mostly small ones. Big ones are okay too, I guess."

"Is anything too big?"

"What?"

"Well, what about painting, dry-walling, insulating, floors…?"

"I been known to take those on."

"But you know how?"

"Affirmative."

"Do you show up on time?"

"I'd need a truck for that."

"When you have your truck, do you show up on time?"

"Now that depends." He smiled.

Everything on this island was slant. "I live on Forbes Road."

"Forbes. Yes, I know. You bought the old Deregard place—we was surprised it went so quick, being as it..."

"Needs work?"

"Well, for sure it needs something. So, when do I start?"

"How about tomorrow?"

"That could be arranged."

"I'll expect you at eight-thirty."

When she got into the house, her eyes went straight to the chair Ernie had sat in the night she moved in. The temptation to lift the phone and get him to come back was overwhelming. It was as though he was still sitting there, legs apart, feet firmly planted on the bare boards. Her glasses misted up. Much as she needed him he couldn't be part of her life, not now the boundaries had been breached.

She spent the afternoon lazing on the couch in the bay window, soaking up the full blast of the sun. She warmed up slowly, one layer thawed, then another—she was amazed by how deep the cold had penetrated. She screwed up her eyes then popped the lids. Now there was a burning red sky and diamond flecks danced round the distant sailboats. She could dump her fears, there was no more need to tread the middle ground—she was home. She sat up and lit a cigarette. She'd come within a hair's breadth of disaster, all set to spend the rest of her life in a holding pattern, on red alert for Alzheimer's, lung cancer, osteoporosis. What she needed to do now was reconnect with what she'd surrendered, and keep everything balanced. She could luxuriate in her very own house, plain old Catherine, no longer Mother, or Teacher, or Neighbour. What would she do while she was waiting for this new incarnation to take hold? Maybe she'd get a library card; maybe she'd collect firewood. Or maybe she'd do nothing, lie, as she was lying now, lie through summer and fall and concentrate on forgiving herself for all the vanished years, for losing the will to work with her own blood. Or maybe she'd go quietly—or noisily—mad.

She inhaled deeply, rolled up her pant leg and contemplated her shin. It was a good American shin even if it wasn't shaved to the bone like a plucked California chicken; the good American hairs had been passed down over a couple of centuries. She had a history and she still had some Mid-west vowels.

She'd never denied being American, but she'd lost track of it. Occasionally she'd considered trading in her nationality but it wasn't important enough to make the effort. Kit bugged her about it. It must have been hard on her, growing up with a parent who claimed no allegiance to the country she called home but it was too bad. Catherine loathed nationalism, particularly the American sort. What part of yourself could you possibly pledge to such an abstract, conveniently political concept as country? She thought Kit's loyalty to Canada excessive, but she never called her on it. It was just as well she hadn't stayed on in England after the divorce, Kit would have grown up English and they'd have become completely alienated from each other.

She lay still, sifting her thoughts until the sun went down, and then, on impulse, she called her brother and sister in Illinois. She got them up and they tried to conceal their sleepy surprise at hearing from her. She wondered briefly if they shared a bed.

As usual Clayton did the talking and April listened on the extension. "How about that, she's back on home turf, Ape, didn't I tell you she'd come back one day? We knew you wouldn't last up there in Can Ada, Cat," (he always called it Can Ada, and this always pushed the same button). "Give it a few more weeks, you'll be right back on the Crescent, banging on the old front door, wanting in. Your room's still here, Ape here got rid of the rug after the dog threw up, didn't you Ape? You know you'll be welcome as an Interflora bouquet."

She sighed. As far as they were concerned, she was still young Cat, the doodler who'd used up valuable family resources for a fancy art school education. She was still little Catkin, full of half-baked ideas and no job worth mentioning. They excused her and loved her in their way, but she could still smell their self-righteousness. She pictured their pleasant, orderly life together, both unmarried, Clayton a retired accountant and April (who was born in December) a retired Home Ec teacher who'd taught for forty years at the Junior High they all attended a block from the family home.

She felt bad about the obvious pleasure they took in the call—she'd thought she might feel more kindly disposed to them. All her life she'd alternated between wishing she belonged to a big, like-minded family and being grateful she was the black sheep. They were loving and concerned but they felt more like spinster aunts than brother and sister. Their Middle America suffocated her—fussy, tentative, proscribed, endlessly and always Right. Like them it had its own distinctive smell. The memory made her nose twitch. This is what she'd escaped when she'd raced off to London so long ago.

She put on a tape of Billie Holiday and let the blues blow the smell away.

She was up at six the next morning putting together the ingredients for a batch of croissants. Eight-thirty came and went. At ten she flicked through the phone book, searching for Mel Mantova's number. At twelve she still hadn't picked up the phone. She went out back and began to pry up the floorboards in the shed, taking out her frustration on the rotten wood. The ground below the boards was wet and spongy. She was alarmed—she'd been expecting to see rock. She stepped over the hole and slammed the door on the new discovery.

Two mornings later, Mel showed up at dawn. She heard the truck pulling in, jumped out of bed and opened the kitchen door wide, bowing ironically. He came in and sat down, carefully removing his baseball cap but leaving his muddy boots on. He was wearing a canvas apron filled with tools so she knew he was here to work. She dumped a plate and mug in front of him and presented him with a soggy croissant. As a concession, she added a knife and a cut glass dish of jam—he would have to earn the butter. He vacuumed up the croissant and treated a second offering the same way, ignoring the jam. He wiped his lips on the back of his hand, brushing aside the paper towel she'd supplied. So far they hadn't exchanged more than a good morning. She saw that he was a good-looking man, loose-limbed, with high cheekbones and good teeth.

"I think we should start on the studio," she said, leading him out to the shed.

He crouched over the hole, peering down through the boards, tugging on his chin. When he got up, he went outside and paced the perimeter of the structure, kicking the foundations. Catherine followed, holding her breath.

"Gonna need to raise her," he said.

"Why?"

"Looks like we have a spring under here. How's your water?"

"You mean the tap water?"

"What's the pressure? Didn't you have your well tested?"

She bit her lip.

"Well that's none too smart. Water has a mind of its own. Often as not it runs dry in these parts, we either got too much of it, or a drought. Then there's the sulphur. Rotten eggs. The house smells fresh so you're probably okay there. Then there's the coliform count—did you have them take a sample before you laid down your deposit?"

She had no idea what a coliform was or how you counted it.

"Well water might look clean, but it's alive. Bugs can kill you if you don't watch out. Parasites. Make a rat's nest of your liver. You need to get your water tested. Shoulda been done before you bought." He grinned at her, his eyes dancing. "What about your septic field?"

"Fine." The word was strangled.

"When was the tank cleaned out?"

"They said it met regulations as far as where it's located." At least she knew that much.

"Probably topped up. I know the folks use' to live here, full of it. You want to get it emptied."

"How much would that cost?"

"Oh, a hundred or two, depends. Did you take out earthquake insurance?"

"No!"

"Just as well. Costs an arm and a leg if you can get it. You're sitting plum on the San Andreas fault, though. Line goes clear through the island. When the big one comes, we're all matchsticks. You ever see the top of Mount Saint Helens?"

She hadn't.

"Best you don't go up there. Nothing left alive except frogspawn and that wasn't even an earthquake. Mountain blew her brains out. Force of two hundred atom bombs."

A volcanic crater opened up before Catherine's eyes, swallowing her life's savings. "Isn't there any good news?" she whispered.

"Sure. Looks like you struck lucky with your water supply if you've got a spring here. Trouble is damp's got to your foundations. See here—rotten as a six-week windfall." He kicked a joist before she could stop him.

"Will the building stay up?" She was ready to weep, but he wasn't done with her yet.

"Couldn't say. Should be looked at right away. And now you're going to hire me without a single reference or recommendation. I could be anyone. You tourists are all the same."

"This is my home!" She couldn't control the childish whine in her voice.

"They all say that. They come here swearing they'll settle, but they're just floaters—once the rains set in, they sink. They walk off that ferry from Seattle and points south, flashing their chequebooks and they pay, pay, pay and don't ask no questions. And they don't give one thing back to the place. We bleed them dry, of course. And after that no one wants to work for a regular wage. I could walk in here, rip you off for thousands, walk out without finishing the job and you'd have no comeback. You'd just up and leave like the rest of them, rent the place out in the summer for a small fortune—if it's still standing, try to get a local to take it in winter at cut rate, then turn him out at the start of summer. You'd be lucky to sell it."

"I could sue you if you walked out."

"You know what that'd set you back?"

"It's every man for himself here, isn't it?"

"You mean it's not like that where you come from?"

"No, people are honest in Vancouver." She took in his incredulous expression. The panic had passed and she was furious. How had he got her to the point where she was ready to sue him before he'd lifted a finger? "So, what do you suggest I do? Where do I start? Do I spend months waiting to interview workers who don't show up and don't want the job anyway? Men like you who'll take me for everything I have. And by the way, I'm not a tourist. I'm a volunteer fireman. Fireperson. And I volunteered for other things, too."

"Yes, I know."

"I suppose everyone knows."

"That's likely."

The longer he stood in her yard, the clearer it became that she was completely at his mercy and he was closing in for the kill.

He shifted his weight. "Well, I'll tell you one thing, there ain't no one round here'll give you an estimate. Nothing personal, but we don't do estimates. And you won't find no one to tell you not to hire so-and-so, even if he's useless as a tit on a billy goat—they'll be wanting the guy to buy a book of raffle tickets next week, gotta look after your neighbour in these parts, then you get good treatment returned."

"So, you think I should do the work myself?"

"You're a girl."

"In your humble opinion where should a girl start?"

"In my humble opinion? Well, for starters you could brew up some fresh coffee. And I don't want no more of them fancy pastries. They were stale anyways. You're gonna have to hire someone to help you if you want to be done before the earthquake. I'll give you a break if you like, seeing as you gave me a lift. I'll be here tomorrow. I'll be early again."

After he left, she rinsed his cup and plate, letting the water run full force, deliberately wasteful, wondering how she'd come to pour her savings into a swamp, hire a torturer and land herself in a mess she'd never be able to walk away from. In all likelihood, the big earthquake would catapult her and her house down the cliff-face before she even found out what she was doing here. Maybe that wouldn't be such a bad thing. Ernie Last would have warned her off. She kept catching herself in the act of calling upstairs.

The gurgle of the spring filled the kitchen. Why hadn't she heard it before? She sat at the table listening, full of woe—this was a sound she'd have to get used to. Then she realized she'd left the tap on. "Faucet," she said aloud, and laughed. "Faucet, faucet." She was in

America now.

Outside the kitchen window, an uplifted band of cloud gave the sun a quizzical look. The cloud stayed put after the dark red disk slipped behind the horizon. It soothed her. How often had she heard Kit telling her to put her mind in neutral? Poor Kit, where was she? She wondered why she always thought of her as 'poor' Kit. Clever Kit, prescient Kit, talented Kit—thank-God-you're-so-far-away, Kit!

A rich rumble spiraled up from her guts. The sun had left a trail of orange flecks on the water.

Mel showed up earlier than promised for his first day of work. He set to right away. "We'll soon get you sorted."

Catherine stayed at his elbow and waited for orders. 'Hold this' 'carry that' 'pass the saw' 'keep the ladder steady.' She was his factotum. He worked rhythmically and she fell into line without bothering to question his assumption that this was the agreement.

All morning she attended him, hosed coffee into the tin mug he'd brought, tuned the radio to catch his favourite elevator music, brought out a box of Kleenex when the dust got up his nose. She saw that he was a deft worker, neat and quick, even graceful, with perfect hand-eye coordination. She also saw that he was turning the tables on her. He was treating her like a green apprentice, the way she'd treated Ernie when he used to hang around her studio. She fumbled a package of nails and watched them scatter in the mud. How could she convince him her hand was normally steady? He snorted as she went down on hands and knees in the mud; the snort was like a bee sting. She was determined to please; the slightest hint of a compliment was snatched up before he could take it back. By the middle of the afternoon, she was exhausted and chastened. She couldn't wait for him to call it quits.

Two days after he started, he had the studio jacked up and she helped him dig a drainage ditch round the perimeter. They were beginning to get used to each other's working methods, and he occasionally threw out a grudging word of respect. "Not a thing you can do about the water problem except stay out of its way," he declared. "We could move the whole structure over to the other side of the lot, but that puts her hard up against your septic field, so I guess you're gonna have to live with her the way she is. I wouldn't recommend it for everyone. We'll build you some steps up to the door and that'll do you as long as you're not gonna start falling down. Steps get slippy in winter, even with treads. And ground water plays havoc with your joints. You have pains in your knees?"

She shook her head. "You get me all turned around, you know that?" It occurred to her that she was flirting.

"That's right," he grinned, "turned around's the best way to be. Walk forward, face back, that way you got all your ducks lined up and no one's gonna shoot 'em out from under you."

CHAPTER ELEVEN

ﻋﻠﻰ

Ernie Last stayed out of the house as much as possible. He became a fixture at the library on Hastings Street, not so much reading as flicking through the newspapers and watching the Chinese men vie for first dibs at their papers, then wait patiently as the victor pored over the unintelligible script sometimes making notes of what were obviously advertisements. Could it be that landlords were advertising for Chinese tenants? One day he wrote out an advertisement for the downstairs apartment. He specified that he wanted an older female, preferably a painter. He didn't call it in. When he was home he sat upstairs, alert for the sound of the key in the front door, the thrum of her heels on the wood floors. He stood in the empty cave of Catherine's apartment trying to imagine her in front of her fridge. He didn't need to rent the place, he had no use for the rent money, his only luxuries were an occasional trip to the movies and the hand-stitched white shirts that were put out for the laundry each week in batches of seven. He prided himself on being a regular man and he asked himself over and over how he could have cast regularity to the winds and let his feelings for Catherine erupt like some teen-aged premature ejaculator.

Unread flyers and free coupons littered the floor of his kitchen, the radio was never switched on; glimpsed through the open door, the T.V. was a dead eye. The outside world had been obliterated as if by some natural disaster. Barely animate, Ernie Last had come to rest between the four walls of his kitchen in the company of the red arborite table, the four folding chairs and the oversized Welsh Dresser displaying a set of his mother's Carnival Glass plates.

⁂

Catherine crouched on her haunches on the stoop and stubbed her cigarette out. She watched Mel measure and saw the wood for the studio steps. There was no checking or re-checking with the rule or the spirit level, the first measure was always miraculously accurate. Within half a day the skeleton of a sturdy stairway was in place. "You're a miracle worker, Mel." He lifted his cap with his thumb and scratched his scalp.

"And you're useless. You been sitting there like a stone frog for two hours, know that?"

"I'm mesmerized."

"That's girl talk. You're trying to tell me you're not a girl? You're the biggest girl I ever come across."

"Is that supposed to be a compliment?"

"Sure is, if you buy it."

"I'm just trying to soak up what you're doing. I'm a fast study. I used to sculpt, I know a few things about wood."

He came over and sat at her feet on the lower step. "I knew the first time I clapped eyes on you that you was a girl," he remarked, emptying tobacco into the fold of a cigarette paper with the same speed and precision as he nailed a plank in place. "You hide yourself behind all that other crap."

"What crap?"

"Well, look at you. And sculptressing—what's that about? You want to see sculpture, you go down to the beach and pick up a chunk of driftwood. If you was to curl your hair nice, put a bit of red on your lips, pretty necklace, maybe take off those glasses and boots."

"What then?" She was incredulous.

"Then?"

"I'm sorry, no, no, no. I don't have to listen to any more of this!"

He stubbed out his cigarette and put it carefully in his pocket. "It's lucky for you, you ain't pretty. For sure I'd get nothing done around here if you was."

"What the hell do you mean by that?"

"Don't take a rocket scientist to know a pretty woman when he sees one." He watched her, knowingly. "Take Ida Mae Rivers who was here the other day."

"How do you know she was here?"

"She said you was a hard sell."

"Oh, she did? Well, I'll tell you something. If you think she's pretty, I think you're blind!"

"She don't know her ass from a rolling pin."

"I'll make tea." Catherine clumped into the kitchen. He was hateful. As she stood at the counter, she eyed the depths of the Brown Betty, as ugly and serviceable a teapot as you could find. There was absolutely nothing wrong with that teapot. Like Mel Mantova it was thoroughly old-fashioned. How old was he anyway? It was hard to judge with black men. His hair was going grey. He was certainly old enough to have heard of feminism. She gave the tea more time than it needed to brew before stepping out into the yard and banging the tray down in front of him. "I'm not falling for your bullshit, Mel. You're pathetic. Embarrassing. If you think you're buttering me up so you can get away with sticking the 'little old white lady' with a huge bill when you're through here, it won't wash. I'm not stupid, and I don't buy it, so lay off the personal crap and get on with the job, okay? Let's keep things professional."

She'd heaped a plate with his favourite fig cookies. He shoved them aside, sniffed and moved his cap round so the peak came down over his eyes, then he scooped up his tools and headed for the truck without a word. In the time it took for a plane to pass overhead, she'd lost her handyman.

⚶

Ernie traced the windows that were left on the white walls where there had once been paintings. She hadn't left any of her artwork behind—he'd never offered to buy as much as a sketch. She could have used the money and he'd failed to help her; it would have been such an obvious gesture.

He left the house tentatively and went in search of something to replace the pictures. He tracked down a coffee-table anthology of twentieth century German artists, bought the book and tried to blow up the two Käthe Kollwitz prints on a photocopier in a nearby grocery store. The man at the till, who had been an aspiring artist in Vietnam, told him he'd get better results if he scanned them into a computer. On his way back to the car, Ernie noticed a store with a small selection of computers in the window. He chose one randomly, added a scanner and paid cash.

He sat in the car trying to catch his breath. An alley sloped up to his right. He noticed a diminishing line of hydro poles supporting a forest of sagging wires linking fat gunmetal converters. He was sure he could hear the hum of electricity. He'd never thought how menacing they were, how alive. Why had no one attempted to hide them underground? A snag of heart-shaped balloons strained to release themselves from one of the wires overhead. They glinted silver against the sullen sky. It was the sort of thing Catherine would remark on. She'd come back soon and he'd be ready for her, this was her signal.

⚶

In clover. The phrase kept repeating itself. She could sit in the window and chew like a cow, save the cud and regurgitate it whenever she was ready. She had a roof over her head, food in the cupboard, money in the bank to buy more; there was no place she had to be, no work that had to be done. For the first time in her life no one expected anything of her and she had no one else to think about. Above all, she had time. No one knew her phone number except her brother and sister and Mel—she wasn't listed. Sometime, maybe soon, she'd give the number to Ernie and her best friend, Mary, but she'd warn them not to call.

She lolled back with a pile of art books at her fingertips. A lifetime's collection, they'd been useful for studying and teaching, but what use were they now? She would sort them slowly and plan which artists she wanted to keep as friends. She slid a volume of bad reproductions of Emily Carr's paintings out of the pile. Growth. No, she didn't want growth—she needed consolidation. Stasis. Had Carr ever reached this point? The sheer Van Gogh-like energy darting through her paintings seemed to say she'd never stopped being rapacious. Catherine liked trees, but not forests. The rain forest in the North-West shrank her—skeletons of trees festooned with ghostly grey lichen like dead-men's hair, new saplings fused to stumps, the living gorging on the dead. Carr had been born to it. Why would an alien choose it as a safe landing place? Her fingers vibrated as she turned the pages.

On this island, unlike the mainland, the bush was manageable, contained on all sides. It would be hard to get lost here. Vancouver was a glass and concrete blip on the rim of a black infinity of trees. With a few exceptions the people she knew managed to live without venturing into them, unless they were testing their stamina. Kit laughed at her—she said she should be living in the heart of Manhattan. She was probably right. Bricks and mortar were good; wood was too easily mutated. But if you were afraid, at least you were alive. Who was it told her there were huge forests under the sea, connecting up, endless connections? It was too much to take in. As long as she stayed put, she could keep her fear under wraps. She pushed Emily Carr aside; she would never try to colonize the bush with her brushes.

She opened a favourite book of Japanese woodblock prints but they were too precious, she wasn't through with Carr yet. She ran her eye over a reproduction of flaring evergreens with a sky that would be worthy of Turner if it weren't so Canadian. The best paintings were angry, but they would be better if the anger weren't so contained. She fought back to the evening of her Last Farewell, when she'd almost lost control; she thought of how she'd contained her anger with Mel. Was there a lesson to be learned? If Emily had let it boil over, if she'd sacrificed sanity and restraint, would she have been a truly great painter? Or what if she'd plumped for calm—pure godliness? It seemed they'd both lost courage when it came to following the forest into the sea. The worst paintings had been conserved along with the best. The text told how Emily's executor had sorted through her work after she died, but her friend Willie Newcombe had recovered the discards. He'd done her no favour. It was like having your dirty underwear displayed. She'd just thrown out Kit's childhood. Who would blame Kit if she tossed her mother's work after she died. It would all go, the good, the bad, and the indifferent, and there'd be no one to reclaim it.

Her head lolled back. She imagined driftwood, tree stumps ten feet across thrown up on the beach like sticks for a dog. She heard waves crash. The sound might be real or it might be the sound of her heart going through one of its occasional arrhythmic dances. Mel was right, this was the real sculpture, hundreds of years of growth cut down, forever changing, reshaping. There were powerful forces at work—nothing was final. How can you make art in a landscape like this? Emily had almost succeeded. The picture on the back cover showed a bulky intense woman, her hair in a snood, pushing a buggy with a monkey on her shoulder. She had dignity and distance. Catherine had distanced herself from people and their rudeness, rudeness like Mel's. It was just as well he wasn't coming back. She didn't need him. Emily would never have put up with a man who called her 'girl'. He was out of her life now and that was where he'd stay.

The book slid off her lap and she lay back, counting the flaws in her unfamiliar ceiling. She'd been reduced to a coy flirt. She'd been flattered. She found him attractive. It was pathetic, and at the same time it was amazing. She needed time to get used to this growing euphoria. It was so much easier to be miserable when you were alone than it was to be happy. She closed her eyes, thinking this must be an enchanted isle—she was living a dream, a midsummer night's dream and maybe she'd wake up wearing an ass's head.

Two of Ernie's sisters lived in Vancouver. Dana called him regularly to update him on news of her friends and neighbours, people he'd never met who were essential props in her life as a single woman. His younger sister Veronica had a large family and no time to socialize. Ernie didn't recognize her voice when she called: "He's behaving like a moron, honest to God, Ernie, you know how it is? He's eighteen—worse than his dad—driving the other four out of the house. They're all gonna end up on the street or into drugs or something worse if he stays. Dana says your downstairs is empty after all these years. We don't have money for rent, but I was wondering if you'd do us a small favour? Well, he is your nephew. What do you say?"

"Let me get back to you."

Ernie didn't need to think. Catherine would be back in time for blackberry season. They'd make jam the way they always did. He had a cupboard full of jam dating back over twenty years. It wasn't surprising she hadn't phoned, she never phoned, she always shouted up the back stairs. Some mornings he dreamed her shout and jumped out of bed.

The new prints did nothing to bring her back. He saw that the walls needed a coat of paint, there were telltale holes and tape marks where pictures once hung, scuff marks from furniture, a cigarette burn in the linoleum. She'd turn right around and leave if she saw it like this.

He studied wallpapers, tested brushes, took home carpet sample books and scoured magazines for tips about decorating. He kept running into a woman called Martha Stewart. He needed Catherine's advice, but he called Dana, and, much to his relief, she urged him to steer clear of her. In the end he plumped for white; white for the living room, the bedroom, the basement rooms and the staircase. Catherine couldn't disapprove of white, but still it wasn't easy, there were so many shades of white. The kitchen needed tiles. Coloured tiles. He wracked his brains, trying to think of her favourite colour—she often wore black and grey. He decided on a deep, inky blue, for the tiles, blue and white for the floor, yellow stripes for the wallpaper. He would leave the kitchen till the end.

He wanted to hurry, in case she caught him with the work half finished, but hurry went against his nature. He cleaned, stripped, sanded and filled every inch of plaster and wood. He discovered solid oak doors and banisters and worked on them with the utmost care, thinking of the look on Catherine's face when she saw these miracles. Wood was almost as sweet as leather under his fingertips and he toiled into the night, unwilling to let go and sleep.

Before the undercoat was on the walls he felt an urge to decorate them, nothing large or garish—a small, illuminated 'C' here, a beautifully executed Catherine there, the letters copied from old German script and from a pristine reproduction of the Book of Kells he found in the children's library. He joined the initials and names with swags of leaves and flowers. When they were finished, he buried them under two coats of paint.

In the hallway, he uncovered the original plaster, stamped with the date 1904, and this presented an even greater challenge. Catherine's name floated along the length of the walls. He got bolder, no longer copying, designing his own script, emblazoning the name from the top to the bottom of the stairs, letting it leak onto the ceiling, the letters growing more and more elaborate, more and more extraordinary as he gained confidence. Floors begged for attention, he levered up the boards and branded Catherine into the undersides, using a wood-burning technique he found in another library book. He didn't need sleep.

He laid new carpet on the stairs, lowering it gingerly over a long line of Catherines. The stained glass windows round the front door were dirty and some of the panes were cracked. He would replace them, but not until he'd learned the skills it took to do the job properly. He wanted to make a design of tulips—she'd once said tulips were her favourite flower.

The fixtures in the bathroom and the kitchen were old-fashioned. Plumbing was demanding and he couldn't find what he needed in books, so he enrolled in a class. He now had the perfect excuse for not having a tenant. The rooms were in a state of upheaval, no one could live there—no one that is, except the person for whom they were intended. He didn't bother to call Veronica and when she showed up on his doorstep he blinked, barely recognizing her. "Go away." He wasn't trying to command, or rebuke, simply to recommend; he could see she didn't understand. He tried to look chastened and when he failed, he simply closed the door, leaving her outside.

⚘

Catherine got off the couch. She was restless. She needed something to occupy her hands, it was too bad she'd been so efficient about unpacking. The night had clouded over, there were no stars and no moon, just a black abyss outside the window and she had no drapes to block it out. There were some cans of emulsion on the window sill that she'd bought for the studio. She levered one open with a pair of scissors and poured a dollop of paint in a tray. The fresh tang stung the roots of her hair. Grabbing a roller she began to paint a wall without pausing to move the furniture or roll up the newly laid rugs. She worked tidily without splattering and the rhythm relaxed her. The wall was dusty and the cobwebs added texture to the finish. She hadn't wanted a white room, white walls gave nothing back, but undercoat was all she had, so undercoat it had to be.

With one wall finished, she decided to tackle all the rest and white out the traces of the house's past. She would get the job done in two days—she was well enough rested, stasis could wait, and if she worked straight through, Mel would see she had spine. But Mel was gone and he wasn't coming back.

As she worked, she realized she could get by without the luxury of a studio. The kitchen would serve well enough, even though it had a western exposure. Westerly light was fine. Bronze. It gave a feeling of decline that might provide an interesting counter to this unexpected blast of energy she was feeling. Late light. She'd make new, latter day art in late light. She'd treat it as she was treating the decorating, begin at the end and work forward. Mel wouldn't understand that kind of logic. She didn't need to prepare fancy meals for herself in the kitchen. She'd work on the table and eat whatever food came to hand. No restrictions, no judgment, nothing and nobody to come between her and her goal. She was on a quest for the equivalent of Georgia O'Keeffe's turquoise blue. She'd do better—she'd surpass it. She was really and truly, finally, in clover.

His tools were still good. Roger laid them out carefully. The colours needed replenishing and there were probably some new gizmos on the market, but his collection wasn't too unprofessional. He arranged them and rearranged them on the trestle Ilona had thoughtfully provided, then he assembled his easel, wondering if wood had been replaced by something more high tech. As recently as eighteen months ago he'd been treading water, his peak experience the decision to buy a time share in Spain for his retirement, his chief delight the chance of a long soak in the bath on Sunday, followed by a read of the weekend papers. It dawned on him that his marriage hadn't prevented him from growing into the type of man he used to hate; if Kit hadn't shaken him up, he wouldn't have noticed.

He was beginning to formulate ideas. He longed to share them with someone the way he used to. Were they outlandish, or simply out of date, workable or not? How could he begin to put them into action?

Desire lodged under his ribs. He hadn't felt anything like it since his student days. It twanged. It demanded his total attention. He didn't even desire Ilona in this way. He felt such gentleness for her that he always apologized before entering her. He buried his briefcase and mobile phone at the back of the airing cupboard.

But still he didn't make a move.

Kit and Ilona weren't adjusting to each other as he'd hoped but there was still a small window of time before the babies were born. He realized with a shock that, whatever he thought of her, he could easily come to rely on Kit. She was his link to the past, the past he'd let go of without a pang, the past that Ilona was encouraging him to retrieve. It hadn't been at all that unpleasant to come face to face with a fully formed adult daughter, flesh of his flesh but completely other. She was still a puzzle, unresolved like most of the brash North Americans he'd met, a bit raw, no centre, no sense of place or belonging, no apparent birthright. But she was attractive—that was a bit of a shocker. He hadn't seen it at first, with her baggy clothes and strange hair, but once she'd turned herself over to the village barber, she'd transformed, if not into a swan, at least into a mallard. She reminded him of his brother Sam when he was young, the same long narrow feet and hands. There was something boyish about her; she didn't shave her legs and she even had the beginnings of a fine, downy moustache. The laugh was on him, because if she hadn't been his daughter, he might have fancied her!

He was sure Ilona would come around, after all, Kit would be more than useful to them after the babies were born. Everything would be righted in the fullness of time and his wife had to be the one priority. She was spending more and more time in bed, pleading tiredness, so he guessed her time was close; once he'd found her curled up in the closet with her arms round a cardboard box, like a cat getting ready to have her kittens.

CHAPTER TWELVE

و

§ St. Agathe, May 21st, 1911

Frances Hodgkins has just left after a jolly hour in the garden. I do so enjoy her company. Over the years, we have talked at length of our respective histories, and I'm afraid we have gossiped mercilessly about all the artists and expatriates who take up residence in St. Agathe. She is not one to suffer fools gladly, but in spite of this I consider her my closest friend.

From the moment Miss Carr arrived in town, demanding to be met in person, claiming that some weakness made walking a problem and that she disliked cabs, Frances took against her. She was occupied with pupils all morning, so she wasn't free to go with the driver to the station, but at the last minute her private pupil took a fainting spell, so she described to me how she clambered up into the seat next to Raoul and enjoyed the leisurely trot inland, her nostrils straining to hold onto the receding smell of the sea. Today is hung over, but yesterday was a perfect day, one of those days the expatriate colony claims is unique to Brittany. A moderately brisk wind sent the clouds into a flurry and the fields, yellowish green with sprouting crops, are smothered in a brilliant scarlet topping of poppies. (It seems to me they are earlier every year.) She told me how she tried to describe these poppy fields to her mother in her regular letters to New Zealand, but the best she could do was to send home a couple of small water-colours, only to receive the response: 'What's all that blood doing in the fields, did someone slaughter a herd?' Her mother maintains a sweetly naïve attitude towards art which aspires to anything other than a cross-stitch sampler. Frances has always maintained that Mrs. Hodgkins is neither sweet nor naïve. She never ceases her efforts to convince her mother that she is not dribbling her life away, that she is not merely creating useless renditions of a nature. Nature, the old lady insists, is a reflection of God's inner eye and cannot be imitated. Fanny doesn't expect praise. She says praise is more than one has a right to expect from any trueborn New Zealander—even from her father, who immigrated as a young man from England where they portion out their feelings a little more generously. Her father would have been proud of her had he lived. It was his influence that made her devote herself to art.

Frances seems happy enough in Brittany: it is picturesque by any standard, and, unlike me, she hates large cities like Paris, though if she were free to choose, I think she'd prefer something with a bit more bite than St. Agathe. She tells me there are parts of the South of France and Morocco where the light and the landscape are so fierce they make it impossible to put one's brushes down. In Aix, she would rise at dawn and keep painting until dark. Here she feels more sluggish, and the burden of teaching gives her all the excuse she needs for not working. This place lulls one to sleep with its soft, feminine curves, its quaintly dressed peasants who might have stepped out of a Breughel, and its pretty harbour bobbing with fishing boats, their brown sails always so inviting. Why brown, I always ask? Fanny's feelings for her pupils ricochet between gratitude, even love, and bitter resentment. These people give her the freedom she needs to paint while robbing her of the energy that painting requires. Without them, she would be consigned to the role of governess, or wife to a small town official back home in New Zealand.

She has been living in Europe for ten years, a good part of that time in France. She likes languages and has a good ear, but though she is fluent in French, I think her accent betrays her origins; she finds it impossible to eradicate those flat a's. To most ears, her English is perfect, barely distinguishable from the King's English, though when she is out of sorts, her accent slips and one can detect a slight bleat. Perhaps it is a result of living so close to sheep. Her father was a British lawyer, and she was given elocution lessons from age five. She made a point of telling me that she was instructed to fall asleep reciting 'how now, brown cow,' rather than counting sheep like the rest of us.

She likes to chat with the villagers in St. Agathe to keep up her French vocabulary. They are hardworking people, and she complains that she must be content to talk to the old ones or the children, or someone like Raoul who would talk to a scratching post if there were no human in sight. Frances told me that on the afternoon they went to meet Emily Carr, Raoul was expounding on the fate of one of the railway workers who'd been found guilty of embezzling company funds. He was very excited about it since crime is rare here, and to actually have acquaintance with a criminal apparently gave him some kind of a leg up. The horses took advantage of the temporary distraction, and slowed to an amble, flicking their ears to rid themselves of flies. A dragonfly zizzed in front of Fanny's nose, hovering, as if attached by some invisible thread, then swooping away towards a ditch covered with bright green algae. As she described it to me, the whole countryside buzzed and drowsed in my head. She described the picnic lunch she had intended to prepare for herself when she got back to the hotel, cold mutton, ratatouille, a crusty baguette, maybe even a glass of Rouge since she had no pupils that afternoon, and no inclination to paint. Raoul's chatter had formed a pleasant counterpoint to the perfect day, and it seemed singularly unimportant that they would arrive at the station after the train left.

Fanny described to me in detail the oversized person who stood, surrounded by paraphernalia, traveling rugs, an easel and mountains of unrolled canvases on the platform. (I had to pretend I had not seen her.) It was a small deception. At the foot of the pile were two wicker cages, one containing an ugly grey bird, with its head tucked under one wing allowing a malevolent yellow eye to stare at the newcomers; the other, green as the algae in the ditch, was screaming and flapping its wings. Raoul immediately identified them as corbeaux, but Fanny doubted it, she'd never heard of green crows. She disliked the idea of caged birds—in truth she was rather afraid of birds (her grandmother believed they were bad luck, and refused to have even a picture of a bird in the house). Frances was sure these specimens would have been more comfortable had their cages been standing in the shade. I agreed, though it was none of my business. She kept returning to the size of the new arrival. She was glad that she hadn't insisted that she stay at the Hotel Bon Ami; their bedsprings have been known to collapse if one merely looks at them.

Fanny held out her hand politely as Raoul grabbed the two cages. Miss Carr snarled at the hand and pounced on Raoul, hissing, "Put them down!"

"Oh, permettez-moi de vous aider, Madame."

"I don't speak French." She snatched her precious squawkers. A green feather landed on the stone slab, and lay at Fanny's feet like a small offering.

Fanny said a shadow passed over the sun at that very moment; she asked me if it might be an omen. I told her I am not given to fancy. Miss Carr stood sentinel over the cages as Fanny helped Raoul to load the crates and boxes into the trap all the while thinking that she had taken this woman under her charge for six weeks and it could turn into a most horrible ordeal. She got a glimpse of a couple of oils as they hefted them. They looked unfinished, but she thought they weren't bad. She doubted they were executed by the owner of that square, furious face, but I assured her they probably were.

There was very little room left in the trap once they had all her belongings on board and Miss Carr insisted on sitting at the back, facing outwards, announcing that her legs wouldn't bend. Raoul and Frances heaved her up. They are not large people and she was stiff as the dead, and weighed as much as a heifer. I missed the spectacle as I had to stay concealed by the railway line. From where I stood, I did manage to see the trap as it passed. Miss Carr was sitting like a wooden doll, her legs poking out in front of her. Her heavy coat fell away to reveal wrinkled wool stockings and sturdy boots and (I could hardly believe my ears), she was singing.

Ilona shone a beam of light on her great-great aunt's letters and bills, always alert for the sound of feet on the stairs—she wouldn't be caught out again. She'd filed them differently this time, there were so many possible orderings. It was stuffy inside the cupboard. Once again she did her best to decipher the physicians' medical notes, extracting them from the job lot Roger had bought from the old hospital. The cramped writing strained her eyes, the medical terms still meant nothing. She pressed the cool cover of the diary to her forehead. She was the keeper of Winnie's excellent grammar and precise script, the letters leaning to the left. One or two t's were crossed carelessly on each page, missing the mark and floating unanchored, as if she'd wanted to say 'be blowed with all this!' Ilona imagined her dipping her pen in the inkpot and clamping the end of her tongue between her teeth as she wrote. This world of St. Agathe had become so familiar that she didn't have to second guess, or wait for events to unfold like a story. The things Winnie talked about weren't put on the page for effect, they were written down as they happened, because they happened, on the day they happened and for no other reason. Her mother was right, they weren't for anyone else's eyes. But it was too late now. Winnie was dead and her secret was in jeopardy. Miss Carr would understand the significance of this better than anyone, after all she wrote books about her life. Ilona wondered if she'd ever divulged any deep secrets in the books. She vowed not to let the diary out of her possession. It was safer here than it had been in the old sewing machine. She wouldn't let go of a single pressed flower.

⚜

It is a warm spring day. Emily stands by the side of the road with her baggage while the dark woman, who claims to be Miss Frances Hodgkins, converses with the driver of the trap who has just brought her luggage up from the station platform. She's forgotten how pleasant the landscape is, and not the least bit forbidding. She'll get lots of good work out of it, and that's why she's here. They are in no hurry to assist her in getting aboard, she has no idea what they're saying and she has not been properly introduced.

She recalls Alice's index finger, remonstrating with her for not trying to communicate with the people in France. Her sister has recently set sail, after their year together in Paris; Emily sighs as she thinks of her goodness. She didn't always manage to stay on her feet in Paris, landing in hospital once; and it hadn't been easy to ward off fears that she'd be shipped back to the dreaded sanatorium in England. She'd spared Alice the horrors she'd endured there, though there were times when she'd wanted nothing more than to spill the beans. When she spoke French, Alice got all her tenses right, which was only to be expected since she was the brain of the family. A sister who speaks French is more than useful in France when one's throat seizes up at the mere idea of a foreign word. "It's just as well you were born with an eye," Alice has remarked more than once. "If you had to rely on your ear you'd be a gonner."

Emily wonders if her grey matter is suspect too, though Alice is too good a pal to point it out. Today, when she wants to concentrate on getting to her destination, her thoughts slip around as if they were buttered. Animals understand her, her family and a few close friends put up with her, but she knows no one can anticipate her. She wonders what this woman will make of her? Her lack of what she has come to call 'charm' only bothers her on days like this, when there is someone to impress. She wishes she could get by without noticing the effect she has on others. At the moment it isn't a problem because she's being ignored.

She eyes the red cart. It looks primitive. Alice would not approve. Alice is a marvelous helper—she even sat in on the classes at the Academy Colarossi, until the model objected to being asked to cover up, and she was barred, leaving Emily at the mercy of the instructor who actually threatened her in torrents of French, waving the leg of a broken easel. (Why did they think that if they shout louder a person will understand?) It wasn't her fault that she couldn't draw from life à la française. She was not used to drawing from life in any language, particularly when the life was unclothed. In the art schools she attended in London and San Francisco, they drew from statuary—marble feet and torsos and occasionally live models who were so well wrapped up it was difficult to detect that their bodies had bones. She thinks of Mr. Geoffrey Church with regret. It was he who recommended the Colarossi. He encouraged her to go in search of something a little different; he thought it wouldn't hurt her work if she were to be in a group that consisted of male as well as female pupils. Mr. Geoffrey Church pointed out that one should not discount the influence of one's peers, whatever their sex. In the event, she had no contact with her fellow students, except for one young man, an American who agreed to translate for her on condition she brought him fresh paint rags every day. She'd ripped up one of her petticoats and spent the evenings hemming the edges of the rags instead of working on her art. Then he found a better supplier; the translation dried up but she was once again free to paint at night, though she had only three petticoats to her name.

Miss Hodgkins, (she wonders if that is indeed the name of the hatless lady who is placing a step at the side of the cart), Miss Hodgkins is supposed to have had the great honour of being the only woman to teach at the Colarossi. This is a good recommendation, but even if she'd been there at the same time, Emily would never have enrolled in her classes. She has no faith in women instructors, though she is a teacher herself. She is the first to agree that ladies are well able to teach children—her sister Alice runs a successful day school—but men are more equipped to convey advanced learning. Art teachers of any stripe are hard to come by in Canada; there are no world-renowned academies such as those that abound in Europe. This is why she and some of her painting friends have been encouraged to give lessons. It has nothing to do with their level of skill.

The lady has still not glanced in her direction. She is helping the driver to load the luggage. She is not wearing a hat or gloves. Emily is now certain that she should have known better than to accept Mr. Church's second piece of advice and enroll with her, even if she is the best teacher of modern methods in France—and where is more modern than France? She should go to him and insist that he teach her himself, here, this moment, in St. Agathe; she should jolly well plonk herself down in his doorway with all her luggage until he takes her on. He said he liked her work. He told her once she was more than merely good, that she might one day be one of the best women painters to be found anywhere. He even paid her the compliment of refusing to let her view his work, while he allowed everyone he considered his inferior to critique it.

Miss Hodgkins approaches her and introduces herself properly this time; it seems they are ready to leave. Emily sees that she is expected to clamber up beside the driver.

"I'll stay here at the back. Fetch me the step," she says. Miss Hodgkins stares at her as if she didn't understand English, then she summons the driver (in French) and together they pick her up and hoist her bodily onto the back of the cart.

The conveyance has no springs. Her teeth trap her tongue, and her eyes are spinning in her head like plates on poles. She tries to concentrate on nice things. The jar of condensed milk that is snug in her Gladstone—it is a shame that French bread is always desiccated, but she's discovered that if she spreads the sticky milk liberally enough and waits at least five minutes, it seeps into the crust and moistens it so that chewing is a pleasure. She jabs her left leg with a hatpin and feels a tingle. Jab, jab. The nerves must not give up on her again. She turns and glances over her shoulder at her new teacher's back. No hat, no gloves, she must be reckless. For a moment she sees a similarity in the shape of the head and the shape of another head, though the hair on that other head was auburn, not black. The shadow of a black bird flits across the horizon, hovering for a moment over the receding railway line, then swooping towards her. She ducks, but it comes in closer.

The patient is lying on an improvised bed in the mortuary in Suffolk with a blue sheet draped round her midriff.

The doctor sticks her carroty head under the sheet; she crouches, parts the patient's legs, feet first, then knees, then, gently, thighs. It is like slitting an envelope when the contents are flimsy. The patient keeps her eyes on the back of the doctor's neck.

A child's coffin is on view and the perfume from a vase of Sweet Peas clogs the patient's nose. Somewhere, someone is playing dirge-like music. The patient recognizes the tune but doesn't know its name.

The doctor probes with a speculum. At the first touch the patient screams. And screams.

The doctor coaxes her up off the bed and into a rocking chair. She produces two silver balls.

The sheet is of no use when she is sitting up. There's no escape.

"Dis is the Roman word for the god of the underworld," the doctor remarks, as if she were commenting on the weather, "when his name is joined with ease it creates unbalance. Dis must be eliminated. Manus means hand. Sturbo, to defile. To defile with the hand. To masturbate." The black bird hovers, then veers away in the French sky. Its shadow vanishes in the bright sunlight, but it remains behind the patient's eyes.

Emily twists round and looks again at the back of the famous Miss Hodgkins' neck. It is long and slender and exposed to the sun. The doctor's neck was no neck at all as she knelt in front of the rocking chair, her head scrunched into her shoulders. She is Raven—red raven, a trickster. The Indians in the Northwest say Raven is a shapeshifter, the great creator who stole the moon, the sun, the stars, who stole fire. Raven stole fire. It was unspeakable. The doctor may have worked miracles on other people, but Emily wants no truck with miracles. The time spent in Suffolk is long since buried and she's been well until this year. Now she's recovered for a second time, reinvigorated, her nerves are just a bit shaky but they haven't given up on her. From now on, she vows, she will be healthy as a horse.

She lets her coat hang loose and wills herself to stop shivering. They are going downhill and she keeps sliding back. She intones a French song to chase away any lingering doubts about her health. She thinks about all the sketches she'll make of this sunny landscape and she will sing if she pleases—it doesn't matter what Alice says about her musical ear.

Fairy Jacques
Fairy Jacques
Dormay voo
Dormay voo
Ring the bell for Matins, ring the bell for Matins
I'm wet through. So are you.

They seem to be clopping down the main road into town. She can see the harbour at the bottom of the hill. She observes that the shops are closed for the afternoon siesta. Someone is playing a pianola. The cart comes to a stop outside one of the shops. The driver jumps down and seizes her by both wrists. She wills her legs to bend, and, with an enormous effort, slithers down and crumples into a useless pile of wool and fur in front of her lodgings. Behind her, Rebecca, still stranded in the trap, yells, *"Merde, merde, allons vite!"* The bird has picked up more of the language than her mistress.

When Raoul brings her luggage upstairs, he drops it any old where. Her trunk sits outside the door where it will have to stay.

She snaps open her brown Gladstone bag and scrabbles for the feel of glass. Prizing the lid off the jar of condensed milk, she dips in two fingers and draws them out covered with the sublime sticky stuff. She licks, savouring the tiny stabs of sweetness, closing her eyes, trying to conserve the pure pleasure of each taste before it grows so sweet it makes her remaining wisdom teeth ache and forces her to stop. She tugs at the door of the wardrobe. It is jammed. She catches a glimpse of herself in the glass. This is always unnerving; she never looks at her reflection unless called upon. She tugs harder and the door flies open, catapulting her image into her face. "So here we are," she remarks, "embarked on another adventure." Even the parrots seem to be temporarily paralyzed. "What do you suppose that person will have to teach us?" she asks.

Emily settles her two birds and their cages on the outside sill, "Some people give me the pip," she remarks to Rebecca (she is thinking of Miss Hodgkins). "And I don't want a word out of either of you, so keep your heads down. Did you see how our French landlady glared?" The green parrot lets out a flurry of invective and Emily shoves the window up further and throws a travelling rug over the cage. "I think she was telling us that one bird can be tolerated but two's a crowd."

She tosses her fur wrap onto the only chair. An oversized orange cat materializes from under the bed, its ears flattened, whiskers quivering, elated by so much provenance; the cat pounces on the intruder in the chair, sending clumps of fur flying, and Emily opens her mouth and laughs so loud her jaw clicks and she has to prise it back into place. She hasn't laughed this hard in months. The landlady comes running upstairs and arranges her lips into an O at the sight of the large Anglaise, marooned in a sea of bags, apparently delighted at the destruction of her beautiful fur. She wonders if the English always laugh at such times. *"Tu es méchante, méchante, méchante."* She chases the cat onto the landing. *"Pardonnez madame, pardonnez-moi, mais c'est pas ma faute."*

"Paa di toot," Emily trots out her single French phrase, smiling at the woman, understanding that she will now be allowed to keep her birds. "Ronron," she says. "I think that means purr."

As soon as the landlady-cum-shopkeeper leaves, Emily invites the cat back in. "If I was cruel I'd grab you by the tail and prove there's no room in here to swing a cat." She takes in the proportions of the room for the first time. "We've got one at home like you. Our puss makes Edith's life a misery when she's down on her knees. My sister Edith, the Praying Mantis—you didn't hear that! She's the missionary who's head of our house. She'd be right at home with that picture of Jesus over the bed, but maybe not the bleeding heart.

Look at the thorns! The French like things to look bigger than life, don't they, perhaps they'll like me. We wrap our hearts up in tissue paper in Canada."

The cat settles on the eiderdown and blinks at the voluble intruder. Emily offers him the fur, but he's lost interest. "You can talk to Rebecca when I uncover her. See what you can do about her bad language. She thinks she's French; we'll have to straighten her out before we get home. It's her bird sitter's fault. The birds were both lonely so I paid a nice young girl to sit with them while I was at art classes and my sister Alice was out on the town. Sister Alice is much kinder than Edith but I'm different than either of them. I think they found me under a gooseberry bush. Anyway I paid this sweet young French person to sit with Rebecca and Josephine while I was out, but it turns out she wasn't sweet at all. She had a mouth like a navvy. I hope it won't rub off on you, puss, if you're going to settle in. I shall call you Monsewer, is that all right? You don't look like a Minou. And remember, parrots aren't very tasty. They're tough old flesh, like me!"

The room is no bigger than a ship's cabin and it smells of boiled artichokes—boiled artichokes remind Emily of soft green soap. She stares up at the cracked ceiling. "This wallpaper's disgusting, do you suppose someone actually designed it? I hate design." She sits up abruptly, banging her head on the sloping ceiling. "No writing table, no room for my easel, no gas mantle—so that means smelly old paraffin. And it costs an arm and a leg. Let's hope it'll all be worth it. It's not even as roomy as the Elephant." Emily smiles at the thought of her beloved Elephant, the grey wagon she uses for camping in summer; why has she relinquished it so easily to summer in France, when it is fitted out with all her needs—supplies of tea, books and chocolates, lots of room for her menagerie? She consoles herself with thoughts of summers yet to come. Next year she'll get her usual tow out of Victoria and park the old girl. Some Clever Alecs have said

Canada can't be painted; Emily is determined to prove them wrong, but not while she is in France.

Her room has a tiny window at eye level and she hauls herself onto her feet and looks outside onto the cultivated cobbles, hammered into position by centuries of cart wheels and clogs.

"Back home nothing is hammered," she remarks to Monsewer. "Back home everything moves and shifts. Even the sky looks fiercer, especially over the Sooke Hills. I don't suppose I'll do much painting in this little matchbox, d'you think this bed's wide enough for both of us?"

§ St. Agathe, May 23rd, 1911

I have not been out for two days as I have been waiting for a man who is supposed to attend to a loose slate. (I fear the French have some difficulty in keeping appointments.) I have a yen to write, and write I will, though I have nothing to confide in the way of interesting events.

We have been coming to Brittany every summer for six years. Personally I like St. Agathe, but my husband leans toward St. Efflame, a small coastal town to the north of here. His preference is mainly fuelled by the conviviality of a certain wine-merchant in the old town together with his excellent stock. There is also the small consideration of the two drinking establishments whose proprietors defy the statutory closing hours by moving their tables out onto the road for the night. Geoffrey is a night owl; if he had his way he would sleep until noon. I told him that I would be quite happy to stay in St. Efflame for artistic purposes, but bibulous activities must take a back seat, since I am the one who must wait up for him and change the sheets after he has rid his stomach of its alcohol stew.

I have no artistic pretensions myself, which is just as well since the house is already overfilled with people (often of Scottish descent) who imagine they are the successors of Englishmen like Stubbs or John Constable. Geoffrey leans rather to the Fauves; we are both greatly interested in the newer French ideas. His close friends are French or Russian, but his pupils are mostly from the British Isles. The Channel serves as a muffler of new trends.

The wife of an artist should never have ambitions—it is a recipe for disaster. In point of fact I am the second wife of this particular artist (the first fancied herself a water-colourist, but she died of consumption before her talent could become a burden. I have seen some of her miniatures and they show refinement). Like his first wife, I have no children. Geoffrey jokes that it is just his luck to marry two barren women. I tell him that I don't feel deprived by our lack of issue.

"All my friends and neighbours say you are an admirable woman Winifred," he laughs, "look at your admirable little wife, they say, she is staunch and stalwart and pale as a lily, with her pressed flower collection, her good works and her tatting." They speak of me as if I were a ruminant, good only for milking. Geoffrey, of course, knows better, but even he doesn't know everything. I am on good terms with most people though I have no intimate friends, unless you count this journal, which is my true confidante. Fanny Hodgkins is a friend, but she is not yet an intimate.

I met Frances when she first came to St. Agathe two years ago. I thought her pleasant, but a little aloof and I haven't changed my opinion. Her moodiness drew me to her. She is one of those expatriates who are permanently displaced—she belongs nowhere and has no corner to call home. I have never met anyone who grew up in the Antipodes who was completely happy, or who, once they escaped, had any wish to return.

Miss Carr, of course, is a different kettle of fish. To hear her talk, there is no place on earth like Canada, in fact heaven has a hard job competing with her place of birth. She is particularly effulgent in her praise of the Pacific Coast. I don't believe she has visited much of the rest of that vast land, but then, who has, apart from a handful of rogues and traders?

After my encounter at the railway station, I questioned Geoffrey about Miss Carr. We rarely discuss his pupils, but I knew he had a high regard for her work, and I knew that he recommended Miss Hodgkins as an instructor. I did not think this wise, but I kept my opinions to myself. A man has very little sympathy for the alchemy that attaches one woman to another, or the bile that keeps them apart. Although I knew little of Miss Carr, I would not have placed her within a country mile of Fanny Hodgkins. The women are too similar, both proud and peppery spinsters, neither one prepared to concede the slightest point, both Colonials and both completely immersed in art to the point where they are lacking opinions on almost any other subject. I judge them to be very close in age, though something terrible has happened to Miss Carr since last I saw her. I wonder if Geoffrey will notice the change in her? For a man who lives by his eyes, he is not particularly observant. I brought up Miss Carr's name while we were eating lunch on the terrace today. He hates anything but small talk over meals—he will not be distracted from his food, so I waited for the sigh to come as he mopped up the last vestige of his sardine salad with the heel of the baguette.

"So why did you suggest that she come here, Geoffrey?"

"They'll be good for one another."

"But Miss Carr is of the English school. You know how Fanny feels about the English school."

"Beggars can't be choosers. All our students are of the English school."

"But Miss Carr is not run of the mill, you said so yourself."

"Miss Carr changed her approach under my influence in St. Eflamme."

"I admit that you did influence her work, but then, you influence everyone's work. How do you know that your ideas have stuck?"

"She managed to reproduce my techniques down to the last brush stroke. The woman's a sponge."

"Sponges dry out."

"Are you implying that my teaching methods are lacking?"

"No, I'm not implying anything of the sort. In any case, you are no longer teaching. I'm simply saying that you are not being fair to her. You know very well that she's more than a mere copyist."

He took a sip of coffee. "You're right. She took what she wanted, what she needed, and, like a true artist, she fashioned it into something entirely her own. But it had nothing whatever to do with the New Art, so it's virtually worthless. I've done all I can for her."

He swiped his napkin at his mouth and got up from the table to take his nap. At three o'clock he will pick up his pipe and head for his studio—every day is the same this year, he is preparing for an exhibition in Paris, and he has cut out all other work. I noticed a speck of sardine hiding in the corner of his lips and I stood up and put my nose to his, while I tongued the sardine into my own mouth. He paused, downed the last dregs of his coffee, thwacked me on the shoulder and asked me to join him in the bedroom at two-thirty. I decided that, this afternoon, I would probably not disappoint him.

The Hydrangeas are coming into full bloom, their blue is quite alarming, someone must have put centimes into the ground round their roots and the copper is working overtime. I prefer the flowers when they are dried, just as I prefer the misty, slightly opalescent light of England to the dancing summer gold of St. Agathe that sends my husband into such transports. My French is improving. I take lessons every morning from a young architectural student who is summering here. I become more and more comfortable in this country—not a difficult task, since it is in my nature to be comfortable wherever I fetch up. I could hardly wish to find myself back in Hertfordshire where I spent my first twenty years. I have a theory that if you are not comfortable in your childhood home, you will be forever an expatriate, a cuckoo in whatever nest you happen on.

After I cleared away and washed the dishes, I brought out my journal. In France it is a journal, in England I call it a diary. Diary is a heavier word, thus, in England, my entries tend to lack air. In England I never record conversations, and generally confine myself to meticulous entries of everyday events. I record the weather and tasks that I have completed. Here in St. Agathe, I am more frivolous. I always make my entries while my husband is having his zizz. It's not that I keep the journal a secret, I'm sure he would have no interest in my views on Frances Hodgkins or Monsieur Matisse, or his other friends. Simply put, this book is my blank slate. I don't pretend to be a literary genius; I try to write down events as I remember them and I am interested to see how close I can come to the truth. I can't seem to make my thoughts untidy—I keep parceling them and trimming them down to a size that will fit the page. At bottom, I suspect I must hope that the entries will be read by someone who will say, 'Oh, what an interesting life, what an impeccable mind, how fortunate to have lived in that place at that time.' And who knows, perhaps I will trap something between the pages and press it, like a flower, thus conserving it for all time. This is an exciting prospect.

I have reported on our two very different trips to the railway station thinking that my curiosity about Miss Carr might be assuaged, but this hasn't proved to be the case, so I will lock this book away, forget about the man who will or will not mend the roof and make my way upstairs to waken my husband.

§ St. Agathe, May 25th, 1911

I found Fanny lying in a hammock on the back verandah reading a novel by Mr. Zola. I made my presence felt and she looked up with a small frown.

"Have you read this, Winnie?"

"You know I don't read French novels."

I sat down on a white wrought-iron chair next to the hammock. It was extremely uncomfortable. She slit the belly of the book with a jeweled paper-knife.

"You must forgive me, I'm just coming to a good bit."

I watched the street as she continued to read. The Hotel Bon Ami is a modest hotel and Frances had positioned herself in a quiet spot, so there was little to attract my attention. "Monsieur Zola was an exceptional man," I ventured. This received no response. "I met him once." This had the desired effect. She tore her eyes away from the page and fixed them on me. "It was in Paris at a vernissage, or a salon."

"When was this exactly?"

"I don't remember, but it was before he died."

"What a bore it must have been."

Fanny is not comfortable at social occasions. I can't blame her, it isn't easy to go to these events unaccompanied, but I was forever encouraging her to take more part in Paris society, it is the only way to become known and to increase the demand for one's work. My husband feels one must work as hard at selling a picture as one does at completing it. Fanny does not want for invitations, her reputation is considerable, but her absence only serves to make people forget her; I suspect that, if she were a man, the absence would have lent an air of mystery, which might have provoked considerable interest in her painting. As a woman, she was merely overlooked.

"So what did he look like, our Mr. Zola?"

She was expecting too much, but I felt I should try to supply the forgotten details. "Our eyes connected once and I think he understood it to mean that I admired him. He had the most extraordinary eyes, like moss agates." I was thinking of the stone that Geoffrey has on his watch chain.

I lost the battle for her attention and she returned to her book, glancing up long enough to throw an English book with ready cut pages into my lap. The author was Annie Swann. I had heard of her, she writes romantic novels, which are much admired in England.

"Where did you get this book?"

"I paid a visit to the Chateau on Sunday. The nice old English governess gave it me, and I didn't have the heart to refuse it."

"You were at the Chateau?" I was amazed.

"Just for tea. Two cups. Bitter Russian stuff, quite revolting. I had my hand kissed several times. The Prince told me he buried his beautiful wife in his drawing room, and has not been back to Russia since. He was talking in glowing terms about a friend of his, a Monsieur Rasputin who is due for a visit. He thought we should meet. I think he was matchmaking. He came to the hotel on Friday to take a second look at my pictures."

"He came to see you here? Perhaps he is interested in you for himself, not for his friend. Did he buy?"

"Such a shame. My bloomers chose to slip down just as he was kissing my hand. He departed, saying 'Better put them on again or you will catch cold.' The hints that he would buy evaporated."

"How dreadful for you."

"Oh, not really, they're ten a penny you know, princes. Russia's full to the gills with them, and they're all for export. Actually, I don't think any of them has any money and they don't know anything about painting. Unlike Mr. Zola—now if I had met him and lost my bloomers I'd have turned to stone! Are you sure he didn't speak to you?"

I had no wish to prolong the discussion. I didn't come to the hotel to gossip about writers, novel writing holds very little interest for me. And I'd fibbed about my meeting with Emile Zola. I was told that he was attending the salon, and I think I identified the back of his head, but I didn't look into his eyes.

"I have come to discuss Miss Carr with you, Fanny." Fanny went back to her novel, and I poked her in the ribs hard enough to hurt. She put the book aside and laid her hands in her lap very carefully. Her fingers are extremely long, and she'd filed her nails into perfect ovals with a raspy metal file, which she has a habit of bringing out when she is distracted or bored by a conversation. I have been known to almost stand on my head to prevent the appearance of the dreaded instrument. She was wearing two rings, one a band of plain gold on her right hand, and the other a large ruby ring studded with white sapphires, somewhat ostentatious, worn on the middle finger of her left hand. It might well have been an engagement ring, though she has never spoken of any emotional attachments. I've never asked her exact age, but Geoffrey puts her at thirty-nine or forty. He makes it his business to acquaint himself with everyone's year of birth, as he fears age. He sees his days ranged out as if on an abacus, rods and rods of coloured beads, which can be moved in one direction only. I've pointed out that an abacus is only capable of registering what is tallied by a human, not a divine hand, that the beads can be moved forward and backwards, and even register up and down. He will not see it. The beads on his abacus are moving forward inexorably, click, click, and the manner of it sends him into a frenzy. Once he is embarked on the subject of time, no amount of chivvying will return him to a good humour.

Frances noticed that I had fallen silent. "Miss Carr is settled in her lodgings, Winnie. I believe she has been resting since she arrived. We have agreed to begin our tuition at ten a.m. tomorrow."

"How did you find her?"

"Do you know her?"

"Not well."

"I found her to be—very English."

"But she's from Canada."

"She has a British passport. She wears it on a string around her neck."

"You have a British passport. Does that make you English?"

She bit her lip. "Her accent is English."

"So is yours." I wasn't going to let her off easily. "Are you accepting her as a private pupil?"

"No. She will join my morning class. She will receive no particular favours."

"Is there any reason why she should?"

"She seems to think so." Fanny brought out her nail file and I flinched.

Emily Carr declined all my invitations to tea when we lived in St. Eflamme, though most of my husband's other pupils accepted with alacrity. They would have weekly viewings of my husband's work, at which they were expected to pass critical judgement. Miss Carr was never invited to these viewings, and, being perverse, it was the only time she ever wanted to come inside the house. Wanted is a strong word, expected is more precise. She would turn up punctually at five p.m. every Wednesday and my husband would, just as punctually, order me to 'keep that person out.' I took her aside and tried to explain why he refused to let her criticize his work any more. "He's afraid—he knows that you have more *je ne sais quoi* than the rest, and he is afraid you will upset them all by putting them in the shade. What is more, he fears you might have some special insight which would not prove conducive to his future efforts." This was no more than a quarter of the truth, but it seemed to satisfy her until the next Wednesday when she showed up again, punctually at five. She unnerved him. He told me once that when he was stooping to look at her canvas, she took off her boot and then removed her stocking. She had a false toe sewn into the stocking where her real toe should be. I don't know what effect she expected this to have on Geoffrey, perhaps she thought he would take pity on her and allow her to come to his Wednesday sessions. He said the sight of it made him feel sick and after that he gave her an even wider berth.

She has no social graces. When her sister was with her, she had an ally who could cover up her gaffes; Miss Alice Carr was classically well mannered. I remember when the pair came to the house after they first showed up in St. Eflamme. Geoffrey, having no knowledge of Emily Carr's abilities, displayed a few of his canvases. Alice averted her eyes and made small talk with me while Emily went into paroxysms of delight. She commented loudly on the light, the colour, the soul of the work; she fell down in a chair and repeated, as if we did not already know it, that the depiction has never had to match the subject exactly; she was brimming with excitement, and all the while Alice and I discussed hats. Emily told me later that the new school of painting upset her sister and she could not even bear to look at the work. She maintained that Alice had exquisite taste and her views were always to be taken seriously. All I can say is that she did not know a great deal about hats.

I closed my eyes and tried to imagine the scene when Fanny was forced to be civil to Miss Carr. I couldn't summon up a single image and the rasp of the nail file became so intrusive that I clutched my temples. Fanny grabbed my arm, her face suddenly alive and full of concern. "Are you all right Winnie dear? I have some salts inside. May I leave you so I can go and find them?"

I smiled. I smiled and I continued to smile as Fanny rushed into the hotel. We have an interesting summer ahead of us.

CHAPTER THIRTEEN

⠀ℓ⠀

Catherine started in before the paint on the walls was dry. Rough sketches spurted onto the canvases so fast she broke out in a sweat. She was well supplied with surfaces—in the last few years it had been easier to prepare them than leave marks on them.

The first day, she covered three canvases, painting whatever her hand and eye dictated. The day after, she started at seven a.m. and worked through to midnight, taking short breaks to refill the Brown Betty, not bothering to change the teabags, not pausing to analyze the huge self-portraits that were taking shape. The figures were mostly naked. The first one she finished was seated in her leather chair in a pose reminiscent of the Welcome Wagon Lady.

When she'd explored all the possibilities of bare skin, she began to dress herself up. A week passed without the output abating. She emerged onto the canvas as a cook, a scullery maid, a chatelaine, always a domestic, the costumes harking back to another time, nothing she recognized, but definitely not today, though the brush cut was always recognizable. She remembered back to one of her teachers in England who said you could always see the vacuum cleaners in women's painting. She would paint perfect vacuum cleaners.

In one study she was kneeling. The price was stuck to the soles of her new shoes, $30.00, and above her head her image was shrunk down and repeated, legs open, blood dripping copiously into her upturned hat. She wished she had a dress-up box like Cindy

Sherman or Rembrandt. As it was, everything came from something she'd seen in the movies. Sometimes the backgrounds were very detailed though mostly she opted for the 'dirty window effect' deliberately blurring the detail once it was in place. There were staircases, studios, the university clock tower with the hands stripped from the clock and transposed into her fists like batons; there were market stalls and domestic interiors, tame skies, tonsured West Coast gardens and tiny little mountains, like ice cream cones, scraped clean of vegetation. She pushed herself further. Linked body parts and objects began to detach and float free. Much of it didn't work, and when she needed a break, she painted over the failures in beige.

At first the faces she made were her main focus; they were exaggerated, not always human. She gave herself a pert little horn instead of a nose, the horn detached, so she painted another and another and she was reminded of of Dürer's rhinoceros, and how he had no idea what a rhinoceros looked like when he drafted it onto paper. She studied her face in a shard of mirror, moving the glass around, cutting the chin off, then the forehead. She didn't recognize what she saw—it was hardly human. She loved it.

Later, she zoned in on one of the many blemishes that had bothered her when she was younger. A strawberry mole on her temple became a purple platter piled with lustrous red berries. A chipped tooth was transformed into a white fence post, a picket fence marched over her cheek like a huge scar where she'd once had a couple of stitches for a gash. Laugh lines became fissures. In one study she was holding onto the four detached legs of a dog, a limp black creature not unlike her brother's pet. Her eyebrows were heavily accentuated like Groucho Marx or Frida Kahlo. Or Emily Carr. But like all her other features, they floated off her face.

The varicose veins became a tangle of vines, thickets, fallen branches, the ones that gardeners call widows. Major arteries pushed through landscapes of thighs and buttocks, sturdy as old growth trees, spouting like geezers; the undergrowth of hair lining the ridges formed by her bones became more and more impenetrable. Slowly, inexorably, the bush crept into the pictures and it was beige. She put the beige forests outside the back door, freeing them to march over the cliff and into the sea.

The days sped by and still she didn't pause to select or deflect. She was dropping into her inmost colours, she'd never flaunted them before. Her excitement increased. "I have never worked coldly." She repeated the words like a mantra.

She signed every painting, even the toss-outs. Her signature changed. It was large and far bolder than it had ever been. It began to pull the eye from the figurative images. It dared the viewer to peer behind it.

When she took a break, she didn't know what to do with herself. She paced the perimeter of the property, stood on the edge of the cliff in the blowing rain seeing the ocean in black and white; she took a chair outside and walked around it instead of sitting down. She picked up her sketchpad and signed her name. It looked foreign in this medium. She experimented with different signatures, running them over the edge of the page, filling every bit of space, covering more and more pages and then she swung back to her painting.

She was running on a moving belt and the gears spun faster and faster. Her pace increased. She stopped occasionally to snack on sardines, stale bread, a can of milk, a few half rotten apples. She knew that her temperature had risen because her skin was so hot and dry. When she napped (usually in the late afternoon) it was on the couch in the window with the light full in her eyes. Her eyeballs were dry and prickly and as soon as she shut out the light, images jostled each other, squeezing out anything but the shallowest sleep. Just as she felt herself dropping off, she jerked awake, and came to in a place she didn't recognize.

It began to rain in earnest, pissing morosely on the windows, thunking on the roof, sweeping across the open sea in grey gusts. The rain neither complemented nor detracted from her mood; it was outside her, existing in its own time, it wasn't even a background. Once she woke with her mouth filled with flakes of charcoal. She realized she hadn't washed or cleaned her teeth, she needed a change of underwear, even her glasses were greasy. None of this mattered.

🐝

A week after Kit arrived, Roger blurted out an invitation to spend an hour with him in his studio. As usual, she was adrift in newspapers.

"Sure, let's do it." She jumped up, scattering her clippings.

He saw how she softened the minute she stepped over the threshold. She sauntered around, touching his few belongings and he trailed her into the back room where he'd hung one of Geoffrey Church's paintings, a French landscape in primary colours, bristling with energy. A stack of Church's paintings had appeared in the cupboard under the stairs. He presumed this must be Ilona's doing, she was trying to encourage him to get off his duff. It must have taken all her energy to sneak them up the hill, energy she should have been conserving. Roger was waiting for the right moment to tackle her on it; this wasn't the time for her to be thinking of his well-being. Kit examined the red hay stooks. "Did you do this one?"

"No, no, the artist's a distant uncle of Ilona's. School of the Scottish Colourists." He dragged a couple more canvases out and propped them up in the light. He hadn't examined them closely at Golding, and now, given play in the empty room, Geoffrey Church's skill was palpable.

"I didn't think it was yours, your paintings are at the house, aren't they."

He waited, hoping for some favourable comment, but her attention moved elsewhere. "Do you paint at all?" he asked.

"Absolutely not." She came to rest on one of the folding chairs and sat on her legs.

He breathed into the silence the way he did with a difficult client. "So, tell me about yourself."

Kit noted how hard it was for him to ask this question. It had taken him more than a week. It was horrible that he was still so disinterested in her, but she'd been waiting too long for this opportunity and she didn't need any more prompting. For the rest of the hour, she regaled him with stories of her theatre company, its beginnings, its triumphs and its forlorn end.

He'd had no idea she was a well-known actress. It sounded as though she was a sort of actor manager like Henry Irving, or Shakespeare. When she'd mentioned being on the stage he'd thought she meant something like the Christmas pantomime in the village hall, which was followed up with a ghastly midsummer musical. He'd never had any interest in theatre, but Kit made it sound quite worthwhile. "You know, to be honest, I wouldn't have known there were any theatres where you come from. I have no idea what goes on in Canada. How come they never make the news? I suppose it snows a lot."

"That's so corny! It's hotter than Mexico in summer."

"Really? A colleague went there for a holiday last year—hired a car. He said they drove for eight hours behind the same lorry and saw nothing but trees."

"You'll have to come visit," she said, enigmatically.

Mercifully, Ilona had them booked for France every summer from now until the third millennium; Kit's enthusiasm for Canada could probably be explained by the fact that she hadn't travelled. When he got back to work he'd ask his secretary to dig up a few books for him to read. There were so many questions he wanted to ask, not least about Catherine, but he held back. He knew that if he asked questions, he would be required to answer them, and he wouldn't know the answers. She'd certainly want to know why he'd neglected her for so long.

The next day Kit stayed for two hours, and after that, the visits to the studio became a daily event. Ilona offered no resistance; she only appeared downstairs at mealtimes, meals that he ordered in, or prepared, with Kit's help.

One morning he decided to bring down some of the artwork he'd stored in the attic. Kit helped him to transport it to the studio. There were boxes of drawings, rolled canvases and sculptures, a stack of drawing by old friends who, Roger explained, now had established reputations. They hung them on the walls of the studio and it began to look like an eclectic gallery. They hauled out boxes of old records and an ancient record player in a fake leopard-skin case. Roger produced a teddy bear; it was a threadbare, eyeless old relic, a dirty grey, faded from blue. Kit threw it in the garbage and he rescued it. He found it a place on a shelf near the Emily Carr cartoon that Ilona had, to his relief, banished from their bedroom.

The doorbell sounded. Catherine glanced up and saw Mel's truck in the yard. She hadn't heard him drive up. She made no attempt to open the door. The bell rang a few times, then stopped, but the truck stayed put.

She heard signs of life in the yard, distant sawing and hammering, but she didn't investigate. She was coming to the end of her screed of signatures. She took out a large, pristine canvas and began work on a spiky-haired child who had a paper streamer round her neck. She was wearing a paper party hat, the kind you find in Christmas crackers. It made Catherine laugh; she'd always loved crackers, though she couldn't think when she'd last pulled one. A few hours later she discovered the child was straining to hold the weight of a living heart in her extended arms. She dug out an anatomy book, tracing the route of the aorta, then went back and worked meticulously on the head which was detached from the body; now the aorta was squeezed between the child's lips like a drinking straw.

She wanted her discoveries out of the way. She knew she had to work fast; she mustn't give herself time to ask questions. The self-portraits were far from flattering but this exercise wasn't about vanity. She was groping towards something deeper. She selected another canvas, painted another outline. Now she applied the paint more thickly until she was carving it, deepening and intensifying the effect, partially covering the background, coarsening the features. This figure wore a crown too, but she enlarged it, it slipped down over the eyes like a blindfold. She laughed, wiping away tears. She'd returned to nudity, but the flesh was different now, much rougher and cruder. She tucked a wine flagon under the little girl's ancient breast.

He was looking through the kitchen window. She had no blind, no way of shutting him out. He must have climbed up from the beach. There was no access to that side of the house except from below; the whole structure was precariously close to the edge of the cliff, far too close considering erosion, as he'd been at pains to point out. She thought he'd probably come to tell her the septic tank was flooding the road, the spring had overflowed and swept half the yard away, the house was in imminent danger of falling into the sea with her and her painted hall of mirrors inside. The thought distracted her. She looked around the kitchen to see if anything had changed and when she looked back at the window, she saw his lips moving on the other side of the glass. She walked over and painted a yellow cross on the glass, covering the lips, then returned to her work. The mirror on the kitchen table reflected the window. His face was still there, he'd moved up a little, so the cross was over his throat. The flesh on his nose and cheeks were light, splayed like a slug where the skin was pressed against the glass. She threw her brush down, strode into the yard and yelled his name.

It took some time. He had to scramble down the cliff then walk up through her neighbour's property. Finally he stood facing her on her swampy lawn, his hands in his pockets, lips sealed. He was drenched and his pants, clung to his thighs, heavy with mud.

"I have all I need. You don't have to stay."

He crept closer and put out his hand, tempting, palm up. The palm was pale. She saw it, magnified; this was how she would paint a black man. Pale palms and pale nails, mouth wide open—was it entreaty or a scream? Strong white teeth. Frances Bacon said the inside of the mouth had all the colours of a sunset. The skin on his palm was scored with deep lines filled with oil or grime or whatever he'd picked up on the job. He'd wiped it off, leaving behind an intricate, calloused, relief map. A new painting was taking shape, a map. What kind of map? This was one too many questions. Already it was losing its impact, it had to come from the blood.

"What is it you want?" She startled herself with the volume of her voice.

"Nothin'," he muttered. "Just come to tell you one thing, that's all. I'm through working for you."

"That's fine, Mel, I fired you. What was all the noise? All the hammering?"

"That was just me."

"I figured." She couldn't be bothered. She pulled her robe round her, realizing his eyes were fixed on her and she was damp and naked under the thin cloth. She flexed her fingers. "Why don't you just pick up your stuff and go home?" She watched her right hand wave him off.

"Home?"

"I don't need you. I'm doing fine."

"I see that." His voice was loaded with irony.

She turned to go back into the house, ignoring the outstretched hand.

"I been thinking about you," he said.

"Well...I guess thought's free."

"Not the kind I have. They cost. See. I've been thinking I need to get you out of my head. I've been thinking I should crash in the studio till I get it sorted."

"You want to move into my studio?"

"Just for starters. After that I can come over here to the house and be closer to you."

"I don't think I need a studio any more, thanks anyway. You said you were through working for me. Go home to Mavis."

"Shoot me down if you like, but there's no way round it."

"What are you talking about, Mel?"

"And I took the pictures you left outside the door. Is that okay?"

"As long as you know they're scrap."

"I know, but I want them."

"Then keep them. Just give me space."

"So, about what I said..."

"Are you crazy, Mel?"

"Me? No way. I mean, look at you—you're a dog. If a man thinks he's hooked on a dog, it must be for real, right?"

"Get away!" She stepped back into the house, and stood with her shoulders pressed against the closed door. No one had showed more than a passing interest in her since Roger, and now suddenly every man who crossed her path had stardust in his eyes. It was crazy, it was still *Midsummer Night's Dream* crazy, or maybe it was darker than that. Maybe she'd wound up on Prospero's island and Caliban was paying court, an attractive Caliban, but still a monster. She glanced at the line of canvases, some dry, some half finished. They were grotesque. She imagined herself calling Kit and telling her she'd moved in with a married black carpenter. A crazy man. It would almost be worth it to hear her response.

She watched from the doorway as he backed his truck carefully into a better parking spot, hopped out gracefully and took a bundle from the cab that looked like a sleeping bag.

⚘

Ilona excused herself from the dinner table, saying she had indigestion. Before she left the room, she replaced the guttering candles with a long life variety she'd found at the post office on one of her increasingly infrequent excursions to the village. There were four red candles, and one smaller green one. Roger and Kit took no notice as she lit them. They were arguing and laughing, the way she was sure they laughed when they were alone in the studio. But that was still secret. They hadn't told her they went there together every afternoon.

Mealtimes in her family had always been orderly. Nobody argued. The table was properly set with fluted fruit spoons and fish knives and forks and all the proper condiments. Her mother placed herself conveniently near the kitchen and her two brothers sat on either side of their father, waiting for him to be served. Ilona had helped with the serving but not the cooking; she'd learned cooking as occupational therapy, and that was how she still thought of it, though Roger never complained about his meals. There hadn't been much talk in her house. "My parents had separate rooms," she told Kit as she walked between them. Kit raised her eyebrows and Roger shrugged, brushing the remark aside; it was another of Ilona's nonsequiturs. He used to find them endearing but lately they'd started to grate.

Her parents had separate rooms. They never talked about this. The boys had their own rooms with their computers—they were computer wizards. Anthony, the youngest was unhappy in his job, she could tell from his face and the sloppy way he tied his tie, but the unhappiness wasn't overwhelming. You got over most things. That was her mother's philosophy. She guessed that boys and men didn't talk about personal things the way girls were supposed to, though girls never talked to her. Her parents would have worried if they'd known the details of Roger's past (particularly the detail that was sitting at the table at this moment, siphoning up his attention); but even if they'd found out before she was married they'd have said nothing, because it was common knowledge they wanted to marry her off.

She went upstairs slowly, watching them through the banisters, Roger, Kit, Kit, Roger. When she got to the bedroom she crawled into the cupboard.

§ St. Agathe, May 26th 1911

Frances reminds me of a pigeon. She is always so well turned out in her neat grey costume, her immaculate white blouses and white gloves, her parasol—and such head pieces! She never wears a smock when she paints, and I haven't seen a single splatter. I think she is far too tightly corseted. If you're plump, you're plump and that's that (this is spoken by someone who is as thin a broom handle, so it is hardly fair). She doesn't bind her bosom so it always meets you halfway, and she walks like a bird with small bobbing steps that you can recognize in the dark from the breathless tap-tap-tap of her heels. Geoffrey says she lacks looks, but I don't agree. Her face is strong, her eyebrows are a little pronounced, but she has the most beautiful dark hair and eyes, and though her mouth is a little too wide, she has somehow contrived to retain most of her teeth and salvage her smile, which is more than can be said for the rest of us.

The summer pupils have now arrived and they are summing her up, looking for assistance from us—many of them are unused to working with a woman instructress. Geoffrey is very gracious, though a touch condescending, I fear. This is the first summer in which he has not held classes himself, and, while this is his choice, I think he occasionally wishes it were otherwise. Fanny certainly doesn't need to filch his pupils; she has a good enough reputation of her own, what with her exhibitions in England and the prizes she has won here in France. Only recently she had five pictures hung by the Societé Internationale de la Peinture á l'Eau, it's a very exclusive group and to my knowledge it has allowed only three female members into its ranks. In addition, she is the first female ever to teach at the Académie Colorassi in Paris. These are accomplishments that Geoffrey cannot equal.

The pupils are a mixed bunch, as usual. Mostly ladies—why is it that they take so strongly to water-colour when it is no less demanding than oils? Amateurs are entranced by its possibilities. I suppose it is the delicate, ethereal quality that attracts them, though Fanny's sketches are very substantial. Emily Harrison, the famous Scottish water-colourist, is in St. Agathe for a short stay, and she called on us and asked whether we thought Miss Hodgkins would be prepared to give her a few lessons. Geoffrey didn't take kindly to this, even though he is unavailable. He told her where to find Miss Hodgkins' studio and sent her on her way. I asked Fanny about it the next day; her answer made me laugh.

"I didn't feel quite like giving myself away to a lady of her years and experience," she said "Why should I part with my dearly acquired knowledge for a mess of pottage? I felt flattered, but should one pass on one's secrets to someone who might make dangerous use of them? A private lesson gives up so much of one's very own self. It's not so bad if one is teaching amateurs, but for sister brushes in the same field? I don't think so." And then (the sting always comes in the tail with Fanny), "Her work isn't very good, I don't know how she has acquired such a reputation!"

I have written this down verbatim as the words might so well have come from my husband's lips; perhaps artists are all equally jealous of their territory. He asked how the meeting went, but wanted to know no more after I told him Fanny refused Miss Harrison's request for lessons. It will be interesting to see if the lady settles here in St. Agathe after such a welcome!

The other pupils are less forbidding. The class is small this summer and Fanny is considerably alarmed. She lives on so little income it quite amazes me. She was forced to give up her room at the hotel and move her bed into her cramped little studio and yesterday I found her at her easel in tears. When she felt my eyes on her, she looked up and remarked "Blessed is he who has nothing, for nothing can be taken from him." I think there is some deeper unhappiness at the root of it, but if I ask she will never tell.

There is the usual gaggle of elderly ladies in the class—most are American though a couple come from the British Isles. A Miss Whiting, who hails from Philadelphia, has hands so crippled with arthritis that I wonder how she will hold her charcoal. The ever faithful Mrs. Parsons arrived last night with enough painting materials to start up an artist's shop and dear old Miss Winthrop is due tomorrow; she joins us every summer, though she is completely without talent. There are two young men, a Mr. Merton who is very dashing and a Sidney L. Thompson who is not. I don't know what the L stands for; Americans seem to need initials, perhaps they feel it gives them more substance. It would be quite infra dig to ask about the L, though I'm sure Fanny will do just that if she is at all interested.

There is a rail strike pending. Soldiers have begun to arrive in town and the officers are demanding the best rooms in all the hotels. Monsieur Aurier at the Hotel des Voyageurs threatened to oust some of Fanny's pupils in favour of the military men, and there was an almighty row, which, naturally, Fanny won. She would be completely indomitable if her French were more fluent though she gets by well enough to cause a deal of alarm. The two biggest hotels in town are great rivals, and, since they rely on the art pupils for business, particularly in the off-season, Frances need only have dropped a quiet word to have her way, but that's not in her nature. She likes her pupils to stay together, so that they can discuss their work over meals, however Miss Carr is not staying at the hotel with the others. Fanny has found her a room over the seed merchant's shop. I suppose this means that she did not have the means to pay for a hotel room at summer rates, but I will not inquire. Perhaps they have the wrong things in common, Miss Carr and Miss Hodgkins. Poverty is never the best adhesive. I do wonder how they will hit it off. Everyone says the strike will be short lived so there is no panic about how we will all get home after the season has ended.

There has been very little rain this year, and for some reason fish stocks are low. I don't know if the dry weather accounts for this or if it is something else; the hauls are disappointing, some say catastrophic. *'Quelle catastrophe!'* One hears the words constantly around town. The French have such a way of wringing their hands. Groups of fishermen cluster outside the cafés drowning their sorrows in absinthe while their boats are tied up, the sails furled. Their children buzz you in small swarms, hands extended, begging, no, demanding centimes, or food, anything to keep them going. It is very distressing. In other years, the scene has been so calm and benign, the women in their wooden shoes and intricate head-gear sitting in doorways making magnificent Breton lace, and on Sunday, the carnivals and dancing. The spirit of these events has not been entirely lost, but it is just a flicker of what it was. Starvation is such an ugly word, particularly when one's own table is weighed down with bounty, but what can one do? There are so many of them, and one can hardly invite them to lunch, so it is best to support them by buying their produce.

Thank goodness none of this misery detracts from the peace of the place. It is no wonder that this little walled town has attracted so many artists and artist's colonies over the years; the light is like crystal, sometimes one fears it will crack, and the sight of the sardine boats out on the blue waters of the bay has inspired more paintings than any museum could accommodate. It is calming to turn one's back on the walls and the hustle and bustle of the market and walk around the bay. The rocks are flat and deeply scored and the white beaches are overhung with sweet chestnuts that provide a home for some exquisite song-birds. When I am in the right mood and not feeling homesick, I wouldn't mind if Geoffrey wished us to settle here every summer for the rest of our lives, though if this were to be the case I would certainly hope the sardines will return.

CHAPTER FOURTEEN

░

They sat on the cheap chairs and drank expensive red wine out of plastic glasses. It felt like slumming, in keeping with the old days. Roger did his best to reconstruct the Old Scene. Kit was fascinated with sixties London so he tried to dredge up memories of Carnaby Street and the Beatles, whom he'd never much cared for. It was hard to convey that he'd been too busy living on the edge to realize it was the edge of hippie London, the edge of history.

"Tell me, tell me everything!" her eyes shone. He realized that most of his so-called memories of the sixties were actually culled from things he'd read since. He could see how the Germans might have stumbled blindly through the Nazi atrocities—when you were penned up in the confines of your own busy, fruitful world, you needed a good reason to look at the bigger picture, even when you were surrounded by the fallout from your oblivion. This was never truer than here, in this room, with his erstwhile daughter. In the last week, the outside world had diminished until it was honed down to the three or four hours they spent in the studio every afternoon.

He'd never encouraged Ilona to probe into the past, for fear of emphasizing the gap in their age and experience. Before they met, he'd hardly thought about it. He put a Petula Clark '45 on the old gramophone, and then took it off. It sounded so 'down home.'

"Tell me about the Stones."

He pondered, recalling a record jacket. "I remember going to some gala at Earl's Court. They were stoned out of their gourds." (Was this true?)

"And what about the folk scene? What about Joan Baez?"

"Sappy. I was more of a jazz man—used to hang around the Marquee and Ronnie Scott's. I liked Dankworth and Acker Bilk. That dates me, doesn't it?"

"Did you groove?"

"Groove? Yes, I probably did."

"Did you rock round the clock?"

"We jived, your mother and me."

"Mom jived?" Kit was incredulous.

"Well, maybe not well. Funny thing how certain dates bring up certain music." It was so obvious, but no one had asked him to spell it out. "I met John Lennon at some party in a grotty cellar in Soho—it was just as the Beatles were coming into their own. I remember thinking he was a bit of a prat. One of the lenses of his glasses was cracked; someone'd tried to punch his eye out. They were always having punch-ups. Those were the days when you didn't have to apologize for taking a swing at each other." She sat opposite him, swigging wine, nodding and encouraging. There was so much to tell. "Have you ever listened to Cliff Richard?"

"Never heard of him."

"Good Lord! He's still around, you know." He looked for a record. "They dust him off for every Royal Occasion—he's the icon of the Great Unwashed. Where the hell's he hiding?"

"Will I like him?"

"I hope not. He's a prancing mummy. Like Mick Jagger and Tom Jones, all lips and cartilage. Their eyes give them away of course—plastic surgery doesn't hide everything. They still have that wily, calculating look. They're foxes, every last one of them.

The English cling to their icons." He stopped suddenly. Of course, that was how she must see him. An old goat with a ludicrously young wife, wily and calculating, propped up by...by what? At least he was still capable of creating and sustaining life; she had to give him one gold star for that. None of it was real, least of all the word father. Here he was, swigging wine with a comparative stranger who had his genes and none of his history. If he'd brought her up, they'd have watched the same T.V. shows, shared quotes from Beyond the Fringe, mocked the same politicians, eaten the same comfort food. He'd have made her listen to recordings of the Goons and answer questions from Round Britain Quiz. Now the only thing they had in common were Catherine's croissants. "If I tried, I might be able to locate some of my old fans," he told her recklessly.

"What?"

"I used to be a bit of a name in the art world. Did your mother tell you?"

"She never talked about you. You mean you were famous?"

"I was on my way."

"What made you give up?"

"Moved on to other things, joined my father and brother in business."

"But why?"

She was persistent. Just like her mother. "I haven't had an original idea for years." This was unfortunately true, but it had never got in his way. "I have other things on my plate now. At least I won't end up an old duffer, dribbling into my beer and telling porkies in the pub."

"But Daaaad!" She had no idea what duffers and porkies were. "Why not give it a try?"

She'd called him Dad! He looked at her and held her eyes, so like his own. "Glaucoma." There. It was out. "It's an eye disease. It can lead to blindness."

"You mean you have it?"

"Don't worry, it's under control and I can still see your pretty face. I've probably had it a very long time." He'd kept it to himself since the specialist gave him the news just after he was married. The truth was, he'd done nothing about it; he hadn't renewed the prescriptions, though he kept intending to.

"Is it serious?"

They both lapsed into silence. Roger thought of Sam—he probably had it, too, though he'd never said anything. The truth was that it ran in families. Things were changing for them both. Sam said once that people like them were anachronisms, they'd had most of the pickings, and now they were sidelined, figureheads glued in place by a few last whiffs of authority. "Speak for yourself," he'd told him. The subject was never raised again. He wasn't about to undercut the advantage he had with his older brother and Ilona didn't deserve to know that in all likelihood she'd hitched herself to a white cane. He was glad he'd been able to confide in Kit.

"So you're not going to use this studio?"

He said nothing. To say no would be too final.

Kit looked around—if he wasn't going to use the place, it was a perfectly livable space. The first thing she'd do would be rent a computer. She'd look up glow coma on the internet and check out exactly what was going on.

It was easy to fill the hours they spent together every afternoon. Roger wanted to bring Kit into his world as quickly as possible; he encouraged her non-stop talk while assessing what to tell her and what to leave out. He saw she had no trouble cramming words into the cracks, meaningless insulation, but consoling all the same. He could barely begin to comprehend Kit's itinerant life and he tried not to let this frighten him. In the house she barely opened her mouth, Ilona's shadow fell over them, though poor Ilona was mired in the final stages of her pregnancy and in no state to offer resistance to any scheme they might dream up. Roger felt no compunction to challenge his wife's need to be alone.

For her part, Kit was overjoyed to have found such an avid and non-judgmental listener. He made her feel fascinating, hanging on her every word, questioning her, helping her make sense of the muddle of her past; he would keep her on track with a single, pointed comment. She knew it was foolish, but she let herself dream of bringing him and Catherine back together. Why not? They were both saddled with unsuitable mates. It would be wonderful if the three of them could live within a stone's throw of each other. Catherine could move into Golding, she'd move into the studio. It was amazing—the more time she spent with Roger, the more she liked him. She kept talking, hoping that, by giving him every last piece of information, he'd feel he was part of their past. She didn't want to leave any pauses for him to start judging her.

"The one thing I'd always been able to rely on was the fact that Mom would be there. She was always there in the house on Lakeview, our incredible plain old house, just a square box, covered with wood shingles. I know it better than any place I've ever lived. I actually feel it in my bones, it's like I own every nook and cranny, every cupboard—the drawers all have their own separate smell, their own separate type of lint and fluff, then there's my bed and my beach mat, and my posters. I have posters going back to when I was in elementary school. I have Dorothy Hamill standing on the tips of her skates, and the Grateful Dead and Popocatepetl—it's a volcano—we went to Mexico with the school—and I have a couple of great posters of Polish theatre productions. I'd love you to see them. Mom preserves everything like a shrine; she'll have packed everything away, but we'll unpack them together. Without her, without a home base in my home town, well, everything's just wavy lines."

Her eyes were full of tears. He thought she'd probably had a glass or two too many. It didn't matter, he liked to watch her lips, to see how mobile they were when she wanted to be emphatic.

"See, I haven't really stayed in touch with her much lately. It's my fault—I'm the one with the cellphone. She won't even get a hotmail account. And now she's moved. I don't have an address or a phone number. Could be we'll never hear from her again."

"That's not likely."

"I should've been there when she retired."

He wanted to squeeze her hand, but he didn't move.

"Can you tell me what I want? I don't want to run any more theatre sweatshops. I don't want to do Improv. I don't want a life with any of the no-hope men I've filled in with. Tell me what I have to do to stop being hungry, Dad."

Sometimes her need was as encompassing and amorphous as a pea-souper.

He stared at the backs of his hands. Hands were dead giveaways when it came to age and his were no exception.

"What's ahead for me? More endless rounds of auditions? More smiling and forelock tugging to useless directors? How long before they stop wanting to get into my pants? How much longer can I go on looking and acting ten years younger than I am just so I can compete in the Biz?"

He blinked at her—she was quite mad, no logic and she didn't care what he thought of her. It was so refreshing.

She found some string and taught him cat's cradle, and he cracked a new pack of cards, offering to teach her to play Snap. He couldn't believe they didn't play Snap in Canada. She was competitive, but no more than him. The game got noisy; she pushed him and he pushed back. It was all very silly and giddy. He saw that this would be his life after the twins were born.

She produced a stick of chalk from somewhere and drew a hopscotch grid on the patio outside the front window. He had no idea how it happened, but within five minutes she had him rolling a stone, hopping over the squares like a clumsy schoolboy.

"Stand in a square, marry a bear, stand on a line, marry a swine," he yelled, but apparently even that was different in Canada. Hopscotch was different, too, but he insisted they play by English rules. A couple of neighbours watched curiously from upstairs windows along the terrace. It didn't matter. "Go, go, go goddamnit." He matched her, bellow for bellow. He was lightening up. It wasn't difficult.

Ilona stood at the gate scanning the street. She couldn't see what they were doing but she could hear their shouts. The whole village would hear them.

He'll grow out of her, she told herself as she waddled back into the house. The pink walls were almost a thing of the past, held up by scaffolding today, like the shell on a giant pink-bellied pupa, tomorrow they'd emerge, vibrant and yellow, like a moth.

She sat on the floor of the bedroom, with her back to the motorboat. The mood of the room had shifted since she'd taken Emily's cartoon down. She stretched out her legs and tried to reach her knees. 'He'll grow out of it, it's only a phase,' she thought, pressing her palm into her side. She had gained almost five stone. She made her ankles move in circles, first to the right, then to the left; miraculously her feet followed. Were ankles supposed to be so swollen? 'He'll grow out of it, won't he?'

They'd told her she'd grow out of it the first time they sent her away. "Don't worry," they'd said. But she did worry. She worried that Kit was here for good. She worried that Roger was going to change into someone she didn't recognize, someone who had no time for her and the babies. She worried she'd always be fat. She worried that there was a fish in the ceiling.

CHAPTER FIFTEEN

꙰

Emily rests on each step as she climbs the narrow stairs to her room. She pulls herself up by the handrail, which must have been recently painted, judging by the blue that comes off on her palm; it's an unpleasant blue, a neither-one-thing-nor-t'other blue. Quite dead. It reminds her of the dining room walls she faced when she was an 'Up' in the English hospital. Whenever she sees the colour, she breathes in mashed potato. Food has been a problem ever since. She smiles, thinking of being released back to Canada—of her sisters trying to feed her up though she wanted to be fed down, of dodging them briefly, escaping to the room over the barn and existing on a diet of oatmeal and apples, of meeting Lizzie in secret, middle sister Lizzie, ever the physiotherapist, massaging and smoothing, performing miracles on her chins. Too bad the miracles were short-lived. The other sisters were at war with Lizzie, there was hardly time to brush off the crumbs of Clara's drop cakes before Alice arrived with meringues. So she'd blown up again and pretty soon she'd outdone her English proportions.

It had been good to feel home under her feet at last. Just the smell of Victoria was sustaining. Smell quickly turned into taste. The sea was slightly bitter like iodine, the rocks pure ginger tea and the conifers had a resinous aftertaste, like the Greek wine she'd tried once. It was a miracle to be home in springtime, to uncover the taste of chocolate lilies, not chocolaty, but metallic— the bronze flowers flecked with gold, masquerading as dry grass.

And there was Camas, Camas as far as the eye could see, a pure blue, never disappointing. The absolute. Impossible to capture as taste or smell.

She wipes the nasty blue banister paint off her palm onto her skirt. She is almost at her door and she stops and breathes fiercely, frog marching forward to August when with luck she'll be home again. She experiences the scarlet of Indian Paintbrush, and then the sharp magenta of Fireweed. Such a sharp, sickly colour to paint but completely forgivable in nature. Practical Fireweed materializing instantly, covering the tracks of forest fires, then hanging around too long till it's forced out to the rim like an old artist pushed away to make way for new growth. Emily has a soft spot for Fireweed.

They cut down one of her favourite firs a few days before she left. A monster, it stood in the way of a new bank. She is still mourning. She thinks of the bleeding stump—children roll their hoops round its edge, it takes eight men holding hands to circle that tree. How long had it stood? Long before white men, maybe before Indians, before Indian Paintbrush ever had a name. In Paris she came up with a new collective noun, an amazement of Firs, and she wrote her friends that if the new fangled post-impressionists had any idea of the size and spirit of real trees, they'd stop fooling with light and concentrate on bulk. Her muscles get heavy and stiff with the effort of transferring bulk to canvas. It gives her headaches and backaches and pins and needles. No one has to suffer this in France.

The bed springs ping as she surveys the years she stayed close to home after they sprung her from the San. It's clear now they have been nothing years, years of sweat, mostly spent in Vancouver trying to find time to paint between the teaching, and sewing and pickling, enduring her scolding sisters who have been reincarnated as saints now she is stranded in St. Agathe. Here, she is Gulliver in the land of the giants, but the giants aren't trees; trees she can live with. The more she looks up, the more things grow. She is deathly afraid that she isn't up to the task ahead.

She stretches out without taking her boots off. She's been walking around for hours scouting out painting spots, limping a little, but that never held her back. She thinks of the hours of walking in Paris, looking and looking and admiring someone else's history. Cities are frightening, Paris more than most. The people in Paris are so intense and so gay. So intensely gay. There are exciting things happening but she has no clever talk, no breeding or sophistication to match them. And the artists who congregate in the cafés and ateliers don't welcome ladies into their midst unless they are particularly eye-catching. She remembers Alice's shining eyes when she came home one day, agog with the news that she'd secured an invitation to visit one of the famous 'at-homes.' They were to spend the next Thursday evening chatting with People Who Mattered. She'd stayed in bed in their hotel room while Alice fumed and fretted, and, she suspected, thanked her for being such a boobie.

There is no Alice to clear her path in St. Agathe. No Alice to share her room. If she is to learn, it won't be from one of those high-flyers, the men who have so much to say that they need to drink and talk all night at tables on the pavement—as if any one of them would take her on! She wants to learn from someone steady, oozing talent, someone who is abreast with the new trends without swallowing them down whole. Someone who speaks English, someone she would never meet in Canada in a million years. Someone who admires her work. Someone like Geoffrey Church.

The thought of Mr. Church makes her sweat. What a spoil-sport he is, after she has travelled so far to sit at his feet. His admiration for Miss Hodgkins seems genuine; she has no option but to follow his recommendation. Before she'd even set eyes on her, her instinct told her that the lady teacher would be a washout. How can a woman have anything to pass on when she has so little access to what matters? Have her own years of teaching girls brought forth any hidden geniuses? None worth mentioning. The pupils will go on producing serviceable sea views and dull flower and figure studies in spite of her bullying. They all leave her classes with a grasp of perspective but their vision remains unchanged. She has no clout, nothing with which to inspire them.

She knows now that her instinct about the new teacher was spot on. This lady, so seemingly ordinary, is blown up with her own importance. She has no understanding of status, and, worse, many times worse, she is from the Colonies. Why did Mr. Church not warn her of this? What could a Colonial possibly have to offer that could not be bettered in Europe? Since it is obvious that the lady won't give value, Emily decides to have some fun and do her best to puncture Miss Hodgkins' balloon. She slips under the eiderdown meaning to take a short nap—then she will nail down the best painting spots before the hoard jumps in and pinches them.

§ St. Agathe, May 26th, 1911

Fanny always allows the new arrivals an extended time to settle in and explore their surroundings. She calls it going walkabout, a strange term, I think. She meets them around four-thirty for tea on the day after they arrive.

This year she begged me to be present, and I agreed since there was no conflict with any of Geoffrey's plans. I know she is always nervous at this first meeting-and-greeting. In my experience there's generally one oddball who threatens the stability of the group. Geoffrey always ignores this, he treats everyone with equal contempt, which they seem to find either endearing or challenging. Fanny doesn't teach in his style. She is shy and inclined to fall silent. I've noticed that she tries to draw the pupils out so they will fill in her blanks. She seems to get on best with the lively, noisy ones, though she gives those who are self-opinionated very short shrift. Geoffrey finds her ridiculously self-effacing, but I don't agree. She is very clear about how things should be done, and she knows exactly what she likes. She knows her boundaries and conveys them to the pupils, which is, in my opinion, as much as you can ask from any instructress. I have often heard them say that she is a very good teacher. For me it is instruction enough to stand behind her and watch her construct a painting. She allows me to do this because I am not an artist. She is not at all corseted behind the easel, though she follows a few rules, unlike my very favourite water-colourist, Mr. J. M. W. Turner who, as I understand it, was never afraid to wash out, reinvent and over-paint until he got exactly what he was looking for. Apparently he never heard anyone say that transparent water-colour was better than opaque, he combines both with complete abandon. Fanny is very strict about not allowing her pupils to follow his example, though I know from the evidence of my own eyes that she has a facility for building up and wiping away that is generally only possible in oils. I watch in silence, and never comment, which is what she seems to require of me.

Although she is so solitary in her pursuits, I know she would welcome a soul mate (she has spoken once or twice of a woman, a fellow artist, with whom she travelled for three months in

Morocco, living as one of the locals; unfortunately that friendship seems to have fizzled). I wish I could find her someone who would be inseparable, like Braque is to Picasso, a constant source of inspiration and a repository of ideas—someone with whom she could work like a twin climber, roped together on a high rocky shelf. I suspect my husband may be looking for something similar, but instead he has to carry Winnie Church, slumped, for the most part over his shoulder, though he puts me down at relevant intervals so I can make tea and starch his shirts and see to his correspondence.

When I arrived, the group was sitting at a long table on the verandah with Frances at the head, teapot in hand. They were warming up. I cast my eye over the eight people. I had an inkling that I had been invited in order to keep Miss Carr entertained until Fanny could assess how she would fit in. Her methods require that the group provide support and encouragement for each other, meeting every few days for group critiques and discussing methods at meal times. Miss Carr was nowhere in sight and I seated myself at the opposite end of the table from Fanny, with an empty chair on either side, and treated myself to an earful of the teacher holding forth on the need to render what we see with complete truthfulness, uncomplicated by emotion, intellect, sentimental or romantic interpretation. (I made a mental note to challenge her on this, using Mr. Turner as an example.) She was speaking of Cézanne now, with enough passion to have everyone sitting bolt upright. She has two modes, the bold and the with-holding, and there is very little in between, especially in public or with strangers. The name Cézanne drew a blank expression from three or four of the pupils as she pounded the table. We were, she said, to punch through beyond romanticism to strip back to the skeleton, to refuse to allow our eye to be seduced and to learn to discriminate and select. I suspect several of the ladies at the table would have been more than happy if she were teaching them how to paint a reasonable likeness of a stag at bay to hang over their fire-places. They were not to know that Frances recently attended an exhibition of Cézanne, and now she could talk of nothing but his use of colour to express structure.

The young man with the middle initial had begun to interrogate her on her views of the new art when Miss Carr arrived, all out of breath and still vastly overdressed, considering the heat. Fanny stopped mid-sentence, fixed Miss Carr with a flat gaze and said, "We are discussing Monsieur Cézanne, Miss Carr, have you got anything to add?"

"Can't say I'm well acquainted with him," she puffed. "Saw a couple of things he did in Paris, but I didn't make much of them. Liked the trees."

"How long were you in Paris?"

"Oh, about a year."

"Good. Then you must have found time to view the work of some of the Fauves. I was just saying how exciting this period of transition is, here in France, how amazing to be here now, at this moment in history. At the turn of the century painting was at a stage of *reculer pour mieux sauter* and now the leap has been made, don't you agree?"

"Sorry, I don't speak French."

"Oh, that's too bad. But you must have an opinion on Fauvism—fauve—it means wild beast."

"Never heard of it."

I heard an audible sigh of relief from some of the ladies. Against all the odds, Miss Carr was attracting a fan club.

"Never?"

"Well, not entirely never. Almost never. It's that fellow Matisse, isn't it? I went to an exhibition, The Independent Salon. The one where the chaps who can't, do. The one where they pull out all the stops."

"And?"

"Amazing." She plonked herself down next to me. Her expression changed from expectant to poker. She'd shut down as tightly as if you'd clamped a lid on a saucepan. I suspect she had quite definite views on these subjects, but she was not about to make a fool of herself by expressing them in the present company. I could sympathize. She sucked her cheeks in and out. I noticed that she wore rather ill fitting dentures; we have been careful not to export our good dentists to the Dominions.

The tea proceeded slowly and painfully. Miss Carr's presence seemed to have put a damper on things, though she never opened her mouth again, except to eat her mille feuilles (without a fork), starting with the hard layer of icing, licking the custard from her lips and drinking her tea more noisily than was necessary. I wondered if she was putting on a show for our benefit. Fanny wound the proceedings down, instructing everyone to meet at the gateway to town at nine a.m. for the first sketching expedition. They were to bring only charcoal and lead pencils.

The company drifted away until I was left alone at the table with Miss Carr.

"I hope this sojourn will prove useful to you, Miss Carr." I said.

"Oh yes," she replied. "I think this will be the start of something quite new."

I looked at her more closely. Her face seemed puffed and blotchy, and I was sure she had been crying.

It had all worked out in the end. "Don't worry," they said, so she hadn't and she didn't and she wouldn't. "It's something that happens to young people," they'd said. (Did this mean it was something that happened to expectant mothers, too?) Ilona wasn't sure if it was still afternoon, or any time at all as she stretched out on the carpet with her head inside the cupboard. In the old days she'd just got on with going completely mad, leaving her body from time to time, not flying but swimming, feeling as though she were forever swimming out of her skin. She'd swum through tanks of warm, sticky water, which was incorrect, since she knew water wasn't sticky. Other people were swimming too, though they weren't all keeping time. Her arms were strong. They whirled like egg beaters. And her eyes were fried eggs, filmed over. Bulging. If you were to prick them, they'd ooze. Oh yes, she tried that, with a nappy pin someone on the ward had left lying around. Someone got into deep trouble about that nappy pin. They'd put her hands in splints, so she couldn't use the cutlery. A nurse fed her, or sometimes it was another swimmer. The food all tasted of seaweed.

She mustn't go to that place again, it wouldn't be fair to take the twins with her. She reached over her head and let the tips of her fingers rest on the box, then inched it out of the cupboard, tumbling some shoe-boxes in its wake. She couldn't think how she'd got there last time. There was a knife, her mother's paring knife, small but sharp. There was the feeling of release, and that had been so comforting.

They said it was just a place, just a place where she could rest long enough to get her over the hump. They told her all she needed was a bit of time off. She didn't mind time either way, on or off. Her brothers were embarrassed. They wanted her to behave like everyone else. They didn't want to admit their sister was mental—well, not exactly mental, but a bit off the rails. The rails ran at the bottom of the tanks, they were tracks left by sea monsters. They ran through undiscovered coral seas. Once, when her brother came to the hospital, not the youngest one (the sad one), not Jeremy but Anthony, they asked if he'd like to feed her and he tried, but his hand shook and he slopped the stuff down her nightie and his face turned bright red and he couldn't hide from her. So they let him stop.

She got on with it, and then she got over it, just as they said she would. In between, there were days when they strapped down her arms, mid beat, they strapped her down and put a rubber gag in her mouth, and she waited for the jolt knowing that after it she'd swim with much slower swimmers. After it, they let her hands out so she could put them in front of her face.

This time she could do it without help. She covered her face with her hands. Through her fingers her eyes followed the lines of the engraved pattern in the carpet. She waited for something to happen, but nothing did, nobody came into the bedroom, time passed, the twins swam, she didn't go mad. As usual these days, she was alone in company.

They'd got her moving again, but her body was stiff and she couldn't stop smiling. Smiling and swaying like the poplars outside the hospital window. They liked it when she smiled, "See, she's happy." "She's pulling through." Pulling through. And then there was the last of the shocks and the world wrenched back into place, and she could look around and see the ward as it really was, with the racks of thermometers on the table in the middle. When she looked at the floor she could see all the way down. She could see through the green linoleum, through the concrete, into the earth, and all its layers lined with stones and rocks and trilobites and euripterids. Earth, rock, more rock, and something moving in the seams, was it water, or air, or fire? Was it growing and swaying and getting hotter? No one had measured the temperature at the centre. Best not to look at the floor. Best to beat up the thermometers instead, throw her pillow at them, and chase the cold silver beads that exploded across the green shiny surface, skittering and weaving between the legs of beds and disappearing between the cracks, down, far down. She could feel the pain from the tiny splinters of glass in her fingertips. Real pain. Real feelings.

And in the end the floor sealed over, and she could breathe again. Everyone said they were pleased to see her back and in such good form.

She twirled her feet. These feet are made for walking and I am made for speed. Watch out Mika Hakkinen, champion of the world. Vr-o-o-o-o-m. These feet are pressing the pedals. Rock paper scissors. Rock, she stays put, paper, she crumples up, scissors, she rips. Kit's scissors had scooted upstairs from the Harrods' bag. Once again she was flooded with heart's ease. The lot had fallen on scissors. Sp-e-e-ed. Go Lady, Go. Scissors are looking better and better. "Don't worry," she glanced at her belly, "I'll always be rock."

⚘

§ May 26th, 1911

We sat together in silence for perhaps five minutes. I am not afraid of silence, even with strangers, but I found myself gripped by a powerful wish to take Miss Carr by the shoulders and shake her until her false teeth clattered onto the plate, which she had refused to allow the maid to clear away. My heart went out to her when I realized that she was distressed, but somehow her manner dispersed all feelings of charity and left me with a desire to escape.

I rose to take my leave.

"Sit down, do!"

She didn't address me directly, but when she spoke, I found myself compelled to obey. Now she looked at me, letting her large, yellowish eyes flick up and down my person, appraising me without any hint of apology. I submitted to her scrutiny, rummaging in my handbag to deflect her gaze.

"So, tell me about Miss Hodgkins."

"She introduced herself to the pupils with some thoroughness. She talked at length about her teaching methods at the Académie Colarossi in Paris. I'm afraid you weren't here."

"But I was at that school. I was there for two months. Your husband, Mr. Church recommended the place. He felt I would benefit from working alongside men since their work has more muscle. But I was twice their age and I had twice as much up my sleeve! Don't talk to me about the Academy Colarossi!"

"I'm sorry." I didn't know whom I was sorrier for, the teacher or Miss Carr.

"Oh, don't bother with that." She dabbed her nose with her napkin. "I'm late because I had to finish off. There was no wash water and it took forever to get through to Madame. How do you act out the word for water? I wish I could be like Monsewer and use my tongue to wash." She didn't acknowledge my look of astonishment. "Well, at least these students aren't babes. Some are perfect dowagers! How do they ever lift a brush without falling into a snore? I suppose they've finished with being wives and think they'd better have a go at something else. They'll go back to America or wherever it is they come from and show at the Women's Guild and have the cheek to say they're painters!" I waited, expecting more, and she obliged. "Don't worry, I'm always late. The early bird catches the worm, the late bird misses it. I'm frightened to death of worms."

What was I to make of this? Her diction was not improved by

those teeth, though one was emblazoned with a splendid protruding gold cap. She was still wearing several layers of clothing with no consideration of the mild temperature. I tried to cast my mind back to the last time she was in St. Eflamme. She came to the house, but she didn't stand out as being so very different from any of Geoffrey's other pupils. She interrupted my reverie.

"Miss Hodgkins—what's her background?"

"Didn't my husband tell you?" (I knew he had not.)

"He told me nothing, except that she was good in spite of being from the Colonies. I wasn't sure I should take him at his word."

"I think you should question her yourself." Frances conducts herself exactly like an English woman, in this respect there is nothing to distinguish her from my friends and acquaintants in London, so I had no idea what Miss Carr was finding to challenge.

"Why should I ask her, when you know the answer and you're on the spot. You're her friend aren't you?"

"Of course." I said, with considerable pride.

"Well? Is it private? Is it something she keeps under her bonnet?"

"If you must know, she was born in New Zealand. In a town called Dunedin, which, I believe, is their equivalent of Edinburgh."

She snorted, and I mean this literally. I have never heard a lady make such a sound. "New Zealand?"

I felt I must defend Miss Hodgkins. "You're right, it is a long way away, but she has been in Europe for almost twenty years and she has gained a considerable reputation here. I don't believe she has any plans to return to the Colonies permanently, though she has family there. Her mother is still alive. There is a sister, and, I believe, a brother."

"Well, good for her." Miss Carr pushed her plate in the direction of a passing waiter and rose, knocking over her chair.

I was left sitting alone at the long table, wondering how I could best help Fanny without being consumed by this mountain of ill will.

CHAPTER SIXTEEN

ﻋﻠﻢ

Roger was searching for a dictionary when he discovered the shelf of children's books among the encyclopedias and almanacs. At first he thought Ilona must be collecting the books for the babies, but they were old and falling apart, and when he examined them he saw that most had his name inside, Roger Rintoul in bold, childish letters. As he opened them, he knew their feel by heart. There was *Milly Molly Mandy* and *Little Black Sambo* and a book about an orange cat named Marmaduke, some Rupert annuals, a set of *Biggles* and a well-thumbed first edition of *Just William*. He pulled them out and put them on the table so Kit could look at them. "Hey, you have to read to me!" She grabbed his arm.

"Me?"

"Please. Make up for lost time."

He felt silly reading aloud the stilted verse in the Rupert annuals. How eagerly he'd waited for the next edition each Christmas, fought with Sam for first dibs—even now he could feel the pull of the stout-hearted little white bear with his checked trousers and red jumper. He couldn't bring himself to open the Black Sambo books, that stuff didn't wash any more. He was surprised that it bothered him, he didn't think of himself as P.C. Rupert was different, he was a white bear, presumably of the polar variety, a bear who a Canadian like Kit could learn to love. He read on. She was curled up at his feet, still as a stone. He leaned over and asked, "What do you think?"

"Don't stop!"

He stooped down to show her the pictures, and she craned her neck so she could see. The position was uncomfortable, so she climbed on his knee. She was heavy, but he didn't have the heart to put her off. They followed the text together as he read. When his leg went to sleep, he gave her a gentle shove and she moved into one of the big armchairs. He followed and they squashed themselves in, side-by-side, laughing and giggling. He put his arm round her. She put her head on his shoulder. She was wearing black tights and a pink shirt with half the buttons undone. He let his fingers rest on the edge of her collar, where the cotton material met the skin of her breast.

Kit felt a mix of emotions. The relief of being here in this place was suffocating.

He opened another book and flipped through the pictures of Marmaduke the orange cat, but he couldn't concentrate. He thought of his cat, Nigger, and remembered how he used to jump up on his lap and sprawl across his knee shedding long mahogany hairs on his grey school flannels. What had happened to Nigger? It must've been something bad because he felt a lump in his throat. He wanted to tell Kit about him but he held back, knowing she'd never approve of a cat with such a name, and anyway he'd been lost for fifty years. His hand moved a fraction. Now he felt her skin rebound slightly under the pressure of his fingertip. He slid his knuckle under her bra strap and felt the knob of her shoulder bone. This bone would never have existed if he hadn't gone to art school—if he hadn't met Catherine.

Neither of them noticed when Ilona came downstairs. She crept into the room and screamed.

Roger jumped up. It was as though she'd caught them in a compromising act, as though it were not all completely innocent, a man and his daughter reading a picture book. Any fool could see this, but he actually found himself apologizing.

"Tell her, Kit. Tell her what we're doing."

Kit was focused on the gashes on Ilona's wrists. "She's cut herself!"

Somehow he got her back to the bedroom. Kit followed and he closed the door on her, but she opened it. There was blood on the carpet.

"Those are my scissors!" Kit pounded on the doorframe.

"Go away."

"Should I call an ambulance?" Her voice sounded thin and childish.

"Go away!" He took Ilona's wrists in his hands. There was so much blood, it looked as though she was hemorrhaging. "Is it coming from between your legs, Ilona?"

"No."

"Did you do this to yourself?" He regretted the question. The answer was obvious.

She nodded then shook her head.

He examined the wounds. Fortunately they looked superficial. "You're sure you haven't started into labour?"

"I'll pull through," she said, brightly. "I'm all right, honestly, nothing's happened." Then she went limp.

"Should I call an ambulance?" Kit repeated, wondering if he'd heard.

"Do what you bloody well like." Some part of his brain registered the sharp tug of fear in Kit's voice.

"Is she crazy or something?"

Ilona was alive, he knew that, and there was movement inside her, so things were all right down there. He fanned her with some papers that were lying on the floor. "Go to the bathroom.

Bring the smelling salts. Green bottle," he barked. He took off his shirt, picked up the bloody scissors and clipped one of the sleeves, making strips of rag which he bound round her wrists, then he buried the scissors in the bottom of the laundry basket, and scrubbed at the carpet with what was left of his shirt, wetting it with the water from the tumbler on the bedside table. Kit delivered the salts and they did the trick, just as his mother had always claimed. She continued to stand in the doorway and he tried to ignore her. When he sensed her absence, he felt better. There was a brown cardboard box on the carpet; Ilona had dripped into it, and whatever was inside seemed to have fared badly. He gathered up the scattering of papers from the floor and stuffed them in the box and shoved it into the back of the cupboard out of the way.

"I think we should call Doctor Haines."

"No. Please, no." The colour was returning to her lips. He sympathized with her fear of doctors and brought out her rabbit from under the bed. She cradled it obediently.

He stayed with her, holding her as close as he could, given the barrier of the babies. He stroked all three of them, circling them with his arms, willing them all to stay calm. It had been a close call. He was such a fool.

He kept a watchful eye on her all night, aware that the light was burning in Kit's room on the third floor.

The next day was Sunday. He brought up a breakfast tray, then got Ilona onto her feet, helped her to dress in a long-sleeved jacket to cover the bandages and took her for a walk, out through the back garden and along the field path behind the house. The path curved back on itself and led down to a road into the village. Her body was stiff, and she was unsteady, clutching his arm like an old woman with no will of her own. He

208

turned back, not prepared to meet any early risers or dog-walkers. They moved along silently, with small, measured steps.

Ilona pulled up just short of the gate. "The trouble with you is you're phosphorescent."

He had to grope for the word, remembering the light that danced on the sea at night. There were worse things she might have called him. "Phosphorescent? You mean me?"

"I mean ghosts. I miss my friends."

"You're going to have to pull yourself together, Ilona. I'm going in to work tomorrow, I can't hang around here all the time." He knew it was harsh, but if he wanted to put a stop to this nonsense he had to be firm, he had to let her know who was the boss. "You must take some responsibility for yourself. Kit will be here to lend a hand. You're going to have to work out your differences and get to know each other. You can be friends."

"Why?"

"Because she's my daughter."

"That's right," Ilona said. "I am her stepmother."

"I'd like you to try to be friends."

"Stepmothers aren't friendly, they're wicked."

"Oh, that's a fairy tale. I'm not going to let you drive her out of my house with your antics. She'll leave when we're all ready and not a moment before."

Ilona smiled. Wicked stepmothers had ways of dealing with their step-daughters. "I'll try," she said.

"Promise?"

She nodded and squeezed his arm and he waited in vain for the flood of relief to come.

Next morning as he prepared to drive to the station, following the same routine as he'd followed at the start of every week, he noted that the painters had swathed the climbing rose in sacking. The scaffolding was like a scab. He didn't remember Ilona asking his permission to change the colour of his house but it didn't matter. Suddenly he couldn't wait to be swallowed up in London. There'd be decisions waiting for him, problems to sort, deals to rubber stamp, the city was big enough to be forgiving and he would be free to forge ahead. A black cat jumped down from the gate, flattening itself as it streaked across the drive, narrowly missing his wheels as he backed out. He shuddered and made up his mind to spend the night at the club. Ilona wouldn't be able to claim he was leaving her alone. If anything happened, Kit would alert him, he could be home in a trice. The business with cutting herself had obviously been hormonal. She was overwrought—who wouldn't be—birth was a scary business and the babies weren't going to be rushed into putting into in an appearance, however strongly he willed it. There'd been too much waiting around, too much tumult. They were all exhausted. He realized he'd got off lightly last time he was a father-in-waiting, Catherine had been nothing if not efficient, taking care of things like a mother lioness. She'd hardly needed to call on him. He was going to have trouble handling this new situation. He'd need Kit's help. Just knowing she was in the house yesterday had kept him on even ground. He hadn't come off well—she'd seen him at his worst, foolish and inadequate, he regretted being sharp with her. He wouldn't ask her to be around for the actual event, but she should be there for the aftermath.

Kit awoke to the abominable dawn chorus and decided the

time had come to leave. It was too much to hope that she'd get any quality time with her father now, and her presence in the house was making everything worse. She lay in bed, heard Roger start up his car and guessed he was leaving for work; she couldn't face a day alone in the house with Ilona. But where would she go? She had two fifty-dollar bills in her billfold and a maxed-out credit card. A hundred Canadian dollars in London would buy her a few subway tickets, a hotdog and a cup of coffee. Should she just lie low and wait for Roger to come home then ask for some of the maintenance money he'd never provided when she was growing up? With a couple of thousand pounds, she could find a bolt-hole somewhere, it was the happening place, the place to go if you wanted to get seriously oblivious. Ilona was in a different orbit—if Roger didn't see that yet, it wasn't her job to tell him, and it certainly wasn't her job to mediate. He'd wanted to take her to Madame Tussauds—he must have been thinking of the chamber of horrors! She'd have to detach, wait it out, come back when things were calmer. But she wasn't ready to give up on something that looked so promising. She couldn't remember ever feeling as centred as she'd felt yesterday. It was as though she'd finally discovered breathing through her nose after a lifetime of breathing through her mouth; Ilona must have seen this and stolen the scissors.

Ilona opened her eyes on Monday morning, sure that this was The Day. Roger had rolled over and kissed her as usual and told her he was going to the office, so it was like any normal Monday morning, except that Kit was tucked up under the best quilt upstairs.

"You can always come home," her mother had whispered on her wedding day. At the time she'd thought it was spiteful, but now she saw it differently. The door was open, just like when she'd come home from the hospital. Her room would still be there, exactly as she'd left it. Last time she'd gone back to school as if nothing had happened. This time it would be the twins who would go to school. She remembered how everyone who was in the know marveled that the shocks had been such a success. She'd sat her exams (and failed them, of course) but her father had found her a job in a travel agency and she'd moved into a bedsit in Kensington. And she'd confounded them all by loving her independence.

She thought back to the cocktail party at her father's office when she met Roger. She was too shy to enjoy parties and he'd seen that and come over and talked to her. It was the week after her twenty-first birthday. They'd liked each other immediately. She'd been complimented before—people thought she was pretty, someone once said she was sassy. The word wasn't in her dictionary but it had a nice sound. No one suspected that anything more disquieting than a missed bus had ever occurred in her life. Roger wasn't her first boyfriend, there'd been Noel who serviced the photocopier, but he had no money. And now here she was with the hearts of two strangers beating inside her, listening as her husband calmly left for work after days spent singing the praises of her step-daughter who was seducing him and plotting against her.

She got dressed and walked up the road to the studio, not bothering with breakfast. She hadn't been there for a while. She saw that the two chairs were placed close together. There were empty wine bottles and a paper bag with discarded plastic glasses. The walls were covered with the art she'd brought up from the house. Her great-great-uncle's pictures were too exotic for a Suffolk cottage—their loud, bilious colours made her jump. They were meant for the house they'd been going to buy in France. She wanted to take them down, but it was too much trouble. Roger had found an old teddy bear. It was a fright. She hoped he didn't intend it for the babies. She laid it on the shelf, face down, and cancelled it. She ran her fingers over the glass that separated her from Miss Carr's cartoon.

There was a hopscotch grid on the patio; she realized this was what the shouts had been about. She stepped outside and took a few skips on it, cupping her belly. 'Hey diddle diddle, jiggle and giggle.' Why hadn't he asked her to play? He was pushing all three of them out of his life, like putting empty milk bottles out on somebody else's step.

Back at Golding, Ilona packed her suitcase. The job was half done anyway, ready for when she started labour pains. There wasn't enough room for all her shoes (a change of clothes, her china rabbit, her shoe collection and her box of papers were all she'd brought with her when she came to live here). She squeezed her red pumps into the case next to her dressing gown, then lay on the bed, thinking she'd stay put to see if, by chance, Roger would turn around when he got to Colchester and come home. She took off the bandages, and laid them on the bed, noting with a little shiver that he'd torn up one of his best shirts. The cuts were crusted in dried blood, but they didn't look bad. The house was perfectly still. She went to the window. Kit was pacing around the back garden. She seemed to be deep in thought. Ilona put on her flower printed smock and her white lacy cardigan, tried to button it over her stomach and gave up, slid the box of papers out of the cupboard, trying not to look at the mess she'd made, stuck the china rabbit under her arm, and, with the suitcase in her other hand, made her way slowly and carefully out to the car.

She stowed the case in the boot and strapped the papers in the front seat, then perched the rabbit on top. Driving wasn't as hard as she'd imagined, once she'd wedged herself behind the wheel. She was careful not to gun the engine.

She drove west and south, through Essex, home to all the newly rich, the people Roger made fun of. She drove through London and out into Surrey. She felt hungry and she realized she'd forgotten about breakfast. It didn't matter because she was on home turf. She waved at Mrs. Das Gupta who was standing in the doorway of the newsagents. A moment later, she wheeled into the driveway of her parents' square white house, within spitting distance of the Thames. (Mrs. Das Gupta had once told her mother she'd never seen the Thames. Shocked, her mother had offered to run her to a bridge a mile down the road. From there you could see the royal swans and the rich red bricks and crenellated rooftops of Hampton Court. Mrs. Das Gupta had thanked her and said she'd go on her own if Mrs. Martin would kindly take care of the shop. Naturally it hadn't happened. Ilona thought she understood Mrs. Das Gupta. History and rivers were immovable, but paper shops, like husbands, could be snatched from under your nose.)

With a bit of an effort, she managed to unwedge herself. She unbuckled the box, picked it up along with the rabbit, and made for the wide, shallow curve of the front steps. She still had her door key but she wasn't sure whether she was entitled to use it. She rang, though she already knew the house was empty; she'd got used to sensing emptiness when she came home from school.

Inside, the house seemed to be dozing. There was a pile of

unopened letters on the mat, so her mother had left before the first post. She crept upstairs to her old room and dumped her case, put the box down next to the bed and the rabbit on the bedside table next to her white leather prayer book, and spun her globe until she found France. St. Agathe wasn't there, so she opened the top drawer of her student desk, found a felt pen and marked it with a dot. Then she shaded in Brittany. It was hard to make the ink stick on the shiny surface. The globe was a twelfth birthday present—she'd asked for a dog. She examined the photo of Form Three on the wall; all the children in her class wore identical uniforms. She couldn't find her face.

She kissed her finger and placed it on the thin lips of the woman whose tinted brown eyes gazed out from a silver frame on her dressing table. The photo was dusty. She'd rescued it from one of her mother's piles of discards and decided it was Great Aunt Winnie. She'd come to believe it, although there was no evidence. She'd always wondered if you could take over someone else's face. If she wasn't there and the twins looked at her school photo and her mother told them she was some other girl, would they believe her? She sat down heavily on her desk chair. Everything in the room was in place; no one had cut her out.

She went downstairs again and checked the biscuit barrel. As usual, it was almost full of her favourites, bourbon creams. She took it to her room and slipped under the pink paisley bedspread. The bed wasn't made up; the mattress was bare. She wasn't sure but she thought she could feel a very small, very slight pain. She leaned over, opened the box and pulled out the diary. It was in a disgusting state. Only the medical records and a few letters in the bottom of the box had escaped unscathed. The marker was still in place in the diary. She dipped into the barrel and split one of the biscuits in two, licking the stiff brown cream off. If she managed to read as far as the secret, everything would be all right, and if she didn't... She breathed deeply.

CHAPTER SEVENTEEN

◦ℓ◦

§ St. Agathe, May 26th, 1911

At nine o'clock precisely, Miss Hodgkins' group assembled and strung themselves along both sides of the wooden causeway leading to the gate into the old town. Frances instructed them to make quick charcoal sketches of whatever their eye alighted upon, each sketch to take no more than ten minutes after which they were to alter their viewpoint and begin afresh. The citizens shunted back and forth along the causeway with their goods, their children and their donkeys, without giving the sketchers a second glance. They are used to these invasions of wealthy would-be artists. It says much for them that, given their present circumstances, they never show the visitors the least disdain.

Miss Winthrop had forgotten her stool, and I offered to go back to the hotel to retrieve it for her, since she moves so slowly. My motives were not altogether pure. Miss Carr had failed to put in an appearance, and I was curious as to where she might be. If I took a circuitous route back to the hotel it would lead me past her lodgings. I had some half-formed idea that I would knock her up if she were still sleeping, and perhaps assist her should she be having difficulty communicating her needs to her landlady. (I was feeling a little guilty on account of my uncharitable thoughts last night.) By craning my neck, I could see that her window was open and her two birds were hunched in their cages, with their backs to the world. I had a word with Madame Lefebvre who was seated in the shop doorway. She told me that Miss Carr had left with her easel and painting sack two hours ago. The parrots were well looked after. Madame is an excellent woman, with a soft spot for animals. She said she was trying them on a new consignment of pumpkin seed and they were taking to it very well. She was happy to have some takers for her merchandise other than the harbour rats. Customers were few and far between this season.

I hurried on, procured the stool, and, having delivered it safely, excused myself to go in search of Miss Carr. Frances appeared not to have noticed her absence—she was too busy setting everyone up. I've learned from Geoffrey that the first two days of these summer sessions are all important. Once the pupils are settled they can be safely left and this allows the instructor uninterrupted time for his own work.

Having no idea which direction Miss Carr had taken, I chose the road along the harbour. One or two boats were putting out in full sail, hoping for some change in their fortunes, but for the most part the water was cluttered with moored craft. I decided to treat myself to a mid-morning pastry, and I turned up a side street heading for my favourite patisserie and found Miss Carr, as round as a cannon ball, perched on the steps of a church, her sketch pad balanced flat on her knee, her easel leaning against the church doorway. I was in two minds as to whether to disturb her and decided to pretend I had not noticed when she called out.

"Mrs. Church? I wish you'd been here five minutes ago. I was having such a splendid talk to a young fisher lad. I believe he wanted money to pose for me—thank goodness he was speaking Breton, not French."

"Oh, you speak Breton?" I could hardly contain my surprise.

"Not at all, but it's much easier on the ear than French, don't you think?"

"Shouldn't you be meeting the others?"

"Couldn't wait for them. I like to get going early. I was a bit late this morning. I'm normally out by six at this time of year, so I can take a break at noon when it starts to swelter."

"Would you like me to tell Miss Hodgkins where she might find you?"

"You can if you like. Won't make much difference."

I didn't remember Miss Carr following this early morning regimen when she was with us in St. Eflamme, but I made no comment. This was a different Miss Carr from the one I once knew.

"I thought I might call on Mr. Church this evening."

"Oh." I was taken aback. "I don't know how he feels about visitors at present. He's working very hard. He has a show in London in September, you know."

"I see." She looked so crestfallen that I felt I should relent and invite her to tea, but Geoffrey's displeasure would cost me too dearly. Why did she have such a capacity for making me feel guilty? "Well, tell him congratulations from Miss Carr. Miss Emily Carr. I don't suppose he remembers me."

"Oh, I'm sure he does."

"He once said I'd be one of the best artists of my day if I stuck at it." And she went back to her sketch, closing me out as if I had already moved on. I was too far away to see whether her work had any merit.

Fanny accosted me as I was taking my evening stroll and told me Miss Carr had failed to show up for lunch or supper at the hotel. My own inclination would have been to leave her to her own devices, but I knew Fanny was worried that she would not receive her fee, so I offered to provide them both with lunch tomorrow. Geoffrey can join us or not as he pleases, I refuse to feel guilty on his account.

My husband is a little jealous of my journal, or of the time I am beginning to expend on it. I must say I look forward to making my entry, trying to reconstruct events as they play out in my mind. Sometimes I plan what I will write, sometimes, like now, I let my hand have its way. Of course I keep the book locked away, but a key is little barrier against prying eyes. Here in France I aspire to write about the things that are too big to be dissected immediately; if I record them undigested, I hope I may come back in a few years' time and make sense of them. Geoffrey, of course, doubts that I have anything in my life that could possibly require clarifying, and he declares he is only interested in what I leave out. This is the best insurance I have against his reading what I have written. I have advised him to keep his own journal, it is very liberating, but he says he is too busy, and he will put me in charge of the liberation department.

§ St. Agathe, May 27th, 1911

It was a cloudy day today but I laid the lunch on the verandah, taking care with the flowers and polishing the best silver, which didn't escape Geoffrey's attention.

"Are you expecting royalty?" he asked as he came into the house from the garden.

"I've laid a place for you," I replied, ignoring the little grunt, which indicated that he had no intention of joining us.

A word about this house. We always rent it when we come to St. Agathe. It is a typical Breton grey stone property, well proportioned, seeming to have sprung out of the landscape. It has three dormer windows, a black, slate roof, a small porch and a spacious white verandah that wraps round the house at the back, so it does not interfere with the simple, elegant lines of the façade. The garden is large and, unfortunately, entirely in the clutches of Claude the ham-fisted gardener who took root here long ago, along with the ancient grape vine over the arbour. I'd rather do without him, he's good for watering and pruning, but not to be trusted with weeding as he knows nothing about flowers and even less about vegetables. The worst part is that he's deaf and dumb so he gets by without learning of his deficiencies. The garden suffers terribly (I always enjoy calling him Clod!). I try to tell myself that it doesn't matter; it isn't as if the place is ours, but after five summers of renting it feels as though we have taken root, too. Geoffrey says we should tolerate Clod just as we do the pink-bellied lizard who lives on the wall over the water butt. (The lizard has more charm, and the garden is not Geoffrey's concern.)

Miss Carr arrived early. As I helped her into her chair, I hoped she might have changed her mind about worms since the lawn was covered in worm casts. She settled in with a great shudder before presenting me with a greasy paper containing an evil cheese that she'd picked up in town.

"It's supposed to be sheep," she remarked, "but it smells like wet dog. I thought it might make an interesting challenge."

I thanked her and took the object into the kitchen where I turned it out on an indigo plate and added a few sprigs of parsley so that at least it would please the eye. From the kitchen window, I spied Frances' parasol bobbing along the crest of the hedge and I left her to make her entry and settle in with Miss Carr.

When I came out onto the verandah again, the two of them were sitting side by side locked in silence. I said something placatory—I'm a great placator, ironing out seems to be my major talent, one of these days I'll burn a hole.

"I was just about to ask Miss Carr if she requires a private viewing of her portfolio," Frances smiled at me. "She doesn't seem inclined to join the rest of my pupils."

"*Bonjour mes élèves,*" said Miss Carr (her pronunciation was atrocious). "That's what my French teacher used to say at the start of class. It just came to me. I always wondered why she called us elves. Then she'd say '*asseyez vous*'—and we would. Sit down, I mean. We were very obedient. Good morning, my pupils! We only had French for a year, Quebec's too far from British Columbia to bother us. So I suppose I'm an elf, still. Not a very obedient one, I'm afraid." She sighed and subsided, as though she regretted her long speech.

Frances said nothing, and I served the soup, a cold concoction with an avocado base. I was rather proud of it. Miss Carr sniffed it and lifted her spoon gingerly.

"Do you enjoy French food, Miss Carr?" Fanny enquired.

"The bread gets on my nerves; it always tastes like brown paper, and there's too much fish."

I had prepared a dressed crab as our entree, so I absented myself from the table in a panic to rustle up an alternative.

When I came back with the crab and a savory omelette, the two of them were embarked on some kind of discussion and I was able to concentrate on finishing my soup, relieved that it wasn't intended to be hot.

"—it's interesting you should say that; we appear to be steering similar courses, though I thought it was a new technique. I'm not sure of the results." I glanced over my spoon and saw that Fanny's eyes were shining. "Have you had any success?"

"Oh, I just dabble. I'll try anything to get where I want to be."

"Me too, me too. I am experimenting with a mixture of pastel and gouache. I find the textural differences, dry and wet, can be ...happy. To portray the sea using a dry medium sets up a sort of juxtaposition that can be...different." Fanny was trying to hold back, but she couldn't do it when she was excited. "The liquid boats, so insubstantial when it comes right down to it, a dry and liquid sky, finding colour through absence of colour, the dark rim around rocks—sometimes it works, don't you find that Miss Carr? I do believe in water-colour as the ultimate medium for expressing nature, but it cannot be all things to all men. Oil can be so difficult, and ultimately quite disappointing, don't you think?"

Miss Carr took a large helping of crab. "Please call me Emily, the family calls me Milly but we'll skip that, shall we? This absence. The absence of colour, which produces colour. Mr. Church used to talk of it. He very much favours outlining his forms in black. I tried it myself. I must ask him if he has developed his ideas further."

"It's a useful technique—interesting in water-colour where it is more unexpected."

"Absence. I've been trying to get more of it. My work's too much there. I want to put everything in. It's as though I only had a day, or at most a week to get it all down. I've been trying to concentrate on absence, but I can't help preferring presence. I can't bear all this awaying, I want everything to be here. Right here. Now. This minute. Know what I mean?"

"Not at all. I love leaving. Moving on. Changing. I look at what they're doing in Paris, how they rally round the Fauves and paint nothing but fauve, and now it's the Cubists and cubes, but I can't seem to hang on long enough to cleave to any of their fads. I find my own way. Leaving's such a drug. Do you know, I don't own anything and I don't want to. Put me on a railway station and you've lost me forever. I have to be free so I'm ready for change. My mother has so much difficulty with all this. I used to try to bottle it up, but I don't any longer. Maybe I'll settle down when I'm her age."

"Where is your mother?"

"In Wellington at present. That's New Zealand. On the other side of the world really. I sent her a picture of me outside the Café de la Paix the other day, but I had to explain away the wine bottle. They're still dry back home, though we women are finally allowed to vote."

"Why would you want to do that?"

"Because our opinions count, why else?"

"Of course." I don't think Emily had thought about this. She was silent for a while and then she piped up. "But don't you want to go back?"

"Never."

"Oh, how could you say that? I can't wait. If I could go back today, I'd promise never to leave again—even if I can't vote. Does that make me a stick in the mud?"

"Oh, I think I've just been taking the leaving drug too long. Absence becomes a way of life. The love of leaving—I like that phrase, don't you? I'd like to do a suite of drawings based on it. Maybe I will—everything scampering off the edge of the page. I never get round to anything much when I'm teaching. I shall go to England for the winter and perhaps to Italy in the spring if I have made enough sales."

I'd never heard Fanny be so frank.

"Do you support yourself by your work?"

"Well, there is no one else to support me."

"That's extraordinary. You have no resource to fall back on?"

"None whatsoever."

"So, it is possible?" Miss Carr's eyes were suddenly full of tears. She brushed them away with her cuff and leaned forward. "Will you walk back with me to my lodgings?"

By the time I'd finished my soup and cleared the dishes they had completely demolished the crab and Miss Carr had made short work of the brown paper baguette. She seemed to have a mighty appetite. I was excluded almost entirely from the conversation and, after they got through the dessert and coffee, they got up and strolled down the verandah steps sharing the parasol and leaving me to finish the omelette. Miss Carr's voice reached me from the other side of the hedge.

"I always like to stoke up when I'm invited out."

§ St. Agathe, June 5th, 1911

Some days have passed since I made my last entry. Geoffrey has had a bad chest that needs poulticing every few hours, and because of his fever he has been unable to complete the landscape that has caused him so much anguish over the past three weeks. As a result, our life has been in turmoil. When things are not going swimmingly for him, everything sinks. Nothing I can do pleases him, the house is a cauldron of problems, cushions are too soft, pillows too hard, paintings are wrongly hung, the terra-cotta pots in the hall are too ugly to live with and must be replaced immediately. The house and furnishings do not belong to us, which adds to my anxiety.

When we are in England, he is much more agreeable and we have none of this nonsense. It is at times like this that I thank my stars we have no children, one child is quite enough in this household. And it is just as well that I have decided against trying my hand at water-colours as I planned to do before we came to France. Geoffrey would seize on them to make a further mockery of me. I feel like a maypole, twirling aimlessly with all my ribbons knotted together. I am finding it hard to be amusing.

I have bumped into Frances a couple of times in the market and each time she has been with Miss Carr. They seem to be getting along famously, and I must admit I felt a little stab of envy, not for their friendship, but for the fact that, for the present, I can have no part in it. When friendship between two girls becomes far advanced—or should I say if, not when—it is impossible to prise them apart in order for a third party to gain admission. The chain is locked, there is no way in. This was my experience at school where I worked very hard to be an insider, and I haven't observed that things change for the better in the adult world. Miss Carr asked again when she might visit my husband. I was inclined to say 'go this minute if you are prepared to wrap him in red flannel and mash up his lunch,' but I put her off with some trifling excuse. I am surprised that Fanny hasn't dropped by at the house, she is usually a frequent visitor. Perhaps she is afraid of germs.

⚹

Frances chases Emily up the hill and half the women in town chart their progress. Fishwives, basket-weavers and lace-makers stand in doorways, arms crossed, heads tilted. A mattress-maker laughs so hard she chokes on the bodkin that she clenches between her lips like a cigar. News of the fracas at the table outside the hotel spreads like a rash, they whisper and shout, *"Écoute!* The teacher banged her fist on the table and made the silver jump. She broke a dish and there were words, English words. She shouted at the fat one and the fat one shouted back." It was moments like this that made the invasion of their streets worthwhile.

The slope is steep and the seed merchant's shop at the top impossibly far off. After the first rush Emily realizes that her legs aren't up to the climb. She rests in a doorway, leaning back against the doorknob. The door swings open and she swoons into the arms of an elderly man in a greasy black cap. Frances stops in her tracks and holds onto her stays to contain her laughter. The old man cackles, everyone is laughing—it is what Emily hates most. She can laugh at herself, draw cartoons of herself, but this kind of laughter is like soap in her eyes. All these peasant women in their long black dresses and white caps remind her of vultures waiting to swoop and Frances Hodgkins is leading the way. "Be quiet!" she shouts, and then, "Shut up!"

Frances snaps her jaw shut. Emily relaxes.

The victory is short-lived. "No one tells me to shut up!" Frances approaches, her rolled parasol has become a weapon. She is still grinning. Emily thrusts aside the helping arm of the old man. His breath smells of aniseed and his fingers are stained with nicotine. Suddenly Frances lowers the weapon and holds out her hand. The gesture is so unexpected that Emily loses her resolve; she responds without thinking, she is smiling, then laughing along with the rest.

"What cuckoos we are!" Frances links one arm in hers, turns her around and together they march back down the hill, singing, "Oh, the Grand Old Duke of York, he had ten thousand men, he marched them up to the top of the hill and he marched them down again."

The locals crowd windows and doorways. They are used to *étrangers* who have all the time in the world to be difficult and demanding. They are used to the foreigners' harsh voices and their strange attachment to animals, but the lady with the parasol, the teacher who has been in their midst for more than one season seemed to be more restrained, her behaviour can be relied on. She gives bonbons to the children and even to the dogs, and has a friendly word for everyone in a French they can all understand. She speaks of the weather and she wastes a lot of time copying views of the harbour onto blank sheets of paper, but at least she works, if teaching people to do the same thing can be counted as work. And now she has touched the fat lady. Foreign ladies generally move slowly like galleons. They do not shout and run after each other on hills on hot afternoons, then turn right around and trip back into town like two plump milk jugs, their handles entwined, turning their heads neither to the left nor right. And singing! There is a local saying equating fat ladies with frogs—if you kiss them you will catch the plague. The teacher is marked.

"You know, that nursery rhyme was one of the best things England ever exported," Frances gasps as they lower themselves back into their seats at the table. "On my last trip from New Zealand our ship called at the Solomon Islands, and I took the opportunity to go ashore. I left the others, they had no curiosity, and I strolled through the settlement. There were some children playing in a ditch. They ran away when I came upon the scene, but they were singing—and you know the song? 'Georgie Porgie pudding and pie, kissed the girls and made them cry.' That's what the Colonisers gave them. A song about a poxy king, King George, a single road, a crushed coral road and not a stitch of clothing to put on their backs. There were giant butterflies high up in the trees, big as dinner plates—the English shot them with guns, don't you hate the English sometimes?"

"My father was English."

"And mine. So what?"

Emily stares at Frances wide eyed. How is it possible for a woman to have travelled so widely, to know so much? The creamer she broke lies on the table, and she mops up the spilt cream with her handkerchief, then stops. The gesture is much too domestic.

"I have plenty of acquaintances back home but I rely on my sisters for company and I prefer to live alone," Emily says.

Frances nods, understanding. "One must live alone."

Emily is ready to unburden, but she holds back. The closest she has ever come to unburdening herself is to Mary, the Indian woman she befriended (against everyone's advice), because Indians don't criticize or judge. She thinks of her two English friends in Victoria, they appear to be soft as marshmallow, but they are tough, always on their mettle, always available for sketching expeditions or for meting out solace over lost sales. Like her sisters, they have no great notion of fun. She realizes, suddenly, that the nearest they come to a laugh is a sharp little intake of breath, more a snigger, though always decorous. Not one of them can hold a candle to Frances Hodgkins in the laughter department. Here is someone to be reckoned with; the lady has a considerable reputation as an artist. She has painted more, exhibited more, won more prizes than any person of Emily's acquaintance, with the exception of Mr. Church, who claims to have done everything that is worth doing. Frances is intimidating, yet somehow they seem to have found a middle ground—perhaps it is because they are two maiden ladies adrift in a land where the artistic standards are so high as to be out of reach. It is a land where the rules are completely different, where the people, at least in Paris, actually welcome the bizarre and unconventional, and possess an openness to change that Frances apparently finds intoxicating, and Emily finds overwhelming. Emily observes that Frances hasn't melded into this society, but neither has she admitted to any desire to do so. She's explained that she needs to earn a living and she has no time to spend debating philosophical conundrums in French cafés, flirting with the men who all seem to find their own ideas so intoxicating that no one else's have the least importance.

Emily makes up her mind to be strong. There will be no more relapses, no more repeats of the illness that has knocked her down twice in the last few years, no more wet dreams. No one, particularly Frances, must detect that she is rancid inside. No one will know of the terrible purges she had to undergo, how certain people felt they had a ticket to enter her darkness. She has not left darkness behind, but at last she has found someone who will decode the novel sensations that threaten to overwhelm her whenever she leaves Victoria. In the heapings of praise she is receiving for her work from her new teacher, she has a buffer against the weekly pleas that she give up art and return home. It is worth the sacrifice of a couple of months in the elephant. She knows what it is to have a true friend and she will hold onto her if it takes her last breath.

Emily grins as she recalls how the mad chase started. Coffee is a newly acquired taste for her, she learned to like it at the Colarossi. She confided this to Frances and went on to tell her how, after leaving her post for a coffee and a cigarette, she returned to find the male model had been induced to remove his clothes. Naturally, she refused to go back into the room. Frances lost her temper, not because she felt strongly about painting from the nude, but because of the refusal to acknowledge that there were times when, for art's sake, prurience must take precedence over propriety. She'd refused to back down, and they'd almost got themselves in a tangle.

"Did you mean three p's, prurience, precedence, propriety?" Emily studies Frances's face as she gathers together the pieces of broken china. She must be careful not to let her sniff out the darkness. Perhaps she wouldn't care, but it is too much to risk. Fortunately she is smiling. She leans across and grabs Emily's hand. "I just had a vision of you, Milly Carr. A young girl at the art school in San Francisco, or maybe at that dreary academy you tell me you attended in London, surrounded by plaster feet, marble torsos and reluctant models in Spanish costume. (They were probably ladies of the night doing their day shift. I'll bet they undressed for their evening work!) And there you were, stuck in front of a death mask, clutching your charcoal—concentrating so hard all your buttons were popping, while you waited, dutifully, for the approval of a second-rate teacher. That's what I saw. You. Dribbling away your family fortunes in one useless exercise after another. Your life has been so constraining, so constricting—so plebeian. You are through and through Colonial and unless you pull up your socks, you'll end up barking mad with nothing to show for it, all alone in your little house on your draughty Canadian island. You'll vanish without a trace. Just beware, Milly Carr!"

What impertinence! What understanding! It is confounding to hear things put so plainly. Emily can't allow her to entertain this, not yet. She flashes back, "We're always most cross when we perceive our own flaws in other people, Fanny." Unwittingly, she has hit the mark. She spies Madame La Directrice looking down at them over her balcony. Up to now, Emily knows, Frances has had a good rapport with Madame, in fact she is receiving free room and board on account of the business she brings to the hotel, but now Madame is frowning.

"I suspect the old harridan's lying in wait for me, she'll probably put me out on the street for breaking her blasted china," Frances remarks, cheerfully.

"Why ever would she do such a thing?"

"Just watch."

Emily sits back, wondering how they have covered so much territory so fast. No one but her family calls her Milly. And no one would tolerate the word blasted.

"Mademoiselle?" Madame disappears, then reappears in the doorway of the hotel. There is a vigorous exchange with much hand wringing and reddening of cheeks, which Emily can make nothing of. It ends abruptly, and Frances motions her into the foyer.

"It's all right. I've said I'll pay for the breakage and I've promised we'll be good in future. She's afraid of her reputation. She's given me two days to find another place. Come on, let's go up to my room." Emily is shocked. How can she take this so casually?

Frances' room is tiny, but the bed is huge and a large black cat lounges on the pillow. Emily reaches out to pat it then realizes it is a velvet cat.

"How very life-like." She sinks down on the only chair in the room and folds her hands to stop them from straying in the direction of the fake. If Frances isn't worried about her impending eviction, then she won't worry either.

Frances snatches up the animal and cradles it in her arms then tosses it up and catches one paw. "Meet Gatto—that's his name when we're in Italy, Gatto Moro—in France, he's Gateau—that's cake—isn't he scrumptious?"

"Don't you have any live pets?" Emily thinks about Monsewer who meows interminably when he's shut out of her room; she thinks of her sheep dogs back home, and of Rachel and Josephine who've been caged up for far too long. She resolves to take the parrots along on her next sketching trip.

"No."

"Then you don't like live animals?"

"Of course I do. I love animals, but it's a mistake to get too fond of a pet, one gets too harrowed when they depart. It must be so awful to have to break oneself of scratching an ear, don't you think? Ay, there's the rub."

Emily isn't sure if Frances is being serious. "If they are to live, they must eventually die." She feels the remark is probably provincial and she takes out her cigarette case with a sophisticated sweep, making sure the gold initials are on view.

Frances accepts the proffered cigarette. They light up and

inhale deeply. Recalling the stains on the old man's hands, Emily puts on her gloves. She thinks she would like to have soft, white hands.

§ St. Agathe, June 6th, 1911

Miss Winthrop told me there was something of a fracas at the hotel. She was taking tea at a nearby table when whatever it was erupted between Miss Hodgkins and another lady. She was not aware of whom Fanny's adversary was since Miss Carr had not attended any of the classes and she assumed she was a summer visitor. I questioned her closely, amazed that Fanny made a spectacle of herself in public, but Miss Winthrop was only able to tell me that Miss Carr took off up the hill like a scalded hare, with Miss Hodgkins waving her parasol in hot pursuit. I tried unsuccessfully to equate Miss Carr's gait with that of a hare and the very idea of Frances waving her parasol made me wonder if Miss Winthrop had been sitting too long in the sun. I was impatient to find Fanny and question her, but when I finally ran her down, she shrugged the incident off, saying there had been a slight contretemps but she and Miss Carr were now on good terms. I relaxed a little when she referred to her adversary as Miss Carr. Obviously they were on less intimate terms than I had suspected.

The hotel terrace has recently been taken over by a rather loud posse of military officers who have been dispatched to St. Agathe on the rumour of a railway strike. I am not sure what good they would do should the threatened strike proceed, but they certainly enliven the place with their masculine display and their colourful uniforms. All the hotels in town are now full to overflowing. When I next joined Miss Winthrop for tea, she was all agog with the news that she and three of Fanny's other pupils had been asked to vacate their digs in order to make way for the military men. They had, of course, refused to leave, and Miss Hodgkins came to their rescue, but not before she had been asked to move out of her own room. This was very bad news indeed and I searched in vain for Fanny to find out what her living arrangements would be. In addition to the room that the hotel allowed her to occupy, they provided her with a rent-free studio in a storage room tucked away at the back of the fourth floor. She would be lost without a place to work.

I took a walk out of town to calm myself, and spied Miss Carr planted in a meadow beside the road. I turned to look at what could possibly interest her in the scene she had chosen. It was perfectly ordinary, a small cluster of oaks, a hedgerow, a distant glimpse of the sea and the turret of a church.

There was an empty birdcage sitting on the grass beside her, and my first thought was to wonder how she got herself out here loaded down with her easel, her paint sack and a bird in a cage. The green parrot was attached to her stool by its ankle, I didn't notice him at first, he blended with the grasses and buttercups and he had his head under his wing. I climbed up to where she was sitting to ask after Fanny, and just as I arrived Miss Carr threw herself off her stool. I'm quite sure she had charted my progress along the road so my sudden appearance didn't surprise her. I stood looking down at her, completely non-plussed, just as I was intended to be. The sun glinted off her gold tooth, setting fire to her mouth. It crossed my mind that I didn't much like her. The parrot's head had emerged from its wing and it stared, rudely sticking its tongue in and out of its beak.

I examined her painting, in order to give her time to get up. She had placed the trees in an interesting triangle and the preliminary oil colour was applied in thick, luscious brush strokes. She was

234

using the shadow well, allowing it to provide depth but also structure and tone—simplifying and emphasizing—shaping the rather
ordinary scene into a small bijou without departing from the essential truth of what was before us. I remember that she always had
difficulty simplifying, but she seemed to have conquered the
problem. I wondered if it was possible that Frances effected this
remarkable sea-change in her work, though it seemed unlikely in
such a short space of time. She was still lying flat on the ground,
blinking those pollen-centred eyes. It was almost as though she
read my mind.

"Your friend Miss Hodgkins, is she to be trusted?"

I was startled by the boldness of the question and the emotion
in her voice.

"Why, yes." What was I to say? Given the evidence of the last
few days, I was beginning to have my doubts. She hoisted herself
into a sitting position, leaving her outline in the crushed clover.

"Good." She picked up a fallen brush, then heaved herself onto
the stool and went back to work as if I had never interrupted her.
The parrot screamed "*Au secours.*"

"Watch your beak, bird." Miss Carr tapped on the easel,
without looking up.

"*Tais toi,*" I added, wagging my finger at the parrot for good
measure.

I wondered whether he was emitting a genuine cry for help and
who taught him to ask? Perhaps it was Miss Carr's landlady. She no
doubt felt obliged to entertain Miss Carr and her birds after the
brushes were put away and there was little to do until bedtime.
Even Geoffrey can't work by the light of a paraffin lamp.
Something must have passed between them. Or possibly Miss Carr
was spending her evenings with Frances and abandoning her birds
to pick up all the bad language that floated up from the bar next

door to the seed shop.

"You seem to be getting along quite well with Miss Hodgkins," I ventured.

"Passably." There was a long pause.

"I don't suppose you know where she is to be found?"

"She's staying in the other guest room at Madame Lefebvre's."

"She's staying in your lodging house?"

"Yes," and then she looked up again. "I haven't shown her my poles yet."

I had no idea what she meant.

"I suppose I shall get up the courage. She says she used to like to paint the natives. What do they call the natives where she comes from?"

"May Ories, I believe."

"That's it. She showed me a study of a head. It was merely a likeness."

I have one of Fanny's Maori portraits in my sewing room at home. It was painted in the nineties before she came to Europe, but it is such a beautifully realized, sad little face, a young darkie, with a baby in her arms, wearing a bright native costume. I paid her five guineas for the portrait and my husband said it was robbery. Now Miss Carr seemed to be confirming his opinion. "I think her portraits are first rate," I replied, preparing to leave. I couldn't imagine why Miss Carr would be painting Poles, I very much doubted that she had visited that country, though there were a large number of Polish and Russian expatriates in Paris.

"I've never been much interested in painting from life myself," she said, "but I'm beginning to warm to it, I can see how the figure can become part of the composition. Cézanne uses fruit in much the same way, not as an end in itself like those monsters your husband has produced."

I was stung by her tactlessness, and I wondered what Fanny had told her of Geoffrey's work—she certainly hadn't laid eyes on his recent pictures. It felt like a betrayal. The parrot repeated '*Merde*' several times, but by now the word was old hat and I stared him down. He is slightly less dyspeptic than the grey bird I remember from the railway station, though he is going bald. I decided to distance myself as quickly as possible.

"So what do you think of my daub, be truthful."

I did not feel like flattering her with a truthful opinion, and, since I am no expert, she would discount my views anyway so I simply said, "It appears to be coming along nicely," and turned my back.

As I climbed down the bank I heard her speaking, presumably to me, though I didn't wait to catch the full drift. "The Gorse and the Oaks are a bit chewed up, but they'll do. They don't measure up to our Garry Oaks back home of course, but they're the next best thing. The bracken's exactly right, and the May trees, but there's no Camas, there's the rub." This confirmed my suspicion that she didn't really need a listener, much less a critic. I wondered how long it would take Frances to reach this conclusion and how she would get on, finding herself in such close proximity to Miss Carr.

§ St. Agathe, June 7th, 1911

It occurred to me as I blotted my last page that I write as if my life revolves solely around Miss Hodgkins and Miss Carr, so today's entry will be closer to those that I make when I am in England. I suspect that I am obsessive. No one has ever remarked on this, perhaps no one has noticed, though Geoffrey once observed, correctly, that I have a tendency to worry. One of the things about which I obsess is time, using it and filling it economically and efficiently.

Today, as usual, I rose at seven a.m., put on the coffee pot and set the table for *petit dejeuner*. In France we eat au Breton, taking our café au lait in the exquisitely glazed bowls that we bought from a Russian potter in St. Eflamme. I heated a little extra milk as is the custom here, sliced a baguette and made sure that the butter was no more than a day old and the confiture was set out in the cut glass dish that has accompanied us from England. I spread a blue checked cloth and found a nosegay of orange flowers for the centre of the table. My husband favours apricot jam but it is not easy to find. I enjoy the ritual of our simple, elegant 'little lunch,' it is so much more satisfying in the preparation and easier on the digestion than the bacon and eggs we have for breakfast when we are in England.

Whether we eat our first meal together depends entirely on Geoffrey's mood. He does not have to speak to let me know whether the day ahead is to be fraught. If I see from his sheets that he has been tossing and turning in the night, and if he greets me with a sigh I know there is trouble ahead. But occasionally he is whistling *'La donna e mobile'* when I bring up the jug of hot water and clean towels, and the whistling gets jauntier as he strops his razor. I have no ear for opera, but I always welcome Verdi into my day. If it is a sigh morning, I snatch my breakfast quickly, digging into the jar for my jam, cooling my coffee with cold milk and drinking it from one of the kitchen cups. But if it is a whistling morning like today, we breakfast together and he outlines his plans for the hours ahead, how much he expects to accomplish and how I can assist him; occasionally he will ask me to solve a problem he is having with a painting, and, when I succeed, he takes my hand and tells me he can't do without me. This is merely talk, but it always gives me a little start of pleasure when he expresses his appreciation aloud. Today he had no news to share with me, and we breakfasted in companionable silence.

After breakfast, I am free until eleven a.m. when I am generally called on to make more coffee. Geoffrey jots down any art supplies he needs on a blackboard, which hangs on the wall outside his studio, and I transcribe the list, taking care not to disturb him if he's started work. I can generally manage to pick up the shopping in one trip to town though occasionally it takes more than one, particularly if the wine-merchant is having an off day and refuses to deliver our order, or if I need to visit the cobbler or the laundry. After this there are chores to be done, the usual rather dull round of cleaning and washing and ironing (I don't do sheets and shirts) and then I am free to tend my flower beds on the days when Clod is ruining someone else's paradise. Twice a week I take French lessons with Madame Lorraine, a retired school ma'am who is very strict and insists that I practice my verb conjugations every day and that I hand in at least three exercises and one short composition at every class. They are returned etched in red. Geoffrey is amused at my despair. It's my ambition to accomplish a clean sheet and when that happens he says he will frame it and hang it in a place of honour. Madame says my accent is good though it has a touch of Lyonnaise. (I had to look up Lyons on the map, as we've never been there.) I prepare lunch and supper and, if there's anything left of the day, I am free to spend it taking tea with the summer visitors I have befriended, or, if I'm lucky, in a long tête-à-tête with Fanny who can always be counted on to make me laugh. It's not a particularly relaxing summer, but I love every minute. I have never been one to waste time though now I am wasting it by the bucketful, moping over the fact that I never catch a glimpse of my old friend. Gaspiller—to waste, it sounds much more pleasurable in French.

I suppose that after Miss Carr's shenanigans, I must seem very boring. I shall look into ways to make myself more exciting, but meantime the ironing awaits and after that Madame Lorraine will be knocking on the door.

🌴

Frances is propped up on Emily's pillows. She has taken off her stays and her jewelry, and her thick dark hair hangs loose around her shoulders. Emily notes with satisfaction that it has a mesh of silver running through it and the temples are quite grey. Emily's hair turned grey when she was in Suffolk, and she's almost forgotten what colour it used to be. It springs out from her head much too vigorously and has to be restrained with a hat or a snood. Frances cares more than Emily about appearances. She protests, sometimes too forcefully, that she is ugly and she hates to be caught by a camera. Emily notes how her hair shines as if it has been attacked by a hundred daily brush strokes, her nose is powdered and her fingernails are shaped to perfect ovals, with shy half moons at their base. She sighs. She knows she's a scarecrow, Alice never fails to remind her of it, but it never bothered her until she arrived in St. Agathe. She decides to have a good scrub tomorrow to see if she can get rid of the paint from under her nails and maybe buy some lip colour, a little rouge and a new hat if she can find something big enough, and cheap—her hair is beyond rescue. She considers earrings, but they pinch. Frances wears long, interesting earrings and changes them according to her costume.

Frances lights a cheroot and blows perfect smoke rings. They have shared a bottle of wine at supper and now she produces another. Emily has been warned against drinking by her doctors, but the warning was unnecessary, she wasn't tempted, since nobody in her circle drinks alcohol. But now she is with a connoisseur. The foul taste of the wine begins to grow on her and she enjoys feeling light-headed afterwards. It is good to be able to get dizzy once in a while and know you'll be over it in a jiffy and it isn't a sign that you're in for another barrage of electricity, or worse.

"What do you think they should name ladies from the Dominions?" Frances asks, watching her smoke-ring loop and writhe into a smudge. "I mean ladies with a capital L, not the other kind."

Emily draws on her cheroot. "Dominoes?" She follows the course of the ash as it falls into her wine. "We should all wear black and white polka dot dresses when we're in Britain. That way there'd be no mistaking us for locals, and we'd save them the trouble of scoping us out."

"What about Dominicans? We could wear black cowls. Or Dominatrixes!"

"What are they?"

"Women who carry whips. We'd carry cat-o'-nine tails."

"My goodness, what a terrific idea. Would we be allowed to use them?"

"We'd be encouraged to use them. That's what they're for."

Emily giggles. She's given up trying to disguise her innocence and Frances doesn't care. Fresh pathways are opening up faster than the new boulevards in Paris. All this new thought has been lying idle, bunging up the front of her brain. Now it demands to be examined, usually as she is falling asleep. Lately she's taken to re-lighting the lamp, opening up her sketchbook, and drawing cartoons, mostly of forty-year-old babies. Her sketchbook is turning into a sort of self-mocking, visual diary. The cartoons unnerve her. They always have. Far from putting her to sleep, they keep her wide-awake.

"If you were an animal, which one would you be?" Emily asks, taking another swig of Rouge, swallowing the ash.

"A zebra," says Frances, "a zebra in a black and white coat."

"A zebra? But that's African. What about a kangaroo?"

"I've never seen a kangaroo. They don't live in New Zealand. I suppose you'd like to be a bison."

"I've never seen a bison. They live on the plains!"

"I'd be a badger."

"Why a badger?"

"Because they're native to England."

"Ah, so you really do want to be English?"

"No, not really. I just want to pass for English. It makes life so much more negotiable. Everyone in England thinks New Zealanders spend their lives herding sheep, and it's true, more's the pity. We've got more sheep than people. We also have albatrosses. I have one hanging round my neck. It's called Dunedin."

"They're supposed to be unlucky birds. What are they like?"

"Big."

"I want to see one. I love the tale of the Ancient Mariner."

"They have an awful lot of trouble finding a mate."

"Like us?"

"No, not like us. We don't want mates. We have our work."

Emily gulps. She's never heard it put so well.

"If they fail in the quest, the males have to circle the icy wastes for two years. Then they come home and try again."

"I'm glad I'm not an albatross."

"Maybe you are." Frances looks at her oddly.

Emily shifts. To deflect the look she asks, "If you were a badger what part of the badger would you most like to be?" The room is beginning to spin.

"The ear? Would I like to be a badger's ear? No, I don't think so. The eye? The arse? Yes. That's it. I'd like to be a badger's bottom. That's what we call ourselves in New Zealand. Badger's behinds." Frances grins and Emily convulses.

"Badger's behinds!" They fall about on the bed, laughing.

"There are so few of us back home," Frances gasps, "and strange ideas aren't welcome in case we lose control. Heaven help us if we ever lose control! Heaven help me, if they ever heard me say arse!" She sits up, suddenly serious. "We've got nothing to give each other back home because we're all much too frightened."

"Oh, so are we. We clump together along the border like lemmings."

"We scuttle art, it's of no value. We sacrifice it on the altar of good taste. He that does not conform in thought and word is outcast. And as for she, she was never incast!"

"We're just the same. They say I'm a scarecrow and I pretend not to hear."

"But of course you do."

"Do you think I should rouge my lips?"

"Don't go back. Stay here. Stay in France, Milly. Think what we could do together."

The room sways. The idea of staying in France with Frances is fresh and lovely and completely preposterous.

"They love everything that's different, here. They actually dare you to be different. They're open. Don't you find it wonderful? In New Zealand, you can't even polish your shoes on Sunday."

"Oh, we spend all of Sunday on our knees."

"Our lips are frozen into permanent O's. We're cold as the penguins' feet on St. Kilda's beach! You should feel the wind there. You haven't felt wind till you've lived in Dunedin." Emily observes carefully that Frances' accent changes when she talks about home.

"We have wind in Victoria, too. And rain. You haven't felt rain till you've lived in Victoria."

"It doesn't rain in Dunedin. It gushes!"

"In Victoria, it torrents!"

"The only drawing they appreciate is when they draw a fire to make it blaze."

"Or withdraw money from the bank."

"But they like it much better when they put money in!"

"We're in the same boat!" Emily stretches out and touches Frances' arm.

"Ahoy there, sailor!" Frances grins. "You know, there's one good thing about New Zealand. I learned to appreciate colour there. Let me ask you something." She takes Emily's hand and Emily draws in her breath, anticipating a question she cannot answer.

"What did you do in Canada when Queen Victoria died?"

"What did we do?" She hoots with laughter. "That one's easy— we pinned a black rosette to the door, and two on the horse, and we wore black ribbons. What next?"

"Back home the whole place went into mourning. I swear it was worse than England. Everything was black crêpe. There were black blinds at the windows, everyone on the street looked like crows. Until you get right down to absolute black, you can't appreciate colour. I say thank you to Queen Victoria and Dunedin first thing every morning. Thank you for giving me colour."

"To Her Majesty." Emily holds up her glass for a refill and Frances grabs it. "This is the most fun I've had since I used to roll on the ground in the orchard." She is almost bursting with the pleasure of enjoying herself.

"That was fun?"

"Oh yes, I put butter on my face and the petals all stuck."

"Sounds wild."

"What's the most fun you ever had?"

"Paris, and after that, Morocco. You haven't seen light and

colour till you've been to Morocco. It bursts your eyes. And it's fun."

"And what kind of fun do you have in Paris?"

"Oh, I don't know. Just being there's fun."

"Don't you like being here?"

"Yes. Yes, I like being in Brittany. I like being everywhere. I like being with you."

"So, we're friends for sure?" Emily grips Frances' wrist.

"Absolutely. And you'll endure, no matter what. You're strong, Milly Carr, it'll take a lot more than the likes of me to put your lamp out."

The following morning, there is no breakfast. They are tucked in Emily's bed like a pair of spoons. There is no painting that day either. Frances peels herself off the mattress to go to work, but Emily doesn't leave the room. She lies on her back, tugging on the long beaded string that keeps the wooden ceiling fan in motion. The effort is too much, and she attaches the string to her good toe and treadles her foot until even this is too much trouble. Being hung over isn't fun, but it is a milestone. Her head won't obey her, nightmarish thoughts crowd in thick and fast, tumbling over each other in their efforts to be recognized then drifting away as soon as she catches up. It's a bit like the aftereffects of the 'cure'. She pushes down hard on the waves of nausea that just miss surfacing, the way she learned in the sanatorium. She is trying to recall what Fanny said about enduring.

Tantalizing. Emily tries the word. It sums up her feelings more or less. About St. Agathe. About her progress with her work. Above all, about her teacher. It is like wearing a blindfold and

245

reaching out, arms extended, and the thing you think you're reaching for is just beyond your fingertips, so close you can feel the heat of it yet too far away to identify. It has no obvious shape or texture or smell and it requires one to have complete trust in the unknown. She craves it, the thought of it makes her itch, makes her want to roar.

She mutters aloud as she sketches in the little graveyard opposite the railway station where there is no one to answer but the dead. She likes to sort out her thoughts in graveyards. In Paris she haunted the cemetery. She crouched in front of the graves of accomplished men, while Monsewers Picasso, Modigliani, Braque and company flitted around the heart of Montparnasse, painting up a blizzard at her elbow. Contemplating the lives of corpses was one way of coming to terms with the cockiness of Paris. They thought they were the bee's knees but even so, everyone in this hoity toity French town would eventually wind up under a marble slab.

The sketches she has completed in St. Agathe are piled on the armoire in her room on top of her most important work; last night she sorted through them and gave them a low pass mark. Some of the landscapes are not bad. She knows she's managed to clear away all the fretting details and find the nub, but she still has miles to go. Thank goodness Frances is still delighted with her, still bubbling with admiration.

There is too much to do, never enough time, the light fades too fast and she lies in bed waiting for it to return and breaks out in sweats. Frances says the sweats have something to do with the approach of mid-life, but she knows better. The sweats are a symptom. Something nameless is going to happen and she must be prepared. Now, this minute she is right where she needs to be, and the wonder of it is that it's not British Columbia.

Rocking back and forth on her narrow stool, she thinks of how she resented the trade she had to make this summer. Any other year, she'd be making her way up the coast, catching whatever rides she could in boats and canoes, trying to find a horse, anything to avoid using Shanks' pony. (Ironically, her absent toe is always a stumbling block.) There is long light in the north—she spends busy hours charting Indian villages and settlements, sketching their totem poles and trying to capture the workmanship in the carved canoes. It takes time to get used to the lack of boundaries, the unending sweep of trees, the surge of the tides, lakes that are neither wet nor deep, merely smooth unending pools of light, impossible to hold in your eye. These summers make winters worthwhile. 'I can't' vanishes, city tantrums are lost in the density of salal, glossy even in the deepest shadow. She is transfixed by the force of it all, she softens up her bristles and lets it leak in slowly, waiting until she is ready to open herself up to it completely. Each year, she needs to learn again to slow her breathing and her rhythms so she can gradually harness the energy and be at one with the sky and trees, and then they will let her transpose them honestly onto paper. It's the only real opening she has ever experienced and now she is on the brink of another, quite different, but equally powerful.

She likes oils for outdoors, their consistency is right, but Fanny insists on the delicacy and power of watercolour, and maybe that's better for France. Watercolour isn't suited to the north, though when she carts her sticky, half finished canvases through the bush when she's on the move, they land up covered in mulch and pine needles and she has all the bother of making preliminary sketches on paper and finishing them off when she gets home. Summers are magical; this one's no different. She always starts out believing there's nothing more to learn, and without fail, by the end, she's proved wrong. This year, the proof has come earlier than usual. Occasionally she is granted a glimpse of infinity—is that too much to hope for in France? Will she be able to hide the excitement in this so civilized place? In the bush there's only the dog to watch her war dances and listen to the strange noises that issue from deep in her chest, and sometimes, even he is one too many. She must pare down her enthusiasm, but how?

She looks down the hill over the ranks of graves to the distant sea. Excitement is a happy disease. She is happily ill. Ill with happiness. She's had private bursts of this sickness ever since she was small, explosive, giddy, feet-off-the-ground bursts—mostly when she's alone. What would Fanny make of this? Here she is, a guest in a part of the world that has been trampled for hundreds of years by human feet and there are eyes everywhere, human eyes, dead and alive, all of them watching, all demanding restraint. It's hard to believe that here in France she's stumbled on something so deep and yet so light and frothy—it's not so much excitement, the nearest word is hope. There are like-minded people in the world, who are not merely kind and well meaning like her sisters, not merely talented, but ambitious as well. There are people like her who've given their whole life to art, who've made the commitment with mind and soul and body and they are here at this very moment. Anything is possible. So much time at home is spent struggling against hopelessness, filling up days with busying—spring-cleaning, whitewashing, rug hooking, useless socializing. Always trying to make ends meet. Footling obligations. Good working time lost, uselessly frittered away. There are people in St. Agathe who have rejected all this flummery.

She wonders if this frothy feeling is what the poets describe as love? No. Then it must be simply a crush. It isn't possible that she, Emily, Protestant, Prissy Miss Milly Carr is in love, but there is no charge for thinking about it and there's no denying she's in awe. The light is fading and she folds up her stool, picks up her painting sack, and makes for the gate where the keeper is waiting to close the cemetery. As she plods towards the road, she anticipates the evening meal with Fanny. She will try to distribute a little of the excitement among her new friends, but she won't let it run over and cause concern. The fat lady's spirit may float, but her feet must stay firmly on the ground guarding against disappointment. The graveyard is a reminder that there is only one thing that they all have in common.

⚜

The following afternoon she is back among the graves. Yesterday's mood has deepened. She traces the gold lettering on the tombstone in front of her with the nail on her little finger, which, because she always forgets to trim it, has grown long like a horn. Albert Duchamp, 1868–1906, born only three years before her and already dead. Married, of course. His wife, Marie-Louise Duchamp, 1873–1893. And what of young Henri Albert, 1893–1894? Did Marie-Louise die in childbirth at the age of twenty, leaving a son? Did Albert love her? Fanny said last night that love is easier for men—they can have it both ways. They are encouraged to absorb themselves in their work, then they come home to fresh pampering, a groaning table, a warm bed. Maybe Albert Duchamp was different. Maybe he was like Abelard, imprisoned by it, dying for it. There are no clues as to how he died, just the dates. Did the Breton peasants in their earth-floored houses, with their monotonous meals, children with no toys, no pianos or books—did they have love? They knew nothing of Paris, or of all the salons and all the art shows they were missing. Did they dream? Maybe they didn't need to, they had centuries of dreams spooling out in their laps.

Emily turns her back on Monsewer Duchamp and plants herself in front of the monument to an old soldier; it is garnished with a wreath of wax lilies. She opens her sketchbook and traps the line of the weathered stone in a few easy strokes. She recognizes the word Colonel on the inscription and as she draws, she sees a desert, camels, she feels bones under hot sand. She closes her eyes and he comes and kneels beside her, his medals knock against each other soundlessly as he places his hand next to hers. She can see through his fingers to the gravel and she feels a cold gust as his dead breath brushes her neck. He is trying to tell her something, but when she looks for his face, it's not there. With an effort, she withdraws her gaze and drags herself back.

She sketches fast, trying not to disturb the other spirits, the gods, and ghosts—graveyards are always so overcrowded. She's learned from the Indians to take spirits in her stride, but such manifestations have no part in a Christian upbringing, so it's hard to know what to do when they appear. Should she pretend she made up the Colonel? She tries to sketch his hand, but she is drawing her own. Her Indian friends would know what this means, in spite of the fact that missionaries like Edith are making sure they get a solid grounding in commonsense Christian Values. The family house is always filled with penitents. Last night, at supper, Emily confessed her pet name for it. She calls it Prayingmantisland; in Prayingmantisland you are upbraided the moment you step off the well-worn track that leads to a virtuous life and you are instructed in what to do to atone. Edith would think it was too late for the good people of St. Agathe. They are the wrong church. Fanny suggested that Edith might consult a shaman. The idea is so funny, Emily snorts whenever she thinks of it. She is betraying her family with every breath, but they are far, far away.

Fanny had showed her some studies she'd made of the little altars beside the road to Quimper. She'd gone there after she'd seen Emily's efforts. In Fanny's hands, the pathetic offerings of stones, grass and flowers float—but not without pattern and intent. Edith would tell her to destroy them and cover the Virgin's face. When she looks at Fanny's paintings, Emily sees that all she's conveyed in her own work is glossy prettiness, even though the eyes of the Virgin are hard and enduring. There's that word again, enduring. The Virgins are not at all pretty. Fanny has come close to uncovering their mysteries—she's detaching their eyes—they glisten like jewels. To the peasants, these altars are markers of something beyond life, something Emily has sometimes stumbled on in the north of British Columbia but never in Victoria, never in Vancouver.

Last night they argued about the relative merits of stone and wood. She thinks of this as she re-reads the simple inscription on the Colonel's tombstone. Spirits live in stone just as much as wood, neither one is more enduring than the other, both are in jeopardy. She can't avoid the spirits in the tree they cut down to make way for the bank. Indians say the white man isn't happy unless he's in control because he does not belong where he has raised his flag. The Indians don't need to control, the eyes on their totem poles are a bit like the eyes of the Virgin, they look dead, but they're alive and, unlike Emily, they have nothing to hide. They're watchful and mischievous and they yield happily to her brush. She sketches a Haida whale on a fresh page. Whales, grizzly bears and eagles—the creatures crowd the poles and the myths. She knew she might incur the wrath of Raven when she tried to catch them on canvas. A wise elder pointed out to her that in Indian lore, the animals have animal minds and souls, not like the white man's myths and fairy stories; he dismissed the three bears at Goldilocks' table, and Red Riding Hood's wolf, saying they are merely people clothed in animal skins. The demons in Indian stories have no need of human skins. Would Fanny understand this if she were to try to explain it? Emily has talked of it to her friend Willie Newcombe at the museum, but there is no one else who wants to listen. The shrines to the Virgin on the edge of the barley fields in Brittany are dark and pagan. At least Fanny understands that. Can she be trusted with the renderings Emily has made in Indian country, images she promised solemnly she'd never pass on? She has never even shown them to her Indian friends in the south, but she actually planned to show them to Mr. Geoffrey Church! She shivers.

"Protestants like the Carrs don't care for shrines," Fanny remarked last night, as she dug into her fruit compôte. "Why should they, when they have no need of them? They've reduced the mystery of the church and replaced it with good works."

Emily is amazed at this insight. She doesn't have Fanny's facility with words, but for the first time, she questions the rightness, the righteousness, of people like Edith, though she knows that if she lives to be ninety she'll still honour her sisters, just as she honours her family's God. She loves Him with all her heart and soul, and even if she didn't, she'd never be brave enough to abandon Him and enter another force field. She feels humbled when she's with Fanny, no one else has upended her like this. There was no time to talk further, Mr. Merton sat down, uninvited, lit a cigar and ordered a pernod.

She topples her stool and creaks down onto her knees. "Lord, give me what it takes to live boldly in your world." Her paintings of the poles are burning a hole on top of the armoire. With the blessings of her Indian friends, she's unleashed the unnamed powers. They are unlike anything she's painted before or since. If Frances sees this, it will prove that they are true soul mates. And if she doesn't? If she doesn't...? The decision is made, she must take the risk.

She levers herself up and the Colonel taps her on the shoulder. When she spins around to face him, he slips away. He's a joker. A trickster. This place is full of them but they're all French!

"So who should I love?" she asks the space where he was. "And don't tell me it's time I hooked a man. I've heard that old saw."

She glances around the graveyard at the elaborate mausoleums sheltering the richer dead, at the children's graves guarded by naked cherubs and angels in flowing gowns. She thinks of her little nieces and nephews, Clara's children. Once Clara was changing one of her small sons under the coats on the hallstand. She asked for a hand because the baby was squirming, but he was naked and soiled and Emily ran off without a word. Clara is the only one of the five who has had the courage to allow her eyes to stray below a man's collar. "We were brought up to believe that children, like angels and grown-ups, should only be viewed when they are covered," she excuses herself to the Colonel but he's disappeared. "And I think that's right, whatever Frances says. It's right to take baths in my under-slip and I'll keep on doing it, even when I am alone in the forest. We were meant to be clothed, if we weren't—if we weren't, we'd be laid to rest just as we arrived on earth. Unevolved. It's take me with my clothes on or leave me alone, I'm afraid."

Out of the corner of her eye, she glimpses a massive crucifix leaning at an angle against the lower limb of a yew tree. The face of the crucified Christ reminds her of the face of the only man who has ever asked for her hand in marriage, a sweet, well-meaning man, whom she cast aside. She lets her gaze drift down below the Saviour's neck and his loincloth slides away revealing his third leg.

Fully extended. She feels Raven's wing on the back of her neck, hears him laughing. Once again she is back in the hands of Dr. Waller at the sanatorium, burning from head to toe as the hand in the white leather glove forces a silver ball up between her legs, ripping the sheet from her midriff.

She's put off the need for a toilet for some time, but now it's urgent—she's dancing on the spot. There's no time to race back and squat over Madame Lefebvre's primitive trough; there's no one around, so she crouches, lifts her skirts, lowers her drawers, sends a hot river coursing over the baked ground. The river branches where it meets the graves. It's a blessed release, but it is desecration. Raven's shadow hovers overhead—he pecks her shoulder. She opens her mouth and roars, then she topples back into the stream.

On the far side of the graveyard a whistle sounds, a piercing train whistle. But the trains are in the sidings—the railway workers are on strike. Emily sees that it is a man, not a train. He is on the path on the far side of the graveyard, looking in her direction. He whistles again. She's a reservoir. She's burst her banks. It is Mr. Merton.

§ St. Agathe, June 11th, 1911

The officers have attracted a gaggle of very lively young ladies into St. Agathe. Presumably they come from Quimper and surrounding towns, they are all well turned out, goodness knows how many birds have expired to provide the feathers for their hats, and they have a great repertoire of songs, which they like to show off regardless of the hour. I have even seen a couple demonstrating the cancan. Of late, Geoffrey finds that he needs an after dinner stroll to aid his digestion, and, naturally, I do not let him go alone. During the day (unobserved by Geoffrey) the ladies and the officers play cards at the café tables. Bridge, I believe, though often I see money change hands and I suspect that they are not playing simply to pass the time. There has been talk in town of setting up a casino, but some of the cooler heads have observed that, with the departure of the garrison there would be no one left to patronize the tables. The peasants are not going to gamble, even supposing they have anything to gamble with, and the painting crowd are too embroiled in artistic endeavours to have much time for cards and dice. This leaves the summer visitors and wives such as myself, who, while we might be happy to have the occasional flutter, would, almost certainly not be extravagant. St. Agathe does, of course, have an elite upper crust. The prince and his Russian entourage might be interested, though they are more likely to go to Paris. There is also the possibility that an unsavory element would be attracted into this quiet little town, and nobody wants that. So the officers must make their own fun.

Yesterday, one of them stopped me on the street and asked after Miss Frances Hodgkins. Naturally I wanted to know his reason for enquiring (one does not give away information about one's friends to total strangers). He gave some vague response, shook his head and walked away. I thought this odd, and when I saw him at a café table today I asked one of the ladies his name. She lacked my discretion, and told me he was Captain Jean-Pierre Morano and he had foreign blood, possibly African. She herself was from Lyons, and I immediately took note of her accent, which was very far from anything I can imitate.

Mr. Morano was tall and blond, not a bit African in his looks. He had a luxuriant moustache and his shoulders sloped precipitously, so that his epaulettes were set to slide off. I placed him in his early thirties and I wondered what possible connection he could have with Fanny. I had not seen her for ages, so I sent her a note inviting her to come to tea tomorrow. I shall try to find a way of asking about him. Can he be a long lost love, I wonder?

§ St. Agathe, June 12th 1911

Crumpets are not to be found in France. In England we normally enjoy them in winter, but something happens to the expatriate palate and it craves delicacies from home, no matter what the season. Here in St. Agathe, crumpets are served in the height of summer at our tea tables, crumpets with lots of butter and good local honey. Geoffrey's sister in Glasgow supplies us with parcels of necessities from home, but our stock is running low. In fact, I was down to the last four, and I planned to serve them to Fanny today, along with a newly baked simnel cake and some home-made cherry jam. I laid the table under the apple tree, her favourite spot, and sat down to wait with a gardening book, which I couldn't bring myself to open. I turned my back on the gate in order to look as though I were not waiting, and I kept my ear cocked for the sharp tap of her heels behind the hedge. All I heard were horse's hooves, the squeak of a peddler's cart and the occasional passer-by, whose footfalls bore no resemblance to hers. I could not believe she would fail to show up. She is always punctual to the minute, and scrupulous about keeping appointments. By ten past the hour, it was obvious that my worst fears were to be realized and I threw a muslin cloth over the food and set out for town in search of her, trying to stay calm, knowing that there must be something seriously amiss.

I came upon her sitting at an outdoor table in a side-street café close to the Fisherman's Club. She was deep in conversation with Miss Carr. I didn't disturb them. I can't describe the swirl of feelings as I made my way back into the centre of town, barely aware of where I was going or what I was doing. I don't think I have ever actually seen red before, but now everything was bathed in scarlet. I had not felt so betrayed since I was a schoolgirl. I needed to let out some air, or I would explode.

The military men were taking aperitifs on the terrace of the hotel, joking with their consorts; I could hear their banter before I turned the corner. I honed in on her man immediately. He was sitting in a prism of light, a little apart from the rest, writing something in a leather bound book. Before I could change my mind, I marched up to him, drew a deep breath, and invited him for tea. He looked up at me, raised an eyebrow, closed his book with a snap and got to his feet, offering me his arm without a word. It was too late to retract the invitation.

We exchanged introductions on the way back to the house (I didn't divulge that I already knew something about him) and I filled the time by chattering about my husband. He seemed to be fairly knowledgeable about art and he had heard of Geoffrey though he didn't know his work. He spoke English fluently with a strong, not unattractive French accent. I asked if he was a family man and his response was intriguing. "Family? What is family?" I let the matter rest. It seemed pointless to provide a definition. He was wearing a handsome engraved ring on his wedding finger and another, more flamboyant sapphire ring on his little finger. It was not in keeping with his uniform.

He had never tasted crumpets. I'm not sure that he liked them, but he finished three of the four and managed a large slice of cake as well. He didn't seem in the least surprised that the table was already spread, or that an older, married woman was feeding him and engaging him in conversation. The talk came to a halt while he ate, and I watched him, waiting impatiently for him to raise the subject of Frances. Finally, it was up to me. I knew I must act quickly, for if Geoffrey were to stand in the window and crane his neck he would see that I was entertaining a soldier in a quiet corner of the garden and he would down his brushes instantly.

"Where did you meet Miss Hodgkins?" I asked.

"Miss Hodgkins?"

"Miss Frances Hodgkins, the artist. You spoke of her yesterday."

"Ah yes, of course. We met in Tetuan."

I had never heard of Tetuan, and I allowed my ignorance to show. It seemed he wasn't going to help me out but then he added, "Morocco."

I knew she had spent some months in North Africa, and I was about to follow up when he said, "I did not know her well."

I felt he was playing with me, holding back deliberately and I decided to wait him out. He glanced around the garden, folded his serviette, dabbed his moustache very carefully as if he were taking a stain out of a delicate fabric and then resumed. "It is simply that I wished to ask her about the child."

"Ah, the child." I'm sure he knew he had me at a disadvantage.

"Did she leave it in Tetuan? Does she continue to support it? I cannot remember if it is a boy or a girl."

"Well, she certainly doesn't have it with her." I tried to absorb this momentous news. Fanny had never intimated that she was a mother. I assumed she had travelled to Morocco in order to deliver the child privately. It is alarming that secrets have such a way of catching up with you in the most circuitous ways.

"I gave him a present. A mounting of butterflies. I am a collector. This is why I remember it so well. I included a species that is extremely rare. I have never come across it since. It was very generous of me. She likes butterflies."

"Are you suggesting that you would like it back?"

"Certainly. Perhaps you would ask her if she still has it?"

"I doubt that she would have your butterflies on her person." He was sinking in my estimation so fast that he was in danger of vanishing down a wormhole. "Were you stationed in Tetuan?" I played for time.

"Oh, no. But I was there on military business. I became a friend of the British consul. Mr. Bennington, do you know him?"

"Why would I?" (The rest of the world seems to believe we British have expatriate connections strung across the world like bunting.)

"Because he was also a friend of Miss Hodgkins. They were often in each other's company. He is a very fine man. Perhaps he is still there."

Bennington. I made a mental note of the name. Was he the father? Unlikely, if she travelled to Morocco to give birth to her son. "I'm afraid I wouldn't know." I wanted him gone. I didn't like him. He had a withholding and acquisitive character, and I was glad that his precious butterfly was irreplaceable. Besides, I needed time to digest his news.

He must have picked up on my agitation, because shortly afterwards, he rose and took his leave, but not without taking a bite out of the remaining crumpet. I assured him that, in a town as small as St. Agathe, he would almost certainly run across Miss Hodgkins (I still had not divulged her whereabouts) and he said he hoped so, although he would be leaving shortly.

I stood at the gate guarding my newly acquired knowledge and watching him walk away with that leisurely loping pace that I no longer found attractive. I have no idea what I will do with this information, but I know I must keep it to myself. I feel, somehow, that now that I have stolen a march on Frances, I can more easily forgive her lapse of memory.

I cut a slice of cake and took it in to Geoffrey, who accepted it without grumbling that I had interrupted him. Poor, innocent Geoffrey, chained in the confines of his studio. How little he understands of the currents and cross-currents that permeate our life in France. I returned to the table and finished the fourth crumpet. Waste not, want not.

⚘

Emily lies like a plank, the bed covers pulled over her head. The old illness is back. She can barely move her legs, her mouth is dry, her head throbs and her heart races. She is a charred forest without a trace of Fireweed. She won't leave her room till after dark even if the dizziness goes away. She will be the dinner-table topic of the day, a colour wheel to be spun and halted at will, divided up, a segment for each of the students. She recognized the man in the graveyard right away. She imagines how Mr. Merton will launch into his story, peppering it with taut American witticisms, a raised eyebrow, the quiet ironic cough. He'll describe how he found her defacing the dead, bellowing, yes, bellowing, her skirts over her head, her patched yellow petticoat, her bare bottom like a split watermelon. He'll spin the story wheel over and over. He'll turn her into a giant dung beetle, arms and legs waving, rolling on her back. It is too good for a single telling. It is shameful, shameful. It serves her right, she has sinned, she has betrayed her sisters, worshipped false gods, dreamed of being held in the arms of a woman and worst of all she was about to betray her Indian friends. Not only was she ready to show the world their sacred poles, she was looking for praise for her own rendering. Now she must pay, and wry, urbane, ghastly Mr. Merton will make a meal of her.

Frances raps on the door at five thirty. "To the trough, little piggy!" she sings.

"Go away."

"Aren't you feeling well?"

"No."

"Shall I eat alone?"

"Yes."

"All right. See you at supper." She does not come in.

Emily covers her head again. Frances will no longer care for her. There'll be no more pickquicks after work, quick snacks of fruit and cheese to cover the talking, the day's events tumbling out so fast, so deep. There'll be no more midnight feasts. It's all over. Mr. Merton will discover Frances, sitting alone with her Camembert. He will pour out the tale of her disgrace and they'll chew on it again and again. It won't be the first time she's been called a witch.

One good thing will come of it. Frances won't invite her to eat with the rest of the class again. At the best of times, she finds it hard to be cheerful in company. Her tongue is no more use than a baguette, when she wags it she spits out crusts. She has no stomach for garlicky French food. She's ordered full meals along with the rest of the group and ended up feasting on bread, avoiding the copious helpings of sardines, the crabs (doesn't anyone hear them scream as they hit the boiling water?), the raw biftek and the awful green peas stewed with onions and sugar, all washed down with a rough cider like the scrumpy her father once brewed in the basement, forbidding his girls to go near it (she drank two cups straight off, and they had to send for the doctor).

Emily comes up for breath when at last there's a rap on the door. Frances comes in without waiting for permission. Her eyes are sparkling; she has a bag of gooseberries in her hand. She tries to tempt Emily, but Emily moans. She peels back the sheets and puts her hand on Emily's forehead. Emily turns to face the wall. Frances gives up.

"We had such a jolly meal, I'm sorry you weren't there. I met

Mr. Merton in Le Pot au Feu, and we ordered crêpes, he bought a bottle of brandy, and some of the other students joined us and the proprietor opened up the back room to give us more space and we had the most entertaining discussion about Turner—it seems everyone admires him, though they are not all sure why. I gave them my speech about breaking the rules and thus inventing new ones. Miss Hawkes thought she admired him because he was so very English. What a stupid woman she is."

"What about Mr. Merton?" Emily breathes his name.

"Oh, Mr. Merton is very taken with him. He spoke of how he has learned from him that reality isn't one thing but a constantly changing attitude to what you see, it fluctuates and gradually you develop your own way of nailing it down, and then this becomes your style (those are his words). Isn't he clever?"

"And what is his attitude to what he sees?" Emily breathes.

But Frances has not understood the significance of the question. "The best thing about teaching is that you learn just as much from your students as they learn from you. Come, teach me something, Milly."

"And what did he teach you about me?" Emily asks again.

Still Frances will not take the bait. She pats Emily's leg. Emily flinches.

"Mr. Merton always makes his points so well. He agrees with me that the object of watercolour is to keep the surface simple and Turner's watercolours are so drenched, so full of complexity."

"Too drenched, you said it yourself, they are too full."

"Mr. Merton has a good eye."

"And he sees everything."

Frances's face is alight. "I believe you're jealous of him, Milly."

"You don't have to shield me, you know."

"You're so moody, Milly dear." Frances gets to her feet, laughing.

"I never know what to expect. That's probably why I like you. Get better soon, we miss you." She cuffs her and sweeps out of the room in a flurry of skirts, taking the gooseberries with her. Emily reads the message without tasting them. She is being told that she is not to play gooseberry in the affaire. Two's company, three's a crowd. If Mr. Merton hasn't exposed her yet, he will certainly do so later. He'll choose his moment and make it a big event. And if Frances is trying to avoid speaking of her disgrace, this is worse. Tact. Only yesterday she said that tact was the deadening hand of Colonialism, and here she embodies what she claims to hate. She is demoting Emily to a common student, with no more cachet than Miss Winthrop, and she is doing it with exquisite, unassailable tact.

Emily fixes on the armoire and its precious cargo, no longer wrapped in the brown paper it travelled in. If she had the energy, she'd get up and take the poles down. She's a splurter, showering her ideas around like water from a carelessly shaken brush. It has to stop. She must learn to keep secrets and stay out of people's way. Hope leaks out of the frames, hope and desire, she must give it back to the people it was meant for, no one else will sample it. It is all tripe, anyway. The whole of France is tripe. The whole world is tripe. She wants, no, she *must* go home. She will get up tomorrow and send a cable.

§ St. Agathe, June 21st, 1911

Fanny called on me today. I haven't seen her for days. My first inclination was to treat her coldly after what I'd learned about her, but she was so agitated that I sat her down in the parlour, helped her dispose of her hat, and began to make tea, refusing to let her speak until she had loosened her belt. It's been a mizzly day, moisture too fine to call for an umbrella, but swags of mist hanging about in hollows and blotting out the midsections of trees. A day to stay indoors and catch up on mending, even Clod failed to show up for his dreaded assault on the garden.

I passed her a cup of tea and she said, "You should have been a mother, Winnie." I came within a breath of saying 'I should have done a better job of it than you.' This was the first time I've clapped eyes on her since learning about her child, and I sat across the table and tried to decide whether the information had changed my view of her. She took advantage of my silence to undo the top two buttons of her blouse. I noticed that the skin was shriveled in the area of her throat. I wondered if the rest of her was showing the signs of aging I have begun to notice on my own body; it is difficult to judge when all you can see are the hands and the face, which, in her case, are remarkably well tended. Her mouth is far larger than most mouths, and, in repose, she has an intense expression that frightens men like my husband, though they avoid her rather than admit it. Her smile always comes as a surprise; it spreads across her face instantaneously, like an egg broken into hot lard.

"I'm having trouble with one of my pupils," she said, at last. "I need your advice, Winnie."

"Which one would that be? I thought they were a rather pleasant crew this year. Surely not old Miss Winthrop? Has she declared herself to be the living reincarnation of Rembrandt again?"

"Hardly. She is too arthritic now to grasp the charcoal. Do you suppose I could persuade her to try to work with it stuck in the gap in her two front teeth?"

"That gap would hold a tree trunk. She seems to have dispensed with more of her teeth this year."

"I'm talking about the Colonial. Miss Carr. Miss Emily Carr."

"Ah, Miss Emily Carr." I said the name slowly. It was a pleasant enough name, inoffensive, not unlike Winifred Church. We are neither of us exotic, is that why Frances consorts with us?

"I don't know what to do. She hasn't come out of her room for two days. She's bribed Madame Lefebvre to bring her food. Madame thinks she's sick but I know she's malingering."

'Well, let her malinger,' was what I wanted to advise, but I merely nodded and asked, "Why would she do such a thing when she's paid good money to take your course?"

"I haven't the foggiest. To be honest, she's more trouble than she's worth."

"Then why trouble yourself?" I asked, triumphantly.

"Because...because. Oh, I don't know. At first we got on like a house on fire. We were kindred spirits, you know, there's only a couple of years between us. And besides, she's a real artist. You've got to admit she can paint, she's the only one who has really applied herself to the craft...but she's got about as much tact as a doorknob."

I tried to imagine a tactless doorknob. "Geoffrey seems to think she has talent." I stalled.

"It's such a waste. She has the personality of a hedgehog. Say one thing that she takes amiss and in goes the head and out come the quills."

A doorknob with prickles. I perked up. It was obvious that Miss Carr had not made as favourable an impression as I feared. "What have you been saying to upset her?" I asked cautiously. It wouldn't do to sound too interested.

"Nothing. One minute she's surly, the next she's all sunshine. People say I have a sharp tongue, but I've got nothing on her. She could use hers to drill for diamonds. And I thought we were so alike."

A doorknob. A hedgehog. A diamond drill. I was beginning to

enjoy this. The colour blazed on Frances' cheeks and spread over her jaw and down through her crêpey neck. Women's necks are quite fascinating. They speak so clearly of how they have lived their lives. If I were an artist, I'd spend time on them.

"You could be as like as two peas but that wouldn't make you complement each other," I extemporized. "A pea should be paired with mint—I always try to choose my friends from the mint patch. Or new potatoes. Now they go well with peas, or lamb, lamb's a fine complement..."

She cut me off with a shout of laughter. "Your mind is forever on food, Winnie, when will you stop cooking!"

I shut my mouth, and produced a plate of macaroons.

"I knew you wouldn't understand," she plaited the fingers on one of the gloves she carried in her belt.

I withdrew the plate. "What is there to understand? You are both grownups. You can each do as you wish. If she chooses to stay in bed for the entire course, it need not concern you."

"But it does. I fear I may have put her there, you see. And besides, I miss her."

"You miss her, now that's more serious."

"Yes. I know it's absurd. I hardly know her. But I've been dreaming about her. About what we might do here together."

"Do?"

"We would make a fine team." I waited, without comment. "The other students are greatly relieved by her absence. She has never joined them, but her painting presence has hung over them like some sort of axe. Now she is safely out of their way, everything's much more relaxed, they have no standard to aim for. It's too bad that I miss her."

She seemed so forlorn that I relented and put a macaroon in her hand. I felt I was wading into uncharted waters and it was time to steer the conversation onto another course, but Frances pre-empted me by flinging the macaroon on the floor and putting her face in her hands. I was not sure if she was crying, and I immediately blamed myself. Had she detected my underlying pleasure at her discomfort? "You think I'm being emotional," she whispered.

"Not at all." (I hope no one upstairs is keeping a tally of my white lies.)

She wiped the back of her hand across her forehead and straightened her back. To my relief, her face paint was still in place though the tears had corroded small trails in the buttressing under her eyes. "I'm not emotional. It's just that she brings something out in me. Excitement—I suppose that's what you'd have to call it. We both feel it when we work. I have never been able to speak of it to anyone who understood. Sometimes it's explosive. Sometimes we are both blinded by it."

"I'm afraid you must think me very clear eyed."

"Of course I don't. Or rather I do. I'm glad you have clear eyes, Winnie. Blinding isn't for ordinary people." She dabbed at her lashes. "We are all three extraordinary women, of course, clear eyed or not. I don't subscribe to the new ideas about women you know. I don't really care if we've got the vote, we can be just as extraordinary without voting." (I shall record that in my diary, I thought, grimly, just in case you change your mind. Ordinary people are at least good record keepers.) "We may be the first in the world to be enfranchised in New Zealand, but I can't think what good it will do any of us when all we've got to vote for is my brother-in-law and a legion like him. He's well meaning but so dull, my sister has to tell him which socks to wear before he can leave the house. I'm perfectly happy to leave government to dull men and to let the women write their boring speeches, but don't ask me to vote for them. My sister was a better painter than me before she married him. I am so lucky to have escaped that Gentlemen's club."

I tried to signal my disagreement with her point of view, but she was well and truly launched.

"You know, someone asked me to be part of an exhibition of women's art just before I came to St. Agathe, and I refused. We will be seen to reflect each other's weaknesses and no one will notice our strengths. Let's take our place beside men of genius, and if we're not as good as they are, let it be noted. Likewise, let them take note if we are better. Personally, I can't imagine what bearing the sex of the artist can have on the picture. To encourage people to look at art in that way is to encourage them to look down their noses at us, don't you agree? You know, it's women who get in the way of most of my sales. They stand behind the man's shoulder just as he is about to snap up a painting, and they say stupid things like 'think of the price, George,' while all the time they're thinking that the money should go towards a new flat iron or a visit to the spa."

"Oh, not all women!" I felt I should jump to the defense of my kind, though I often had to prevent Geoffrey from spending our savings on other people's art. Last year he tried to buy a very ugly painting behind my back. It was done by our friend Henri Matisse, but I still put a stop to it. I hated the muddy greens and yellows and angular lines, there were none of his usual curves, none of the tingling blues and pinks that I so admire. Even a good artist like dear Henri can, on occasion, go sadly wrong. I made Geoffrey return it to the dealer. He came home with a canvas by Modigliani that was even worse. I think that some of the members of that circle would benefit from a pair of spectacles, then at least they might recognize a face when they see one. Perhaps this is why I like Frances' work so much; though far from realistic, no one would ever claim that its subjects are unidentifiable. Women should encourage their men to buy her work. I've heard it said that her style is too close to Derain, but I don't agree—her style is her own and unlike anyone else's, though as far as I am concerned, the more they compare her to Derain, the better, if it means that people will look more closely. One day I will persuade Geoffrey to invest in one of her paintings instead of always leaving it to me, then he will be able to take the credit when her prices soar and her work is worth more than his friends'.

Frances was now launched into one of her 'isn't it awful to be a woman' rants. I hear it often, which is why I haven't bothered to make a note of it until now.

"It's awful being a woman and an artist." (It always starts like that.) "I wouldn't recommend it to anyone, not anyone, especially if they have the misfortune of starting out in New Zealand. Or Canada, come to that. Canada sounds equally ghastly. They have no people there, and how could anyone succeed unless they can shoot? I've tried to be firm with Milly. She must stay in Europe. I will help her. She must stop being emotional, stop thinking of herself as Cinderella, get rid of her nostalgia for her ugly sisters." Fanny began to pace the kitchen, measuring it toe to heel as though she were about to order new flagstones.

"And she has brought these terrible pictures of totem poles with her. Carted them all the way from British Columbia! She keeps them hidden. I took a peak while she was downstairs attending to her birdseed. She guards them with her life. They are the ugliest things imaginable, garish colours, huge, grinning, feathered monsters planted like slabs of meat among the trees."

"Oh, you mean she's been painting her parrots?"

"No, they're wooden. Very primitive. They scream. One can almost hear the sacrificial drums. She has to stay put in Europe for the sake of her sanity. She can't live cheek by jowl with such monsters. They'll put a hex on her. Maybe she's already hexed and that would account for her strange behaviour. You've heard of voodoo? Magic? There was a good deal of magic in Morocco, but we knew better than to meddle in it. The safest thing is to respect it and keep your distance. Brush up against it and you're tainted, touch it and you're a gonner. Just think of our Maoris. They are beautiful people to look at, especially the women. I love their surfaces and would paint them forever, but I would never presume to poke around underneath. I have a good idea what I would find, and it would bring nothing but misfortune. But Milly? Oh no. Milly never hears a squeak until it's a scream. I can see the attraction of those terrible creatures, Lord knows there's not much else to paint in that wilderness. I might have been reduced to a similar plight myself if I'd stayed in New Zealand. No good will come from them, but if I were to tell her that, she'd explode. I shall stay away from the nasty things. Far away. I shall simply refuse if she suggests that I look at them."

Her pacing increased in velocity and she began a sort of private game on the flags, talking as she jumped from square to square. (I am doing my best to recall these conversations accurately.) "Women have never made it as artists because we give in so easily to our emotions—it is our emotions that hold us back, not men. It's always been the case. She'll never learn any different if she goes back to British Columbia. I ask her what she can accomplish there and she says you don't accomplish, you cope. She must stay in France. It's the only place. I've told her I'll help her to rent a studio in my building in Paris. We can be partners in paint. Sister Brushes. We can be best friends. We will hold the fort against Picasso and his set." She sat down at the table again, put her chin on her outstretched arms and began to pick at loose threads in my crocheted runner. "You have nothing to prepare you for the awfulness. You try to make a living on your own, you have to, but you need, you need food, you need shelter, you need paint. Brushes. You never stop needing. There is nothing to prepare you for what it will be like. I'm offering to shield her from that—don't you see?"

I served her another cup of tea, trying to contain my discomfiture at this outpouring. It was too much to hope that it was over.

"An artist couldn't possibly allow the sort of distractions that you live with, Winnie, not if she is serious. I mean you are forever making tea! But I know what you think. When a woman lives alone or with another woman, everyone suspects she is...well, you know—especially in Paris. In Paris, it's a fad. There are salons where they gather. Steamy female covens! I'd rather die than rub noses with another woman, wouldn't you? Miss Stein thinks I'm the most dreadful prude, but I don't care. If one can't even have a best friend without setting tongues clacking...you don't think I am one of those, do you?"

"Of course not." I assured her, with every confidence. "No woman who has given birth is, to my knowledge, a lover of women."

Her head jerked back.

"I was speaking metaphorically," I extemporized, "about giving birth—giving birth to...art." It sounded dreadfully lame, but to my surprise, she swallowed it.

"Oh, how I do go on. I came to ask your advice on how to get Milly out of her room and this is where I end up. It can't be healthy. She's not healthy, you know, and she was making such progress. I can't think what I said. What could I have done to her?"

"Would you like me to visit her?"

"Oh, if you would. Root her out. And could you perhaps persuade Geoffrey to see her? That would buck her up no end."

I promised to see what I could do, though I had no great expectation of persuading Geoffrey of anything at all when he was in the throes of a painting spasm.

She got up and made for the door. Not a word of apology about our missed appointment, not a single question about my health or well-being. I wondered if she would notice if I swooned. What possessed me to offer to visit the dratted Carr woman and when did she start to call her Milly? "Do you have any intention of returning to Morocco?" I asked, wishing, all of a sudden that she was far, far away, attending to her duties as a mother, rather than pretending to be a man.

"Morocco? No. Why should I? It was wonderful but I'm finished with it."

"Just like that?"

"Just like that. Why do you ask? It's wrong to return to a place from which you have disengaged, don't you think? It always disappoints."

"It must be nice to finish with your own flesh and blood so easily." I responded, and closed the door on her, ignoring the rapping that followed.

I refuse to believe that she would be so callous. Underneath all her cant, she's a good woman. I've never had reason to doubt it.

Geoffrey popped his head into the kitchen to see what the commotion was about and I told him it was an importunate fish merchant. Geoffrey nodded absentmindedly and returned to work.

§ St. Agathe, June 22nd, 1911

I ran into the two ladies from Manchester in the market today. They were arm in arm, shopping with one basket. They told me that Miss Hodgkins cancelled classes due to a migraine and I said I was not at all surprised. They looked at me like greedy starlings, and I imagined what they would make of my comment after I had taken myself off.

On my way to the seed merchant's I passed the hotel and noticed that the military men were sitting around in subdued clusters shuffling their cards. A small, rather pert lady in a somber purple costume with a crisp white bib had replaced the posse of entertainers. She was taking tea with one of the Pooh Bahs, an officer with a waxed moustache whom I'd noticed whenever I passed the hotel. He laughed louder than the rest, tickled the ladies and gesticulated and stamped his boots so hard on the boards that I feared for the safety of the hotel's verandah. Now he was completely transformed and I guessed the lady was his newly arrived wife. I had to smile and the smile lasted me all the way up to Fanny's studio on the second floor of the seed merchant's building, where I planned to enliven her day with the news.

"It is work, work, and more work. It has nothing to do with inspiration." She hissed at me out of the corner of her mouth as I popped my head round the door. She was scrubbing at a canvas with a saturated paint rag, her hair, usually so neat, spiraled down her back in a long, bouncy curl. I didn't take the time to explore her new premises, but closed the door quietly and, following Madame Lefebvres' directions, made my way up the narrow, dank smelling stairs to the third floor landing where I was confronted with Miss Carr's tin trunk and a door marked with a crudely painted number 2.

I knocked. There was no response. I knocked again and a muffled cough told me that she was inside. I said her name. I said it matter-of-factly, with no give-away intonation. "Miss Carr?" I paused. "It's Winifred Church. I've brought you some pudding and I wondered whether..."

I'd used one of my silk scarves as a carrying sling for the dish of rice pudding, and, as I spoke, the knot gave way and the dish crashed to the floor, shattering into a dozen pieces. The door flew open.

"What in the name of Beelzebub?" Her eyes travelled down my body to the mess at my feet and she burst out laughing. She was clothed in a mishmash of shawls, covered by something that looked like a mackintosh. I stepped over the pudding and pushed past her into the box room. The shutters were closed but by the light from the landing, I could see that the bed was tumbled. The room smelt strongly of wet human—not so much a smell as a stench. There was a pile of dirty crockery under her bed and the rest of the room was almost entirely taken up with stacks of sketches and paintings; they propped up the walls and inhabited the table and the chair, the dresser and the top of the armoire— the only real piece of furniture the sweltering cubby hole allowed for. Miss Carr opened the shutters an inch or two letting in more daylight and closed the window; she made no attempt to clear a space for me, and I wondered if I was supposed to sit on the bed. I remained standing. I expected her to push me out, but she seemed inclined to talk.

"Light's too blarey. Nothing against light. When I growl at the sun I feel a low-down, but you need tin eyes to bear it in this town. Sorry if I growled at you. Not your fault. I'm in disarray, as you see. Even Monsewer is steering clear of me. I'm a bear today, not fit for anyone's company. I don't like being found in disarray. I can't seem to put my hand on my dressing gown. Do you find it cool in here? I find it cool."

"Are you well, Miss Carr?"

"I'm a good little charlady when I'm well. You're neat yourself, if your home is anything to go by. I found it sparkling in the days when I was welcome."

I felt called upon to reply but nothing occurred to me, so I continued to stand as she harangued me. "You wouldn't believe it, but there's nothing I like better than settling in for a good clean. Polish the cutlery, wash the nets, beat the rugs. I can't wait to get cracking again. Don't tell that to Frances Hodgkins, she'd have me put in jail. Can't wait to get out of here. I pant, do you know that? I pant to get out, like a pup cooped up in a hat box. I'm tired of this French smell. You know, we found two cockroaches in our hotel room in Paris. When we complained, they told us we were lucky there were only two! That's the Frenchies for you"

I cleared some paintings off the chair and perched on the edge. I wondered how I was supposed to cheer someone up who appeared so cheerfully determined to be disagreeable. In the best of circumstances, I would have found it hard to relax, but with my pudding sitting outside the door, I was in genuine distress.

"Take as you find," she said, leaning over and knocking on my knee with her mottled fist. "I'm not as rude as you think, in fact my friends think I'm a push-over. I'm just in need of a bit of good old housework. All these lodgings are too much for a body. I long to be at home and busy, away from all this thinking about art, all this chasing after shading. It's thickening. Soups up your brain. Turns you into a slug, and you leave nothing but paint trails over the paper. I thought it was what I needed. I despise all the dumpy little housewives back home, all busy catering to hubby and brood. Saturday afternoon painters! And I despise them even more when they turn up in France!"

"Why don't you try getting dressed? I'm sure lying around is much more—thickening. Why don't you try taking the sea air?"

"Where would I take it to?"

"Well, Miss Hodgkins thinks you're making good progress in your painting."

"Miss Hodgkins! So she's been talking about me, has she?"

"Only in so far as to say..." I felt trapped. I tried to plan a polite exit but how was I going to step over my pudding and get out onto the street? "Fanny thought you might be ill."

"I was, but that was years ago. You can tell Fanny that apart from the odd moment, I'm completely well, thanks all the same."

"I'm glad to hear that." It seemed impudent to ask what she was doing in bed in her mackintosh if she was feeling so well.

"I still like puddings, though. That was a kind thought. Do you put cinnamon in yours?"

"Nutmeg, vanilla and a little grated apple, occasionally I add an egg."

"Sounds good. I'm sorry I missed it."

"I'll make you another," I offered, rashly. "You must come to the house and I'll serve it properly."

"Oh, I don't think so."

Unable to let well alone, I added, "Mr. Church is looking forward to meeting you again. He's been working himself into a lather over this upcoming show. In some instances less is more, don't you agree?" I sounded like such a dry stick, and that's how I felt. She was sitting there like a milk jelly, huge and wobbly, and rather repellent and I was perched at her extremities, a stick insect, all arms and legs. I suppose it is often this way when you discover a person in her home circumstances. It's like winkling a snail out of its shell and wishing you had never succeeded.

"That's good. We could exchange recipes for vinegar, you and I." It seemed she was being deliberately nasty, and once again I fell silent. "I've been sitting here for two days going through all the vinegars in my head. Have you ever tried to make balsamic?"

"I'm afraid I haven't."

"Nor me. Do you know how?"

"No, but raspberry vinegar is rather good and our raspberries are coming into season."

"Well, I have to fill my time here with something. The trains are on strike, so a body can't leave. Maybe we could make raspberry vinegar together."

The idea appalled me. Fortunately she didn't pursue it.

"The Atlantic has a different whiff than the Pacific. It's whiffier. The sun makes things worse. I won't go out in the sun."

"Then we'll wait for a rainy day." I was off again, walking into my own traps. I would pray to the god of fair weather.

"No. I mean I will only go out after dark. Trouble is the days are so infernally long."

"But why wait until dark?"

"Reasons." She moved her legs from under the blanket. Her mackintosh parted and I saw that she wore short pink bloomers under her nightshirt.

(I am doing my best, but my recollection of conversations may not be entirely accurate. I'm afraid I am too easy on myself when recording my responses, not wishing to reveal how stupid I am, even to the person inside who can't be fooled!)

"I'm sorry about Frances," she announced, attempting to cover her exposed knee. "I'm sorry about Frances and me. You know when you get along with someone? Really click, like two cogs—when you find your talk in their mouth and your hear in their ear...?"

I felt sad. She has such an off-kilter way of expressing herself, no wonder she has such trouble in being understood. It was a shame that I'd had so little truck with her. She shifted her weight and the blanket slipped off the bed, revealing a picture face up on the bottom sheet. It looked like one of the totem poles I had heard about. I leaned over for a closer look and Miss Carr sprang at me then relaxed. She made no attempt to explain why she had a picture in her bed.

"You're always looking, aren't you. I've always thought you see more than you let on."

Her tone was quite stinging, so I came back, "Looking is free." She stared at me for a long, uncomfortable moment, daring me to view the painting, then she pulled the blanket over it.

"The Indians have no word for art."

"Nor do the peasants. Or at least, they have no understanding of it." I felt I was almost forgiven.

"The peasants' weavings are streets ahead of anything the members of the Victoria Craft Guild can do, and as for the lace, I'd love to bring the whole flock of them over from Victoria and have them walk around and peer through people's windows. That'd rattle their looms! The trouble with being around the peasants is they make you feel so darned guilty about using up your time on something that's so useless in everyday life. I never feel that way when I'm working in the Indian villages. Useless, I mean."

"I'm afraid I wouldn't know."

"I don't want useless. I want someone to tell me I've made him look with new eyes. I can't be a betrayer. If one is neither Indian nor peasant one may copy but one may not steal." I followed her gaze in the direction of the armoire, where there was a stack of paintings. I assumed these were what Frances had referred to the other day. I knew I was being pushed aside. The road to forgiveness had forked again. "Now if Mr. Church had told me he thought my best work had merit, it would have been worth all the time I've spent in this dump."

"I'm afraid I can't guarantee his opinion."

"You're right, I've been wasting my time. I don't suppose that even he would understand, though he's a man of the world. Rest assured, I would never have shown those paintings back home...even to a Finch or a Pine Siskin. I was on the wrong track, I was almost ready to blurt."

I couldn't understand her. I had only glimpsed the canvas in her bed, it was certainly bizarre, but no more bizarre than much of the work I saw in Paris this year—they have a new concern with African artifacts. "Why do you worry about this? You have so many other paintings."

"You tell me."

"Is it for the sake of your Indians?"

"Some things just are. The difference is that the people who made what I have merely represented leave things alone, but I keep on meddling, I keep on thinking *permanent*. It's to prove I'm up to areness. If you have areness, you can't have absence. You have your place. So much art is nothing but absence, just pretty pictures—oh Lord, I hate it. Just once, I wanted to know that I'd produced something significant, I suppose I wanted to be sure I'd keep ticking—I'm such a goose."

I had no idea what she was talking about but her words had an impact nonetheless. "I suppose you mean presence?" I ventured.

"If you say so. If I need someone to tell me that my poles are good, then I think I should pack up my brushes. I had to find their poleness and that meant painting them the way they're not, I just needed to see if someone else could comprehend it. I sit in the forest and I feel this great dumbness of the soul, do you know what I mean? If I sit long enough, it sometimes shifts."

I fought off the shivers. For a while, I lost her. I was aware that for most of my life I have suffered from 'dumbness of the soul' and I have sat and sat, looked and looked without attaining anything. My mind flew to a time when I came close to understanding presence. I couldn't begin to tell Miss Carr about it, but I decided then and there to try to write it down, to put it in words since I can never paint it or share it. Perhaps if I allow the story a presence, it will help to make it more bearable. I have relied for too long on absence. I think Miss Carr and the picture in her bed may have done me a service.

§ St. Agathe, June 23rd, 1911

When we met, Geoffrey told me he liked my thin wrists, he said I had skin like see-through muslin. And he liked my surprisingly broad shoulders and my profile. (I have a slightly hooked nose and he is the only person ever to set me at ease about it.) He told me long after we were married that he had not been interested in marrying a beauty, or a woman of great wit—I suspect the truth is, he selected me because he thought I was a virgin. He could not have been more wrong. Before I met him, a school friend of my eldest brother had already used me as a sampler. I do not deserve pity, since I was not averse to being used, and my brother's friend could not be said to have abandoned me since he knew nothing of the outcome.

My mother chose to ignore my condition and my father and brothers never looked at me closely enough to notice my shape. I didn't talk about it to anyone and I stayed at home during the gestation where I read my way through my father's meagre library, and painted in watercolour. I left school at fifteen in order to help my mother run the house and I was always reluctant to go to the social events in our village or travel further afield to attend the seasonal balls and fairs where one was always on display like the prize yearlings at the county fair. When I reached eighteen, there was talk of my coming out, but it was quietly dropped after my mother became aware of my condition. She acknowledged it in subtle, and sometimes not so subtle ways. I remember she offered to help me let out my skirts, and suggested I drink a glass of milk each evening before retiring. She had learned that if one remained quiet and tried one's best not to disturb the ingrained pattern of events in our household, things would take care of themselves. I have to admit I have often taken a leaf out of her book.

My mother was a solitary. She could not sleep at night without the aid of valerian drops and she became less and less inclined to run the house, so gradually I took charge. My father was a much-respected doctor with a practice in Harley Street, which he attended two days a week. He continues to practice even today, though he has closed his registry to new patients. My eldest brother has followed in his footsteps, as has his friend. My second brother, Gregory, is an officer, serving in India. His honours come so thick and fast that I have trouble keeping up. It was he who introduced me to Geoffrey, and they still exchange letters, though their lives have taken them in directions that seem to preclude friendship. Gregory tells us that there is a war in the offing and warns us that France may take the brunt of it, though how he can fathom this, out there in India, is beyond us. Everything here is so peaceful that it is hard to take him seriously. Geoffrey points out that the railway strike, coming on top of the dearth of sardines, do not exactly add up to peace in St. Agathe, but I argue that this has caused a slowing down in activity. The town is in stasis. When I saw the French officers at their card games, with their chirruping entourage, I often thought of my brother Gregory, though I doubt he ever thinks of me—which is just as well, for, if he had been more curious, he would have discovered aspects of me (possibly known to my elder brother) that would have convinced him that I was not a suitable partner for Geoffrey.

I didn't see a doctor in the whole nine months of the gestation. My mother remarked that the coming of a child could often hurt and that was as much as I knew about giving birth. There was no one to ask.

When the pains hit, they were worse than anything I could have imagined. This was more than mere hurt. It was as if someone were rotating an iron tiller inside me. Fortunately, it was the cook's day off and the daily woman had left an hour early. My mother was in her room as usual, and I knew better than to disturb her. I don't know where the men were.

I tried to go upstairs to my bedroom, but the staircase was too long. I can see it now, carpeted in red with a gold medallion design, stretching up as far as up went, an impossible climb. I went blindly through the nearest door, which happened to lead into the kitchen. I grabbed a knife from the draining board. I don't know what I had in mind, or, if I do, it is nothing I can set down. I stumbled out into the kitchen garden. It was winter; there was a light rime of frost on the ground. The brussels sprouts were all picked but the stalks were still standing like a field of knobbly walking sticks, and there were some blackened tomato plants with a few split red pustules of fruit clinging to the vines. And there were orange Chinese Lanterns—I don't know what they were doing in the vegetable patch. I remember the colour because it was cheerful. I stood on the hard black earth and it bore my weight, I could move across it without leaving a trace.

The pain would leave and I'd relax, thinking it was over and then it would come back double strength. At each spasm, I gripped my thighs together tighter, trying to fold myself up like a fan, willing it to go away.

I stumbled into the potting shed and curled up on some sacks at the back, under a small grubby window that faced into a lilac bush. I remember looking at the tight brown buds and trying to think of Lilac blossom and spring. I remember singing to myself. The song was 'The British Grenadier,' the ta-ra-ra-ra marching rhythm seemed to help. I remember beating my palms over and over against the floorboards. I remember the whoosh of water pouring from some place between my legs, soaking my knickers and I remember being thankful that I wasn't staining the carpet. I touched an opening and experienced a huge downward pressure as if I was being sucked into the earth. I remember thinking that there was nothing like this pain. Since that time I have heard women who have given birth gossiping about it, saying how very easy it is to forget once a short time has elapsed. I have never been able to tell them they are wrong.

I removed my undergarments and folded them, then I stood up and tried to shake myself out of the vice. I seem to remember that I thumped down on my knees again and as I did so the thing slid out onto the sacks. Fast. Absolute. But it was still attached to me. I cut the cord with the knife. There was blood running down my stockings. My blood. Our blood.

It whimpered and opened its mouth. Its lips were the pinkest pink, scored with deep lines. It was slippery and covered with blood and lard so I knew it must have been crushed inside me as my organs crashed around. I remember trying to hold onto it and being afraid that it would slip out of my grasp. I remember sucking its cheek. I remember a foot with five perfectly formed toenails. I don't remember its sex. I think I remember feeling its tiny cock but if I put my memory into my fingertips I can feel the cleft that would make it a girl. I don't remember the moment of its death, but I remember the relief. I held it and watched its colour change, and finally I put it down on the ground. And I remember noticing it was getting dark—I have no idea how long I was out in the shed, but there were frost flowers forming in the vapour on the window. It was bitterly cold. I remember kneeling beside it until all the heat had gone out of it, and getting up, and choosing a spade from the rack on the wall, and taking it round the back of the shed and digging a hole under the lilac bush. I dug as deep as I could in the stiff soil.

It is a white Lilac. Double. The smell is always overpowering. Always surprising. I believe it is still alive. I will not have Lilac in my garden. When Clod refused to cut a bush down, here in St. Agathe (purple, not white, but lilac nonetheless), I did it myself, making my palms bleed with effort, then I rubbed them in the soil, hoping I would be struck down with tetanus.

Nobody told me how long your body goes on weeping, the blood flowing out of you, the milk dripping. And then, somehow, it ends. There is no dividing line between after and before, no day when you wake up dry. There's no moment of letting go. You never forget the pain because it is the only time in your life that you are really and truly present. You simply get on with living. You try to live safely.

Geoffrey is right. I may not be a believer, but I am a survivor.

I feel committed to continue with this journal, although it has changed now. It is no longer safe. If it is discovered, the life I know will never be the same. Geoffrey would cast me out. Perhaps, as the days pass, the wounds I've opened will heal and I'll want to tear out the pages and consign them to one of Clod's bonfires. Some of us choose to live dry, and some, like Miss Carr, choose wet. I am dry and cold. If we could predict the outcome, we might try to do more to affect the humour. I shall keep this book secreted, away from the shelf of volumes representing the years of my recorded days, even though I am sure none of these books have ever, will ever be touched.

St. Agathe, June 24th, 1911

Looking back I see I was too anxious to complete yesterday's entry. I rejoined Miss Carr in mid-rant. My rice pudding was still sitting outside her door. She had made no attempt to remove her mackintosh.

"Frances talks about Picasso and his clique in Paris—they've got hold of some of the African primitive stuff, and they're bent on conjuring it into something new." She was flinging her words at me as if she knew that I had not been giving her my attention. "I never want to be a conjurer. My poles are supports, and it's what they support that matters. That's what I cannot reveal."

"Supports can cave. Like the bones of a newborn child."

Fortunately she was too absorbed in her problems to see that I was buckling under mine. "Edith thinks all my Indian pictures should be burned, she's right, but for the wrong reason. She says they're pagan. She's intent on converting every last tribe to Jesus, if he can find room for them in heaven. Now, that was nasty, wasn't it?"

"Yes. We appear to be nice, while we are actually being quite the opposite, I think." I moved to uncover the painting on her bed, but she stopped me.

"Poles are meant to rot and go back to the earth. They're not intended to be art. Tricksters. Jokers. The Indians like to laugh, though it is sometimes difficult to twig their humour."

"Do you believe in hell, Miss Carr?"

"Of course. I'm a Christian."

"I suppose it's safer to stick with the punishers—better the devil you know."

"I don't hold with everything that passes for churching. I don't believe I've told that to anyone before. And I certainly shouldn't tell it to someone with a name like yours, should I?"

That made me laugh and without more ado I invited her to come to supper on Tuesday. I told her I would make sure Geoffrey was home and I made a note to provide a lot of food so she could stoke up.

"How late do you eat?" she asked.

"Around seven. Will that suit you?"

"No, it doesn't suit. Make it nine."

"Geoffrey would never wait so long for his supper."

"Then ask me to come for a nightcap. He'll like that, it means he won't be stuck with me for hours. We can drink cocoa and chat."

"Very well then. Nine o'clock. But he doesn't like cocoa."

"I will not bring my poles. I don't want his opinion now. And I certainly don't need Frances to look at them."

"Oh, but Fanny has seen them." It slipped out, I don't know how.

"She's seen them? When?" Her face contorted.

I simply shook my head. I felt drained. I got up, re-pinned my hat and adjusted my veil. I thought it safer to let myself out than to compound my clumsiness. As I left, she was levering herself out of bed.

Today, with hindsight I see that we are both stuck with our punishers. I have no idea who her demons are, or what she has done to bring them down on her. Things that seem small to the outside world can be mountains when you have to face them by yourself. I doubt if she will come for cocoa but I will have my work cut out convincing Geoffrey to be social after nine if she does arrive.

꿔

Emily drags her trunk into the room, ignoring the fallen pudding which has lain outside her door all night. There is no space to move around once the door is closed, so she perches on the bed and begins to pack her pictures, rolling, smoothing and flattening as much as the surface allows. She leaves her poles where they are. Outside the door, Monsewer keeps up a constant yowl. She worries about tender paws and fragments of glass, but not enough to investigate.

She sees that she is going to have to search out another

container to house everything. She's been prolific. Few of the sketches speak, but they are so merry, full of air and energy that her mood lifts. How could she have ended up like a spent paper bag? And Mrs. Church is not a bad little soul. She feels nostalgic for the brown-sailed sardine boats already and she hasn't even left town. She holds up a painting of a pile of kelp, stranded on the quay. She's captured the light on the slippery surface. Thirty years ago, she used to run her tongue over kelp, popping the golden brown pods with her eyeeteeth. Chow brought up bulging slings of the stuff up from the beach and forked it into the flowerbeds where it turned into stiff black lace. Sometimes he let her balance the pole on her shoulders. She puts her tongue to the painting and stabs.

She's hungry. She hasn't eaten for hours. There is no food in the room and it is still too early to go out. But maybe it isn't. Maybe she can show herself briefly. When the strike ends and she is no longer a prisoner in this town, she'll be able to post letters home and tell them she is leaving. Then it won't matter a fig what people think or what they have seen her do. It won't matter what Frances really thinks of her work; Miss Hodgkins' opinions are of no consequence anyway. She's nothing more than a would-be, a would-be man, a would-be European, a would-be teacher. She does not deserve a moment's attention. The sketches are good, she already has some nippy ideas for developing them and she'll do it when she gets back home. There is only one thing left to accomplish, she must decide what to do with the poles. They're burning a hole in the top of the wardrobe.

She buttons her mackintosh, brushes aside Monsewer, steps over the pudding and goes downstairs in search of hot water. She passes Fanny's room. The door is open so she is not home. It will be good to get back to London where they have plumbing. It will be good to be clean and tidy. From London, it is a short hop, skip, and a jump back to Victoria, her passage is booked for October, but that can be brought forward with a small infusion of funds from home. In Canada, cats have an outside life, here they stay home, or they will end up as food for the pigs. Madame downstairs seems to be saying that it is the wrong time of day for hot water, so Emily stomps back to her room, strips down and wafts the contents of her talcum powder box over herself, patting it under her breasts and arms and between her legs and toes, creating a small dust storm. The stuff is in her hair, whitening the few remaining dark streaks, and she has a glimpse of what she will see in the glass in five year's time. The talcum hangs in the air, alighting on her poles. She suddenly sees the answer. When she goes, she will leave them here, in the company of the bleeding heart. They will find their own way in the world.

She dresses and goes outside. The sun is disappearing but the dazzle still makes her eyes smart and she races for the shadow. As she does so, she has to sidestep to avoid colliding head on with Mr. Merton who is escorting a large, tousled sheepdog along the centre of the road. It is an English sheepdog, like Shep and Driscol and Domino who are all waiting patiently in Victoria. She is sorely tempted to stop and throw her arms round the dog's neck, but the need to hide from the human on the other end of the leash drives her into an iron-monger's doorway. Mr. Merton takes his hat off solemnly, and she sees he is mocking her. She turns to look through the window into the shop and after he's passed, she presses her cheek against the glass. The display of axes is very tempting. She waits for him to disappear from sight before scooting down the hill to the bakery where she orders half a dozen dainties smothered with brightly coloured marzipan. At the last minute, she points to a tray of profiteroles and holds up three, then five fingers. Her mouth fills with a foretaste of the custard fillings as the shop assistant eases them into a box.

CHAPTER EIGHTEEN

⁓

Ilona held onto the mattress. Her body rippled, in tune with the feral pain. It was the kind of pain she'd been longing for all her life. She wanted to bite down on it, remember it in her muscles. It was so real she could never mistake it for anything else. Another wave rolled through, then another, she couldn't fight it off and she didn't want to. "Come. Come. Come." She propped herself up and timed the intervals, the way she'd been taught. She wished she could remember why she was doing it, she knew her memory used to be better before, but before what? The batteries in the clock on her dresser were dead, the hands stuck at seven. She didn't have a watch so she had to count, trying to keep the pace slow and steady, one, two, three… it seemed they were quite far apart. She flopped back on the pillow with a second pillow clamped between her knees. Her mother would know if she was ready, she'd asked if she could be with her when the babies were born. Ilona couldn't believe she'd follow through. Mrs. Martin had poor circulation, cold hands and she hated hospitals. "Mummy, pleeeeease." The voice seemed to come from outside her. She clamped her teeth on the last of the bourbons, hard, like a dog biscuit, but sweet, and chocolatey. Alexander and Matthew Rintoul. They had names; they had a room and a twin pram and matching blue rompers. People would help her—it wasn't at all like Winifred Church's experience.

This was the first time she'd been able to read that part of the diary without crying. Now she saw that Winnie was a murderer. That was the family secret. She'd always thought of it as a mistake before today; her mother acted as if it had happened in this house and the baby was buried in the vegetable patch.

There was no need to worry about the twins, everything would be over very soon, they would flow out of her, along with her milk and blood; everything would keep flowing. This was no secret. Flowing. Swimming. Everything had worked out well for Winifred Church in spite of what she did. Everyone always pulled through—this little space of time before everyone's lives changed was frost on the pumpkin. But did frost kill the pumpkin or did it turn it into a golden coach?

She tugged at the binding of the diary and ripped out the pages she hadn't re-read, found a plastic bag and pushed the rest under the bed along with the medical records (she knew she wouldn't want to read those in hospital). She pulled the bedspread down to cover them. The handful of unread pages had escaped the blood. She dropped them into the box along with the rest of Winnie's papers. It was time to move.

She roamed round the house shifting things and putting them back, straightening rugs that were already straight, replacing the empty biscuit barrel. The only thing that was new since she'd left home six years ago was a pink flowering Azalea on the bureau. Someone must have been ill. The long dinner table with its twelve upright chairs in padded red plush was empty except for a sparkling white cloth with the corner turned back to reveal a white matinée jacket, a ball of wool and a silver crochet hook. Ilona picked up the jacket. It wasn't quite finished, but it looked small, barely big enough for a kitten. Her mother once tried to teach her to crochet but she couldn't get the hang of it. Which baby would fit into this thing? She ran the metal hook along the soft scab on her wrist, but she had no compunction to gouge, the contractions were enough, they were delicious. Her body was a den for two lions and how they were growling! There was a pile of travel brochures on the arm of a chair. Bermuda, Trinidad—if they were thinking of taking a trip, they hadn't asked her advice.

She wandered out into the back garden. The stocks gave off a sweet, sickly smell that sent her stomach into a roll. She needed a seat. She walked round the side of the house and found herself back on the driveway, next to the car. The bonnet was still warm. She leaned over and caressed it, rubbing her belly against the grill. The heat was lovely. She pressed the release and the top peeled back slowly revealing the upholstery, white as pith. She looked down into the driving seat and wondered if she could climb in without opening the door. It might be less of a squash. She doubled over, and jammed her palm into her side to spread the hot stab. Control. Control. Breathe. Breathe. She hurried back into the house, grabbed the box of papers, and picked up her china rabbit, forgetting her case. Too bad—it would follow her later. She knew she had to get to a hospital though she didn't know which one. There was no time to drive back to Suffolk.

She gave herself a couple of minutes to strap the box into place and seat the rabbit so he could see through the windscreen, then she drew in her breath and squeezed behind the wheel. Next time, she thought, next time I'll be thin. Her belly felt different—something had shifted. She rubbed her thumbs down her cheeks, then pressed hard on her sweaty temples.

She started the engine and inched forward, stopped, letting the car roll, listening to the quiet crunch of gravel under the tires. The pain seemed to subside with the forward motion. There was a hospital in Kingston-on-Thames. It shouldn't be hard to find the H sign beside the road once she was heading in the right direction.

She floored the accelerator, flinging gravel onto the flowerbeds, and looked back to check the bald spot she'd left on the drive.

Her water broke close to Thames Ditton. She remembered being taught about what to do when this happened but she couldn't recall what the teacher said. She wasn't prepared for the force of it, the fact that it would end up in her shoes and spoil the leather seat. She whispered, "Shame," but she felt none, though it was a shame about the upholstery. She couldn't get out of the car now. "Shoot," she whispered. "Shoot!" Her panties were saturated. She would have to keep driving. The pains were faster, more fluttery, then, suddenly, more intense, the downward drag was hard to resist. "Don't push, don't push, dear."

She drove off the highway and through the village, then round and round a little roundabout, one hand on the steering wheel, one hand gripping the rabbit's ears. Round and round screeching the tires—if she did it enough, surely someone would bring her to a halt, a lollipop man would step out and stop her. Who was that man with the brown dog in front of the shop with the orange awning? Why didn't he look up? Bump, bump, bump. Why so many speed bumps? Roger called them dead policemen. Did they have speed bumps in France?

No one waved her down, so she selected a street that led in the direction of the river. She thought of Mrs. Das Gupta, blissfully numbering newspapers in her corner shop and she put her foot down hard. "I will show you the Thames," she said.

The people in the pub saw the white sports car careening down the boat ramp towards the water. The people at the table outside the pub had an even better view, they watched helplessly as the car bounced off a Volvo, then hit a concrete abutment before rolling over and ending up at the water's edge. The ducks made a great commotion. There was a lot of screaming, beer glasses shattered, chairs overturned, several patrons called 999, a young man in a cricket sweater kept repeating that he had his St. John's Ambulance certificate, a man on a passing pleasure boat shouted instructions that nobody heard.

CHAPTER NINETEEN

The rain persisted. Catherine welcomed it. Now she had an excuse not to venture outside. Mel was sleeping on the property. His presence in the yard and the studio affected her mood and shifted her focus, the outpouring of work didn't let up, but now the blemishes and birthmarks were less obvious, the faces were altered to become younger, more open, the veins less pronounced, the hands smoother, the breasts filled out. She saw that the painting was freer, looser. Large areas of canvas remained blank; she sketched in new ideas and the work started to be as much about space as about the relationship of parts. Shapes floated confidently, the colours muted; she worried them less, and, unlike her earlier efforts, they rested easily within the limits of the canvas. She began to feel more lucid. She knew this was an anomaly brought on by lack of sleep and hunger, but she didn't care, she liked it. She didn't care about the quality of the work, though she guessed it was good; she was out in front, ahead of herself.

She'd reached the bottom of her food supply. There was no toilet paper, no milk or coffee. She knew she'd have to go outside and cross Mel's path, but she put it off. She needed to rest more—her body twitched and her thighs leapt in her sleep. When she paused, she picked books from the shelves and read randomly, barely taking in the meaning of the words. She opened a book of essays and read that Darwin looked for oddities, misfits—he scorned perfection. The writer quoted him, 'You can't demonstrate evolution from the perfection of a gull's wing.' She liked that. There was no challenge in perfection.

She made do with the remains of a bag of noodles spiked with fish sauce, ignoring the display of Quaker grits in the pantry. For some reason the former owners had left the shelf loaded with the red and blue oval drums. She had no idea how to cook grits and she couldn't be bothered to read the instructions; when the noodles ran out, she tore off one of the lids, poured half the contents into a pan and added water and salt, regretting that she'd spoiled the symmetry of the display. She forced the slush down and it stopped up her hunger. She pushed herself harder, although she was snatching more and more rest. The work continued to be airy and light but the bones in her skull felt heavy and they seemed to be vibrating. She had the sensation of zooming forward, a feeling of elation she recognized from art school days. She was back in touch with the student who had the most potential in the entire art school, the world at her feet, never once worrying about the future, even after she got pregnant. She had no idea of time or how much of it had passed. How easy it was to come under the influence of the island, how simple to adapt. Darwin would be proud of her with her multiple imperfections.

The phone rang as she lay on the couch feeling weak and dizzy. At first she couldn't place the insistent burr and when she picked up the receiver, she didn't recognize the voice. "Who is this?"

"Mom? It's me."

"What?"

"Are you okay? You sound far off. It's taken forever to find you. How come you haven't gone home? I couldn't get a hold of anyone. Ernie's phone's still hooked up but he's not picking up. Is he with you? Auntie Mary's still out of town. No one knew how to get a hold of you. Anyway, I found you."

"No one has my number."

"I called Chicago."

"They didn't! I told them not to!"

"It's me, Mom. Kit. Mom, it's urgent."

With a start she realized she'd hardly considered Kit since the move. None of the paintings recalled her. "Where are you?" she asked, blowing her nose on a paint rag.

"I'm in England, of course."

"In England?"

"Listen, you've gotta come over here. Quick. Now. I need you, I'm desperate, Mom. Listen, write down the name of the village. It's in Suffolk. The house is called Golding. Got that? Don't phone, just come. And ask at the store or the pub, they'll direct you, okay? Get a cab from Colchester or Ipswich. You've gotta come, Mom. I'm in the worst trouble. The worst trouble I've ever been in. I can't stay on the phone." Catherine caught the cry of a young baby and scribbled down the address before the line went dead.

'These are the patterns in a sunflower,' she read from the open book in her lap. '1,1,2,3,5,8,13,21, each number is the sum of the two that precede it. Divide it by the number that follows it and we have 0.618. The ratio of 0.618 is the Divine Proportion, the Golden Section, the ideal geometrical proportion as used in architecture, found in many plants and shells.' Golding. She underlined the name. "All the world gleams golden," she said, aloud, and then she lost her breath. She knew she could breathe if she wanted to. It was a choice. Everything was a choice. I have never worked coldly. She opened her mouth and heard herself keen—it sounded like the faint mew of a cat stuck on top of a telephone pole. Surely the divine had no end? But something divine had snapped. Her breathing kicked in, but the keening continued until tears washed it out. She couldn't place the time when she'd last cried. She couldn't even get to the place where she'd been before she'd broken her own rule and answered the phone. The poem nagged her, 'Golden gleams the western sky...all the world gleams golden.' She'd learned it at school. She tried to retrieve the author's name—Walter, Walter, Walt? Mel appeared in the doorway, looking worried. She waved him away. She was past the point of being able to get up, so she set herself adrift and cried until darkness and exhaustion sucked her up.

When she was finally through customs at Heathrow, Catherine made her way to the tube station. She was grateful for the ancient carriage (one of the last of its kind, she heard somebody say), seats slashed, slatted floors providing a bowling alley for discarded bottles and beer cans. It was the England she remembered, grubby and down at heel. The familiar glimpses of moist red roofs and identikit suburbs gave her hope that she wouldn't feel like a stranger after so long. She got up and examined her reflection in the darkened window of one of the doors, barely recognizing the wraith with yellowish bags like bruises under her eyes. She pinched the swags of skin under her arms. Her jeans bagged. She'd had to drape them around her and fasten them with a brooch, but it seemed to have gone missing. She lost her reflection as the train burst into light again. Gardens. What was with the English, that they tended their gardens better than their children? She tended neither.

The brief snatches of familiarity ended at Liverpool Street. The station had transformed from dingy to upscale. It had an oddly European atmosphere—the precinct full of shops selling exotic cheeses, Belgian chocolate and futuristic umbrellas. Cellphones had replaced bowler hats. She wandered round, dazed, listening to the rattle of her suitcase wheels on the flagstones, looking for the yellow fruit-cake with scarlet cherry pockmarks that train riders used to gobble down at stations. Someone on the station was actually making an announcement in French. The commuters were no longer pasty white.

Mel's last kiss was still on her lips, the kiss planted just as the gangplank was due to be raised on the ferry. For a first kiss, it couldn't have been more public.

She sat on a bench. A clock told her it was nine o'clock; she thought this must mean nine p.m. It felt late in spite of the throngs of people. She had no sense of how long she'd been travelling. She pulled out her pen and her sketchbook, stared at the blank page and wrote Fuck. The word looked pathetic and inadequate. The enormity of her blasphemy couldn't be broken down into silly little words. The pain of leaving her work was still so strong she didn't know if she'd be able to continue to support it. She'd been painting her mother's hat—floating, headless—the red hat she wore to church, the hat no one was allowed to touch.

The morning after the phone call, she'd finally invited Mel into the kitchen. He'd spent a long time looking at the paintings, shuffling from one to the next without saying a word, until finally she'd had to instruct him. "What you see is an old woman with varicose veins, a skin like an ashtray and such a fixation on herself there's nothing going on in the world outside her window." She'd waited for him to negate this, but he hadn't. He'd simply grinned. She'd decided he didn't get it—why should he—she didn't get it herself. She wanted to hear him say the work was brilliant, but he merely touched her arm. And now she couldn't be shot of him. He'd bypassed all her resolutions. She was in such need of kindness and good advice and he'd found the chink in her rhinoceros armour. She'd had no number to call Kit back. Her instinct told her the trouble was real. Should she have come to England? Should she have stayed? Why was it suddenly impossible to function alone? She felt his lips again—foreign, yet familiar, warm and slightly salty.

The lone cab outside Colchester Station might have been waiting for her. She parroted the address Kit had given her and sat back, abandoning herself to the intoxicating smell of stale smoke—it was good to know the English still welcomed smokers. She was whisked along miles of unfamiliar highway on the wrong side of the road with fields and hedges looming darkly on either side. There was a cloudy moon and a couple of stars hanging low, almost touching a hump of ground to her left. She felt suspended, like a yawn that refused to be yawned.

She could just make out the thatched roof on the darkened house when they pulled up. As she fumbled for the fare, she asked the driver to wait, in case there was a mistake. She felt foolish lugging her case up the path, standing on the doorstep, prodding the bell in the middle of no-man's land. The three-note peal was deafening. How could Kit possibly be behind this door? She was probably waking a guard dog.

It took a succession of peals before a light went on and she heard footsteps. The door was on a chain. Someone let out a screech. "Mo-o-om."

She waved the cab away, the door opened and they flew into one another's arms.

Kit sniffed her throat as they swayed together in the hall; she snuffled along one of Catherine's arms, coming to rest in her armpit burying her nose in her parka, then detached herself and stood back, holding both her hands. "You look like a hick, Mom!"

Catherine shook her off.

"I mean it. I don't recognize you. Where's all the padding gone? You're all bony, like you came from a fire sale—a parka in summer?—where'd you dig up that suitcase?"

"Sorry for the clothes. I dropped everything. There wasn't time to dress up. I threw all my good ones out when I stopped teaching." Catherine saw their reflection in a mirror on the hallstand, the back of Kit's head with her own face looking out over her daughter's shoulder, a young face, the potato skin miraculously peeled back. She saw her next painting and her imagination reached for the smell of paint. "I'm totalled."

"You came," Kit said, grabbing Catherine's arm and leading her through to the kitchen where she filled a kettle. The room was well fitted out, but it didn't look as though anyone ever ate in it.

"I couldn't get back to you. You didn't leave me a number—fortunately the cab driver was used to picking up from this place. You're still in trouble?"

"Guess so."

"Where am I?"

"The English always have tea, I guess you know that. They think it's the solution to all life's problems. They drank gallons after the funeral. You should've seen them. There was all this wine, and they drank tea. In china teacups. Typical, isn't it?"

"Who...?"

"The mourners. The family. I didn't know any of them. They all wore hats."

"No. I mean, who died?" Light was starting to filter through. "Not your father!"

"No. Not him."

"Whose house am I in?" She cast around, "Don't tell me it's his. Not Roger's! He's here?" She was shouting.

Kit shook her head. "Shush! He won't sleep in the house. He doesn't want to come over the threshold. Okay, so it's his. Well, that can't make any difference after all these years, can it?"

"Oh Kit, you don't know what you've done!" This must be how it felt to be shell-shocked. "Who's dead? Have you had a baby? I don't want tea."

"Good." Kit shut off the gas. The baby started to cry somewhere upstairs.

"Why didn't you tell me you were pregnant?"

"It's not mine, Mom. It's Roger's. I call him Dad now, you don't mind, do you? I guess it makes the baby my half brother?"

"Wait a minute, I'm skipping."

"He doesn't have a name yet. I call him Pip."

"Start again, Kit. Tell me this is a bad dream."

"He's in some kind of state...I dunno, he's kinda lost it."

"Roger?"

"Dad. He's swallowing pills. He doesn't want to come home. He has this studio up the road, only it's not really a studio, it's more of a cottage. Ilona rented it for him as a surprise. He's staying there."

"Ilona?"

"Yeah. She's the one that died."

"Such a name." Catherine stared at the too-solid granite surface, and put her elbows on the counter, head in her hands. "So his wife died in childbirth?"

"Yeah, something like that."

"What does that have to do with you, Kit?"

"I killed her." Kit jumped up, ran into the hall and hefted Catherine's case up the stairs. Catherine followed as fast as she could and reached out to grab her, but Kit dodged her grasp, opened the door on what looked like the master bedroom, deposited the case and vanished.

Catherine sat down heavily on the bed. The mattress was hard. She reached for the switch on the bedside lamp. There was a photo on the night table. A young girl in a high collared grey suit that reminded her of a Salvation Army uniform was leaning on an old man's arm as if she were holding it down to stop it from floating away. They were posing against some kind of fortress with a sunny continental harbour behind them. The photo stood on a doily. She hadn't seen a doily since she was last in England. She pulled it out and balled it in her hand. Kit was suddenly standing in front of her again. Her cheekbones looked more pronounced, she'd had her hair blunt cut in an unflattering style. "I can't take this in, Kit, I'm in a time-warp."

"That's him," Kit pointed at the photograph. "And her. Ilona. On their honeymoon."

"Married?"

"Yes."

"But how...?"

"—old is she? Twenty-three. She was having her birthday the day I got here. I crashed it."

Was it supposed to hurt that he'd married a child? It was just information. "And you say she passed on?"

"No. She died, Mom. She had a really bloody death."

Catherine shuddered. "I'm...I dunno...that's Roger in the photo?"

"Don't you recognize him?"

"I suppose I do. No. No, I don't. How did she die?"

"Pretty well instantly. It's amazing they saved one of the twins."

"Twins?" This was a nightmare. "I'm sorry."

"They said she was in labour. She drove into the river."

"Suicide?"

Kit's eyes filled with tears. "Don't know."

Catherine sat motionless and cradled her in her arms. Kit tried to pull away, but Catherine hung on, hearing herself say, "Darling." Then she said it again. "Darling," over and over. She'd called Kit darling when she was teething, and many times when she'd sat with her, comforting her after a bad dream, but never after that.

✲

Ernie Last worked at his projects methodically. The downstairs apartment was looking brighter, the floor was laid in the kitchen, the blue and yellow gave the room new life but the old appliances dragged it down, so he replaced them with the most up-to-date models he could find and he installed a dishwasher and a microwave to ensure she would have no excuse to leave again.

He couldn't escape the knowledge that the unfurnished rooms were unloved. He knew she wouldn't appreciate him buying new furniture, and he fretted. As the décor changed, she seemed less and less present. He sat in the basement in the evening, whittling as he used to when she let him in. He whittled female figures about eight inches tall. Each one bore a crude resemblance to Catherine, some had her owlish glasses, others her brush cut—they were all unclothed but this wasn't obvious, as the bodies and legs weren't well defined. A close observer would make out the nipples and a scratch of pubic hair. He stood the figures on the floor of her former studio, marching shoulder to shoulder. Some he arranged on the new kitchen tiles like chessmen, some he clumped together in the center of the living room. The apartment felt less empty, and, as he added to the figures, he felt her return coming closer. Any day now, she'd be calling for him to drive down to the States to pick her up. He was patient, she knew that; she could rely on him not to disturb her; she would be happy to know how busy he was.

Catherine shifted her weight around the unyielding futon, checking the illuminated dial of the bedside clock radio every ten minutes. Leaf traceries and swooping winged shadows flitted left to right, right to left on the blind, backlit by the streetlight. She doubted if Kit had changed the sheets. She was sure she could hear grunts and creaks coming from the mattress—the sound of sudden release.

The morning light, when it came, was timid. There were hours to fill before she could get up. She tried to anticipate her meeting with Roger—she could smell him in the bed. Should she run? Get up and go? There was a telephone by the bed. She made a note of the number.

She tested herself, trying to retrieve details of their domestic life. What did they eat? There was a fish and chip shop on the corner of the street—skate and chips on Saturday night, smothered with tart H.P. sauce the colour of wet bark. She remembered the bones, like umbrella spokes. Did she cook? Who bought the groceries? Who went to the laundromat—no, the laundrette—she remembered that word. Painstakingly, she reconstructed the layout of their flat. All the details were gone, all the basics of togetherness, wiped out. When or where was Kit conceived? What about morning sickness? They'd slept on big square pillows in 1964 when they went to Austria and tried to ski without paying for lessons. The pillows in this bed were exactly the same. She buried her nose in one and pulled it round her ears. She needed to get things straight. His current wife had died—was this his second wife? His third go around? His fourth?

She let go of the pillow. Roger was a sporadic lover. When he was on he was completely on, and when he wasn't, he told her to "go whistle." Harsh. 'On' times were urgent, he'd acted as though he'd burst if he didn't satisfy himself instantly. It used to work, too, she remembered feeling as if she'd been burnished. She liked his body, he woke up all her sleeping places, the arches of her feet, inside her elbows. There hadn't been anyone since. It was too long—too long to be having these thoughts. Too confusing. They'd been a good fit though no one else saw it; he was all she'd needed. She let her mind drift back to Mel. What did a married man have to offer? She had no business thinking of him in her ex-husband's bed. She had no business being here.

She remembered the big jar of pickled onions on the counter in the chip shop; in those days you slid your fingers in, the onions were slippery, sometimes it took several dips to snag one. She couldn't bring back the street outside the shop, A,B,C, D...she went through the alphabet, trolling for its name. On the way home, she always unwrapped the newspaper, sampled the chips and picked the flesh off the fish bones and Roger was always furious, she could see his livid face, much thinner, no grog blossoms round the nose like the face in the photograph.

Where did they catch the bus? Which tube station did they use? She was helicoptering memories in and coming up with shoddy bits of collage. That's what Tom Gilbert, the best teacher in art school, used to say in his critiques. "This part's alive, but that part you're helicoptering in." She'd used the same line on her students. That was the trouble with good teachers, you let them poison your perceptions without questioning them and then the poison got passed down the chain; art lives and breathes deception so why cover it up? And what's memory if it isn't art? If Tom were to walk in on her now, she'd tell him not to crash people's helicopters.

Catherine screwed her eyes shut, trying to short out the dreadful mistake she'd made in leaving home. What a fool, to jump the minute Kit said, "I need you." She would never be able to pick up the pieces when she got back, she'd be forced to work coldly.

The baby cried. She heard Kit creep downstairs, presumably to heat milk. What would become of him? Roger had been completely uninterested when he was introduced to his newborn daughter—there was no reason to believe he'd change now that he had a son. Someone should step in and arrange for a nanny. If the house was anything to go on, he'd acquired some loot and in doing so, he'd lost his taste. She counted the danglers on the mini-chandelier on the ceiling.

She got up, groped her way to the ensuite bathroom and sat down to pee without putting the light on. Too late—the cold shock—she realized Roger was up to his old tricks. He never bothered to lower the seat. On the way back to bed, she pulled the blind up a few inches and knelt to look through the gap. The streetlight was still on, though daylight was well established along with the dawn chorus, something else she'd erased. There were other thatched roofs in sight so she knew she wasn't in the middle of the countryside, though there was no noise, no traffic—the villagers—if this was a village, were still sleeping, not a night owl among them. She kept watch until a woman walking a waist-high poodle crossed the road, appearing out of nowhere. Satisfied that she was not alone, Catherine padded out onto the landing. A nightlight burned in the room at the end of the corridor and Kit sat cross-legged on the carpet just inside the door. A wing of hair hid the noisy bundle in her arms. Her washed-out T-shirt read www.luv.me. She looked up at Catherine and smiled a sweet, contented smile. It was not an expression Catherine recognized.

"Think I'll take a shower."

Kit nodded. "Help yourself to towels," she said. "Make yourself at home."

The shower was sweet, hot and forceful, unlike any English shower she'd known, and, to her surprise she discovered a towel-warmer by the sink. Heated bathrooms? Along with all the other changes, they were no longer scourging themselves. She stepped out, wrapped herself in one of the big fluffy towels and went on a tour of exploration.

The window at the end of the landing looked out onto a pop-up picture of rolling countryside with pop-up trees and a strategically placed stream that probably burbled if you got close enough to hear. It seemed both unremarkable and extraordinary. The population of England had almost doubled since she'd left. How did they all fit in and still maintain even a shred of open space? She'd heard they'd cut down all their hedgerows, yet the hedges were still in place, darkly dividing one green or gold square from another.

Downstairs in the kitchen, Kit had laid the baby on the counter.

"He'll roll off." Catherine scooped him up automatically and felt his dry diaper. Kit sat at the table holding an enormous yellow coffee cup in both hands. She didn't offer Catherine any coffee. Her face looked ashen and she had panda eyes.

"How long since you slept, Kit?"

"Dunno."

"How old is he? Pip? Is that his name?"

"Philip, well, he was supposed to be Alexander, but that was before. I called him after the Duke of Edinburgh."

"You're joking!"

"No. I like it—I cut his picture out of the paper the day before...that day."

"When was the baby born?" She would have to proceed cautiously, Kit had the word FRAGILE tattooed on her forehead.

"Ten days ago. He wasn't exactly born. More like ripped out."

Two small purplish fists waved in Catherine's face. She couldn't help touching the fingernails, marveling at their perfect form. He had a boat shaped birthmark at the base of his neck like Kit once had. She explored the over-large skull, feeling for the hole that all babies have. His skin was warmer than she anticipated. He smelled sour. "I don't want to hear the details."

"No, I didn't think you would, you never do, do you?"

"Okay—how long has he been with you?"

"I'm not sure. When did I call you? It was before that. They kept him in the hospital to check him out. They say he's fine, not even bruised. He was full term. He's sweet, isn't he? Everyone says he's a survivor."

"What happened to the other one?"

"I don't know. I don't think they were identical. Someone said he was decapitated by the steering wheel." Her expression didn't change as she imparted this bombshell. "I have to learn about babies."

"There were two and one died and they weren't identical." Catherine missed a breath. "What about the mother's family? Can't they take over?"

"Dad asked me to stay. I forgot that you didn't like babies."

"That's not fair. You're not being fair, Kit, I came, didn't I?"

"But you wouldn't've come if you'd known I was here."

"Probably not."

"See!"

"And when I get here, the first thing you tell me is that you killed this young woman."

Kit put her nose in the yellow cup and shut her eyes. Catherine saw tears oozing from under her lids but she didn't trust them. Kit had been an actress from the time she could crawl, often to an audience of one; Catherine was always fooled into thinking a child so young couldn't help but tell the truth.

"Kit, I need to know the truth."

"Okay, okay, I may have exaggerated."

"Oh God." Catherine sighed. Kit's way was to bring down the curtain and walk from unpleasantness, and this invariably caused more grief. Catherine knew she had to tread carefully, but she had no idea what she was treading on. What role had been allotted to her in this drama? "Just fill me in. How did Roger coerce you into this situation?"

"It's okay. It's not a situation and there's no coercion." Kit wiped her eyes and the tears were gone. "You can ask him yourself, Mom. Chill out."

"I didn't even know he'd gotten married again."

"But you could've guessed."

"I didn't trouble to guess. How many wives has he had? Oh, forget it, it doesn't matter. Tell me about Ilona. Was that really her name?"

"She was from this incredibly hoity-toity family. They live in a place called Surrey. That's where they held the funeral. They made me think of those stiff-upper-lip British drawing room comedies, but they weren't even witty—they were total androids. They just assumed that because I was from Canada, I had to be dumb, and they spelled everything out 'terribly, terribly' slowly. It was embarrassing. And they acted like Ilona wasn't even related to them—they were more concerned about people parking in their neighbour's driveway, and keeping the dog off the lawn and why the red wine wasn't 'enchambré,' than being real. Talk about the big chill. It was a cremation. Dad wasn't even consulted—well, two cremations counting the other twin. And her two stuffed-shirt brothers just stood there saying, 'Thank you for your concern.' They were like tin soldiers with their hair plastered down and these black ties, and black pointy handkerchiefs in their breast pockets, like little black pointy teeth. I tried to wind them up but they didn't get it, they just gulped. And her father made this speech. He said they'd meant to name her for this mystical Scottish island and they got it wrong and called her after an Italian porn star instead. Dad was gutted. Apparently the guy told the same story at their wedding. And her mother's something else—well, you'll meet her. She's about the same age as Dad, or maybe younger, you can't tell under all the enamel. Red lipstick up to her nostrils and big hats and stuff. Poor Ilona, she was such a great person." She stopped and held out her hands in a hopeless gesture. "I guess that's it."

"No. No, that's not it. It's not even the tip of the iceberg." Catherine picked up the baby. "Is he hungry?"

"No. He's overflowing. I've been pouring milk into him all night. It just comes out the other end."

"Do you have formula?"

"Of course I have formula."

"Where?"

She waved her hand at a cupboard. "I have this girlfriend who went to India last year. And she was up on top of this tower like Rapunzel, she was leaning over the rail, blissing on the scene and there was a family on one side of her and they held their baby out over the rail and it peed into the wind and she caught it smack in the mouth. And they didn't even say sorry. See, they don't diaper their babies—it's not a bad idea."

"It's a bad idea." Kit was going full throttle. She needed to be slowed down.

"...but you know, I was reading in one of these English colour supplements about this high school experiment to stop girls having babies. They make them carry a nine pound rock around for a month. They have to sleep with it and eat with it. If they want to put it down, they have to find a sitter. Apparently it really works. They go right off motherhood. I cut the article out. I have all these articles. Weird, eh?"

"Weird," Catherine sighed.

"Oh Mom, it was so...so...I can't begin to describe it. I mean, I can't even think of her as dead. It's just so...disgusting. So incredibly...I mean, poor her. She was probably an amazing person. I didn't do enough. I didn't pay any attention. It was my fault."

"What should you have done?"

"I don't know...more."

"Is that what you mean by killing her?"

"Not exactly."

"Are you in trouble? I was thinking about what you said all night."

"It's just that I was hanging with Dad. And I said she was crazy. Well, she was crazy. You must see I can't just crap out and leave him holding the baby." She pushed her cup aside. It blazed like a sun on the granite tabletop.

"Listen, if you take this child on, you're going to have to see it through and that's a lifetime commitment. You have to understand. It's not a nine pound stone. You could be saddled..."

"Like you're saddled with me?"

"I'm not. I just want you to consider the implications. In thirty-five years you could be sitting at this table with this same kid, and he'll be in trouble, and you'll be completely out of your depth and you'll have to cope and you'll be..."

"I'll be seventy!"

"Exactly."

"Don't worry. I'll be dead. You know your trouble? You're too indulgent. Whenever I wanted rapture, all I ever got was indulgence."

"Oh, grow up. Why do you still act and talk so immature?" Catherine needed air. She had a strong sense that Kit was regressing, time was moving backwards. She got up and carefully placed the baby in her daughter's lap, his head a few inches from the golden cup. She remembered how Kit used to hold buttercups under her chin to let her see the yellow reflection, and prove she liked butter. She remembered the tiny baby who'd kept her up, night after night, who snapped the painting thread just as painfully then as now. And Kit still had no idea of the rupture she'd caused.

She found her way through the strange front yard with its fake wood fences and dry bamboo water shoot. Neither direction beckoned, so she turned left and walked up the hill. In daylight, she saw that the walls of the house had recently been painted, scaffolding poles were piled in the driveway, waiting for pickup. Golding was the sort of English relic they'd always joked about—it even had roses round the door, golden roses of course, almost lost against the golden walls. She thought of the doilies and the chandelier and shook herself. She had to stay detached from this sanitized version of Roger and the enormity of what had happened to his wife. He had failed in the fatherhood stakes again and now he was dumping the fallout in his daughter's lap. Where was he? Surely he wasn't going to abandon Kit in his ersatz English paradise? He'd always believed in happy endings. All the world gleams golden.

She passed a terrace of workers' cottages. The drapes were open in the one at the center of the row. A man in shirtsleeves was watching T.V. and swigging something from a red can. He had his back to the window. The yard was cramped, it took only a couple of steps to reach the window. It was an ordinary room, a familiar room. She'd seen its like many times when she lived in England, a standard lamp with a fringed shade, a gas fire, maroon overstuffed furniture, flowered carpet, china shepherdesses. She peered at the T.V. screen. It looked as though a stage magician was sawing his assistant in half. She looked closer and saw it wasn't sleight of hand. A woman's body was being dismembered in full colour. The camera closed in on the saw blade as it hacked through her thigh bone, then it pulled back to show the butcher's face, utterly concentrated on the task. She was watching her first snuff movie. She stood, frozen, confronting her own painting process on film.

A door slammed. She glanced up as a man stepped out of a front door further along the terrace. She followed his progress as he turned along the street towards her. He passed without appearing to notice her. Gagging, she scrambled back into the street and turned in the opposite direction. After a few steps, she sank down on a wall, willing herself not to throw up. She had witnessed the grisliest act of desecration on a real woman's body—but was it real? The body was being dissected, then speared by a movie camera that paralyzed at the same time as it called for action. The woman was a fly on a pin. She had no personality, no name. Surely the viewer could be excused if she felt nothing. Film could do that—it wasn't like painting. She mustn't let it affect her.

The village high street opened up in front of her, like the opening shot of a new scene. Ordinary shops in an ordinary community, poised and pretty as a calendar—a second hand bookstore, a green-grocer—a post office with a window full of notices written on post-cards. Yet nothing was ordinary. Who knew what was going on in all these back rooms? She paused in front of the post office to read the messages, waiting for the words to stop dancing, expecting a musical cue to tell her what she should be feeling. Postcards were relics, like everything else around here. Someone wanted somebody to do the ironing, preferably on Friday mornings. Someone had a tricycle for sale, a room for rent, two elderly terriers requested a dog walker and a tinted blue card called for a live-in nanny. She read it over twice and realized it gave Roger's number. The writing wasn't Kit's or Roger's. She read it through again. It was too bland, there must be a hidden message.

Turning away from the shop window, she banged her head on a hanging basket and just missed falling over the swinging tin adver-tisement for Walls Ice Cream that was placed strategically to trip pedestrians. The English were great at creating obstacles where none existed previously, then finding ingenious solutions. Everything was geared up for another sleepy day. She looked around. Nothing could go wrong, short of not finding a walker for your terrier—unless someone willed it all to change course. She'd been crazy to think Kit had had anything to do with the death of Roger's child-bride. And women in snuff movies didn't really die. It wouldn't take more than a day to get Kit organized and out of here. With luck she could get off without ever meeting Roger, go home and pick up from the kiss. Mel had come on the scene to remind her it was unhealthy to spend her life alone, dismembering herself and her past. She started walking. The nausea receded.

When she got back to the house, Kit and the baby were nowhere around. She dragged her case into the small bedroom on the third floor, which she'd decided last night was probably a maid's room. It was stuffy, but at least there were no doilies or happy family pictures. She hadn't slept for forty-eight hours and she collapsed on the bed fully dressed.

※

Kit roused her with breakfast the next morning.

"How long have I slept?"

"It's tomorrow!"

She jumped, rocking the tray, remembering the nine-year-old who brought her burnt toast and rubbery scrambled eggs on Mother's Day. This time the toast wasn't burned: it was replaced by three wafers of Ryvita in a silver toast rack, some butter and two wedges of orange. Ryvita always made her think of vinegar and brown paper.

"Are you more comfortable in here, Mom? Don't you have any p.j.'s?"

Catherine stretched, sending the dangling parchment lampshade into a swoon. "Lord, I've slept. You're sure it's tomorrow already? I haven't been much use to you, have I?"

Kit flung her arms round her. "I don't want you to be useful, Mom. I just want you to be here. It's okay. Dad's gone away. I dropped by his studio yesterday and persuaded him to get out of town. He's completely wasted."

Catherine was instantly awake. "Where's he gone?"

"Spain."

"When's he coming back?"

"I told him I'd give him the nod."

"What nod?"

"I said to decompress, let things settle down. He's not going to be any help round here the way he is right now. He can take as long as he needs. It's okay, you won't have to see him."

"Things aren't going to settle down, Kit. Not as long as he's out of the country and you're here with his child. He has to take responsibility. He's useless! Surely you've figured that out? Useless as tits on a billy goat."

"What?"

"You know what I mean."

"You don't know him, Mom. He's not like you think. I mean, what do you expect? He's lost his wife and kid. I know you don't want to hear about it, but, look." Kit dumped a cardboard box on the bed. "I brought this from Dad's studio. The police or someone brought it to the door after the accident. Apparently it was in her car. There was her watch and her rings and her purse—and this. And there was a china rabbit, all in pieces. Most of the stuff that didn't get thrown out of the car got a bit wet from the river. The watch took a hit, it stopped at 3:15, and the ink's run on this label, look, but the contents seem to be pretty dry. Dad's not up to dealing with it."

"This has got nothing to do with me, Kit." Catherine nudged the box off her ankles. "Your father's going to have to come right back home."

"Open it. Read. It's only papers. They're not about Ilona. Maybe you can sort them out. That'll be useful. Look, I have to buy groceries. Enjoy your breakfast."

"But what about the baby?"

"I'll take him with me. Luckily the house is full of baby stuff. Two of everything." Catherine lay back. The morning sun streamed through the leaded window, a golden rose knocked against the outside pane stirred by a breeze. She poured herself a cup of thick espresso coffee, drinking in the smell. Occasionally Kit got things exactly right. She would dip into the box when she was more in the mood.

CHAPTER TWENTY

⁓

The paint on the stairs was barely dry and Mel was sitting, rolling a cigarette, half hidden behind Catherine's parked Valiant, when he heard a vehicle stop on the road. He slipped into a better position so he could see without being seen as the tall white-haired man opened the gate, pushed past the Rhododendron and walked up the front path, his neck stuck out, his head moving around like a turtle. He knocked at the front door, politely enough, and then, having waited for a response, he banged with his fists. Mel slipped behind the shed as the stranger stepped onto the path leading out back and stood, looking up at the studio. He put his foot on the bottom stair and Mel noticed he had good boots, cowboy-style boots with engravings over the pointed toes, not something you'd pick up from a catalogue. "No you don't. Who you looking for?" The guy looked puzzled. "Best get moving." Mel kept his voice as low as he could. "Lady's not home at present."

"Where is she?"

"Who wants to know?"

"I drove down from Vancouver."

"So?"

"I'm her landlord."

"She owe back rent?"

"No! That is...I just came to see how she's doing—when she's coming back. I'm holding the apartment."

"That's not a good idea."

Ernie turned to the back door, tried the handle, looked through the window into the kitchen. The wash of colour that met his gaze knocked him back. He stood, trying to absorb the shock of it. Mel was at his shoulder. "I see she's been working."

"I'd say."

Ernie lunged toward the glass. He'd spotted the large nude, breasts flattened—it was the image he'd had with him ever since the night of her party. She must have known it was his. "Did you have something to do with this?"

"What do you mean?"

"Why did she do this?"

Mel shrugged. The guy was obviously missing a couple links in his chain; his lip was trembling. It was embarrassing. "I think it's time you was on your way, man." He tried to be gentle.

"Where is she?"

"Right now? As far as I know, she's in England." The white guy let out a sigh like a collapsed inner tube and Mel suddenly felt sorry for him, he'd come a long way. He should have phoned first. "There's some coffee in that flask before you take off," he offered.

"Thanks." Ernie didn't move. He thought of her living room in Vancouver gradually filling up with wave upon wave of spiky brush-cut heads. When he lay on his side on the floor, one or other of her features repeated itself. And here she'd taken herself apart in her new kitchen. Here was her head, over and over, not always attached, not always complete. Here were parts of her body, floating free—pieces of clothing. And there was the nude. Complete. She must have known he'd watched her that rainy night. How could he face her now? And who was this man who was acting like a watchdog? This wasn't what he'd looked forward to as he drove down, when he waited impatiently for the ferry, got on board, paced the loading deck until one of the deckhands shouted at him to get back from the edge. He dreamed she'd be lying around, moping, and then, at the sight of him, she'd realize her mistake and jump at the opportunity to backtrack. She'd apologize for not calling and leaving her number. What a fool, to dream! You couldn't backtrack. Backtrack. It was a nonsense word. Like love. "I love her, you see," he said flatly, looking Mel in the eye, as he backed up into her drive, preparing to turn around.

Mel wasn't sure he'd heard right. "You're spinning your wheels, fella." The back tires on the truck were slipping on the muddy drive—no tread. He watched as the vehicle took off. He hadn't been home since she left. The kiss was all over the island just the way he'd intended at the time.

⚘

When Ernie hit the Interstate, he turned right instead of left, headed south and kept driving. His life was no longer about boot making, it was about plumbing and sisters—a nothing life. Without Catherine he'd turned into a nobody. He decided to keep on driving till he reached Mexico.

⚘

Kit knocked, and pushed the bedroom door open. Catherine hadn't moved for hours. The tray with its mix of crumbs and rinds lay abandoned on the floor, the papers from the box were strewn across the quilt.

"What's going on?"

Catherine blinked. "This is amazing, Kit. Do you know what this is?"

"A bunch of old mail, recipes, mostly bills."

"And a diary—or a fragment. Written in 1911." She picked up the pages of Winifred Church's diary. "Is this blood? Where's the rest?"

Kit shrugged.

"Oh come on. Look, someone's ripped it apart."

"I told you—it was Ilona's. It must be her blood. I thought it would be something for you to do. Don't get so excited, 1911's not old, not over here."

"Where's St. Agathe? Get the atlas out."

"What atlas?"

"Oh, Kit. It's Emily Carr. And Frances Hodgkins! And I think it's genuine. I must've told you about them."

"Along with all the others."

"According to this, they were there together. In France. Oh, get the atlas out. This is the time when Carr did her French paintings— and Hodgkins—I know that name so well, but I can't place her."

"It's weird, this is the third time Emily Carr's come up since I got here. There's a place a few miles from here that used to be a nuthouse, and now it's luxury apartments. And before all that it was a T.B. hospital and Emily Carr was a patient!"

"In this village?"

"Dad said the mortuary sold for about three hundred thousand pounds. Do you know how much that is in serious money? Who'd live there? It must be haunted."

"Would you take me there?"

"And Dad has this sketch of hers in the studio—he got it at a sale. He remembered you talking about her."

"He remembered me talking about Emily Carr?"

"That's what he said."

"And he owns a sketch? You know she's never been at the top of my list, but she's been on my mind lately."

"It's just a cartoon of a bed and a nurse and a birdcage. It was thrown out when they stripped the building."

"Were there more?"

Kit shrugged.

"She wrote a book about being in that sanatorium, it was called *Pause*. I have it somewhere—I was only thinking about her yesterday—well, not yesterday but—you say Roger has one of her sketches? And this diary. I mean, it's synchronicity. It's an incredible find. Maybe this is why I'm here. You have to look for the missing pages."

"You can see the drawing for yourself. It's nothing. Why don't we walk up to the studio and take a look? It's just up the road."

"Oh, no."

"He's in Spain, Mom! We won't run into him. It's just a little cottage at the end of a row. Just up the road."

Catherine flinched. "I saw a guy coming out."

"When?"

"I don't know, I was watching a snuff movie."

"You?"

"I have to think, Kit. You're throwing too much at me."

Kit prodded her sharply, "Maybe you need some more sleep."

"I want to go through this stuff properly. Then I'll take you out for a meal. Then I want you to take me to that hospital. We'll find someone to sit with your nine pound living stone. By the way, did I take over your room?" She noticed Kit's bag on the floor.

"You're finally you again, Mom!" Kit waltzed out of the room, grinning.

§ St. Agathe, June 25th, 1911

I didn't sleep well after I closed these pages last night. Whenever I dropped off, I dreamed of the abandoned kitchen garden and my father rattling around in the unused rooms of the old family house. In one dream, the house was consumed by a fire, but it didn't burn. In another, my mother was sitting at the kitchen table. I dreamed she sat there for days, everyone walked around her and she never blinked and no one noticed her. I won't even chronicle the rest. I haven't been home since I married. We meet my father for lunch at Claridges at Christmas and on his birthday. He always pays the bill, which is not strictly necessary.

I have always been of the opinion that feelings, when sifted through the mesh of time must eventually settle, but now I am beginning to doubt it. If you prod and poke under the surface, everything festers. It's like teasing a hangnail, and ending up with a whitlow. So what is the answer? Feelings put into words have presence, like pain. Perhaps the presence, once it is acknowledged makes you more alive, perhaps even a little *damp*.

I feel oddly close to Miss Carr this morning. I hope she spent a better night than I. I am annoyed at myself for letting the cat out of the bag about her precious pole pictures, I think they were something special—could she not have guessed at Fanny's opinion? It is hard to accept adverse criticism of something that has cost you a good deal, but it happens to us all at some time, as my husband will attest. He tells his pupils, "If you're only looking for praise, or you merely want to give pleasure then you should be a pastry cook." I suppose the answer is that one should never put oneself up for examination until one feels more dry than wet.

Fanny will be expecting me to report on my meeting with Miss Carr, but I won't go looking for her, to do so would be disloyal, besides, Fanny has not played fair with me of late. No. I will say nothing. I owe her nothing. It will be best if we have no contact for the present, I won't even waste my contempt on her. I will concentrate my attentions on Miss Carr and try to part her from her mackintosh, and in the meantime I will stay at home and begin my lists. Perhaps this pole business will be the ultimate test of her friendship with Frances.

There's a lot of planning ahead. Our sojourn here is coming to an end; we will be leaving earlier than usual to prepare for Geoffrey's show. There is the yearly ritual of closing up this house and of airing the house in Mecklenburgh Square. If the rail strike continues, we will have to think up a way of transporting his canvases to Paris. The town is full of horses, and I'm sure someone like Raoul would be willing to tackle the journey if he is allowed to take his time, but we will need something larger, speedier and more reliable than a ramshackle trap. I don't think this has occurred to Geoffrey yet, and I won't worry him with it.

§ St. Agathe, June 26th, 1911

I spotted Frances Hodgkins and Mr. Merton having supper outside a fish restaurant in the old town tonight. I suppose I was looking for them, I only cross over the ramp into the old town when I am on business. I was restless. I'd left Geoffrey a plate of cold meats and a salad and taken off, seeking some relief from the heat of the day and from my lists.

They didn't spot me. I can't explain why I didn't immediately make myself known, but they seemed to be very intent on their conversation. Their heads were almost touching until Frances threw hers back in a great guffaw of laughter. I heard Miss Carr's name mentioned. Mr. Merton was regaling Frances with a story and, since it obviously concerned Miss Carr, I felt it incumbent on me to listen.

I stood behind an awning and glued my eye to a rent in the fabric.

"Most extraordinary," said Frances. "What would have made her so surly?"

"I have no idea. I haven't had a chance to get to know her. I've barely even set eyes on her. She had her eye on those axes as though she wanted to reach inside, seize one and chop me into pieces. I wish she would let me approach her, she seems quite lively. Maybe she thinks I have horns."

"I don't think she's particularly fond of men—with a few exceptions of course. She has a sycophantic connection with Geoffrey Church. I can't imagine why, the man's such a bore and a charlatan, always cozying up to the rich and the famous. I don't know how poor Winnie puts up with him. I suppose it's because he's all she has. And he's not a bad artist. She's such an obliging soul—she simply asks to be tramped on. 'Do this Winnie, get that Winnie.' He turns her into a skivvy. People see her as a well-decked-out drudge and it's entirely his fault."

"We men are not all so unkind." Mr. Merton smiled and put his hand over hers.

My eyes misted over but my ears were unaffected. I wished myself far, far away. He was at least ten years younger than Frances, but in spite of this, her tone was suddenly mellow, and her voice was lower by half an octave, and I had thought she would not notice him! The pair of them disgusted me. It's true that listeners never hear well of themselves, but I deserved better from Frances. It was so unfair. She understands no more of marriage than of motherhood. And what about love? What did those two people know about love? Frances Hodgkins is a dried up old spinster. She is not a real woman and Mr. Merton is almost certainly a pansy.

I stepped out from behind the arras like Polonius, but I was not dead for a ducat, though Frances pointed her fork at me. I pulled back a chair and took a seat at their table almost falling over his large smelly dog. I was trembling and I didn't trouble to conceal it.

"I know about you, Frances Hodgkins," I said.

"I beg your pardon?"

"I know all about your bastard child and how you abandoned him to the Moors to be brought up as an infidel. You should make sure that your own house is in order before you pass judgment on others."

I don't know how I managed to get the words out. I raced away before she had a chance to respond, but she came after me, tripping on a cobble and tugging at my skirt to steady herself. It was all I could do to stop myself swiping her with my handbag.

"Winnie, Winifred Church. What are you talking about?"

"Making a fool of yourself. That man's playing with you, can't you see it? Do you know how old he is?"

"Winnie!" She pinned me against the wall. Her eyes were sparking and her hat swung, clinging to a strand of hair on the back of her head. I concentrated my attention on the large jet pin that held it captive. It's funny how you take in details, even when you are quite beside yourself. And I was. Beside myself, I mean. Quite literally. I saw myself, a small frightened mouse, flattened against the wall beside my own much larger body. An apparition. A doppelganger. A *drudge*. Perhaps it was on account of this out-of-body experience that one half of me was so unlike my usual self, shaking with terror and, at the same time giggling, madly silly. I wanted to spit in her face. I wanted to impress myself on her, so she'd carry the impression like a scar, a lifelong brand, something she would always remember.

"Winnie, just tell me what you're talking about. What is all this about a child? And who are the Moores? Do I know them?"

"I met one of your accomplices. As a matter of fact he ate your crumpets. In my garden. He asked after the child."

"What child?"

"Why, your child, of course. Don't tell me you've forgotten!"

"But my dear, I have no child."

"No, not any more, you haven't."

"Not now. Not ever. I have never had a child, Winnie."

It could have been me who was making this denial. Me, or my doppelganger; it simply didn't wash. My jaw was trembling. My eyes were misting again. I suddenly hated myself for being so wet, and I know that she hated me for it, too. Emotion is anathema to Frances Hodgkins.

"Who was this man, Winnie?"

"Captain something. I don't know."

"One of the officers?"

"Captain Morano."

"Jean Pierre? He was in town? Well, why didn't you tell me? Why didn't he call on me? I knew him in Tetuan."

"He despises you."

"No, that's not possible. You're mistaken, Winnie. And he must have been referring to P'tit Jean. My godchild. Has he seen the boy? He must be walking, talking by now? One of our attendants gave birth while we were in Fez and I took to the baby, he was so sweet. I got it into my head that I'd adopt him and give him a Christian upbringing. She was a young serving girl and it was a terrible disgrace—she wasn't married. Fortunately she was away from home. The British Consul, Mr. Bennington looked into the possibility of my adopting him. It was out of the question of course, so I appointed myself his unofficial godmother. I know the Mohammedans don't have such a concept, but the girl trusted me. Whenever I can, I send money in care of Mr. Bennington, to be kept in trust for the child. I heard that the girl's been married off to an older man. Wife number six or seven most likely. It's quite barbaric. I hope she has the child with her. I hope she has not been completely shamed. I must send another installment, I have fallen down in that respect."

I tried to release myself, but she had me well and truly flattened, with her arms braced on either side of my body. I knew that I was being made to endure a terrible penance.

"I would have spirited the child away, Winnie, but even I wasn't capable of that. Oh, I wish I'd heard what Jean Pierre had to say."

"He said he was awaiting the return of his butterflies."

"Oh, nonsense, he can't have meant it. They are long since discarded. It was a generous gift, but the Moors believe butterflies should fly free. They pin their prisoners' heads to spikes on the city walls. Now that is a different matter." She laughed, leaning in closer to me, so I could barely breathe. "He didn't leave a forwarding address?"

I tried to escape but I couldn't, I could feel her breath on my face. "I'm not the horrible person you think me, dear Winnie. I'm sorry you overheard something that was not meant for your ears. I might have been exaggerating just a tad, you know me! I quite like your husband as husbands go. Well, don't tell me that what I said was news to you. You've been married to the man for how many years? Forget what you heard. Words don't always carry the intended meaning when they fall on the wrong ears. Won't you come back and join us for a glass of wine?"

She relaxed a little and I squirmed from under her arm. My only wish was to be free of her, to be spirited away, far, far, far. Just then, the dog seized my ankle. Fortunately I was wearing my lace-up boots so he didn't get much of a purchase, but it gave me the excuse I needed, sometimes dogs have their uses. Mr. Merton seized the mutt's collar and offered his arm but I refused all help, saying I was in a hurry. As I limped away (an exaggerated limp), it came to me that I would not speak to Frances Hodgkins again. I might write her a letter once we were finished with Geoffrey's exhibition and if I did, I would tell her exactly what I thought of her.

I am running out of space. Tomorrow I shall go into town and choose another book. There is news that someone has stolen the Mona Lisa from the Louvre in Paris, now that is something to record! What effrontery to think this small life should deserve so many words.

⚘

Catherine glanced over the diary again, lingering on odd sentences and copying them into her sketchbook—*'one should never put oneself up for examination until one feels more dry than wet,' 'men are not all so unkind,' 'they pin their prisoner's heads on spikes,' 'feelings put into words have presence, like pain.'* She wanted more.

She drew a triangle on a blank page with a name at each point, Emily, Frances, Winnie. She joined the names with a circle and put her own name in the middle. A triangle within a circle that joined Frances to Winnie, Winnie to Emily—no point of entry for Catherine. The intricate, spidery branches of friendship criss-crossed, exclusive and invisible to all who were not caught up in them, diverted by daily happenings, the presence of men and children. Had Winnie or Frances had children? How accurate was Winnie's account? Had she stayed with Geoffrey Church, and what had become of him? She seemed like a bundle of contradictions, the rest of the diary would throw more light on her. And where did Emily fit? She'd never read anything about a friendship with Frances Hodgkins and she knew nothing of Hodgkins' work. She'd never imagined Emily had much room in her life for love but maybe she was wrong. No one could exude so much passion in paint and not know love, however much they denied it. And what of the paintings she was so obsessed with? Had they survived? Gilly might be able to throw light on some of this. Gilly Tannenbaum, Associate Dean of Arts, feminist scholar, red-haired, Australian, over-reachingly ambitious—onetime friend. What had happened to all the old friendships? What had taken their place? Catherine grimaced, thinking of her paintings, abandoned facing her kitchen wall. They weren't ready for examination, they were wet, not dry. But they were good. All this business with the baby would unravel eventually, but eventually was too far off. The baby was crying, as usual.

She stacked the blood-spattered papers, preparing to put them back in the box when a thin, folded page slipped from between two larger sheets:

Army form B15681

No 24653/L

Madam,

I regret to have to inform you that a report has this day been received from the war office that no. 24553/L   Rank Ag/Sgt Name Geoffrey Henry Church, Regiment—4th Artillery was wounded in action. Place not stated. On this 3rd day of April, 1915.

I am at the same time to express the sympathy and regret of the Army Council.

Any further information received at this office as to his condition will be at once notified to you.

I am, Madam, your obedient servant.

The writer's signature was not legible, but his title was Officer of the Records. The paper was pristine, no tearstains, no sign that Winifred Church had read and re-read or crumpled it. He must have been a casualty of the First World War. That question had been answered quicker than thought. The clues to the past were everywhere if she could only read them, and they were pointers into the future. The trouble was, there were too many ways to interpret, too many possible implications. Her head was bursting. The dead held onto their secrets and lies, even when they painted or wrote them down—you had to rely on the intelligence, the integrity, of the interpreter. This was the trouble with the present, too. The crying had stopped. What did this mean?

Kit picked up the baby and held him up to the light. His skin was translucent, and soft as bubbles. She took off his diaper and he peed. The pee came out in an arc. It was a miracle. He waved his left fist. He didn't like to be trussed up, it looked like he was going to be left handed. She was left handed. He didn't look or feel like an Alexander.

She unbuttoned her shirt and slid her bra up. She had nothing to offer him, but he seemed to like snuffling round her nipple. "We have the same blood," she whispered, running her tongue round his ear lobe, butting it gently with her tongue stud. She was getting bolder with him; she wouldn't have dared put the bond into words a little over a week ago when they picked him up at the hospital. Roger hadn't been able to look at him, but she'd been transfixed. It was the first time she'd ever been in charge of anything so small and dependent. She tongued out a speck of yellow crud from the corner of his eye. It was shocking. Awesome. She was going to prove to the world that she could step in. "I'm going to be your Mommy."

The doorbell rang and she opened the door with Pip in her arms. He chose that exact moment to squall. She put her hand over his mouth and took it away quickly as the woman on the doorstep stretched out and touched her arm. Kit realized with a shock of fear that she was from some kind of agency. The State was here to claim him. The woman wasn't very old, she didn't look fierce, but it was the friendly ones you had to watch, she'd learned that long ago. The best stage directors were rarely friendly, they charted their course at the first read-through, the despots hid behind compliments, waiting to pounce when you were most vulnerable.

The woman stepped inside, unasked. She said she'd come to check that everything was all right, that Kit was coping and that she had everything she needed. She said it was a routine call. Kit hung back as the woman looked around without hiding the fact that she was checking up. Together, they looked up at the ceiling. There was a greasy smear, and a daddy-longlegs in the stairwell. Kit apologized, knowing the woman was putting her down as a bad housekeeper. She tried to distract her by inviting her into the kitchen; too late, she remembered the dirty dishes in the sink. The woman wore a nametag. It said Helen something, she couldn't read it without getting up close and she didn't want to put the baby down to fix her contacts—you were probably supposed to have perfect eyesight to look after a newborn.

Kit offered the coffee that was left from breakfast, not wanting Helen Something to get too comfortable. It was cold but she drank it without a murmur. She wondered if this was a good or a bad sign. If it was some sort of test of her cooking abilities, she'd failed. There'd been no opportunity to take out her tongue stud, so she mumbled through half closed lips. "His grandmother just got here from Can...no America." Now the woman would know for certain she was incompetent—she didn't even know which country her own mother lived in.

Catherine chose this exact moment to go to the bathroom. The sound of movement upstairs seemed to be enough to reassure Helen Something that there was someone else in the house who might be more competent, and, after checking that Kit had all the essentials, and she knew about sterilizing and vaccinations, she left, saying she'd look in again next week.

"I have everything I'm going to need, thank you Helen," Kit said, and when the door closed she added, "and I won't open up if you come back."

Kit tried not to let go of the baby. She knew it was stupid, but she was scared he could be snatched when she looked away, or wriggle off of his own accord and vanish like a silverfish. Twice a day, she laid him on the scale in the nursery and marveled that he was actually gaining weight. She guessed that women who'd given birth were more confident that their child was real and substantial, after all, they'd felt it grow inside them for nine months. She vowed to make up for those missing months. He was a gift, intended for her, and she tried to stop expecting that the giver would come back to punish her. Now she understood why babies were swaddled, and why women in some cultures wore them on their backs, even when they were slaving in fields in terrible heat bent double like Quasimodo.

꙳

Catherine came into the kitchen. The postman had been and she'd scooped up the pile of mail that Kit had abandoned on the hall table. Kit appeared to be in an absent, dreamy mood and experience told her she'd have to hold off and wait for a mood swing if she wanted to talk about anything serious. She dumped the mail on the counter and Kit rifled through it, pulling out a bulky, registered envelope.

"That one's addressed to Ilona. What should we do with it?"

"I signed for it." Kit slit the envelope open. It contained a red passport. She opened it and showed Catherine the photo. It was a typical passport photo, not very flattering, Catherine guessed. Ilona's eyes looked wary, veiled.

"She's using Dad's name." Kit sniffed the new paper.

"Well, she was his wife."

"You didn't use it. You didn't give it to me."

"Oh Kit, it was such a long time ago."

"I should get a passport for Pip."

"Why? He's not going anywhere."

"Not yet."

Catherine watched Kit put the package away in a drawer and turn her attention to a can of lurid tomato soup. She had the baby strapped to her back. He looked like a chrysalis.

"I'm going to stay home, Mom. I don't know any baby sitters. You go out and explore. If I can get him to sleep I'll look for the rest of the diary, okay? Take Dad's car. See, I've drawn you a map, the place you want is on top of the hill. You need some air."

Catherine was glad of the opportunity to escape alone. Kit's behaviour was beginning to alarm her and the comment she'd made earlier about being too indulgent still stung. Kit had no right to demand rapture. Rapture was for Hollywood. She needed to get away on her own, make some plans. "You're sure you won't come for the ride?" She glanced at the map; it showed a couple of intersecting roads and not much else.

"Don't look too closely. I don't know the area well, and I've never been to that place."

"You have no sense of direction anyway."

"You said it." Kit tore the map in half. "And do you mind putting that cigarette out?"

CHAPTER TWENTY ONE

℮

Catherine ground her teeth as she tried to come to grips with the ass-backwards left hand drive and the unfamiliar controls on the silver Audi. She pulled up just outside the village and asked the way from a couple of teenagers. She didn't know how to describe what she was looking for, and she couldn't understand their accent when they responded. One of them pointed across a busy road and she followed his finger and turned off into a lane that headed straight up one of the only hills in the county. The lane narrowed and she found it hard to judge the width of the car. Twice she got too near the bank and heard the scratch of twigs on paintwork. She almost ran into an elderly woman pushing a bicycle loaded with bags of groceries and she shouted for directions. This time, she understood what she was being told, and the woman offered to pedal ahead of her and show her the way once they got up the worst of the slope.

The bicycle was a ramshackle crate with a huge basket filled with bags of kitty litter. As they ground along, she had to concentrate all her attention on holding the clutch in place. She was directed to pull off the road onto a driveway and ignore the Private Property sign, and the old woman was freewheeling down the hill by the time she'd wrenched the door open to thank her. Catherine relaxed back in her seat, recalling how often she'd been surprised by unexpected kindness when she lived in England.

Lime trees arched over the long drive, letting in pillars of sunlight. She parked out of sight of any buildings and walked the last part, crossing her fingers that she wouldn't be turned back. She had no idea what she was looking for, or why she was there, but outside the confines of the car she began to feel a sense of adventure. The clock on the clock tower had stopped at seven o'clock. She tried to envisage the sanatorium as someone might have seen it when they arrived in a carriage at the turn of the century. It would have looked austerely modern. She paused and watched a bee working on a stem of purple Canterbury Bells, silent bells, emitting a vibrant, expectant pulse in the afternoon sun. She scanned the grey walls. This architect had left his dull thumbprint on schools and public buildings all over England. Everything looked benign and cared for—the place smelled of money.

She veered onto a path that led round the back. From this angle, the building was more prepossessing, a stately stone semi circle, perfectly proportioned, its tall windows looking out over the patchwork of fields and woods. She wished she could think what Emily had said about it in *Pause*. She remembered the book as a thin hardback. The blinds were down on many of the windows, suggesting absentee owners. She imagined the windows unglazed, open to the elements. Who would buy a luxury home in a former house of death? The building was on the crest of the hill, but it would be raw here in winter with the North Easterly winds whipping across the open fields.

She scrambled over a retaining wall, bracing herself to be turned back at any moment. She was afraid to be seen looking through the windows, so she sat down on a turf bank, assessing the view from the vantage point of someone inside one of the rooms. The field below was full of bumps and burrows, the grass was parched for want of rain. She couldn't see any sign of rabbits or gophers, but there was a chestnut pony tethered to an iron fence to her right, and she spotted some sheep in the distance and horses browsing in another field. She'd been transported to Suffolk against her will, and now she was following the trail of an artist whose doorstep she'd lived on for more than thirty years without considering her; the sunny afternoon felt suddenly chill. Why was she wasting time on Emily Carr?

She lay back on the grass, lit a cigarette and let the idea of rapture play in her mind. Rapture was risky. It was the opposite of solace. She knew which she preferred, but Kit was providing neither. Had she ever tried? Somewhere along the way they'd missed each other. Catherine closed her eyes.

She woke to someone shaking her arm. She kept her eyes shut for a moment, aware that she was waking from a dream. When she opened them there was no one there. Suddenly she was completely awake. She saw flames.

Roger phoned while Catherine was out. He was in Sheffield, not Spain. He said he'd got off the train there and taken a room in a pub near the station.

"Where exactly are you calling from, Dad?" Kit had been snoozing.

"There's not much here, actually. They seem to have pulled most of the factories down but they haven't put much up in their place."

"I thought you were going to a resort."

"So did I."

"I'm sorry you can't talk to Mom, she's out on the trail of Emily Carr."

"What?"

"She read that diary. It was in the box Ilona had with her."

"Oh, get rid of it!"

"Too late. I don't suppose you know where the rest is? It would make her day."

"Are you telling me your mother's there with you?"

"Of course. What did you expect? She arrived the night before you left. I wanted to break it to you gently but you took off."

"Is she staying at Golding?"

"Yes. Oh, and Pip says hallo."

"Who's Pip?"

"Daaa-aad! Don't zone out on me!"

"You mean the baby? He's called Alexander. We decided on that."

"Well, why didn't you say?"

"Didn't I?"

"Philip. It means lover of horses, like in Prince Philip. Dad, I don't think this is a good connection."

"I can't abide horses."

"That's not the point. Why don't you come home? Mom can't wait to see you. You're gonna have to come home soon."

"Just get rid of her—"

The line went dead. She waited, knowing he'd put the phone down. From where she stood, with the receiver in one hand and the baby tucked under her arm, Kit could see a road atlas on the shelf alongside a row of recipe books. She searched in the index for Sheffield. The baby limited her movements—it was like the time when she had her elbow in a cast. 'The Full Monty' was set in Sheffield. All the guys in the movie wanted to be strippers—Roger was a good name for a stripper. Sheffield looked to be plum in the middle of England, miles from the sea.

Back in the kitchen she washed Helen Something's cup, thinking that if things went well they'd be able to take Pip back to Canada in a few weeks. They'd move back to the old apartment and re-decorate. He'd sleep in her old room and play with her toys; she'd move into her mother's studio, which was once her playroom. Catherine would probably want to move upstairs with Ernie, they hadn't had a chance to talk about that relationship yet. There was something right about bringing up a child in the house where you'd grown up yourself. It all made perfect sense. And it made perfect sense that a few short weeks ago she'd never have considered being a mother. Lives could be changed in a heart-beat. Catherine was a wreck. She looked like a wraith and she smelled like an ashtray, it showed how unhappy she was, cooped up on a godforsaken island in the States. Ernie was probably driving her crazy, he'd be wanting to get back to Canada—hopefully he hadn't put the Vancouver place on the market.

She sat down and let the baby lie across her arms. He was awake, but he wasn't fretting. She lifted his English vest and traced the veins scrawled over his skinny ribs. Pip was going to bring her closer to Catherine. All her friends envied their casual, hands-off relationship but it had always felt incomplete. It was her fault. She'd taken too much for granted. Pip was helping her realize the value of her mother. Some character she'd played in another life said clichés like this were parings off the collective unconscious. She didn't care any more that she might be losing the urge to be original. Good riddance!

✳

Catherine shrank into the house, tiptoeing past the kitchen where she could hear a radio playing. She was shaky, still in shock.

She'd been lucky not to set herself and the entire county ablaze. As long as she lived, she'd wonder who or what had tugged at her arm to awaken her in time to see a line of fire licking the dry grass where she'd let go her lighted cigarette. The flames were close enough to singe her, yet she'd felt nothing, smelled nothing. Moving faster than she'd thought possible, she'd stamped the fire out. Her sneakers were scorched, her pants smoke-stained and she'd left a patch of charred, smouldering grass behind. She'd seen no one, met no one. There was no explanation for what had awoken her.

Sitting in the car, she watched through streaming eyes to make sure the fire was really out and mouthed a silent thank you to her protector. It took a while before she could get it together to start the engine. Normally a careful driver, she cut the turn onto the road too close and clipped a tree while she was trying to light another cigarette. She didn't stop to examine the damage until she parked the car next to the yellow house; the sight of the dent brought on another fit of shakes. She kicked it, wishing she'd totalled it, and Roger along with it, then she got in and re-parked closer to the wall so the dent didn't show.

She showered and changed her clothes. The baby was fretting again. Babies she'd encountered before never cried so much. Kit had been happy and contented. She wondered if maybe this poor little brat had an inkling of what had happened to him. Could he be crying for his brother? She'd heard tales of how surviving twins go through life forever searching for their other half, like lovers looking for their true match.

Back in her room, she sipped a stiff drink. She felt wonky, too full of unabsorbed business. This house was unhealthy, Kit needed to get out, there were ghosts, Ilona, for a start, a pale presence as strong as malt scotch, and Winifred Church, a sharp-eared listener. And then there was Emily Carr. She knew she had nothing to fear from Emily, she didn't believe in ghosts but she did believe in jet lag and that was the reason she was still so shaky; if she could only work out how to gain Kit's trust, everything would fall into place. The baby's cries had died down and the radio was turned off. Kit was singing. She remembered taking her on a day trip to Victoria when she was six years old. Totally uninterested in the scenery, she'd stood on the deck of the ferry and sung the National Anthem, drawing a crowd. She had perfect pitch but Catherine had still felt embarrassed. All that was so long ago, she'd shed the old life, but it wasn't so easy to shed a daughter. She had to find out what had really brought Kit to England. Had something happened to her theatre company? What had gone on between her and Ilona? They must talk soon.

Outside the window, the leaves on the climbing rose had black spots. She released the catch and leaned out. The flowers were blowsy, each with a double frill of fading petals, and there were clusters of tightly clenched buds with small green aphids on the sepals. The aphids were busy. The flowers didn't even have a smell, they were too well bred, like Roger's family. A man walked by the house, chin up. He walked heel and toe down the line in the middle of the road carrying a bag that said 'Torquay United'. She wondered whether Torquay was united. She wondered if she was getting drunk. She couldn't think where her pills were, or when she'd last taken one.

It was beginning to get dark as she shut the window. The colour had drained from the roses. She guessed it must be around nine o'clock and she reset her watch. Kit hadn't disturbed her and she'd lost track of the distant song. She was hungry, so she stumbled downstairs to the kitchen. Kit was curled up, asleep on the floor with the baby in her arms. She stood over them for a while then backed out of the door.

⁂

Roger was living in a room in a pub near the station in Sheffield. The view from the train had lured him as he was heading up to Scotland, in search of something more solid and tangible than Spain. He stood alone in the public bar with his scotch, replaying his conversation with Kit, idly watching the other drinkers as they watched a boxing match on a huge screen over the bar. They shouted at each other and egged the boxers on, uninhibited and ribald, so different from the customers in the Fox and Hounds.

He was stuck here for now. He wasn't ready to go back. In its astonishing ugliness, the city was helping to settle the hurt and confusion that had built up in him since the accident. He looked out of the window onto the dismal street. Sheffield was underwhelming and it made no apology for its looks. The scattered buildings in the vicinity of the pub, many of which belonged to some university, looked as if they'd been discarded. There were stacked up car ramps, metal clad walls, walkways roofed with blue plastic and screened in wire mesh. A bad-tempered patch of garden was attempting to house cabbages and sooty bamboo, but the beds were planted with bus tickets and empty drink cans. A sprawling plastic bus station gave a sense of destiny, but no sense of destination. It was called Interchange. He'd wandered round it, marveling at the names on the departure boards, Meadowhead, Fullbrook, Brightside, Wisewood. Was this where the city's dreamers escaped for pastoral relief?

He could see the railway station from where he was standing. It was close to the urban sprawl, yet it stood apart, a million miles away in what it represented. The solid, Yorkshire stone exterior marked it as a respected Victorian monument to progress, symbol of a city reaping the rewards of industry. When he arrived, he'd been bemused by the inept metal and glass additions to the station's interior—some joker's idea of modern improvements. The sheer hill behind the station was another clue to today's cynical lack of faith in the future and in good design. It was lined with skeletal blocks of flats, neither high nor low rise, neither old nor new. Spare, unrelieved by any form of decoration, they gave Roger hope. Nothing in his life could possibly be this bad.

He didn't stray far from his room once he'd established that the town center offered much the same fare as the area round the pub. He noticed a preponderance of shops selling bathroom fittings. The headlines scribbled on a newsagent's hoarding announced an urban renewal project, and he felt a stab of regret. He thought of his newly painted house with a shudder. Someone much wiser than he had discovered the basic human need for ugliness. What he was finding in Sheffield was not the cliché grim north of soot and flat caps but unabashed honesty, free of the baloney of his in-laws, evenings at the club, picnic hampers from Fortnum and Masons', speedboats and fast sports cars. He'd felt something close to honesty when he was with Kit, playing hopscotch and reading Rupert Annuals, but now he understood that even this was a sham. He didn't want to think about her, she had no place in his life. She'd usurped almost all the time he could have spent with his wife in the last weeks of their life together. She'd diverted his attention and made him turn his back on Ilona's needs. Because of her he'd lost a child. He couldn't forgive himself. And now she'd further violated his trust by bringing Catherine into the house. It was a lesson in getting one's priorities straight, and Kit was not, never had been, a priority. Ilona hadn't liked her—why hadn't he been more sensitive to this? With a bit of luck the advertisements she'd placed for a nanny would bring some results so he could send Kit packing.

A troupe of rowdy young louts raced by the window on their

way to some watering hole. It was all so much less complicated here in Sheffield. Nothing and no one came between him and the pure, unmitigated simplicity of ugliness. He suspected that this was why Ilona had cut her wrists. She'd wanted to pare back to the bone. This was what Cézanne had been aiming for with those last ghostly bathers, so ugly and yet so prescient. And Picasso with his Weeping Woman—all his ugly women—shocking at the time, but shock wears off and leaves honesty behind. Roger hadn't produced one tear over the monstrous thing that had happened to him.

For two days he spoke to no one except the person who served breakfast and appeared behind the bar in the evening. He hardly noticed her at first, a young, bony person. She was civil and efficient and unprepossessing.

He put through a flurry of calls to Sam. His brother wasn't much of a talker, so the calls were short but he didn't want talk. He needed a detached presence, someone who wasn't embroiled in his affairs and didn't drown him in sympathy. Sam had been his best man twice. He'd wished him all the luck in the world at his wedding, saying if there was anything he could do to help he'd be there with bells on. He wasn't too swift in the tact department. Just after that conversation Roger overheard him joking that the only reason he could think of to throw your lot in with a girl so young was to have someone to clip one's toenails when one was too far gone to bend over.

It didn't matter what Sam thought, no one could get inside his skin and understand what he felt. He couldn't think of Ilona, dead or alive. It was as though she'd gone off on a bit of a holiday—she'd be back shortly and their life would carry on as normal, whatever normal was; they'd hardly been married long enough to establish a pattern. He had to accept that it was too late to take up painting now even if his eyes healed. There was the baby to support. Men were supposed to get excited about having a son and heir, but he felt nothing but dread. He'd been excited not so long ago about the daughter he'd discovered, and where had that got him? The space between Kit's arrival and where he was now couldn't be spanned. He said his son's name aloud a few times, "Alexander, Alexander, Alex, Al."

He tried to imagine having a baby in the house without Ilona to take charge. He'd have to get used to her absence just as he had when Catherine left. Ilona had worked so hard—all those months of preparation, the nursery, the twin pram, the plans for a conservatory, the spanking new front garden and the new paint job. It would all have to go, he couldn't bear to think about it. As soon as he got back, he'd have the house changed back to pink. Maybe he should sell the place. Get something in London. Buy a flat in one of those blocks looking down on the station here in Sheffield. Well, why not? A holiday flat. A place to escape to on weekends. A place to be unhappy in. He could bring Al and his nanny. She'd have to be easy on the eye since he'd be coming home to her every night. He couldn't face sharing his table with a po-faced oppressor like the one he and Sam had endured when they were boys.

The real solution would be to get over his revulsion and persuade Kit to stay. The main obstacle to this plan was Catherine. All of a sudden he couldn't move forward or backward without bumping into his ex-wife. Everything that had happened to him lately could be traced back to her.

As soon as she walked in the door Catherine saw that this cottage had light, it was an ideal studio and bore no resemblance to its neighbour. Kit led her to the simple pencil drawing, badly framed and tacked to a wall at the top of the stairs. She looked at it for a long time, testing the blister that had formed from the burn on her ankle. She tried to loosen the tack and broke her nail.

"Why didn't he get it properly framed?"

"Don't be so down on him, Mom." Kit had the chrysalis strapped to her chest. The light hit her from behind, making her hair glint and softening the lines of her face. Catherine gazed at her daughter. She had a radiance that was never there before, it was eerie; she mustn't delay much longer before she brought her back to earth. "Those pouch things make kids' legs go bow legged," she remarked.

"What do you think of that one?" Kit pointed to a picture in a recess next to the fireplace. It wasn't well lit but Catherine recognized it immediately. A man crucified on the arms of a woman. He'd painted it to spite her after they'd had a row about money and she'd been happy to leave it behind, along with everything else. Without thinking, she'd reproduced the idea in one or two of the sketches she'd made recently, only the limbs of her figures were disconnected.

"What do you think?" Kit was watching her closely.

"It's okay."

She glanced up at the Emily Carr sketch, expectantly. It looked so ordinary. She recognized some of the other paintings on the walls from their student days but he hadn't saved anything of hers. "He changed his style again," she nodded at a cluster of paintings with bold, sharp outlines.

"Those aren't his. They're by some distant relative of Ilona's."

Catherine examined the signature on a painting of a blue sailboat on a jade green sea. "Geoffrey Church, 1912. It's Winnie's husband."

"Who's Winnie?"

"Winifred Church, of course. The diarist. So Roger must be in the know. He must know where the rest of the diary is."

"I'm sure he doesn't."

"Well, how did he get hold of these pictures?"

"Who cares, Mom? They're ancient history."

The baby started to fidget and Kit grabbed a teddy bear and waved it over his head. Catherine snatched it out of her hand. One eye was missing the other was hanging by a single thread. She burst into tears. It was her bear. It was John!

🔆

After driving a few miles in the direction of Seattle, Ernie turned around and headed back to the border, hoping he'd be arrested and jailed for speeding.

He was home just before midnight and he peered through Catherine's darkened window, trying to conjure up the light from the old fridge. He should never have replaced that model. He went inside and plugged in his electric drill. Hundreds of Catherines offered up a wooden welcome. He picked up one, then another and drilled a hole through their chests. He took his time, making sure the job was done properly and not one was missed, then he herded them all into a corner of the living room and left them in the dark. He paced about his apartment, knowing he wasn't finished. He opened his store cupboard and grabbed an armload of blackberry jam, neatly labeled and dated from 1991. He dropped a jar on the way downstairs and it bounced, refusing to break. In the living room, he opened the lids, smashing the wax seals with a screwdriver. He poured the jam over the pile of wooden figures.

'The fixture of her eye has motion in it,
As we are mocked with art.'

He remembered the lines from *A Winter's Tale*. Kit had played Perdita in a school production and he'd listened to her lines night after night. He'd gone to every performance, marvelling each night when the statue came to life. His statues were not going to come to life.

CHAPTER TWENTY TWO

‏ℓ‏

There was no word from Roger. Kit worried about him, but Catherine relaxed into his absence. She was beginning to get onto a more normal footing with Kit. It still hurt to hear her refer to him as Dad, but finding the teddy bear had softened her attitude; rather than fret she decided to wait him out and cross her fingers that Kit didn't tire of her newfound obsession with motherhood before he got back. Kit's obsessions had always caused grief, hard earned money squandered on stamp collections, ski passes, time spent ferrying her to riding lessons, ballet—the enthusiasms almost all vanished before the season was out. She was predictably unpredictable which always made Catherine feel vulnerable. The worst that could happen, or perhaps the best, would be that Kit would take off and leave her holding the baby.

On an impulse, she called home. She needed to talk to an objective listener. She had to look up her own number and she geared herself up to hear her recorded message. Mel's voice gave her a jolt. It lowered a pitch when he realized who was on the line, though it was still raspy with sleep. The moment she opened her mouth, she knew it was all too complex, she couldn't talk—not to a stranger, even if he was an intimate stranger. She kept her tone brisk and outlined the situation, telling him she would be away longer than she'd thought.

"That's okay. I'm fixing your studio."

"That's good of you, and it's good of you to stay over. So everything's okay there? My life's work hasn't fallen into the sea?"

"Not yet. That guy came round, though. The one with the cowboy boots, white hair."

"Ernie? Ernie was at my house?"

"I sent him off. You owe him rent or something?"

"No. Nothing like that. He didn't stay over, did he?"

"He didn't even get inside!"

"Well, if he comes again, don't upset him, he's an old friend."

The pause was electric. "Mel?"

"I'm thinking."

"Listen, if there's an emergency, you have my number."

"Yeah, I have it."

They chatted a while longer, both trying to be casual. Catherine was the first to break down, "I can't wait to get back."

"It hasn't changed. Nothing's changed, yet."

"Good." She put the phone down gently, troubled by the yet. Was he ready to give up? She should call Ernie and warn him to stay away.

Kit cleared her throat. "You look like the cat that ate the canary, Mom. Was that Ernie Last?"

"No."

Kit frowned. "So who was it?"

"Just a friend. The guy who's taking care of my house."

"It didn't sound like he was just a friend."

"Is that right?"

"So, you're not with Ernie?"

"Whatever gave you that idea? You dramatize everything, it's time you got back on stage!"

"I told you, I'm through with theatre. Don't you believe that?"

"I don't believe you'll stay in one place."

"I won't have any option."

Catherine watched as she shifted the weight of the child. "Well, your theatre lasted longer than most of your hobbies, maybe now you can earn a proper living."

"Don't say that, Mom. I loved it. It was more than a job, and you know it."

"Well, it didn't breed happiness. That's the least I want for you."

"I'm happy now. You're getting to sound like a mother hen. You're not in love, are you?"

"Not at all. I just don't want you to be hurt. If Roger does one more thing to threaten your well-being, I'll fight him, I'll fight him if it takes my last breath."

"Don't worry, he won't."

"Maybe you can find some kind of work with children."

Kit nodded and nuzzled the top of the baby's head.

Catherine woke in her box room each morning, hoping that this was the day they could plan their escape. Kit didn't expect her to help with the baby, but she was more and more drawn to him and happy to relieve her, glad of this brief window in which to re-establish an easy, companionable mother-daughter relationship. They shopped together in the village, chatted with the locals, People 'oohed' and 'aahed' over the Turnip, without actually touching him. She was sure they all knew what had happened to Ilona, but no one mentioned her name though they were anxious to express their concern about Roger. They were passing the Fox and Hounds when a florid man in a checked shirt and blazer ducked out and told them what a splendid man Roger was, what a devoted husband. Catherine smiled and accepted the compliment. Obviously Roger had mutated. It was a relief to learn he had such a firm base of support in the village. Life was not perfect, but for the present it was sweetly predictable. She wondered if soldiers felt like this before a battle, this strange lassitude, this perfect sense of living in the moment.

She'd nicknamed the baby Turnip because he was round with whitish blond hair and his skin had a delicate mauve tinge, particularly his feet and hands. He was an English turnip, not the orange North American variety. It was strange to hold an infant again, strangely familiar. During the long evenings when he was sleeping, she tried to dredge up interesting anecdotes, remembrances of Kit's childhood. She put off asking about Ilona.

Kit described her arrival in London. Catherine listened, horrified not so much by the scene under Waterloo Bridge, as by what she was not being told. Drugs and drug talk had always been off limits; she stuffed the oblique references into 'pending', knowing that the file was full. The problem with adult children was that they were inconsistent, they slid in and out of needing and ignoring and they didn't think they should give any warning signals when they changed directions.

That evening Kit broke their unwritten rule and talked about Roger. The most painful part for Catherine was hearing how they'd read his books together. Bedtime reading was her domain, he'd deliberately taken himself out of the running. She had to pinch herself, wondering how she'd allowed the unquestioning love she used to feel for her daughter to atrophy from lack of use. Surely now they could learn to like each other and be friends. To Catherine's relief, Kit dropped the subject of her father as suddenly as she'd brought it up. They fell back into their old habit of playing word games. Kit picked out some British expressions and Catherine topped them. Everything they liked was 'brilliant' (copacetic was worn out, so they trashed it); they giggled and 'sussed out' 'pear-shaped' 'tossers' and 'twitchers', 'slagged off' 'anoraks' who were 'pants'. When Kit steered the game to sex words, Catherine tried to back out, but Kit wouldn't have it, so they reeled off 'shagging', 'bonking', 'balling' and 'getting your leg over'. Kit came up with 'parking the pink bus' and when Catherine countered with 'rogering', Kit missed the beat. Catherine waited, but the game was over and there was dead air between them. Catherine drew a deep breath, "Did something happen, Kit? Between you and your father? Did he do or say something?"

"Mo-o-o-o-m!" Kit's shout startled her. "You don't really think that, do you?"

Catherine shook her head, uncertainly. "Maybe he did and you didn't get it. It's all in the tone of voice. I used to get so frustrated with the English. They talk through irony and innuendo. You wouldn't understand, you haven't been here long enough."

"I do understand."

"I had an English friend once who told me to listen for the music in the silence between the notes. And their humour always caught me out, the way they distance themselves by putting themselves down. If you stand back and mock yourself, no one can get the knife in before you fall on your own sword. Roger's like that. They're a thin-skinned bunch, the Brits, they always reminded me of channel swimmers, larding themselves with alcohol and words so they won't feel the cold."

"But I'm not like that."

"No, you're Canadian, thank God. We generally use words to convey information. You're sure he didn't try anything?"

"Just stop. Stop being so goddamn patronizing! If he did say something..."

"If he did?"

Kit laughed suddenly. "I'm never going to understand him. Is that what you're trying to tell me?"

"Well, I never understood him, so why should you?"

"Because I'm not you! You hate him."

"But we understand each other, Kit, we speak the same language, you and me."

"Do we?"

"Try me."

"Okay, I will. Do you still masturbate?"

Catherine drew a quick breath. "Still?"

"You do!" Kit jumped up. "Brilliant! At least you communicate with yourself! I was always a bit scared of you, you know, when I was a kid. You seemed so...far off. You knew so much—and you never had a man."

"I didn't want you to feel sidelined!"

"I always thought of you as a brain. Maybe if I'd known you were juicy. You never mentioned sex."

The baby whooped, claiming Kit's attention and Catherine took the opportunity to break away. She went to the window and hid her tears. She'd taught her child to be scared of her. It didn't bear thinking about. *This person has no juice!* Was it written on her body? Couldn't Kit see that she was changing? The changes were sweeping her away and it was hardly a month since the Last Farewell. She was turning into a woman who wept! "Be patient with me Kit. I can't stay here much longer. We have to go home. Together."

"I was always scared you'd die when I wasn't there." Kit's voice had gone up an octave.

"Why would you think that?"

"I used to try to imagine what it would be like without you. I couldn't. Oh, don't cry!"

"I'm not!"

"I want you to live forever."

"I'm sorry I never made an attempt to put you in touch with Roger. I guess it was a mistake."

"What do you want to happen to you after...if you should, you know, die? Have you thought of that?"

"No."

"Have you made a will?"

"There's no need, you're the only one I have."

"Me and Pip, we're two now, not one. That makes three of us."

Catherine felt a sharp crack in her neck as if something had snapped. "He's your half brother, he's nothing to do with me, alive or dead. I'm not contributing to his support. Don't fool yourself into thinking you're more connected than you are. Roger's a shit. If he doesn't call by the end of the week, I'm going to make travel arrangement, for you and me and no one else!" She walked out of the room, realizing she'd just lost all the ground she'd fought so hard for. Friends? Things had been going too well. Friends don't peck at each other's flesh.

⚕

The girl who served breakfast every day grew tired of waiting for Roger to make the first move. She introduced herself. Her name was Brenda—he hadn't noticed her before but now he saw that she was skinny with dyed red hair and a long neck like Kit's.

She laid his bacon and eggs down. He smelled her sweat as she leaned over him to slide the ketchup across the table. He wasn't sure if he was expected to supply his name and, if so, how formal he should be, so he simply said, "Thank you," adding, "Brenda," as an afterthought.

That evening she was behind the bar. She kept his pints coming, and he drank deeply, though he no longer cared for beer. He asked when she had time off, thinking she'd take ten minutes and sit down with him at a table in the saloon and listen to his woes. "I've got a day off tomorrow," she said, "we could go for a curry, you must be choking on what we serve you here." He couldn't believe he was being picked up. He didn't speak to her again, but watched out of the corner of his eye to see if she flirted with the other men. She was efficient and she seemed at home in her body. He noticed that she never smiled.

⚚

Catherine had the idea of tracking down some of Frances Hodgkins' paintings and looking for Emily Carr's books. She kept returning to the two women and their life in England. What had kept them here, or, in Carr's case, sent her scuttling back to Canada? Had they managed to ignore the insidious English light and the saturated quiet of centuries of village life? She could feel it seeping into her own consciousness. She was shrinking, bleaching, losing the grist of the Pacific North West. Over breakfast, she informed Kit that she was going up to London. These were the only words that either of them spoke before she left the house.

She drew a blank on both Frances and Emily in the bookshops on Charing Cross Road. British readers apparently hadn't encountered Carr. The Tate had a couple of Hodgkins' paintings in its collection but they were in storage and not available for public viewing. The staff was unhelpful and not for the first time she contemplated the fate of artists who were locked in the vaults of art galleries. It was like being consigned to darkness for eternity with an occasional glimpse of light for good behaviour. She stumbled on a recent edition of Frances Hodgkins' letters in the Tate bookshop, bulky and too expensive but she bought it anyway, hoping it would give her a clue to the missing parts of the diary. Frances must have talked about Emily Carr.

She'd intended to use the afternoon to fill in some of the blanks of her life with Roger, locate the street where they'd lived, maybe even find the house, but the world of the diary was more compelling. She dipped into the introduction to the letters as she sat on a park bench in Pimlico. It was a surprise to find Frances had been such a big hit in the art world; she'd been one of the most recognized artists in England in the thirties and forties, while Emily struggled in Canada, virtually unknown. Frances had turned her back on home and settled in England and Catherine intuited that she'd vanished from the map because she was never more than a Colonial upstart, in spite of everything she'd achieved. Catherine felt a thrill of discovery as she delved into Frances' world, but she looked in vain for letters dated 1911. It was as though those six weeks of summer had been wiped out. She went back to the introduction to find out what happened to her after she left St. Agathe. She didn't marry Mr. Merton, in fact she didn't marry at all. She died in direst poverty, in a mental institution, painting to her last gasp.

Catherine closed the book, feeling upset. Emily had finished up slightly better than Frances, though her heart gave out. She figured they were almost exact contemporaries. Their lives paralleled each other so strangely that they must have been more than merely teacher and student. But where was the evidence? She wanted them to remain friends.

A group of noisy children had set fire to the tires on a bicycle that was leaning on an empty fountain in the centre of the square directly opposite where Catherine sat. She got up hastily as the foul smoke billowed in her direction. She wasn't ready for London and she wasn't ready to return to Suffolk.

She made her way back to the Tate, where she hunkered down in the café with the book of letters.

'Often I felt like giving up—if I had known what lay before me I should never have had the courage to begin,' she read. *'Everyone will have the satisfaction of remarking how much I have fallen off, which, after all, pleases*

people more than success sometimes.' Catherine swigged her lukewarm tea. Where was progress? Back home, they still made a sport out of cutting down tall poppies. She closed the book with a snap. Her life was different from Frances Hodgkins'. Life in the art world had advanced. It was too early to go back to Suffolk, so she made her way to the British Library and spent the rest of the day looking up references to Frances and Emily Carr.

᛫

Roger had no idea how they ended up in bed. The evening was a blur, a cheap Indian restaurant, too much lager, too much sputtering on about his recent past, things he shouldn't have said, ramblings about Ilona's beauty and Kit's unwanted attempts to seduce him, not everything was true, but truth was like stomach-ache, he wanted to be rid of it. The vindaloo reminded him of the take-aways they'd had after the fateful birthday party, when he was still in charge and blissfully ignorant of what was to come. He lay by Brenda's side talking but not touching. It felt like emptying a pond, Ilona was lying on the bottom, but no matter how often he said her name, he couldn't bring her to life.

The talk became more random and eventually Brenda rolled him towards her. She seemed to know what she wanted and he was too bagged to divert her intentions.

Either she was putting on an act or she was deeply affected by his lack-lustre performance. She shuddered with pleasure and when he pulled out of her, she straddled him and fondled him gently, pecked him with her lips until he could feel a dull roar starting way down inside and moving up relentlessly. His body turned into a wick. The final eruption was painful, nothing like the single hot spurt of joy he experienced with Ilona, and he tried not to cry out but the sound burst from him, a huge, slobbery sob.

"I want it to go on," she whispered. He rolled over, groping for his glasses, fancying a cigarette though he didn't smoke. After a while she snuggled into the crook of his arm and he studied the tendons in her shoulder. He played her vertebrae lightly, stroking them like the keys of some alien instrument and caressed the dark hairline where the red dye was growing out. He imagined the painting he could make of her.

She pulled away from him. "You've not asked about me," she said, and he was seized with panic, thinking she might have some kind of disease. He concentrated on the Yorkshire vowel sounds as she began to talk about her life, and distracted himself from what she might be about to tell him by thinking of the Estuary English spoken by his colleagues no matter what part of the country they came from. Everyone spoke it, except old farts like himself and Sam who had nothing to gain from the classless society. "There was a divorce," he heard her say. She was wire thin, her hip bones stuck up like the handles on a wooden tray his mother used to serve tea on. She was sometimes very intense, taut, sometimes slack, like a cat. Warily he asked about her plans for the future. She said she wanted to go to London and try her luck as a singer. She said she sang in the bar on karaoke nights, there was going to be one tomorrow. "You'll come," she said, and she told him about a factory lad from some-where near Manchester who'd been discovered at karaoke; he'd made it big in the music world. He was singing Italian opera now with no training, just a musical ear. "I can't abide opera," she said, and she tickled him. Sam was the last person who'd done that, when they were left alone together in the nursery. It had been torture.

She came to his room every night after that. He spent the early part of the evening in the bar, enduring the horrors of karaoke, losing his shirt to the domino players, watching Brenda whose face became less skeletal, more sculpted as he got used to it. She dressed quite plainly in high-necked sweaters and low-heeled shoes and he never managed to catch her smiling. He didn't look at her mouth when they were in bed, he thought her teeth must be false but he didn't ask, and he could never get up the nerve to ask about sexual diseases or how she handled birth control. Occasionally she wore an uncharacteristically gaudy pair of earrings, they jangled when she moved her head. When he asked her to take them off she obeyed immediately. He realized he had power over her. She told him she'd fancied him from the moment he walked in the door. She said he was a lost guppy. He let it pass, thinking she meant puppy since a guppy was a fish. He wanted to believe that he was the first, though he knew this was absurd. He thought about her all day, staying in his room, watching quiz shows and veterinary programs about injured swans and abandoned tortoises. He wanted her with him all the time, but she had some sort of life outside the pub, a mum who was 'poorly,' a brother who was on probation. When they were together she went into painstaking detail about all this and he told her about the sick animals he'd seen that afternoon on T.V.

One day he took a bus into Derbyshire. The bus went via Hope, to Castleton, a place someone in the pub recommended for its caves and its local semi-precious stone. He was amazed by how quickly the scab of Sheffield was left behind as they entered a rolling landscape of moors, densely brown, tinged with purple and spiked with sharp green bracken and outcrops of rock; the bus swooped up over the top of the moor and down through dry-walled fields and dark woods. Unable to wait for Hope, he got off at another village and followed a path to a river. One of his knees locked, so he sat down on a stile and stared at a couple of sheep who promptly turned their backs. He now knew about scrapey and he checked the flock for signs of lameness. He was in a lush valley that sloped up through an oak wood to the moors, and the sun highlighted a distant cliff. He felt uncomfortable and out of place and the murmur of water was sending all the wrong messages. He walked back to the village, found a toilet and a gift shop and picked out a silver ring with the blue local stone that looked like lapis.

That night he asked her to come home with him. She asked, "Will your daughter be there?" and he said no, she'd have gone back to Canada with his ex-wife. It was only a small deviation from the truth. She said yes, yes, she didn't mind a baby so long as it was just the one. He gave her the ring, relieved that he wouldn't have to impose on Kit any longer.

⚱

The great Diplodocus dominated the stately vestibule, its vast tail held up with wires instead of muscles. The explanatory tablet said they used to think the Diplodocus dragged its tail but now they knew it held it up in a curl. Kit wondered how they knew? Would they know she had two webbed toes and she'd never given birth when they dug up her skeleton in ten thousand years? She'd come up to London to avoid being in the house with her mother.

It took time to complete the circuit of the giant beast. She woke Pip and swung him round into her arms so he could squint up at the animal's jaws. The Diplodocus didn't look comfortable exposed in his public lair. She moved to an alcove where a petrified tree stump was on display. The tablet said it was millions of years old. The surface was polished and jewel-like and she sat the baby down on it. It originated in America and you could count the growth rings. She wanted him to feel America and to feel the arrested growth, feel what the accumulated energy of two hundred and fifty million years was like, let it enter his four week old bones through the chakra at the base of his spine and fill him up. No one seemed the least interested in what she was doing. The museum was thronged with school classes and French bus parties. She would get Pip to appreciate the immensity of time, so he'd never stumble around groping for milestones as she had. Having him was a miracle—she didn't need to look for community now, community was everywhere. In his one short month on the planet he'd shown her she wasn't a failure.

She pointed out a giant Glyptodon, a kind of Armadillo as big as an igloo. The patterns on its shell and its legs and feet were works of art. "We'll tell Mom she has to come look," she whispered, holding him close to the glass. "See the pattern, thousands of thumbprints, regular as that paisley scarf you've seen me wear." He stretched his hand and wiggled his fingers. "This is where art got started, Pip, you need to be in at the beginning. If you miss out on the beginning you have no hope of understanding what's to come."

She showed him the Great Bustard, a bird that had vanished from Britain no more than a hundred years ago. She pointed out the horns of a woolly mammoth that were found in Ilford, a few kilometres from where they stood. It was quite young, a mere 170,000 years. A group of people next to her were giggling at the mammoth, a man tipped his toe in its direction and said, "She's an Essex girl." Kit waited for more, but they drifted off. It wasn't right to laugh at the beast. She held Pip up and showed him the vaulted ceiling of the museum and its towering walls.

She paused here and there in the halls to read to him about fossils and ape men and plants and minerals, but there was too much writing; some of the exhibits seemed tacky, and the stately building was full of tourist shops and cafeterias. She kept coming back to the vestibule with the Diplodocus and the Moa bird, all extinct except—and here was one of the wonders—the Coelocanth, thought to be long gone, and here he'd been fished up not long ago, blue and glistening, out of the sea off Madagascar. "So you see, Pip, life keeps surprising us."

She made up her mind to bring him here again next year, and the year after. "I'll sit you on the tree stump every year and you'll have another ring. I want you to feel you belong in history, I want you to be calm and strong and durable. We're living, beating parts of nature, you and me. I promise I'll keep you close till you're ready to go out on your own."

An elderly couple paused and listened to her. They laughed. "Way to go!" the woman said. She was American, like the petrified stump.

CHAPTER TWENTY THREE

~e~

The day Kit took the baby up to London, Catherine slept in, revelling in the freedom from tension. She realized how important it was for her to live alone. She'd need to have her house to herself when she got back home.

She lay back, squinting at the blue and gold squares of window, then sat up in bed and started to transcribe the notes she'd made at the library. It was odd to be a fan of an artist whose work she had no chance of seeing. What an irony that Hodgkins' drawings and paintings had almost all ended up in New Zealand. Patrick Heron wrote that Frances Hodgkins was the greatest living painter, the best woman artist ever to have worked in England, she made her own rules, she spoke out about her ideas, but not until she was well into middle age. Patrick Heron was one of Roger's heroes, she wouldn't allow this to make his opinion less valid. She copied out the story about how the old lady was taken to Wales to paint when she was in her seventies. When they were on their way, her companion, an art critic, described a view of the mountains that was obscured from the train. He went to fetch her at dawn the next morning, but her bed was empty. He searched frantically and found her perched on a rock in the middle of a stream, painting invisible mountains, the ones he'd described to her in the train, and he said it was the best painting she'd ever done though it looked nothing like the real thing. It reminded Catherine of Dürer and his imaginary rhinoceros and of her own fanciful self-portraits, done without the help of a mirror, with pieces of barely recognizable body parts and clothing floating, unfettered by attachments. Frances had produced self-portraits along the same lines, deconstructing herself, her belongings, her red beret, a belt, a rose, a china shoe, separate, yet contained by an abstract shape and a green, life-giving border. Frances had such faith in her imagination, and little interest in the viewer's response. Catherine felt buoyed—Emily Carr must have taken so much away from her six weeks in St. Agathe.

And then, inevitably, there were critics like Virginia Woolf's brother-in-law, Clive Bell: '...hers is essentially feminine painting, gay, intelligent, never pushed an inch beyond her scope. Miss Hodgkins' pictures so often charm us, the least little bit artificial maybe, influenced possibly by a man, but illuminating in the exact best sense of the word. She is at her best when she is most herself and therefore most feminine.' She read that Virginia Woolf had possibly modeled the character of Lily Briscoe in *To the Lighthouse* on Frances. If they were friends, why hadn't Virginia defended her?

She called Mel at lunchtime knowing she'd probably wake him, but too impatient to wait any longer. Her resolutions to let him know she wanted him out of the house evaporated when she heard his voice. They chatted about nonsense things, a sort of gentle wooing, simple and uncluttered when they were separated by so many miles.

"I turned your pictures to face out. I hope you don't mind. I thought you were punishing them, leaving them facing the wall— like the teacher used to do to us kids when we were bad."

She smiled. She felt wicked, curled up in Roger's armchair, drinking his Malt whisky and running up his phone bill and happily giving permission to whatever small favours Mel asked. He was right. Why would she want to hide her art? The call was like a good massage, the future was suspended and the benefits would be temporary but profound.

Mel told her a woman had been trying to get a hold of her. Acting on instructions, he hadn't given out the number. It was Gilly Tannenbaum, the Associate Dean. Mel said she'd been very insistent. Catherine decided it was worth a call back, if only to see if she'd guessed right and Gilly had some insight into the Emily/Frances connection.

"So, when do we expect you?" he asked.

"Soon. I've run into a bit of a snag here. Kit and I aren't speaking."

"Do you need to speak?"

The question threw her. "Maybe we've said enough. Maybe I should just pack up and leave her to work things out in her own way." She rode the pause.

"It's still happening at this end," he said, finally.

"That's good." She hung up. Silly, but good. Very, very good. It was a silly game—they had nothing in common. No good-looking, capable man would fall for a crone like her, and certainly not in the time it took to build a flight of stairs.

⁂

She heard Kit come in, and listened as she turned on the radio and fussed in the kitchen. When she came downstairs, Kit was standing at the counter, deep in the parish magazine. She tickled the Turnip's nose and he sneezed. She tried to lift him out of the corduroy bag on Kit's back but he was cemented in, his fat thighs tripling over the tug of the fabric. She stroked his cheek with the back of her finger, wondering who would break the silence. She felt much better disposed to the world after talking to Mel. The baby looked at her solemnly, pursed his lips and blew a spit bubble. "There's no getting around it, you're a killer." She glanced from the baby to Kit who grinned and held up the magazine.

"Look, they're having a fête on Saturday."

Catherine turned the radio off.

"I heard village fêtes are neat, like carnivals. I was in this English play about one once. It was hilarious. The hoi polloi get to rub shoulders with the upper crust—you know they still have lords of the manor here? Why don't we go? I want to see the villagers tugging their forelocks."

"We're in the age of New Labour. The villagers are all townies."

"Are you sure? Things don't change deep down, whatever their P.M. thinks. Look at how they fawn over royalty."

"They're not alone!"

"Oh, Mother, I don't fawn, I just cut their heads off and put them in a Harrods' carrier bag." She put the parish magazine in Catherine's hand. "So what do you think? It's only a few steps from here."

"I don't want to go."

"Oh, come off it. Be a sport! Toodle de doo."

"Stop sounding like Roger, it doesn't become you."

"So you're up for it?"

Catherine searched the pantry and pulled out a tin of Roger's oysters.

Kit pushed the bread across the table. "We have to dress up. That's the rules. Locals have to come in costume, you can only be in mufti if you're from away."

"Well, we're from away."

"No we're not, we're living here. So that's it, we're going?"

Catherine sighed.

Ernie couldn't settle. The floor lurched. It was like walking on a moving belt. He'd locked the downstairs apartment and he didn't go into it again. A sweetish smell seeped up through the floorboards. He opened all his windows to let it out but it persisted like the smell of decomposition. And there was a constant background drone—he recognized her voice, although he couldn't make out the words.

The only solution was to get outside. He walked the neighbourhood streets, then further afield, circling the sea wall, crossing the Lions Gate Bridge, staring sightlessly into the choppy waters of the inlet, tramping across town to the Endowment lands and stumbling through the forest along rutted trails without noticing mud holes, dogs, logs, mountain bikes. When it was dark, he went home to the smell. The only solution he could see was to get rid of all traces of Catherine, pull up the stair carpets and chisel out her name, rip out the tiles, the floorboards. He walked for a day considering what to do about the Catherines trapped under the paint on the walls. He could paint them over again, but this would only seal them in place. They were there forever. His mind wheeled back to the paintings in the island kitchen, her face, her breasts, his image. She'd taken back what was his and passed it on to a black man.

⚶

Catherine hoped that creating costumes together would temporarily divert Kit's attention from making further plans for the baby. Kit decided to dress up as a Dresden shepherdess because it was 'naff' and Catherine toyed with the idea of dressing as Emily Carr. Embracing Emily, actually becoming her for an afternoon was a creepy idea, but she wondered if it would lay her ghost, like drinking to cure a hangover. She'd had a couple of fire dreams since the incident at the sanatorium, waking up in flames and feeling a presence hovering over her. The dreams were hard to chase away. She wasn't used to dreaming.

She knew that appearing as Emily would make no impression on the villagers, she'd simply be seen as a lumbering old frump in a hairnet, they'd probably think she wasn't dressing up at all. It would make more of a statement to go as Frances Hodgkins. Frances had been quite a dresser in her old age. She'd taken to wearing bangles and cheap baubles, white cotton stockings with sandals, short skirts, a red wig topped with a beret. Some said she thought the costume made her look young and gave her friends and critics less reason to dismiss her. She frightened off children. A solitary end meant choosing between bag lady and clown.

Catherine had only memory to help reconstruct Emily's costume. She went through Roger's wardrobe looking for an over-coat and found a stiff khaki greatcoat; it looked like something he wore in his student days. She tried to picture him in it, but drew a blank. She felt in the pockets for clues and came up with a loose button. The coat wasn't Emily but it would have to do.

She scoured the shelves in the village chemist's shop for a hairnet. The obliging sales assistant rummaged in the back and finally produced a substantial pink snood. Emily and pink didn't jibe, so Catherine bought a package of indigo dye. She couldn't think what to put on her feet. She tried on both pairs of beaten-up sneakers she'd brought with her and asked Emily's opinion. The answer was immediate. Emily didn't think much of the baggy jeans either, so she rifled through Ilona's closet. It was the first time she'd been into the master bedroom since the night she came to Golding. Ilona had accumulated countless pairs of shoes. Some were stored neatly in boxes of tissue and looked unworn, some had shoe trees in them. The shoes ranged from elegant to sporty and they were all child-size. Who would dispose of these clothes? Ilona's smell lurked in the folds of the fabric, a light, spicy perfume. She brushed a couple of dark hairs from the shoulders of a pale blue jacket, then searched for them and put them back. She found a dowdy maternity skirt with an adjustable waistband that would serve her purpose, then she dug into the recesses of the cupboard, wondering if Ilona might have concealed the diary somewhere.

Downstairs, on the back porch, she discovered three pairs of Wellington boots. Two obviously belonged to Roger; the other pair was new, and tiny. She tried on the men's boots, waded across the kitchen and decided they'd do if she stuffed rags in the toes. Kit came out onto the porch and watched her.

"I hope I'm not going crazy in my old age, Kit."

Kit laughed. "I think you need to bulk up, you've lost so much weight. Wasn't Emily fat?"

Fat was a bad idea in the middle of a heat wave when she would already be wearing a greatcoat. She decided to settle for a more wraithlike version of Emily and immediately sensed her disapproval. In fact, she would disapprove of the whole exercise, but by now Catherine was too deeply involved. "Perfection isn't always the final answer," she told Kit enigmatically, "read Darwin." Kit watched, amused, as she blew out her cheeks and stomach. "By the way, if you want to help Roger, why don't you give Ilona's mother a call, tell her to come over and pick up her clothes."

"Good thinking, Mom, maybe you're not going crazy after all."

Two nights before the fête, Catherine was wakened by another fire dream. Unable to get back to sleep, she got up at dawn, plucked up the clothes she'd selected for her costume, stuffed the boots and coat in a plastic bag and steeled herself to tramp up to the old sanatorium, turning her back on Roger's damaged Audi. In the early hours, she'd convinced herself that she needed to seek permission to continue with her impersonation, but now, as she left the village behind, she was ready to go home and forget it. The early morning mist was lifting like smoke. It was developing into another hot day.

The driveway was deserted again, and she got behind a tree to slide out of her jeans, bundled up her sneakers and the rest of her clothes and shoved them between the roots of the tree. The coat was stifling. She tried to imagine an ice pack in the lining.

Instead of approaching along the drive, she climbed a barbed wire fence and took to the fields. She viewed the burned patch. Even from a distance she could see new grass-shoots pushing through. She broke through a hawthorn hedge, circled round to the back of the building and stood looking up at the three-storied façade. The top floor windows were casements, rather like the window of her room in Roger's house. She resisted the temptation to place Emily in one of these rooms and put her on the ground floor at the end of one wing, from where she could feed her caged fledglings. She narrowed her eyes, trying to imagine her lying inside, gazing out. She felt like a scarecrow in the heavy coat and outsize boots, but as far as she could see there were no onlookers other than the birds, looping high overhead like fragments of burned paper.

Suddenly she felt waves of fear coming off the building. She saw a melon face in the window. She took in its contours as you might see every detail of a stranger's watch without being able to describe the arm it was on. Sweat rolled down her back, and with it came an all-encompassing weariness. She recognized it. It was not the kind of tiredness that accompanies physical exhaustion, but the numbing, leaden kind that comes with depression. She'd felt alone many times in her life, but she'd never felt this kind of desolation.

She turned her back on the building and made her way down the sloping field, slipping inside the boots. She stumbled on a rabbit hole and fell, rolling a little way. She was winded but not hurt. When she finally got her breath, she threw off the coat and cradled it in her arms. Somewhere, not too far away, a dog had caught her scent. It barked excitedly. She glanced back, realizing that she had probably seen the occupant of the apartment standing in the window she'd assigned to Emily. The barking got louder and she pulled herself together enough to scramble back over the fence onto the drive. She looked for her clothes. They were gone. In a blind panic she scrabbled among the scrub trees, tripping on roots and finally found her bundle right where she'd left it. She slipped her feet gratefully into her sneakers and shrank back to her own size, seeing that her imagination had fed her something akin to the faces on the canvases she'd painted before she left home; according to Mel, they were now looking at the world, not the wall.

When she got back, she shut herself in her room and lay flat on the floor. Her blue bear was abandoned on the bed. She reached up for him and flattened him against her chest. "I just had an Alice in Wonderland experience," she told him. "I've fast-forwarded, or I've regressed, either way I think I'm still in transit."

⚓

Kit appeared in the bedroom doorway with the local paper and more news of the coming fête. She barged in without asking. Catherine was still on the floor and Kit nudged her gingerly with her toe. Catherine told her flatly that she was abandoning her plan to dress up.

"Oh, come on, Mom, you can't fink out, it's gonna be fun."

"No way. Emily doesn't want to be accessed."

"You're weird. You've been acting weird since you got here."

"I don't like her, she's on my back."

"She's gone, Mom, she's dead. You're not gonna bring anyone

back from the grave just by dressing up in a few old clothes. If that happened every actor in the business would be haunted."

"I can't do it. I can't defile her."

"She's just a memory, you don't defile memories, you defile people. She wouldn't have cared anyway."

"What do you know?"

"Why deny us both a bit of fun?"

"But I felt this presence, up at the sanatorium. I didn't tell you, but I think she saved my life. I could have burnt the place down."

"What are you talking about?"

"Oh, nothing!" Catherine got up. "I've had enough of Emily. I don't even like her!"

"Then just laugh her off, she would've—she made cartoons of herself, remember?"

"She had a sense of humour. I don't."

"Come on! You were the one who laughed at me when I was scared at Halloween. You were the one who said there's no ghosts, only spooky people wearing sheets. Was Emily dressed in a sheet?"

"I'm sorry, I want to take this lightly. But I even dream about her. How can I romp around in those clothes and send her up?"

"Pretend you're a hobo. You're the practical one, remember? If you believe in ghosts then what about Ilona, wouldn't she be haunting us? Oh, by the way, we're invited to their place tomorrow. I said we'd drive over. You'll come, won't you? I can't face her horrible family on my own. I said we'd stow all her stuff in the trunk or is that the boot?"

Catherine nodded, unable to summon up the energy to argue. It was unthinkable to impersonate Emily as she'd lived, but it was probably okay to stay on the surface and parody her, just as Emily parodied herself. Surely she'd forgive this small intrusion.

⚶

Gilly Tannenbaum picked up the phone on the first ring, answering gruffly, "Associate Dean." Her tone lightened when Catherine said her name.

"I've been trying to track you down for a week, Catherine Van Duren! I have news. Good news. Great news."

Catherine held her breath, imagining Gilly's red head bobbing, her big gummy mouth shiny with lipstick, the flamboyant earrings. "The Logan's been looking for you. They want to give you a solo. They've asked me to curate."

"A solo exhibition? Me? You're joking—the Logan Gallery?"

"Who else? High profile, gilt-edged catalogue, critics, all the bells and whistles. When can you get back?"

"Do they think I'm dead?"

"Of course not. They've tagged you, don't ask why, just buy champagne. What are you doing over there in England anyway? Is it true you've moved to the States?"

"I'm going to a garden fête disguised as Emily Carr disguised as a hobo."

Gilly laughed. "That's why you made the trip?"

"Would you be interested in some of my current work?"

"You bet. Just tell me where to find it."

"It's at home. I've moved all my stuff down to the San Juans. I bought a house. I'm coming back as soon as I can. Meanwhile you can drive down and take a look if you like. I have someone caring for the place. I'll warn him you're coming—he thinks he's a guard dog." She gave Gilly the phone number, remembering, too late, that she'd planned to keep it to herself. She needed time to absorb this news. She hadn't had a solo exhibition in years. Why would one of the leading galleries in Canada be interested in her now when there was nothing to indicate that her work was about to appreciate? A retrospective was usually mounted to confirm public taste, and there was no taste to confirm in her case.

"Are you still there, Catherine?"

"You bet—and I've got one small request to make. Will you be my executor? My daughter's been telling me off for not having a will."

"You're not about to turn up your toes, are you?"

"No. I intend to outlive you!"

"Not good."

"I mean it, about being an executor."

"Sure, if you trust me."

"I trust you to shred the trash, okay? Just save the good stuff."

"Why are you being so morbid?"

"It's just that someone died here. A young woman, my exhusband's wife."

"Well, what's that got to do with you?"

"I just agreed to ferry her belongings back to her family. Oh, it's complicated but it has nothing, nothing, nothing to do with me." It was good to hear herself say that. "I'm going to make a will as soon as I get back, okay?"

"You are hilarious, Catherine. You get great news and you want to make a will. You're so serious, it's funny."

"I know. That's what I was just telling Kit. Emily Carr had a sense of humour." The room swam. "I might have to get an exercise bike and start drinking vegetable juice."

"Is that what retirement does for you?"

"No, but it's changing me—for one thing it's making me superstitious."

⚘

Kit drove the car while Catherine sat in the passenger seat, trying to navigate. Things went well until they reached the London sprawl.

Roundabouts were intimidating, the endless snarl of traffic was both too fast and too slow. By the time they'd worked their way across central London and reached the outskirts of Surrey, Kit's face was ashen. Catherine took over for the last few miles, deliberately ignoring Kit's request that they look for the spot where the accident had happened. The baby slumbered happily, strapped into his car seat beside a heap of Ilona's dresses. Kit begged to be let out so she could sit with him, but Catherine kept going, grimly.

They found the square white house surprisingly easily, parked on the half-moon drive and announced themselves by sounding the horn. An angular woman with thick gray hair appeared at the door. Catherine urged Kit to get out of the car. She suddenly felt intimidated and frowsy. The woman was wearing a long skirt, a loose red Japanese kimono jacket and a lot of chunky gold jewelry. She raised her hand and Catherine saw a flash of fire-engine red fingernails. The woman didn't come down the steps to welcome them, but stood, looking down solemnly, her hands loosely at her sides as Kit fumbled with the baby. She held out her arms to take him as she mounted the front steps, but Kit held on tight.

Catherine got out of the car and started unloading the boxes of shoes from the trunk, piling them haphazardly on the gravel.

"I'm sorry, my husband's at work and the boys seem to have done a bunk." The woman's voice was loud and pitched low. "I'm Mrs. Martin." Catherine's head was in the trunk and she responded by waving her foot, then changed her mind and strode up the steps, leaving the boxes where they were. She knew her grip was too strong as she shook hands.

They sat at the dining table on the uncomfortable red chairs and ate what were described as 'nibbles'. Kit described them later as zoo food. It was lunch time but nothing more substantial than a gin and tonic was offered. Kit pushed hers aside and sat with her eyes glued to the baby as Mrs. Martin unfolded a cloth, spread it on her lap and dandled him, cooing over his head. Her makeup had been applied lavishly, flattening her features, obscuring any real expression. It stopped slightly short of her neckline.

Catherine excused herself from the table to get on with the unloading. She could hear the baby making 'wa' sounds as she worked, as if he were overawed, too. She watched through a crack in the door as Kit took him in her arms, claiming he needed to be changed. She couldn't believe this elegant, stick of a woman had raised three children of her own. The frostiness might have something to do with the fact that she wasn't willing to raise another. She wondered if Mrs. Martin was aware that she was Kit's mother, or if she thought she was the hired help.

Kit stepped out of the dining room and whispered, "Can you believe that woman? This is the first time she's seen Pip outside the hospital."

"Maybe she's traumatized," Catherine murmured.

"Ever try to traumatize a tank?"

"She thinks I'm a complete frump."

"She'd change her mind if she knew about your big show."

"No—it's in Canada. It wouldn't count."

Mrs. Martin nudged past them and led the way upstairs to a room on the right of the landing. "This is Ilona's room."

She disappeared as Catherine staggered up and down the stairs, her arms loaded. While Kit changed the baby she stowed the boxes away as neatly as she could, pushing aside the bulging plastic bag under the bed. "Someone's going to have to clear this room out and it won't be me." She placed the honeymoon photo face down on the dresser next to a faded picture of a sharp-featured woman in a ruffled blouse. A photo of a school class hung on the wall over the fake fireplace, along with two of Ilona's school portraits, showing a dark, solemn little girl with a school tie, grey wool sweater, hair in stiff bunches that stuck out like brushes. They were dated two years apart but the images were identical apart from a missing front tooth. Catherine sat back, feeling she'd been given an insight into Ilona's arrested childhood. Ilona's fingerprints were on none of the surfaces. "Did you have anything to do with her death, Kit? It's time to be really honest."

"Yes." Kit wouldn't look up.

"What?"

"If I hadn't come to England, it wouldn't have happened."

"Is that all?"

"Isn't it enough? It's what brought us here, isn't it?"

"I don't know why we're here. If I'd been home that day when you came to Vancouver... You're saying we're both responsible?"

"I should heat this." Kit pulled the formula out of the bag.

Catherine poked her head out of the door, looking for Mrs. Martin. She was leaning against an antique chest along the landing, her body curved backwards. She turned her head slowly, trapping Catherine in the doorway. "She used to sleep with her eyes open," she said, "it's not that I don't want the boy in my life. And there was his twin, you know. I never thought she should have children but people said it would be the making of her. She was in this house just before it happened—she ate an apple and she finished the bourbon creams. She had a sweet tooth. If I'd only been home—" Tears had pineappled the carefully contrived upholstery on her face. Catherine took in her slender crossed ankles, tiny feet clad in patent leather pumps. At some other time, in some other place she would have tried to help; as it was she was overtaken by a crushing wave of selfishness, an undertow of love for her daughter, a desire to sweep her up and run off to a warm beach with palm trees and placid, blue water where no one would find them.

Golding's dark interior seemed positively sunny after the atmosphere of the square white house in Surrey. They both felt the urge to be occupied when they got back, so they took time selecting the finishing touches for Catherine's costume for the next day. There were two baby carriages in the laundry room, both big enough for twins. Catherine picked the sleek, upright perambulator, not a popular vintage any more in Canada, but unfortunately still too modern for Emily Carr's time. She arranged an armload of stuffed animals in the pram and topped them off with her blue bear, then extracted him. He had too much dignity for this little charade. Emily would never have pushed a giraffe and a stuffed hippo round the streets of Victoria, but Ilona hadn't collected any toys that approximated domestic animals. It didn't matter. Catherine knew she could only go along with the pretence as long as it was a deliberate parody. Kit dug out a fanciful rag creation from a pile of baby gifts: it was a curious shade of puce, with a long blue tail and one glass eye. She pinned it to Catherine's shoulder with a diaper pin. For the purposes of the fête, it could stand in for Emily's monkey. Her costume was complete except for a pair of wire-rimmed spectacles that Kit found on top of Roger's bureau.

"You look like you belong in Pigeon Park with the winos, Mom."

"Maybe the lady would appreciate that." Catherine was quite pleased with herself. Enough time had passed since she'd been up at the sanatorium; nothing untoward had happened, it was time to slay the dragon. She would go out and have fun with Kit, the village green wasn't exactly a tropical beach, but at least they'd be able to forget themselves for a few hours, too bad if no one guessed who she was meant to be. She took a few tentative steps, then capered up and down the hallway hanging onto the pram. Kit was right, she did take life too seriously.

Kit looked on, grinning. "Any minute now you'll be leaving the ground. You're not meant to be Mary Poppins!"

A song came to Catherine. "Remember this, I taught it to you when you were little, I don't have my books, but I still have some tunes." She started tentatively and line by line the song took off:

'Oh, soldier, soldier, won't you marry me
With your musket, fife and drum?
Oh, no sweet maid, I cannot marry thee
For I have no coat to put on.
Then up she went to her grandfather's chest...'

⁂

Brenda was neatly dressed in a pleated skirt and a royal blue sleeveless top that made her hair fiery and her arms look pale and thin as oars. Roger held back from touching the vaccination scar on her shoulder. Her knees were welded together and she was knitting ferociously, pausing only to adjust some kind of counter on the end of one of the needles. He'd already taken several walks up the train and they were only halfway to London. People were talking into mobile phones, scoffing sandwiches from triangular plastic boxes, sipping coffee from waxy cups, working on laptops; no one else was knitting.

He wondered how he could reward Kit. Would she accept money? Perhaps he could pay the rent on a modest flat in London, near enough to Suffolk for them to meet occasionally, but not close enough to remind him of what had just happened. The future wasn't nearly as bleak as it had seemed, Alexander would be well taken care of. With Brenda at the helm, he could even face Catherine, should she still be in residence.

CHAPTER TWENTY FOUR

⁂

Catherine was still singing to her audience of stuffed animals when Roger walked in. She backed out of the hallway, dragging the pram into the scullery, slammed the door and stood, gripping the handle, concentrating hard on her knuckles. The apparition in the hallway couldn't have been Roger. He was too affluent, fleshy cheeks, roughened skin, and he had a beard. And where were his black eyebrows, where was his hair? He was wearing a tie. He had a paunch. In the moment it had taken to assess him she'd also taken in the skinny, awkward looking woman with bright red hair who stood at his shoulder. She tore off the snood and looked around wildly for a comb.

⁂

Roger took a step towards Kit, not knowing whether to embrace her or shake her hand. He bent over the baby, "You've grown, you little rascal. Look, Brenda, this is Alexander. Oh, and this is my daughter, Kit."

The baby's face folded as the beard brushed his cheek. Kit swung him into his father's arms.

"How's he getting along?"

"He's been fine, Dad. Mom and I had a ball with him. She was just dressing up."

"Yes?"

"For the fête."

"Ah, yes, the fête. What fête?"

They were stranded in the hallway. Kit watched as Brenda swiveled her head, trying to get accustomed to the darkness inside the yellow house with its straw thatch held in place by wire netting, like the hairnet the crazy old woman with the pram was wearing. The smell of burned milk, the pictures hanging like the postage stamps in her brother's album—she'd never seen so many pictures on one wall. She needed to go to the lavatory.

They followed Kit into the kitchen and sat at the table.

"Take your jacket off, Brenda." Roger barked. She stumbled out into the hall again, hung her coat on the hallstand then set off in search of a loo.

"We didn't hear from you, Dad. Where have you been?"

"Sheffield."

"All this time?"

"Yes. That's where I met Brenda."

"Well. Good." Kit looked around for Catherine. Roger looked for Brenda. The baby spat.

"Is it how I'm holding him?" Roger shifted him to the other arm.

"He probably needs changing."

Roger handed him back to Kit. "I haven't had much chance to practice. I was in a bit of a state, wasn't I?"

"It's okay now. It's all sorted. Everything's brilliant. We'll work it out, don't worry."

"Well..."

"Mom agrees with me. She's been brilliant. You owe her."

He cleared his throat.

"I think you should take her out to dinner tonight."

"Put me in the picture. That was really your mother?"

Kit burst out laughing. "Of course."

"But her hair! What was that thing on her shoulder?"

"A monkey."

"Oh." He looked doubtful.

"I'm glad you're home, I can't tell you how glad I am. I'm just so happy we're all back together. You and me, Mom and Pip."

"Oh yes, you call him Pip."

"Mom calls him Turnip! I think we should all compromise with Tip. Or Tuppy."

"Listen, Kit. I'm really grateful to you, believe me. I don't know how I'd have managed." He pulled out his wallet. Fortunately he'd stopped off at the bank near the station. "I don't want you to feel you have to go, you're welcome here, you know that, but I've got it sorted. I'm pretty sure I'll be able to work things out with Brenda." He put down a pile of £20 notes. Was it enough? Too much?

"You and her?"

"We sent her things down, they should be arriving tomorrow."

Kit grabbed the money and ran out of the room with the baby under her arm.

⚶

Catherine washed her face, changed into clean jeans and padded into the kitchen. She'd been prepared for the fact that he'd be an old man, but not this. It was as though the years had deposited a rime—she thought of lichen growing on dead branches. He seemed to be having the same trouble with her face, judging by the way he sat, lips drawn back over his teeth in something between a snarl and a smile while she eased herself into a chair and threw him inconsequential tidbits of information about the week she'd spent in his house. He finally suggested they should go to the village pub, jumping up right away as if he had her on a string and she'd follow unquestioningly.

Bemused, she saw he was still agile. He'd always been limber, never needed to exercise.

At the door they ran into Brenda, on her way down from the bathroom. Roger instructed her to make herself at home, shouted upstairs to Kit to show Brenda around and shunted Catherine out of the house before she could protest.

This was the first time she'd set foot in the Fox and Hounds. The restaurant section was busy. She scanned the room to avoid looking at Roger. It was more up-scale than she'd imagined. They had a menu and a wine list. She settled for pork pie and salad because it was the first thing that caught her eye and Roger ordered the same. He said he was relieved she hadn't outgrown her taste in food and she took this as an insult. The salad was limp and the dressing in its paper container was ill-disguised commercial salad cream. Things had only changed on the surface. As he relaxed, she got more used to him. The long forgotten mixture of anger and pleasure swept over her as he sipped his wine and poured out his sob story. When he came to the part about bringing Brenda on board as a live-in nanny, she wanted to get up and hug him but she made do with congratulations. Things were working out better than she could have hoped.

He saw that she was old. He knew she was retired, but he'd never imagined her flesh being old. He couldn't get used to her face, so he concentrated on her hands. At least they were still strong and competent, spade shaped nails, no rings, a sprinkling of liver spots: a competent old woman's hands. He couldn't get used to her voice either, the sound was the same, low, a bit breathy. It should have changed like the rest of her. It used to turn him on. The accent sounded much more American than he remembered. And she wore her hair like an American G.I. All this unnerved him and he decided he'd better do most of the talking.

She listened as he spoke of Brenda and her family. She encouraged him every time he paused for breath, hinting that he should consider a more formal relationship with Brenda if he wanted to provide a solid future for the baby. As he talked, she planned their escape. All that concerned her was that she should get Kit away before he changed his mind. She envisaged them both at Heathrow, in the holding tanks where passengers sweat out the eternity before boarding. She would be waiting for her flight for Seattle, and Kit would be ready to board an Air Canada flight to Vancouver, or maybe Toronto. Any place was fine as long as she got away fast. Later they could meet up on the island, but not yet. There would be too much to do, preparing for the show, settling scores with Ernie Last. And she had to face Mel, assuming he was still around. Roger didn't seem much interested in how she'd got to Suffolk, or how she'd spent the last half of her life. Catherine didn't expect interest. She was equally uninterested in how he had become the staid, elderly man whose foot had just brushed against hers under the table—an accident of course, and one he corrected immediately. Ilona's name didn't come up. She thought of Mrs. Martin's collapsed face and realized Roger wouldn't stay in touch with that family. Mrs. Martin would never get to know her grandson, just as he'd been denied his daughter. "I don't suppose you know anything about an old diary written by someone called Winifred Church? I gather it belonged to your wife. I'd like to try to track it down, in fact I seem to be a bit obsessed with it. I think it might be important, historically. Have you heard any mention of it?"

He was barely listening, "No. I don't think so."

"Was there any mention of France—St. Agathe? It's in Brittany."

"It's where we spent our honeymoon."

"Oh. I'm sorry."

"Don't be. We had a good time. At least she had that."

"Was there something special about France?"

"She loved it—wanted us to get a summer place there. I would have gone along, I just wanted us to get over the birth first..."

He ordered another bottle of wine, his voice too loud. Catherine lit a cigarette.

"It's just like old times, isn't it." He did his best to sound convincing. He knew she would think him shallow. "I mean, once you've got over the passage—the strangeness of time? I mean, so many roads not taken. I hadn't imagined it, I hadn't imagined this would be so easy." She patted his hand. His flesh felt scaly.

⚶

She picked at the dry bread roll. It was just like old times, totally one-sided only now she had the advantage of hindsight and he could no longer draw her into his world, though he'd very nearly succeeded again without even trying. "Thank you Brenda," she breathed.

"What's that?"

He had hair growing out of his ears. She hoped Brenda was not put off by it. "Everyone's flawed," she remarked.

He nodded and smiled.

"I promised to go to the village fête with Kit tomorrow. I was going to dress up as Emily Carr. You remember Emily Carr? You have one of her sketches in your studio, Kit showed me. She figures in that diary."

"I got a shock seeing you in my old national service uniform."

"The coat? Is that what it was?"

"I was one of Her Majesty's Best, don't you remember? Two whole years in army supply."

"Why'd you keep the coat?"

"Why keep anything?" He studied her wrists.

"And you kept the spare button."

"Did I?"

"I won't need it any more. We'll be on our way first thing tomorrow. Emily Carr's been giving me the run around lately, I'll be glad to shake her off. I don't suppose you believe in ghosts?"

"I can't believe you're asking me that. Catherine Van Duren, the world's great debunker."

"Not any more, it seems."

"Wasn't Emily Carr from British Columbia?"

"Yes, but I'm not. I've gone back to live in the States."

"Come on, let's pick up another bottle of wine and go up to my studio. You can tell me more." He was suddenly seized with the need to confide in her about his health. She'd know what to do, she always did. "I want your opinion of those Geoffrey Church paintings I've got. I suppose you've seen them? He's a minor artist, but I think he has a place. The Carr's worthless, you'll see that for yourself—or have you seen it already?" He paid the bill. "I don't remember telling Kit she could take you to my studio."

"You didn't know I'd be here. Neither did I."

"Well, I'm getting used to it." If only he could talk to her about the dead child. Maybe she'd have an explanation for the aversion he'd just experienced when Kit put the live one in his arms.

"Thanks. So, they sell take-out wine in pubs now? They didn't in our day." She had to stop saying 'our day,' it was too intimate.

"Oh, you can arrange anything, you know that. Everyone's on the fiddle."

"Not in Canada."

"I find that hard to believe."

"So do I." She laughed, "I keep making those claims."

He took her arm as they walked up the hill to the studio. It was pleasant, amicable—precarious. The closeness was completely unexpected. How foolish to have worried about this encounter, and foolish to speculate on what might have been. Best to simply grab the moment. On a warm night like this, with a full moon, anything could happen. He noticed how her eyes lit up and her body tensed when she talked about her upcoming show and he remembered how her obsessions used to turn him on. The further she'd pushed him away, the more he'd wanted to curl up in her warmth.

Catherine was thrown when he took her arm. She thought he'd at least be ashamed of his behaviour around Kit, did he even realize how embroiled she'd become with him and his life? At least he had the good sense not to bring up the subject of his recent tragedy. He skirted the subject of Kit as well. Maybe it was too soon to discuss her, or maybe thirty-five years was just too long. She couldn't imagine why he felt easy enough to touch her, she was sure she'd done nothing to encourage him, but she hadn't encouraged Ernie either, or Mel come to that, and this hadn't changed the outcome.

Three men coming on to her in the space of three months after a thirty-year drought didn't make any sense. Were the gods planning to touch every man who crossed her path? Ghosts and gods—the universe had her in its sites and it seemed there was no escaping. She let Roger's arm stay where it was as she tried one last time to talk about Kit.

"I'm concerned she might have formed an unhealthy attachment to the baby."

"What do you mean, unhealthy?"

"I mean she's too involved with him. And with you."

"Oh, don't be so stupid!"

Furious, Catherine shook off his arm. She recognized the familiar note of finality in his voice. The subject was closed. They'd reached the two steps that led to the concrete apron in front of his studio. She noticed a hopscotch grid and wondered how long it had been there. They stepped over it, both avoiding the lines. She glanced along the terrace and saw that the curtains weren't drawn and the blue glow of the T.V. lit up the front room in the cottage next-door-but-one. She was ready to go back, but Roger opened the door and placed his hand firmly on the small of her back. A blast of cool air hit them from the interior.

"You'll have seen these." He put on the lights and gestured to the wall.

She wandered round, pretending to look at the paintings. He brought out more of Duncan Church's canvases, arranging the lights so she could see them. "Feels like old times," he said, opening the wine.

The new Church paintings were quite powerful, the images rimmed in black, like stained glass. Catherine looked at them closely. "I can see how they might have influenced Emily Carr."

"You're still on that old hobby horse."

"We have unfinished business."

"Ilona was quite closely related to this Church fellow, you know."

"Yes. I know. I have the letter saying he was missing in action... you should probably keep it. I'll give you what's left of Winnie's diary, too. It's all yours now."

"No, I don't think so. Was she a painter, this Winnie? I don't think any of these are hers."

"No. She was just a facilitator."

"Useful person to have around."

"Very."

"I chucked it in, you know, painting. Too many distractions."

"And now you have one more," she reminded him, cruelly.

"I think he's taken care of."

"Oh, Roger!"

"I'm awful, aren't I?" She thought he was glib. He'd blown his opportunity to talk about the babies. "Self-centred bastard, I always was. I'm going to do better from now on."

She remembered how he used to read her thoughts and get round her by being honest about himself, admitting his faults before she could throw them in his face. Since that time she'd thought that honesty was the most insidious weapon of all, but it still worked on her.

"See that one over there?" He pointed out the female torso with the crucified man on her breast. "I painted that for you, remember? Why don't you take it?"

"I already have." He put the light out. A full moon shone through the window throwing a shaft of light on the floor. Both together and without consulting each other, they moved their chairs closer and sat, contemplating the light, acknowledging that nothing substantial had changed and nothing ever would.

They finished the wine and sauntered back to Golding hand in hand. At the gate they ran into Brenda.

"I've been rushing round the village looking for you everywhere. They thought you'd been in the pub, I thought you must've gone into the city, but the car was here and your daughter's gone, she called a taxi. She's taken the baby."

Roger denied that he'd said anything to make Kit do a runner. He insisted on talking about kidnap. Catherine looked to Brenda to help her make him see how unfair this was. Brenda sat with her eyes glued to the knitting, discarded in her lap.

"What did you say to her, Brenda? What did she say to you?"

"Nothing. I told her I was here to take care of them. The baby and him."

"And what did she say to that?"

"Nothing. Well, I didn't do anything wrong, did I? She had a bag. I saw her put nappies in it. And bottles."

"The baby's Kit's half brother. It can't be kidnap."

"I'm calling the police." Roger jumped up.

"Not yet. I told you. She'll come back. She never leaves the house without baby supplies. She's probably just gone for a walk."

"Children are stolen by family members every day, it's the commonest form of kidnap." Brenda kept her head down as she made this pronouncement.

"What do you care, anyway?" Roger turned on Catherine. "You call him Turnip!"

"Why don't we all go to bed?" said Brenda. Catherine sighed. This was the most practical thing anyone had said for hours.

"And not call the police?"

"And not call the police," Catherine said firmly. "She'll be back by morning."

Catherine stayed at the kitchen table watching as Roger consigned Brenda to the nursery. She heard Brenda whisper "I showed her your ring—well, I didn't do anything wrong did I?" She didn't hear Roger's reply. What a fool she was to have let him lure her out of the house. She choked back her fear. Kit had softened and found a real joy in life by taking over this mothering role and she'd refused to see it. The baby should be fine as long as Kit kept a clear head. Should. The word was full of doubt. Would. Would was her life-raft. How could Roger be so hypocritical as to pretend he cared where the baby was now? Kit took after them both. They were all three Walkaways. She took out her sketchbook and drew a triangle joining Kit to Roger to Brenda and framing her name. Catherine Van Duren.

Roger came down to the kitchen in the morning as she was making coffee. He was wearing a stylish silk dressing gown but his feet were bare. He still had hair on his toes. It was seven a.m.

"I'm giving her till half past," he said, checking the kitchen clock. "At half past I call the police."

"I'm going up to London. I'm going to search some of the places she might be."

"What places?"

"Places she's talked about. A record store in Notting Hill, the Natural History Museum."

"You think you'll find her in a museum?"

"It's worth a try."

"Well, who does she know in London?"

"I don't know, didn't she tell you?" Catherine tried not to snap.

"She must know some Luvvies, some theatre types."

"I don't think so."

"Well, you were with her while I was gone. What did you talk about?"

"She talked about the baby. She was mad about him. And she made lists, extinct birds."

"Lists?"

"She cut things out of the paper."

"I know. It upset Ilona."

"It was nothing. Just murders and royalty, stuff like that—"

"Murders!"

"People are interested in murders, that's why they make head-lines. Oh, you deal with it. He's your kid. They're both yours! She can't have gone far, she doesn't have any money." Catherine pushed past Brenda who was propping up the doorway decked out in a pair of see-through pyjamas.

"She talked about murder and you didn't question it?" he yelled up the stairs. "The police'll have a field day with this!"

"Well, why didn't you stop her if it was so terrible?"

"I don't pry into people's personal papers."

†

Kit's bag was still in her room. Most of her clothes seemed to be in place so Catherine was certain she couldn't have gone far. She searched the drawers for money and found her passport. It looked as though it had been put through a washing machine. She didn't know if Kit owned a credit card. She'd given her £50.00 for groceries the morning before. She checked the nursery. Brenda had slept under a blanket on the floor. Otherwise it looked undisturbed. Back in the kitchen she checked the fridge. It was almost empty. Brenda and Roger watched her.

"What are you doing now?" Roger's voice was thick.

"This is our daughter Roger, you can't charge her with kidnapping."

"Try me."

"Then maybe she'll charge you with abandonment—twice over!"
He flinched.

"Please. Just give me a few hours. Just hold off till I call you." She shoved him aside and hurried out of the house.

The woman with the poodle was sitting on the bench at the bus stop, a straggle of potential passengers stood in line, their eyes glued expectantly to the curve in the road.

CHAPTER TWENTY FIVE

C atherine reached London feeling hopeless. What was the use of following a two-day old trail? She spent a fruitless hour in the Natural History Museum asking the keepers if they'd seen a woman with a young baby. They were very kind, but she knew the question was redundant. She called Golding. There was no news, no sign of Kit and the baby. She told Roger to do what he had to in order to get them back.

A short walk from the museum brought her to Kensington Gardens. She examined the sightless statues and circled the round pond where Peter Pan presided, reminding her of Kit and her eternal quest for youth. Young women pushed babies in prams like the one she would have taken to the fête if things had gone to plan; the nannies met and exchanged greetings like greedy geese, hungry for adult contact. The feeling of dread was overwhelming. She called Golding again, using the last of her change. There was no reply.

She couldn't bring herself to go back to Suffolk so she booked into a cheap hotel in Earl's Court. She didn't want any hassle with the police. She had no identification with her, and she was afraid they'd ask for a passport so she feigned a British accent and registered in the name of Miss Emily Carr. The small deception alarmed her. She was an imposter. The desk clerk had an impenetrable foreign accent, but even so she couldn't believe he was so easily fooled. She bought a phone card and called Golding again from the lobby. This time Brenda answered. She said the police had come and taken down details and she added, "They're taking it dead serious. Roger's worried about the tabloids getting wind of it. That'll give her something to cut out of the paper, won't it? Maybe she'll do it in her jail cell."

Catherine went back to her room. It was small with one tiny frosted window streaked with dirt, not conducive to clear thinking. She went over everything they'd talked about since she'd arrived at Golding, looking for clues. She didn't think Kit would ever hurt the baby but she'd never been successful at second-guessing her. She'd seen how vulnerable she was, how close to the edge, and she'd done nothing to restrain her. They were no better than strangers.

She took deep breaths of the stale air to slow herself down. Surely if she'd had a credit card, Kit wouldn't have spent her first night in England under a bridge.

Waterloo Bridge!

She took the District Line to Embankment. The train took forever, stopping between stations, halting interminably after everyone was on board. A recorded voice repeated, "Mind the gap" and she heard 'mind gap.' The man sitting next to her was one of those raving loonies she remembered running up against in London. He kept repeating the same thing, "I haven't seen an angel since I was knee high, but I'm going to see one in King's Cross." Everyone in the carriage ignored him but he didn't notice, his eyes were glittering with anticipation. She hoped he'd see his angel and she tried to smile at him, but the best she could manage was bared teeth.

She got off at her station. The Thames was brown and puckered and the curvy broad-lipped fish on the bronze lamp standards mocked her. It was hard to believe that this river was now home to salmon. She wondered why they bothered about reintroducing endangered species. In a Darwinian world, the strongest would survive: the rest would die. The Turnip was one of the strong ones,

he'd proved it in this very river—he could survive like the salmon.
She was sure he was still alive. She looked under the bridge. There
were a couple of men necking and the evidence of hundreds of
pigeons, but nothing to mark it as a nocturnal hangout. Kit must
have found shelter on the other side.

The sun was low and the pasty face of Big Ben glowed as she
walked slowly over the bridge. Everything seemed to be in decline.
There was a surprising apron of sand outside the grim monuments
to culture on the South Bank. The tide was out.

The area under the bridge was cavernous, a clearing-house for
hell, with dingy neon-lit corridors marking the way to unknown
destinations. There were a few abandoned sleeping bags, beer cans
and food wrappers and a couple of bodies lying motionless under
filthy rags. Two young girls were playing cards, crouched against a
wall. It wasn't obvious why anyone would choose to stay in this dank
place on an evening like this but she guessed they were runaways.
She approached them and crouched down.

"Listen, I'm looking for someone." She tried to keep the urgency
out of her voice. They didn't look up. "Have you seen a young
woman with a baby, well not so young really, she's thirty-five, brown
hair, Canadian, a white baby. Mauvish white."

"Could be anyone. Who wants her?" The girl didn't bother to
look up.

"A friend." She had the presence of mind not to admit to being
Kit's mother. "Was she here? Did she spend the night?"

"Could have."

"Where did she go? Is she still here?" Catherine's thigh muscles
twitched, ready to pitch her forward.

One girl looked at the other. "Ilona?"

"That's right, Ilona," Catherine fell onto her hands. "Where did
she go?"

"She went to the airport. Must've left last night." The girl still didn't look up.

"But she doesn't have money."

"Some friend you are, then."

Catherine shook. There could only be one reason why Kit was calling herself Ilona. She'd taken the new passport; she'd probably taken the baby's birth certificate as well, it hadn't occurred to her to check. Would they let her on a flight with the baby? Surely not. But he was so new, too young to have been issued a passport. And Kit knew all about make-up—she passed for ten years younger than her actual age and she could get herself up to look like Ilona's passport picture. She would easily pass for English. How much attention did officials pay to young white mothers? She was an actress, she'd improvise a believable story. Catherine swallowed hard, trying to force her heartbeat back to normal. She had no idea what to do next. Surely the police would check the airports? She should probably call Roger. Who else would know that the new passport had arrived posthumously? She felt bone tired, yet lighter, with the thought that Kit might have escaped safely.

Roger wanted nothing more than to be left alone. He didn't know if Brenda really liked babies, she said she did, but all women said that. He hoped she understood that she was on probation. She followed him round on an invisible thread. If she would only agree to stay out of his way while he got things sorted, if she would put a couple of meals on the table (though he had no appetite), push the Hoover over the carpet, or whatever it took to keep things running he would feel more comfortable about having her in the house. He tried to explain, but she gave no sign that she'd understood.

The policewoman who interviewed him asked a lot of awkward questions. She wanted to know if the social services had been involved. He guessed she'd probably report him, but he didn't know what for, he only knew he was being punished. He couldn't tell her much—he didn't even know Kit's address in Canada and now Catherine had disappeared as well. The woman's expression didn't change as he talked to her but he guessed she was feeling contemptuous, she'd think he'd walked away from his newborn son. Catherine thought the same. When he said Kit was a well-known actress, the policewoman looked disbelieving. He'd expected a male policeman, a man might have been more sympathetic. There was one sitting outside in a marked car alerting the village to his problems; no doubt men were banned from dealing with cases that concerned babies, it must be considered dodgy territory. He tried to make it clear that the only thing that mattered was to get Alexander back. The baby's name stuck in his throat, he wanted to use it, but it tripped his tongue. Kit had stitched him up. He told the policewoman this in a roundabout way. She asked a second time how he felt about the child, and like a fool he said, "How would I know, I hardly set eyes on him." He wanted to add that he'd wear him in his top pocket if it would convince the world he was a good father. He'd do anything.

After the policewoman left, Brenda came on to him. She unbuttoned his shirt. He supposed she wanted to comfort him, but he was disgusted. He told her to fuck off. When he saw the expression on her face, he wept.

Catherine bought another phone card, found a call box and called Mel. She counted the rings, catching her breath in joyful anticipation of the sound of his voice. When he picked up and heard her greeting, he butted in. "I've been trying to reach you. It's a disaster here. The place is turned upside down." She put the receiver down. She couldn't deal with an earthquake on top of all the other catastrophes.

⚶

Gilly Tannenbaum spent the night in Catherine's bed. The mattress was shaped to fit a different size body and her back ached when she got up at dawn. Her dreams had been confused. She remembered waking herself up, laughing. She went through to the kitchen to view the destruction in the morning light. What she saw was no laughing matter. Rags of painted canvas were strewn across the floor, paints had been squeezed out or spilled over all the surfaces. She hadn't had the heart to ask the handyman to help clear up the mess last night. He'd seemed unnaturally distraught. He said he'd spent most of his time on the phone, trying to reach Catherine before Gilly had showed up. As far as Gilly could make out, there wasn't much that Catherine would be able to do to put things to rights, most of the paintings were beyond repair; only one was relatively intact, a rendering of swirling objects, some of which she recognized as articles of clothing Catherine wore regularly. They whirled round a small still-life of a man who was spread-eagled across the canvas in the shape of a letter T. It was unlike anything she'd seen Catherine paint before and from what she could make out, the rest of the paintings were also a significant departure. She felt a pang of disappointment that so little of this new crop could be included in the exhibition, but it was a relief that the earlier works were still stored, untouched, in the back room.

"Did Catherine take any photos of these?" she asked as Mel let himself into the kitchen.

"I don't know."

He looked as if he'd slept in his clothes. He inched his cap back, it had mined a deep indentation in his forehead.

"Are there any more that you know of?"

"That bastard! If I'd been here—it's my fault. He musta been watching. I don't leave the property, but my wife, she has this niece and she wanted me there at the birthday party and I said sure, why not, see, I like the kid. And that's when he struck."

Gilly was taken off guard. She'd assumed the man was a recluse since he'd hardly said a word last night, shrugging his shoulders in mute defeat when she announced that she'd be staying. "I do think we should call the police," she heard the voice she used to upbraid a student.

"That bastard!"

"If you know who did this?"

"There's only one person did it."

"Who?"

"He was here in his cowboy boots, I know that."

"Would he have taken any of the paintings? Could we get them back?"

Mel shrugged, defeated.

"I'd like you to help me load the stuff from the back room into my van. That way we can keep it safe. I'm not sure it will all fit, I'd forgotten the installations." She pointed outside to her late model SUV.

"Over my dead body."

"I came down to collect them. Catherine gave me permission. I'm curating her exhibition."

"We're not doing nothing till she's back here."

"And when will that be?"

He shrugged.

"I can't stay around."

"Suit yourself. I'm not goin' anywhere."

Gilly was silent, wondering how she could work around him. She needed to get back to Vancouver for a meeting later that day, but she didn't intend to leave without what she'd come for. The paintings couldn't be left here, they had to be crated and sent to Toronto. There was the catalogue to write, the inventory to draw up, time was not on her side. "Listen, I'm her executor."

"You trying to tell me she's dead?"

"No. I'm trying to tell you she gave me authority..."

"And you listen to me. I have the authority round here."

They stared at each other, furious, then Gilly burst out laughing. "I don't believe you!"

"And I don't believe you either, so that makes two of us." He was walking out, when he stopped suddenly. "I have these other paintings, up there in the studio."

"Hers?"

"Not mine!"

"Can I see them?"

He nodded.

He manhandled the paintings into the kitchen, delighting in Gilly's shudder. She took her time examining the sepia marches of trees. "She said they was trash," he said, watching her intently.

"Brilliant." She murmured. "I'll take them with me if I may."

Ernie Last took a room at the Sylvia, a matronly hotel looking out over English Bay, close to the urban forest of Stanley Park in downtown Vancouver. He phoned his sister.

"You can let your kids live in my downstairs if you like. You can move in upstairs if you like. I mean it. I've moved into a hotel. I don't live there now."

He thought he might take a walk past his old shop. The lease hadn't expired and he was still paying rent till the end of the year. Maybe he'd take the Royal Bootmaker sign down and touch it up.

Kit called Ernie from Vancouver airport and when there was no response she took a cab to the house. His curtains were drawn, he didn't answer the door and there was no sign that he was home. She laid the baby on the lawn, wrapped her denim jacket round her fist and broke a back window, checking for signs of the Chinese neighbour. She climbed into the kitchen of the empty downstairs apartment, unbolted the back door and brought the baby inside. She saw the kitchen had been newly renovated. Ernie was obviously planning to rent it soon. She felt hyper from lack of sleep. She'd made lists on the plane but there were so many possible courses of action and she'd been too worried about her reception at Customs to concentrate on much else. She wandered through to the living room and froze.

The walls were freshly painted. Someone had scrawled on them. At first she couldn't make any sense of the words. Catherine's name was everywhere, written in crude letters, crossed out frenziedly, in huge red x's. The word Bitch was scratched into the wall. Whore. She stared, uncomprehending, riveted by the pure, unadulterated madness that had been let loose. Her eye travelled to the corner of the room. What she saw there made her scream and cover the baby's head. The small, life-like figures were piled on top of each other, doused in something that looked like blood. Someone had tried to set them ablaze.

She dashed up the back stairs. Ernie's stuff was still there but there were sheets over the furnishings. It looked as if he intended to be away for a long time. She picked up the phone. It was still connected. She dialed Roger's number. The phone rang and rang and finally a neutral English voice kicked in. "The party you are calling is not available, please leave a message after the tone."

⁜

When Catherine cut Mel off, something connected. She knew where she was going. She'd been inching towards it in her last paintings, but this time she heard the pop in her head, the pop she was always waiting for, the signal that almost never came. Completion. She had finalized an idea, not a painting, an idea big enough to keep her going for years. She was finally connecting with 'it'. She knew that it was pure because there were no words to describe it. She squeezed her eyes shut. It had taken an earthquake to shake the pieces into place, and now, at last, she was completely alive, closer than she'd ever been to the real thing. Emily Carr called it 'areness'. She had to run with it, get back to work at once, before it let go its hold. And she had to locate Kit.

She slid into a McDonalds and ordered a coffee from the sleepy child behind the counter. The place was closing. She paid with some coins from her pocket and sat at a turquoise table on a turquoise plastic chair firmly bolted to the floor. She looked around. She could have been in Vancouver or Venezuela, the conformity of the look and the smell of McDonalds was exactly the same everywhere and it was what she was reaching for, the common thread. Enough of difference and separation. Tonight the world was a vast McDonalds. It was like flying over the Rockies, the window of the plane filled with white peaks and valleys, all joined and multiplying into infinity, as uniform as Styrofoam cups.

She would call Ernie and ask him to keep an eye out for Kit. She wished she'd been nicer to him but surely he'd have forgiven her by now? If Kit had taken off on an early flight she'd be there by now, assuming she was headed for Vancouver. At all costs, Catherine told herself, she had to stay calm and stay put, in case she was wrong and they were still in England. Kit would be tinder dry and she mustn't spark her. Everything possible had to be done to keep the baby safe. If they'd managed to leave the country on Ilona's passport, it was illegal. Kit could find herself in deep trouble. The first priority should be to get Roger to call off the police.

Back at the call box she dialed up her friend Mary in Vancouver. Kit had contacted her last time she was in trouble, maybe she'd do it again. Mary's voice on the answering machine invited her to leave her name and number. "Emily Carr calling in the summer of '99," she announced, in her fake English accent. Then she hung up. Mary would get the joke when it was explained to her, meantime she'd enjoy the mystery. She called Gilly Tannenbaum in her office. The secretary said she was 'away from her desk.' When Catherine said her name (her real name) she noticed that the secretary's voice became instantly respectful, but she couldn't offer any help in locating Kit. Finally Catherine dialed Ernie Last's number.

Kit didn't hear the ringing upstairs. She was rooted to the spot in their former kitchen, mesmerized by the slow drip of the tap and the little beads of water bouncing off the sink. She took out her tongue stud and dropped it onto the metal surface.

Roger put Brenda on the London train. As he was getting back into his car, he noticed that someone had dented his rear mudguard. He looked around the station yard for witnesses. There was no one about.

Back at Golding, he walked the empty house, tramping up and down the stairs, fetching up in Catherine's room. The smell of new paint hung heavily in the air. He opened the window and noticed a pink spot under the sill that the painters had missed. He banged the window shut. He felt wretched about his car. Any decent person would have left a note. He glanced around. Catherine was neat. Nothing was out of place in the room. He rifled through a pile of papers, stacked tidily on the dresser. She'd left a sketchbook on top; it fell open at the word 'fuck'. She'd never used that word. Neither had he. There were no sketches, but she'd drawn a triangle with his name on the left point and the names Mel and Ernie on the other two. They were all joined by a circle. He hadn't considered there might be other men in her life. There was another triangle on the previous page with the names Emily, Frances and Winnie. He read on, plunging through the notes, looking for his name. She'd obviously been doing some research, she'd made notes on Emily Carr—apparently she had spent six weeks in St. Agathe—this was interesting. There were pages of signatures, Catherine's name written in every script imaginable—and she'd spelled out 'defining identity through art!', and then written something that looked like a quote: *'The artist's main purpose is to demonstrate to herself by the authority of her work that her world is not an illusion, not an invention—that her world is real and she is a real part of it.'* He needed to talk to her, the need was so pressing he felt it physically. But he saw with absolute clarity that she wasn't going to come back.

He pulled a yellowing letter from the pile of papers. It announced that Geoffrey Church was missing in action. He ripped it up. They were all missing in action. Who cared? He half recognized the log pattern on the quilt on the bed, tightly tucked round a blue teddy bear that rested with its head on the pillow. Pulling it out by its snout, he stood for a moment, then went down to the room he'd shared only yesterday with Ilona and fell into bed without bothering to remove his shoes. He pressed his nose into the animal's fur.

⚰

Catherine sat on the bed in the anonymous hotel and counted the stains on the wall over the broken T.V. The burning pain in her stomach reminded her that she hadn't eaten for hours. She'd stayed in, not wanting to show herself to the hotel staff, but now she crept down the back stairs, avoiding the front desk. The hotel coffee shop was closed, but she found an all night grocery store and selected some cookies, a small can of baked beans with a pull tab and a yellow bottle of Lucozade. The bottle hadn't changed since she was in England in the sixties, she remembered taking the stuff to people in hospital to give them energy. When she went to pay for the items, she realized her wallet was missing. She searched her pockets, emptied her purse out on the counter and went through it again, trying to douse the hot spurts of adrenalin. If it was a pickpocket, she hadn't felt a thing, hadn't even noticed that her purse was lighter. It must have happened while she was using the telephone. Her address book was gone as well. Now she had no way of getting in touch with anyone. No identity. She returned the food to the shelf and went back to the hotel.

There was no point reporting the theft to the police, they'd treat it as a mosquito bite, and she didn't want them linking her to Roger and Kit until things got back to some sort of normal. She realized she should get help from the people in the hotel to cancel her credit cards, but this would alert them to the fact that she was a fraud and she had no way of paying for any more nights under their roof. She felt light headed. Her chest was heavy and constricted. She reached into her bag for her puffer, realizing she hadn't taken any pills that day, and maybe not the day before either, but her fingers refused to recognize the familiar shapes of the containers so she assumed they'd been stolen too. She knew she had to phone Roger, if only to let him know her suspicions about Kit and the baby. She stretched out on the bed. All these problems about credit and addresses were superficial. The good news was that no one was permanently lost and the muddle would sort itself out. The best news was that, by taking this break, she'd found a definitive way into her work. As soon as she was able, she would walk away from all her obligations, go back home, shut her door and paint. As she closed her eyes, she imagined the next day's headlines in the London newspapers that Kit had been so intent on mutilating. WHO IS EMILY CARR? MYSTERY WOMAN FOUND IN EARLS COURT HOTEL.

TWENTY SEVEN

֍

§ Victoria, 1934.

"Oh we are wonderful fools, we worry about getting old, we fret at every new ache, we plant gardens and then resent them for keeping us chained to home rather than glorying in the certainty that they'll continue to bloom when we're away. I'm going to camp for the summer, Willie. I'll need some help getting the Elephant out of here. I don't care what Lizzie says, and be blowed with the doctor. I've made up my mind and nothing's going to stop me. Don't you agree?"

Emily gazes at Willie Newcombe. She doesn't expect a response; she uses him as a sounding board. Sometimes she spouts complete nonsense, but he never interrupts. He says she is eloquent. She can't think of anyone else who would agree.

Willie examines his fingernails. He always shrinks into the stuffing of the armchair when he is called upon to make a judgment. Not that he lacks intelligence, he has too much of it, he simply lacks the means to express himself.

"I want you to help me put all these chairs on pulleys. I want to raise them up," she announces.

"You want them on the ceiling?"

"Yes."

"But why?" He blinks his pale eyes. "Aren't chairs meant to be sat on?"

"I need the floor space. I'd like to be able to choose who plunks himself down in my studio. We'll rig them up so they can be pulled down without a fuss if I want someone to stay long enough to take the weight off his heels."

"Will I be allowed to take the weight off my heels?"

"Willie, I need you."

"But will I be allowed to stay longer?"

"Meaning?"

"Meaning I'd like to. Stay. Longer. All day. And...longer."

"What for?"

Emily's gaze puts him under the microscope. "To be with you. To be near you. I'd like you not to put my chair on the ceiling."

He is her long-time trusted right hand, all of twenty years younger and she is sixty-three, a wobbly mountain who needs...who needs nothing, except an occasional helping hand with framing and making crates, packing the pictures and sending them off, assisting with the jobs that require more than one set of muscles, arranging for the Elephant to be towed to its chosen site. She can still cut down a dead tree, build a wall, shovel coal into the furnace, scrape all the plaster from a peeling wall, repair and paint a staircase. All these things get done when she isn't making rugs and artifacts and selling them to anyone who'll buy them. The pots sell well. People seem to like the Indian motifs; she copies shamelessly these days, there's only so much she can do to buy time to paint. She has enough money to pay a chimney sweep and a roofer when she needs one, she can feed her boarders, but sometimes there isn't much more than a couple of dollars to feed herself after she's fed the animals. She certainly can't afford to pay a handyman and where will she find anyone who is as reliable as Willie? Why on earth would he want to stay with her full time? She knows she'll have to find a way of placating him. The silence has gone on too long, but she can't think of a thing to say. Fortunately he breaks it.

"Please don't stare at me. I'm sorry I brought up the subject. You said you want us to figure out a way of putting the chairs on pulleys?"

"Oh, I have it figured out."

"Then it shall be done."

She breathes a sigh of relief. She's off the hook this time, but he'll return to the subject again, he's like a beagle once he gets the scent of something. What will she say next time? What a bother. It occurs to her that, with less tea drinking, there will be more time to paint. His patience and long suffering is a drain and he sluices up her small quota of good will. If he were more of a firebrand, if he would only stand up for himself. She watches as he mops the crumbs off his plate with his forefinger. She knows he is trying to study her face without appearing to look. She has made a decision. Does it show?

"I'd rather you didn't come here again, Willie," she announces, surprising herself with the finality of it. She shakes the shoulders of his gabardine. It is time for him to leave. Now that it's out, she feels as if someone has let out her belt. "Take your clothes with you and don't come back. We're not good for each other. I don't want to be unkind, but you let me take advantage of you. I boss you about and I've had enough of it."

She watches him disappear down the path, a slight, paper-white man. She will miss observing him as he skips along the sidewalk on his way to her house from work, in his stiff collar and black museum suit. She will miss his work clothes, which have hung for so long on the peg behind the pantry door that they've taken on a life of their own. She will miss the space he takes up in her studio, but one can't spend one's life missing. Life has to be lived, jobs have to jobbed, she has to figure out a way to get the chairs hoisted up and she'll make a good fist of it. And she'll have to stop shipping her paintings out now she's dispatched her crate maker; that will cut down on costs. There isn't much point to it anyway, the paintings stay crated in galleries and museums for months, sometimes for over a year while the curators and so-called experts out East make no effort to respond to her queries. Then the work is returned, most often without being dignified with a reason for rejection and she has to arrange for it to be picked up, and pay for the return freight. Willie will do her an enormous favour by staying away. She still has her pen, at least manuscripts are light and easy to dispatch. When they bounce back, they can be filed away and not left in the middle of her studio, giving her splinters. No, she has no need of a frame maker. A handyman is only useful when you need his hands and hands should be kept at arms' length. He's a nice man. Poor wee Willie, the world isn't exactly brimming with nice men, it's brimming with men like Mr. Geoffrey Church. She learned that, a long time ago. The world is brimming with contradictions, too, and she's been told more than once that she's the biggest contradiction of all.

She sits in Willie's chair in her own room in her own house exactly where she belongs. There are too many things bumping up against her, bursting with their own importance. She dodges them by shutting her eyes, skipping all the unpleasantness of the past, shrinking herself down, speeding back in time but not in space to the primary colours of Small. To Emily, no, Milly, who is five years old, then further back still, to where she is no more than a few cells swimming in a woman's womb, to the place where everything is connected. The forest under the sea.

THE END